IT WAS PAST MIDNIGHT

Matt's footsteps stopped outside the door to her hotel room. "Ammie?" he called softly. "You up?"

Ammie scrambled to a sitting position on the bed, her gaze snagging on her clothes, which lay draped across a chair in the corner. She should get dressed. But wasn't this the very moment she'd been longing for? The chance for Matt to notice she wasn't a little girl anymore. Trembling, she tugged the sheet up to cover her breasts. "Come in."

Matt opened the door, his eyes adjusting to the dimness of the room compared with the lantern-bright hall. "I don't know what happened earlier tonight, Am. If I said something to upset you, I'm sorry. I—"

Ammie struck a match and lit the hurricane lamp on her bedside table.

Matt's eyes widened. "You're not dressed."

"We've known each other since I was five years old, Matt Grayson. There's nothing either one of us has that the other one hasn't seen." She said the words, though her heart was racing madly. Lord above, what was she doing? She'd never done anything so brazen in her life. It was as if she were trying to seduce him.

Her heart hammered. *Was she?*

WISH ME A RAINBOW

Jessica Douglass

Wish Me a Rainbow

A DELL BOOK

Published by
Dell Publishing
a division of
Bantam Doubleday Dell Publishing Group, Inc.
666 Fifth Avenue
New York, New York 10103

ISBN: 0-440-21187-5

Printed in the United States of America

Published simultaneously in Canada

October 1992

10   9   8   7   6   5   4   3   2   1

RAD

For my editor, Tina Moskow,
who believes in rainbows—
and makes others believe too

☘ / Chapter 1

Amelia O'Rourke checked the northern horizon for the fourth time in as many minutes. Blast! Where was he? She'd expected him back two days ago—yesterday at the latest. Had something gone wrong? Had he been hurt? She lifted her black Stetson, threading trembling fingers through her tumbled mass of flame red hair. Where was he?

It had been nearly six weeks since Matt Grayson and two of the Shamrock Ranch's top hands had headed up the Chisholm Trail toward Wichita, Kansas, to buy a hundred head of half-wild horses, horses to be saddle-broke and resold to the army at a tidy profit. But Amelia knew only too well that it wasn't the money that had lured Matt, but the opportunity to get away, escape, to free himself— for a time at least—from memories too bitter to be borne.

Except that it wouldn't work. She had tried to tell him so the night before he left, but he had been in no mood to listen.

Images, raw and painful, rose up to haunt her. Images of Matt his dark hair disheveled, his blue eyes blazing with hurt, fury, as he endured yet another of his father's towering rages. Only the intervention of her own father had kept Matt and Zachary Grayson from coming to blows. One more ugly scene in the unending nightmare of ugly scenes between Matt and his father since the death of Matt's brother, Clint, four months ago.

Amelia's eyes burned. She should have gone with Matt. To hell with what he and her own father had said! She should have gone with him—at least then she wouldn't be worrying herself sick now about where he was and how he was doing.

Again she glanced northward, ignoring much of the awesome vista that had been her front yard for fourteen of her nineteen years. Shamrock land. Her father's land. Thirty thousand acres of north central Texas blanketed by rolling plains, scattered woodlands, and sweeping prairie. Land ideally suited to Shamus O'Rourke's dream of raising Texas longhorns, land blessed by an abundance of water, crisscrossed by a dozen natural streams. From here, Ammie could see the ribbon of cottonwoods that lined the closest of those streams. But she saw nothing, not even a plume of dust, that suggested the approach of riders.

Dragging in a ragged breath, she headed toward the corral. Despite her tenseness, she had to smile at the whinny of welcome that greeted her from the blaze-faced chestnut horse inside the rough-hewn enclosure. "No, I didn't forget your carrot, Tulip," Amelia said, patting the mare's silken neck even as her practiced gaze slid over Tulip's swollen middle. She judged the mare still had another month to six weeks before her foal was due.

"You think you deserve pampering, don't you?"

The mare bobbed her head.

Amelia laughed. "I'm not so sure about that. I still haven't forgiven you for running off and dallying with that handsome roan in the south pasture." She had wanted to breed Tulip with Jupiter, one of Matt's prize stallions, but Tulip had had other ideas. Twisting slightly, Ammie proffered her right hip in the chestnut's direction. "But since you're eating for two . . ." With a happy snort Tulip daintily tugged free one of the two carrots in Ammie's rear pocket.

Amelia scratched the mare's ears, while Tulip crunched contentedly on her carrot. "One more look can't hurt, can it, girl?" Allowing herself no time to reconsider, Ammie clambered up to the corral's top rail.

Steadying herself with one hand atop an anchor post, she straightened.

"Maybe you oughta try climbin' up on the barn," a familiar voice drawled. "That ways you could likely see all the way to Kansas."

Ammie turned to glower at the bowlegged cowboy heading in her direction. "I don't recall asking your opinion, Smokey."

The Shamrock foreman grinned, the ever-present cheroot at the corner of his mouth extending one side of that grin all the way to his right ear. "A mite touchy today, ain't we?"

Ammie started to bite out a retort, then stopped herself. Smokey didn't deserve to suffer her mood. Smoke Larson had been with the ranch as long as she could remember, starting out as a ten-dollar-a-month wrangler and working his way up until he was second only to her father. Even now, the only difference between the two men was the actual ownership of the ranch. When it came to having the respect of the hands, Smoke Larson was dead equal to Shamus O'Rourke.

Ammie adored him, and the feeling was mutual. Nine years ago, when her mother died, it had been Smoke, even more than her father—who was suffering his own grief—who'd brought her through the pain. Smoke—and of course, Matt.

"I'm just a little worried," she told him.

Smokey stepped up to the corral rail. "Matt'll be all right." His suddenly gentle tones were at odds with his weather-roughened features.

"I never said he wouldn't be." Ammie hopped to the ground, hating how defensive she sounded. She could hardly admit to Smoke that it wasn't Matt's ability to handle himself that concerned her. It went deeper than that, deeper than she could even yet acknowledge.

"You and your pa at it again?"

Ammie let out a sigh of relief, grateful that Smoke had misinterpreted her distress. Even so, she didn't relish the change in subject to her recent skirmishes with her father. "Seems like me and Pa are always at it these days. I'm beginning to see what poor Matt has to endure with his father."

"Whoa, now," Smoke said, his voice mildly scolding. "Ain't no comparison between your pa and Zak Grayson. Your pa can be mule stubborn, but he ain't mad-dog mean."

Ammie folded her arms across her chest, chastened but defiant. "Stubborn isn't the word I'd use. Bullheaded, dictatorial, unfair—now, those words I might consider."

To her consternation Smoke chuckled. "At least you come by it honest, Red."

"Come by wha—?" She gasped, planting her hands on her hips. "I am nothing at all like my father," she said. "How dare you suggest such a thing!"

Smoke only laughed harder. "You even hold your head the same way he does—cocked to one side, your jaw juttin' out like a slab o' granite."

Ammie stomped one booted foot. "This is not funny!"

"Whatever you say, Red." He kept right on grinning.

In spite of herself Ammie felt some of the tension drain out of her. "You're awful. You know that?"

Smoke nodded. "Been told so a time or two."

Ammie smiled. "Thank you."

"My pleasure." The warmth stayed in his eyes, but his expression sobered. "You gonna tell me what's eatin' ya, girl? Or do I haveta keep guessin'?"

Ammie sighed. "I wish I knew."

"This ain't about your pa courtin' the widow Denby, is it?"

Ammie stiffened. "How many times do I have to tell you? He is not courting that woman. He's taken her to a social or two, that's all."

Smoke was clearly unconvinced, but he let it drop. "All right then, if it ain't Mrs. Denby, what is it?"

"I told you, I don't know. I just—I just wish Matt would come back. You remember that awful fight he had with his father the night before he left."

Smoke nodded. "Maybe Matt's bein' gone helped Zak see things with a clearer head. Maybe he don't blame Matt so much anymore for what happened to Clint."

"He'll blame Matt forever," Ammie said bitterly. "It's Zak Grayson's way. Just like it was his way to favor Clint over Matt, even though they were both his sons." She shook her head. "I should've gone to Wichita."

"You gotta trust your pa, Red. He knows what's best."

"Best for me? I don't think so. Not any—" She stopped, her eyes narrowing with sudden suspicion. "Did Pa say something to you? About why he wouldn't let me go with Matt? Did he?"

Smoke puffed on his cheroot, looking decidedly uncomfortable all at once.

"Dammit, Smoke, answer me! You're as bad as Pa. You both treat me as if I were still a child. I'm nineteen, for heaven's sake!"

"Your pa loves you more'n anything in the world. He wants what's best for you."

"Then he should have let me go with Matt."

"Maybe . . . but—"

"Ain't you got some work you should be doin', Smoke?"

Ammie whirled. Neither she nor Smoke had heard her father's approach.

"Mornin', boss," Smoke said, giving Ammie a sympathetic look. They both knew she was about to get an earful.

Shamus jerked his head in the direction of the bunkhouse. Smoke took the hint.

Ammie faced her father squarely. Years of Texas sun had done no favors to his chiseled features. Green eyes that had once sparked as bright as her own were now all but swallowed up by a webbing of squint lines. Sun-bronzed skin resembled aging leather. An oversize brown felt hat covered gray-streaked orange hair that thinned precipitously across the top of his head, and Ammie sometimes found herself wondering if he now had more hair in the bushy moustache that obscured his generous mouth. "Don't you go gettin' mad at Smokey, Pa. He was just—"

"I know what he was doin'," Shamus O'Rourke cut in. "And I ain't mad. Leastways, not at him."

"You got no call to be mad at me either. It's the other way around, you know."

"I'm not going through this Matt business again."

"But you've never even said why—"

"I don't have to say why. I'm your pa."

"And I'm a grown woman. Maybe I don't have to listen to my pa anymore."

The sudden hurt in those pale eyes made Ammie instantly contrite, but pride kept her from taking her words back. Turning toward the corral, she made an exaggerated display of giving Tulip her other carrot. The silence grew heavy, awkward. Ammie cleared her throat. "I'm sorry, Pa. I'm just worried about him."

"I worry about him, too, Ammie." Shamus shook his head, then his gaze shifted off into the distance. "How old were you—three? four?—when me and your ma first come down to Texas after the war?"

"Five," she supplied. "But I don't see what that—"

"Our nearest neighbors were the Graysons. Times were rough back then, real rough. Sometimes I think if it hadn't been for the Graysons, for Zak . . ." He didn't finish. He didn't have to. Ammie knew the story by heart. She never tired of it.

The ink at Appomattox had scarcely been dry when Shamus came south to Texas from Pennsylvania, looking for dignity and self-respect for himself and his family. For all the North's rhetoric about fighting for freedom, Shamus, second-generation Irish, had been repeatedly turned away from all but the most menial work after the war.

Things hadn't started out much better in Texas. The locals' hostility toward anything or anyone Yankee ran hot, even deadly. There were threats, veiled and otherwise suggesting the O'Rourkes should head back to where they came from and fast.

The irony was that her father had never considered himself much of a Yankee—or even much of a soldier, for that matter. He'd been conscripted into the war. "We killed one another for five years, then we sat down and talked. We should've just talked and skipped the killing," he often said.

During one particularly hellish battle, the second battle of the Wilderness in Virginia, her father had gotten separated from his company. Terrified, surrounded by blood and death, his thoughts had been filled with his young wife and daughter and the agonizing belief that he'd never see them again. That was when he had stumbled into a clearing and an equally isolated rebel soldier.

"Battle instinct won out over common sense," Shamus told her.

They both fired. The reb missed. Shamus didn't.

Instantly, he was on his knees, tending the reb's wound, praising God when he saw that it wasn't serious. The soldier, a Texan, bore Shamus no grudge. "I'd 'uv done the same to you, if my damned Henry hadn't jammed."

Dark was falling, and Shamus couldn't get the Texan to

a field hospital until morning. So the two soldiers, who minutes before had tried to kill each other, spent the night spinning stories of life back home. Shamus never forgot one particular tale that the reb told of range cattle "runnin' wild, there for the takin'" in Texas.

Those tales and the burgeoning northern market for beef had led Shamus to the abandoned Texas homestead that he christened Shamrock. Shamus's fire and determination became legendary in the area, but Shamrock might still have succumbed to the hatemongers if he hadn't received a public invitation to stay from the very man who had spun those Texas tales. The wounded reb turned out to be one of the most powerful citizens in the state.

That Texas tale-spinner had been Zak Grayson, owner of the Diamond G. Zak Grayson, recently returned war hero. Zak Grayson, the rebel soldier Shamus O'Rourke had shot.

From that day on, the O'Rourkes were Texans.

Of course, the political overtones of that bright summer day had meant nothing to five-year-old Ammie. For her, it had simply been a chance for a buggy ride to meet the neighbors: the stern, dark Zak with his delicate blond wife Emily, and their two boys, the snobbish, too-serious Clint, age ten, and the delightfully devilish Matt, eight. Ammie and Matt had taken to each other at once. Even so, Matt might have balked at having a tagalong girl around on a permanent basis, if Clint hadn't unwittingly stepped into the mix.

As a child Ammie had loathed dresses, and her mother had kindly indulged her by sewing her trousers instead, albeit always with a daisy embroidered on her rump. Clint couldn't resist making fun of her tomboyish attire. But instead of running shrieking to her parents when he teased her, Ammie had summarily kicked him in the shins. Right then and there, Matt later told her, he'd decided he'd found himself a friend for life. "Anyone who can get the better of Clint can't be all bad," he'd said.

The memory coaxed a bittersweet smile to Ammie's lips. In the ensuing years she and Clint had come to an understanding of sorts, though she had never been as close to him as she was to Matt. She and Clint had been planning a surprise birthday party for Matt during the month before Clint died. Instead, Clint had been buried on Matt's birthday.

Ammie shuddered, forcing the thoughts away, and returned her attention to her father, whose voice had grown wistful, oddly sad. "You and Matt took to each other like nobody I ever seen. I was tickled for you both."

"He's my best friend, Pa."

"He's a man growed, Ammie. He's not that eight-year-old boy anymore."

Ammie frowned, confused. "So?"

"So, you wanted a reason why I wouldn't let you go with him to Wichita. That's the reason."

"Now you're not making any sense at all."

His next words came blunt, hard. "The kind of pain Matt's in, he's going to be lookin' for comfort wherever he can find it. In a bottle—or in a bed."

Ammie felt her cheeks heat. Her father had never been anything but straightforward with her about male urges, but hearing him tell her that Matt would use a woman with no more regard than he would a bottle of whiskey felt like a razor's edge to her already frayed nerves.

Her voice shook. "If Matt is drunk and in bed with some trollop, then it's your doing as much as his. If I were with him, he wouldn't have to look to someone else for comfort."

Her father let her words hang in the air for long seconds, then said, ever so softly, "Exactly."

Ammie gasped, taking a step back. "That isn't what I meant! Matt would never—" She gaped at him, discon-

certed, flustered. "Dammit, Pa, Matt's my friend! How
can you even *think* such a thing?"

"Because you're my daughter, and it's my duty to watch
out for you, even when you're not watchin' out for yourself. I seen the way you been lookin' at Matt lately. It's
not the look a friend gives a friend."

Ammie couldn't have been more stunned if she'd been
struck by lightning. "That's crazy. I don't look at him any
different than I ever have."

"Things have a way of changin' in this life, whether we
want 'em to or not."

"Not this, not my friendship with Matt." She noticed
then that she was trembling and realized with a shock that
she was no longer certain whom she was trying harder to
convince, her father or herself. "Please, Pa, why are you
doing this? Why are you saying these things? I thought
you cared about Matt."

"I love Matt like he was my own. But . . ."

"But what?"

"But I love you more, Ammie. You're all I've got."

"You make it sound as if I should be afraid of Matt."

"No, no, darlin', that isn't what I mean at all. It's just
that—that Matt's always been a wild one, unsettled, reckless. And that's only going to get worse now that Clint's
dead."

"You don't know that."

"You saw the fight Zak and Matt had. I'm surprised one
of 'em didn't pull a gun. I don't want you mixed up in
that, Ammie. I don't want you hurt."

"Matt would never let anything hurt me."

"He'd never mean to."

"I can't turn my back on him. Not even for you."

Shamus looked away. "The choice may not be yours to
make, Ammie. Matt may have made it for you."

A sudden coldness coiled in the pit of Amelia's stomach. "What are you saying?"

"That Matt and I had a little talk before he left." Her father didn't look at her.

Amelia was too afraid to be angry. "Oh, Pa, what have you done? What did you say to him?"

"I told him not to come back."

☘ / Chapter 2

Matt Grayson reined his black gelding to a halt. Ahead of him the churning hooves of a hundred head of horses continued to kick up dust, as Will Hennessey and Jess Johnson hazed the animals on toward the Shamrock Ranch. Matt guessed they weren't more than an hour away now. That was the reason he had pulled up. For the first time in his memory the thought of reaching the Shamrock was not a welcome one. Even less welcome was the thought of returning to the Diamond G.

Lifting his trail-stained Stetson, Matt swiped at the sweat and grime on his face with the sleeve of his faded blue chambray shirt. He should get moving again, resume his position riding drag. Instead, he kept the gelding at a standstill, ignoring the widening gulf between himself and the herd. He had a decision to make, a decision he'd been putting off for six weeks. This would be the last chance he'd have to make it.

Tugging off one black leather glove, he raked callused fingers through sweat-damp dark hair. His mouth was set in a hard line. Only the accelerated beating of his heart gave away the uncharacteristic nervousness that threaded through him. He yanked the glove back on and let out a low curse.

It was high noon in the middle of a dusty Texas road, and he was about to make a decision that would affect the rest of his life. Yet even after all these weeks on the trail thinking about it, he still had no idea what that decision would be. Would he ride on, or would he turn back?

In other words, he thought grimly, was he ready for yet another showdown with his father? Or was he going to turn tail and run?

"You wouldn't be running," Shamus O'Rourke had insisted the night before Matt had ridden out for Wichita. "No more'n I was runnin' when I come to Texas after the war."

"It's not the same, Shamus," Matt had snapped. "You came here to build a new life, a new home for your family. But the Diamond G *is* my home. At least, it's supposed to be." At that moment, he'd wanted nothing more than to bolt for his horse and ride and never look back. But he'd stood his ground, even after his father had mounted and ridden out of the Shamrock ranch yard in a blind fury. One more failed attempt to make peace between them.

Shamus's weathered features softened, his voice laced with the same caring that had ever been there for the second son of Zachary Grayson. "He'll get over it, Matt. He just needs more time."

Matt swore, then apologized for doing so. "Clint was my brother, Shamus. Aren't I entitled to some of that same time?"

"I wish it was different, Matt."

Matt looked away.

Shamus shook his head. "I told Ammie this supper tonight wasn't a good idea."

"I don't blame Ammie, Shamus. She was just trying to help." He'd had a standing invitation to supper on the Shamrock every Friday night for years. But this week Ammie had changed the night to Thursday because of Matt's trip to Wichita. Matt hadn't thought anything of it, until he'd walked into the dining room tonight and come face to face with his father. Obviously hoping to play peacemaker, Ammie had invited Zak, then purposefully neglected to tell either of them the other would be there.

The inevitable explosion occurred.

"We avoid each other at the Diamond G," Matt said. "I only set foot in the house if Pa is gone. I sleep in the bunkhouse."

Shamus rubbed thoughtfully at his carrot-hued moustache. "Then maybe startin' over is the right idea, Matt."

"You that anxious to get rid of me?" The question had more bite to it than he intended.

"It's not that at all, and you know it." Shamus cleared his throat, shifting uncomfortably. "But it is—it's hard for me to put it all into words. I don't want to make things worse for you. I know how hard it's been since Clint died. But—well, after this business tonight, I feel like I have to say something."

"I'm listening."

"It's about Ammie."

Matt frowned. "What about her?"

"She's takin' on too much of your pain, Matt. I'm scared she's going to get hurt."

"My pa and I might knock each other's heads off someday, but neither one of us would ever hurt Ammie."

"That's not the kind of hurt I mean."

Matt straightened. "What are you getting at?"

Shamus paced in front of the corral. "Ammie expects to go with you and the boys to Wichita. I want you to tell her no."

"What? Why? She's gone along on dozens of these kinds of trips."

"That was before she—" he stopped.

"Before she what?" Matt prodded, not understanding any of this.

"Nothing. Never mind."

"Shamus, you can't really think I would ever hurt Ammie."

"Not on purpose, no." Shamus lifted his hat, rubbing his hand over his balding head. "I'm asking you as a friend not to take her with you. But if you do, I want you to promise me something."

"What's that?"

"I want you to remember all the years you two have had together, how precious those years have been. Keep her safe, Matt."

Annoyed and vaguely hurt that Shamus would even consider such an admonition necessary, Matt said only, "You know I will."

"You know you will what?" a familiar, defiant voice said, coming up behind him. Ammie had apparently decided she'd acquiesced long enough to her father's request that she stay in the house. "Zachary Grayson should be horsewhipped. Has anyone mentioned that yet tonight?"

"Ammie . . ." Shamus's voice warned.

Matt waved him off. "It's all right, Shamus. I'm used to Ammie's delicate ways." He forced a crooked smile. Amelia O'Rourke had been his friend as long as he could remember. He looked into her green eyes and winced to see his own pain reflected there. Maybe Shamus had a point about her staying home. Matt knew how upset she was by the rift widening between himself and his father. He should have suspected she would try to do something about it.

"I can't believe Zak ruined everything," she said.

"It's all right, Ammie. I'm used to it."

"Well, you shouldn't be. Blast the man! Fathers aren't supposed to hate their sons."

Matt stiffened—the words cut deeper than he would have thought they could. After all, Ammie had only voiced what he'd been thinking for a long time now. "I'd better get some shuteye," he said, pushing the thought away. "Will and Jess will want to head out early tomorrow."

Ammie caught his arm. "I'm sorry, Matt. I shouldn't have said that."

He didn't look at her. "Forget it."

She didn't let go of his arm. "So what time are we leaving in the morning?"

Matt looked her in the eye. "We aren't. I don't want you to come along on this one, Ammie."

"What?" she gasped. "What are you talking about? We had it all planned!"

Matt flicked a glance toward Shamus, who shot back a grateful look. "Your pa and I decided it wouldn't be a good idea for you to spend six weeks on the trail with three dusty cowboys. Besides, there's always a chance of a freak summer storm." Ammie was terrified of violent weather. Nine years ago, her mother had died in a flash flood.

"You'll be with me. I'll be fine. I want to come."

"No. I need some time alone. To think. Please understand."

She crossed her arms, scowling, but Matt saw surrender in her green eyes. "I'll miss you," she said.

"I'll miss you too." He chucked her under the chin, briefly disconcerted to realize that she was almost as tall as he was. When had she sprouted up? When had—? His thought was fleeting, unfinished, as Ammie continued.

"Could you ride to the creek with me?"

"I need to turn in."

"Please?"

Matt relented. He wondered at the sudden, sharp concern in Shamus's eyes, but when the man made no comment, he and Ammie mounted and rode out. He supposed Shamus was worried that if Ammie got him alone, Matt would admit that he was considering not returning to Texas. He and Ammie had often talked over the things that bothered them most. They didn't always agree with each other or solve each other's problems, but just knowing the other was there to listen had somehow helped.

That night, though, Matt had resisted his temptation to

share his doubts, his confusion with her. And now these six weeks later, he was glad he had. This was a decision that he alone had to make.

He patted the gelding's neck. What was there to keep him in Texas, anyway? He had enough money of his own for a stake. Even if he didn't, it wouldn't matter. He could hire on anywhere. He was a top wrangler, damned good at what he did. He was a pretty fair hand with a gun too. Maybe he could work for Wells Fargo. Maybe . . .

Damn! The Diamond G was his birthright. He'd put his sweat and blood into that land. He had as much claim to it as his father did—maybe more. Zak Grayson had fought off Comanches and carpetbaggers. Matt's battles had been with Zak himself.

How much longer could he wage war with his own father? How high a price was he willing to pay?

Matt's fists tightened on the reins. *Fathers aren't supposed to hate their sons.* Maybe Shamus was right. Maybe it would be better for everyone if Matt Grayson didn't come home.

With smooth, even strokes Ammie cleaved the waters of Shamrock Creek, reveling in its coolness, while overhead the blazing Texas sun trailed fingers of light through the sheltering canopy of cottonwoods that lined either side of the stream. The lacing of leaves culled away the fiercest of the heat, leaving her bathed in shimmering warmth, the water itself dappled in flecks of gold.

She had been right to come here after the argument with her father. As ever, the peacefulness of this place soothed her, relaxed her as nothing else could.

No more than a half-dozen feet wide and a foot deep along most of its course, Shamrock Creek collected into a significant pool here among the cottonwoods and willows, reaching depths of four feet or more and stretching to fifteen feet wide. This was her place, hers and Matt's. It had been since they were children. They came here, separately or together, whenever they needed time to think, be alone, or get away from whatever was troubling them.

Amelia reached for an exposed tree root to help pull herself out of the water. Glistening droplets trailed down her slender naked body to dampen the pungent grasses at her feet. She felt free and uninhibited as she picked up the coarse towel she had brought from the ranch. She could have been Eve, standing in the midst of Eden, surrounded by trees, grass, water, and wildflowers.

The only thing missing was Adam.

Adam in the form of Matt Grayson?

Ammie's body tingled, a scarlet blush starting at the tips of her toes and not stopping until its heat seared her cheeks.

Not the look a friend gives a friend.

No. Her father was wrong, dead wrong. Matt Grayson was her best friend. She was worried about him, concerned—scared. That was why he was so much in her thoughts lately.

Wasn't it?

Reaching for a fresh calico shirt and denim trousers, Ammie pictured him in her mind's eye—his lean, hard muscled body, his dark hair skimming the collar of his shirt, his midnight blue eyes bright with laughter, dark with hurt. Her body warmed anew, and it had nothing at all to do with the day's temperature. Yanking on her clothes, she sank down in front of a cottonwood. What was happening to her?

Not the look a friend gives a friend.

No.

Against her will, her thoughts drifted to that twilight night six weeks ago when she and Matt had come to this very place.

He'd been in no mood for conversation, so they had sat amongst the trees sharing the companionable silence that only long friendship can know. Finally, though, Ammie had succumbed to the need to draw him out. He'd been keeping too much inside himself since Clint died. She had learned over the years that if she didn't prod him just a little, Matt could easily shut out the whole world.

Except for her. Matt shared bits of himself with her that he never shared with anyone. He trusted her completely. He always had. And she held on to that trust as the rare and precious gift that it was.

"Matt," she began, twisting a tuft of grass around her fingers, "I'm sorry about tonight. I shouldn't have tried anything so stupid."

"You were just trying to help."

"I really thought if you and Zak could just sit down to a meal together . . ." She let her voice trail off.

"Don't put yourself in the middle of this, Ammie. Not this time."

"I can't help it, Matt. I care about you too much to keep my mouth shut. Dammit, if you just told Zak the truth about that night in Abilene, that it was—"

"No!" The word was sharp, final. "I wish to God I'd never even told *you* what happened that night."

Ammie's eyes widened, the sting of his words like a slap in the face. He must have noticed, because he rushed to add, "Not because I don't want you to know what happened, but because I can see how much it hurts you not to be able to tell my father. I shouldn't have put you in that position."

"It's all right."

"No, it isn't all right. Nothing's all right, not anymore. That's why I took your pa up on his offer to go fifty-fifty with him on this horse herd. Maybe being gone for a while will give my father the time he needs . . . to get over Clint."

She knew he didn't believe that, not for a second. But she didn't press him.

He climbed to his feet. "I'd best get back."

She rose to face him. "There's something you're not telling me."

He shook his head but didn't quite meet her gaze.

"We've never had secrets from each other, Matt." She gave him a shaky smile. "Well, not too many, anyway."

He seemed about to say something, then changed his mind. Instead he forced a grin. "It'll be good to be in Wichita again. Saloons and painted ladies. Maybe I'll sow me some wild oats."

Ammie turned away, pretending to fuss with the cinch on Tulip's saddle. She remembered all too well the saloons in Wichita. She'd been in a few herself, bailing out her father when his thirst for whiskey had outflanked his judgment after a long trail drive. But she wasn't thinking about her father. She was thinking of the beautiful women who draped themselves over drunk and lonesome cowboys and imagining one of those drunk and lonesome cowboys to be Matt Grayson. The image was suddenly beyond bearing.

With his dark good looks, Matt had turned many a feminine head. Ammie had even aided him on a few of his conquests, happily acceding to his requests to prepare picnic lunches and help him memorize bits of poetry. But no young lady had ever yet sparked more than a passing fancy in him.

She recalled the afternoon they had spent ascribing various attributes to their separate notions of the ideal woman and the ideal man. Matt detailed his dream woman—kind and compassionate like his mother had been, but with a mind of her own—while Ammie had dolloped in for him a spirit of adventure, a woman who wasn't afraid to get her hands dirty or to go skinny-dipping on a hot summer afternoon.

It wasn't until much later, on a moonless night when she couldn't sleep, that Ammie realized how much she had unwittingly contributed bits of herself to Matt's "dream woman"—and how closely Matt himself resembled her own notion of an ideal man. It had taken hours to convince herself that such fantasies meant nothing.

And now he was leaving for six weeks, and she was standing here with him on the banks of Shamrock Creek trying very hard not to visualize him in the arms of a Wichita saloon girl.

On impulse she caught his hand. "You wouldn't want to shortchange any of those ladies now, would you, Matt?"

He frowned. "What do you mean?"

"I mean, we haven't done any practice kissing for a long time." Practice kissing was a game they had played a time or two over the years. They had invented the game just after she'd turned sixteen and Terence Kessler had tried to kiss her at the River Oaks spring social—tried, then stopped, claiming kissing a fish wasn't what he'd had in mind. Mortified, she had run to Matt. Matt had soothed her the best he could, but the only way he could get her to stop crying was to promise to give her kissing lessons. The rare sessions they'd had these past three years had always ended in hysterical laughter. Right now, though, Ammie didn't feel much like laughing. "You don't want your painted ladies to be disappointed, do you, Matt?" she teased, though her heart was pounding strangely.

"I've never had any complaints."

"Ah, but practice makes perfect. Or so you've told me."

Matt looked at the ground. "I don't think it would be a very good i—"

Ammie rose on tiptoe and twined her arms about his neck, pressing her lips firmly against his. At first his mouth was stiff, unyielding, but slowly he began to relax. Matt had ever been a most patient, dedicated instructor. His hand came up, brushing the hair back from her face, then he cupped her head with both his hands, his mouth growing more insistent, demanding. Ammie felt a delicious warmth creep over her, sifting to every tiny part of her. She threaded her fingers through his hair, a low moan escaping her throat.

Abruptly, Matt pulled back, his expression flustered, bewildered. Ammie tried and failed to slow the trip-hammer beat of her heart. She too was stunned, confused, yet tenuously, fragilely awed.

"Practice really does make perfect, doesn't it, Matt? . . . Matt?"

"I need to get back, Ammie," he said, his voice sounding hoarse, distant. He started toward his gelding.

"Matt?"

He turned. "What?"

"N-nothing—" she stammered. "Never mind. Just— just take care of yourself, hear? In Wichita, I mean."

He had ridden out, and she had not stopped him, though everything in her had begged her to try. If ever in their lives they had needed to talk, it was at that moment about that kiss. But they had not. There were too many other things to worry about that night. Matt had indeed been hiding something.

And now six weeks had passed, and Ammie knew what that something had been. She stood barefoot, brushing off the stray bits of grass that clung to her denims. He would be back. He *had* to be back.

Picking up her boots, she upended them, giving each a sharp thump as was her habit. Still, she jumped, startled, as a small garter snake tumbled out of one of them.

She grimaced, watching it disappear into the tall grass. Just what her Garden of Eden needed.

Well, at least the little varmint hadn't tried to strike up a conversation with her.

Amelia tromped over to where she'd left Tulip tied to a shrub. She patted the chestnut's neck. "He's coming home today, Tulip. No matter what my father and Smokey say, he's coming home."

The mare whinnied, giving her head a toss, then nuzzled the rear pocket of Amelia's jeans with her nose. "Don't you ever think of anything but food?"

The mare snorted.

Rolling her eyes, Ammie pulled a bedraggled carrot out of a saddlebag and fed it to the mare. "I don't know why men think being pregnant is a delicate condition. You're about as delicate as a freight train." Ammie mounted then, guiding the mare away from the creek. When she rode clear of the trees, she couldn't resist another northward glance.

She gasped. Dust! An enormous, billowing ribbon of dust! With a glad cry, Ammie urged Tulip into a gallop and headed for the road. In minutes she could make out Will and Jess. Her heart leaped, and her gaze slipped past them. The smile that had been meant for Matt froze.

Matt was not there.

Keeping Tulip at a run, Ammie rode to intercept the two Shamrock hands. They saw her and waved. She waved back. Reining in beside Jess, she tried to keep a note of hysteria from creeping into her voice. "Where's Matt?"

"Why, welcome home, Jess," Jess said in a good-humored mocking tone, his gap-toothed grin showing white in his sun-dark face. "It's so good to see you. We missed you."

Ammie was in no mood. "Where's Matt?" she repeated.

Jess's smile disappeared. In its place was a frown of concern as he studied her. "You all right, Miss Ammie?"

"Where's Matt?" she shrilled.

Jess turned in his saddle, casting a nonchalant glance over his left shoulder. "Have you gone blind, girl? He's right—" The words stopped. "Well, goldarn. He was ridin' drag, I swear. I just seen him, couldn't have been more'n fifteen minutes ago."

"Then where is he?"

Jess shrugged. "He's a big boy. He'll be along."

Ammie wanted to scream at him. Didn't he understand what was happening? But of course he didn't. Matt wouldn't have confided in Jess. Briefly she considered going after Matt. Fifteen minutes wasn't much of a head start. Then her shoulders slumped. If leaving was truly his choice . . .

She gripped the saddlehorn, ordering herself not to cry as she rode alongside Will and Jess. Her wrangler's instincts took over, and she helped the two men drive the horses into the ranch yard.

Will galloped ahead, throwing open the gate of the main corral. Ammie gave no notice to the choking dust. An aching emptiness was already clawing at her insides: Matt had turned back. Matt was gone.

As the last of the horses were hazed into the corral, Jess dismounted and closed the gate. Woodenly, Ammie joined him.

"Come to think of it," Jess said, "I guess it was a mite peculiar that Matt asked to ride drag this mornin'."

"Why?"

"It was Will's turn. Besides, who'd *want* to ride drag, if'n they could avoid it?"

A man who wanted to quietly disappear, Ammie thought bitterly, though she said nothing.

She looked up to see her father hurrying across the yard from the barn. Abruptly, she spun away, fearful that she would say something she would later regret. Her father might have suggested to Matt that he leave, but the choice to follow through on that suggestion, she knew, had been Matt's alone.

Shamus called out to her, but she quickened her pace until she was all but running toward the house. She didn't want her father to see her cry.

She'd reached the porch when she caught the sound of

approaching hoofbeats. Hardly daring to breathe, let alone hope, she turned.

If she could've looked into a mirror, she knew she would have seen a smile on her face that stretched from one ear to the other.

Thundering into the yard astride his big black gelding, four mares running reluctantly ahead of him, was Matt Grayson.

☘/Chapter 3

Ammie sprinted back toward the corral, arriving just as Matt secured the mares with the other horses. He grinned down at her from Drifter. "Those little ladies decided to make one last dash for freedom. I had to convince them otherwise."

Ammie pretended the tears in her eyes were from the dust. "Hi, Matt." Was that croaking sound really her voice?

"What do you think, Ammie?" he asked, dismounting.

Think? Her mind whirled. About his coming back? About his scaring her half to death? About—?

"About the horses," he added, when she didn't answer.

Ammie pressed her hands to her temples, desperately trying to regain her composure. Matt had no idea how upset she was. And this wasn't the time and place for him to find out.

"They look good, Matt," she managed. "Real good."

He was still grinning. "Glad you think so. I'd turn the lot of 'em loose if you didn't, you know."

That he held her opinion of horseflesh in such high regard had always pleased her—but then, she *was* a damned good judge of horses. Right now, though, horses were the furthest thing from her mind. She had to get Matt away from here. They had to talk. Now.

Still, she told him no such thing as he dismounted and strode toward her. Instead, she was scandalized to note that she was actually drinking in the way he walked—all smooth, animal grace despite hours in the saddle. Ammie shook herself inwardly. This madness had to stop!

"Got 'em for twenty dollars a head," Matt was saying. "It'll take a month of hard work, but I'm bettin' we'll get a hundred each for 'em from the army once they're full broke."

Shamus stepped out to offer Matt his hand. Matt accepted. "Glad to have you back, Matt."

"Glad to be back, Shamus."

Ammie detected no hidden irony in either of their voices, but there was a wariness in both men that had never been there before. She hurt for them both. Shamus excused himself then and went off with Will and Jess and Smoke, who'd emerged from the bunkhouse, to inspect the horses further.

Ammie stood alone with Matt, feeling an awkwardness that made her furious. "My father . . . told me about . . . I—" Her words were cut short by a sudden howling from somewhere off to her left. Bounding out of the barn and across the yard was a lop-eared, black-tan-and-white hound.

"Pickles!" Matt hunkered down to accept the dog's stampeding-buffalo style of greeting. Matt still ended up on his back as Pickles swarmed all over him, the dog's whole body wriggling with excitement.

Ammie had to laugh. Pickles had adored Matt since the first day she, Matt, and Zachary Grayson had found her half-dead in some brush nearly eight years ago. Hardly more than a pup then, half her right ear had been missing and her haunches had been ripped open in a losing battle with coyotes.

Ammie's smile faded as she recalled what else had happened that day.

It had been a typical Texas August: hotter than hellfire. What had not been typical was that she, Matt, and Zak

Grayson had been out together hunting deer. Zak rarely took time away from the ranch—at least, not to spend it with Matt. Even then, the tall taciturn rancher and his fourteen-year-old son had seemed to be almost constantly at loggerheads.

But not that morning. Matt had been positively glowing with the idea of having his father all to himself. Clint had broken his arm in a fall from a horse the week before and was under doctor's orders to take it easy.

"You don't have to invite me along," Ammie assured Matt. "You and your pa should go alone." Her penchant for adopting all manner of wild creatures since the tender age of three hadn't exactly made hunting her favorite activity anyway. Not that she hadn't gone hunting with Matt before—sometimes even with Clint joining them—but she'd never taken a shot at anything in her life except for an old bottle or two lined up on a fence rail.

"I want you for a witness," Matt said. "When I finally show my father I'm better than Clint, at something anyway."

Ammie kept her opinion of this notion to herself, though it worried her whenever Matt tried to prove himself to his father. Such occasions had a way of taking unexpected turns, usually for the worse.

Their quarry that day was a particular deer, a cagey old stag that Zak Grayson had already tried numerous times to track near enough for a clear shot. This day Matt was in the lead, maneuvering, shifting, changing their course time and again to keep them downwind, until at last they angled to within a hundred yards of the wary buck.

Zak's palms were sweating so badly, he had to wipe them on his trousers. "You did good, Matt," he said, his gravel voice giving a peculiar edge even to a compliment. "Real good."

Matt beamed, shooting a victorious wink at Ammie.

Eagerly, Zak readied his rifle. "He must stand six feet at the shoulders."

"Pa," Matt said, "Pa, let me. I can get him. Please."

Zak wavered, eyeing his elusive prey. With obvious reluctance, he stepped aside. "Don't miss. I want that buck's head on my wall."

Ammie couldn't take her eyes from the deer. Standing at the edge of a clearing, the buck was surveying its territory like a medieval lord surveying his fiefdom. A twelve-point rack of antlers crowned its magnificent head. Such a proud beast deserved a more dignified fate than adorning the Diamond G mantel. "He's so beautiful," she murmured.

Matt sighted his rifle.

Ammie held her breath. Matt needed this, wanted it so badly. "So beautiful."

Matt shifted the barrel ever so slightly.

He fired.

Missed.

The startled buck bolted into the trees and vanished. Ammie let out a gasp of relief.

Zak cursed, cuffing Matt in the shoulder so hard, he knocked Matt to his knees. "Stupid!" he shouted. "Blind stupid! Do you know how much I wanted that animal? Have you any idea?"

Matt said nothing.

"Bah!" Zak spat. "I'm takin' you home. I should've known better than to let a boy do a man's work. Even with one arm Clint wouldn't have missed."

Ammie was heartsick. She knew that Matt had missed the buck deliberately, because of her. She thought about telling this to Zak, but the man had even less affinity for sentiment than he did for failure. Telling him would only make things worse.

The three of them trudged in painful silence back to where they'd tied off their horses. It was then that they heard a yelp of pain coming from some nearby brush. Zak levered a cartridge into his rifle. Ammie rushed to investigate, Matt on her heels.

"Careful," Matt said, shifting his body in front of hers. "You don't know what it might be." He pulled back several branches to reveal a pathetic heap of bloodied black-tan-and-white fur huddled in a small nest of grasses.

"Keep clear of her," Zak ordered. "She'll tear you to pieces."

"She won't hurt me." Ammie dropped to her knees beside the injured pup, trying to figure out which wound to tend to first. The pup whimpered and licked her hand.

"Likely one of the pack that's been bringin' down my yearlings," Zak said. "Get clear of her, Amelia."

She held up a hand in protest. "Please, Mr. Grayson, she's just a puppy. I can save her. I can train her."

"Get back! Both of you!"

Ammie's lower lip quivered, but she started to back away.

Matt didn't move. "The pup's too young to kill stock. If Ammie says the dog can be saved, she can be saved. Anyway, it's her right to try."

Zak stiffened. "A dog that attacks cattle once will do it again. Get out of my way, boy!"

Matt straightened. "No."

Ammie knew even then what that single word would cost Matt. After missing the deer, he was ready to do anything to get back into his father's good graces—anything but back down from something he believed in.

A long minute followed before Zak Grayson slowly lowered his rifle. Ammie could see the rage in him, feel it—not so much because he'd been denied the killing of the dog but because his son had defied him. Ammie knew Matt would pay dearly for that defiance later.

Working in swift, abrupt movements and saying absolutely nothing to each other, Zak and Matt rigged a travois

for her to transport the pup. Zak then mounted his gelding and waited. Matt started to mount, but before he
could, Ammie hurried over and gave him a quick, grateful
hug. He gave her a sad smile. She knew he wasn't angry
with her, but he was probably regretting that he had
asked her along. They separated then, Ammie taking the
pup home, the Graysons heading for the Diamond G.

Back at Shamrock, Ammie concentrated on the dog.
Luckily, the hound proved to have a rather fearsome will
to live—or maybe it was her insatiable appetite. Nothing
could die that ate that much.

Ammie was certain of it a week later, when she went to
the barn to check on her patient, only to discover the pup
missing. A hasty search found her in the root cellar, where
she'd somehow worked free the lid from a barrel of dill
pickles. Like a hog at a trough, she was happily chomping
away.

The name stuck.

That same day Matt came by for the first time since the
hunting fiasco. "I was worried about you," she told him as
they sat on the ground in front of the barn, petting the
recovering hound. "Your father was so angry."

"Let's not talk about it, all right?"

"All right." It was blisteringly hot, and she suggested
one of their favorite diversions—skinny-dipping.

"Not today, Am."

"Why not? We can take Pickles. She's limping some,
but—"

"Not today." He all but snapped the words.

Ammie frowned but gave him a good-natured poke in
the ribs. "All right, then what do you—" Her eyes widened when she saw him wince. "Matt, what is it?"

"Nothing."

"Matt—"

"Leave it be, Ammie."

"He beat you, didn't he?"

Color rose in Matt's face. It was all the response she needed. Tears welled in her eyes. "It's my fault. I'm sorry, Matt. I'm sorry. I—I should have let him—I should have let him . . . shoot . . . I—"

"No! Don't say that! Don't ever say that. It was worth it, Ammie. Honest." He scratched Pickles's good ear. "Pickles is a great dog."

"I don't understand it. Your pa never beats Clint. Why is he so mean to you?"

Matt's only answer was to continue to pet the dog.

Amelia forced away the poignant memories. How could eight years ago seem like yesterday? So much had changed, and yet so much hadn't. Matt and Zak were still at loggerheads. She sighed, watching Matt wrestle the still-ecstatic hound. "I think Pickles missed you almost as much as I did."

Matt looked up, his brows furrowed. "What?"

Ammie shook her head. "Forget it. It was nothing."

Matt climbed to his feet. He was grinning, but Ammie had a sudden suspicion that his jovial mood was a pretense and had been since he'd ridden into the yard. He must at least suspect that she knew of his plans to leave Texas, but he wasn't about to bring it up first. Instead, he kept his voice light. "Hope you haven't gotten into too much trouble this past six weeks—without my guiding influence, I mean."

Ammie grimaced. "As a matter of fact, it's been precisely six weeks since I've been in any trouble at all. What does that tell you?"

"That your father doesn't keep nearly as sharp an eye on you when I'm not around."

Ammie thought about that, realizing with a start that Matt had spoken the truth. Her father did seem more aware of her when Matt was over visiting.

Not the look a friend gives a friend.

"Tomorrow's Friday," she said, quickly changing the subject. "You coming to supper?"

"Wouldn't miss it."

"I suppose that's why you came back." She'd meant her voice to be teasing, but it sounded sarcastic even to her own ears. Damn. They needed to talk. "Matt, I—"

Shamus stepped over, interrupting. "Got the paperwork on the herd, Matt?"

Matt nodded. "In my saddlebags. I'll get it for you."

"Oh, no, you don't," Shamus said. "You're not gettin' off that easy. We're partners on this one. Fifty-fifty. Bring the papers up to the house, and we'll go over 'em together."

Only Ammie saw the kindling of alarm in Matt's blue eyes. Quickly, she moved to intercede. "Now, Pa," she cajoled, "Matt's had a long, hard ride. Your musty ol' paperwork can wait. How about I rustle us up some of that lemonade I made this morning instead?"

Shamus shrugged. "All right. I'll be in later." He went on toward the barn.

Matt flicked Ammie a brief, grateful smile.

Her heart gave a familiar twist. She knew him so well—probably too well, to his way of thinking. But she wasn't going to chastise him, not this time anyway, about the one thing he did have in common with his father—an overabundance of pride.

Instead, she linked her arm in his and steered him toward the house. "It's good to have you back, Matt."

There was a long pause before he said. "It's good to be back, Ammie." The sentiment was proper and polite, and she knew with a sudden sick certainty that he hadn't meant a word of it.

She tried hard not to give in to a wave of melancholy. She told herself he had indeed had a long, hard trip. He was tired and irritable. He would come around. What mood could she expect him to be in when his inevitable return to the Diamond G and his father was still ahead of him?

Besides, her melancholy wasn't nearly as disturbing as another emotion—her new and steadily intensifying awareness of Matt Grayson, the man. She knew her cheeks were flaming even now, as she tried and failed *not* to notice the feel of hard muscle rippling beneath the blue chambray of his shirt sleeve. She was not used to this preoccupation with Matt's body. She wasn't even certain she liked it. It felt almost disloyal somehow. Yet not even thinking herself disloyal made the awareness subside. In fact, what she wanted most in the world to do right now was to reach out to him, to smooth her palm along the plane of his jaw, to turn his face toward hers and tell him how miserable her life had been these past six weeks without him.

But she didn't. She couldn't.

Not yet anyway. She took a deep breath. Maybe if she got him settled in the kitchen, they could sit and talk. Her heart thundered. Maybe.

Neither of them spoke as they mounted the three wooden steps to the veranda of the two-story house. Their boots made scuffing noises on the planked flooring. The house itself was mute testimony to Shamus O'Rourke's steady success over the years. The first story, built of fieldstone twelve years ago, then expanded four years later, was now the lower level to a wooden second story that had been finished just last year. Ammie had only the vaguest memories of the sod structure they'd called home their first couple of years in Texas.

She shoved open the oak door with its three rectangular panels of leaded glass and walked inside. Matt followed, Pickles galumphing behind him. The hound had attached herself to Matt like a burr, perhaps fearing that if she let him out of her sight, he would disappear again. Ammie knew the feeling.

"Come in the kitchen, Matt," she said, praying her voice didn't reflect her nervousness. "We'll have that lemonade."

"Sounds good."

Matt crossed the spacious main room ahead of her and tossed his gloves and hat onto the horsehair settee that fronted the hearth. Ammie found the gesture comforting. Matt had always felt as much at home here as she did. At least that hadn't changed.

The fieldstone hearth, once part of the original outer wall of the house, was open on two sides, serving in winter to heat this room and the dining room opposite. The settee was representative of most of the furnishings in the house: It was sturdy enough to please her father, yet it had a certain charm that had caught her mother's eye. Draped over the back of the settee was a beautiful patchwork quilt, replete with embroidered daisies, all worked with loving care years ago by Penny O'Rourke. One of Ammie's fondest memories was sitting in front of that hearth with her mother, both of them cocooned in the quilt, giggling and telling each other scary stories that wouldn't allow either one of them to go to sleep until dawn.

A rosewood Seth Thomas clock graced the mantel above the fireplace, flanked by two exquisite wood carvings sculpted by Smoke Larson. One carving was of three horses at full gallop, and the other was of a grizzly bear poking its head into a tree stump in a perpetual search for honey.

On the wall above the fireplace her father had mounted the Sharps carbine he'd carried during the war. He took it down for an occasional cleaning, but Ammie had never known him to fire it. She suspected this particular gun's presence was more philosophical than functional. A grim reminder: It was with that gun that her father had shot

Zak Grayson. "A gun never proves who's right," her father often said, "only who's the better shot."

Ammie rounded the fireplace, strode past the mahogany dining-room set, and headed into the kitchen. She wasn't certain what had possessed her to make lemonade that morning, but she was glad she had. She crossed to the counter beneath a gingham-curtained four-paned window and poured out two glasses from a half-full pitcher. Her father, it seemed, had already helped himself to his share of the tart refreshment.

"Hope that tastes as good as it looks," Matt said, plunking himself down onto one of four rough-hewn chairs that banded the kitchen table.

Ammie handed Matt his lemonade, then slid into the chair opposite him and took a sip from her own glass. "Hope so, too," she said. Her eyes were locked on his beard-bristled throat as he made short work of the lemonade. What would it be like, she wondered, to lay her fingers along that very male, sweat-slick flesh—to touch . . . to taste. . . .

She coughed, sputtered, choked, almost upsetting her glass.

"You all right?" Matt asked.

She managed a nod, her eyes watering. This was getting ridiculous. She should tell him—just *tell* him—and get it over with.

Her heart pounding, she leaned forward. "Don't you know, I'd have missed you forever, Matt Grayson."

Pickles had laid her head on Matt's thigh. Matt ruffled the dog's ear, then glanced across the table, his dark brows furrowing in puzzlement. "What'd you say, Ammie?"

She closed her eyes but could not bring herself to repeat the statement. Instead she said lamely, "You get dust in your ears out there?"

"Ammie, I got dust everywhere." He grinned, peering

down into the open neck of his shirt. "This cowboy needs a bath."

Her heart skipped. "We could go swimming at the creek."

He shook his head. "I'd best head home. Get it over with." He set his empty glass down and rose to his feet. "Ride with me?"

She was beside him in an instant. "Love to." It was a leisurely one-hour ride to the Diamond G—surely she could manufacture some courage along the way.

They went back through the house, Matt pausing to retrieve his gloves and hat. He started toward the door, then hesitated, his gaze snagged by the piano in the far corner of the room. He cast a sad smile at Ammie and crossed over to it, then sat down on the brocade bench. His long, rein-callused fingers caressed the keys. She knew what he was thinking. The piano had been his mother's. From Emily, Matt had learned a love of music that still burned bright inside him, six years after her death. Ammie and Matt had often sat for hours, just listening to Emily play.

Early on, Matt had shown a natural talent for the piano himself. He would hear a piece played by his mother and soon be able to play it back precisely, even embellish it if he chose. The piano was the one thing that had brought the Graysons together as a family. Zak adored listening to his wife play. Those times were among the few when Ammie remembered seeing a look of contentment on Zak Grayson's otherwise implacable features.

The day of Emily's funeral, though, Zak had stunned the gathering of mourners by announcing that the piano would be sold.

Ammie had seen the stricken look on Matt's face. Shamus had seen it too. He stepped in and told Zak he would buy it. "I've been meaning to have Ammie try her hand at some of life's more ladylike refinements," he said.

Later, Shamus had taken Matt aside. "You're welcome to come over and play anytime you like." He clasped Matt about the shoulders. "Maybe even give Ammie a lesson or two."

"Ammie's tone deaf and you know it. Pickles could learn to play before Ammie could." Matt blinked back tears. "Thanks, Shamus."

The day the piano had been delivered to Shamrock, Matt spent the night. Shamus got out his fiddle, and the two of them had played until the sun came up.

There were times, later, when Matt had played for her, beautiful songs he'd made up himself, melodies so haunting, she would sometimes dream about them.

Like the one he was playing now.

"You all right, Ammie?" Matt asked.

She shook herself. "Fine," she lied.

He stood and stretched. "We'd best go."

The front door opened, and Shamus strode in. "The horses look top-notch, Matt. Real good."

"Thanks, Shamus."

Shamus stepped over to the piano. "I'll get my fiddle out tomorrow night, and we'll raise the roof a bit, eh? Mary loves music."

"Mary?" Ammie bristled. "You're not telling me—"

"She'll be joining us for supper tomorrow."

Ammie fumed inwardly. Mary Denby was the last person she wanted intruding on her evening with Matt. But she wasn't about to start another argument with her father. She managed a polite nod. "That'll be just fine, Pa. But don't wait supper for me tonight, all right? I'm riding along with Matt to the Diamond G."

Shamus O'Rourke must not have wanted to start another argument himself. He frowned but said only, "Just be sure you're back by nightfall."

Grinding her teeth, Ammie followed Matt out the door. Matt paused on the porch steps. "You get the feeling your father wasn't real keen on the idea of your riding along with me?"

"My father's head's been getting stuffed with a lot of fool notions lately," Ammie grumbled. "No doubt compliments of Mary Denby. I tell you, things are getting serious between Pa and that woman."

"I thought you liked Mary Denby."

"I do." She folded her arms across her chest. "That is, I did." Mary Denby had been the River Oaks schoolmarm for the last several years of Ammie's schooling. Mary Denby's husband had been alive then, and things had been different. "I just don't like her and Pa getting so—so friendly."

"You can't be sure that's what's happening."

"Yes, I can. Didn't you hear him? He calls her Mary now instead of Mrs. Denby."

"What difference does that make?"

"It makes all the difference. A woman knows these things."

"What woman?" he asked, genuinely confused.

"Me, you idiot!"

He shook his head, contrite. "I'm sorry, Ammie. I guess I don't think of you as a woman. I mean—well, you know what I mean."

Ammie let out a cavalier laugh, but underneath she felt a stinging hurt. She had almost convinced herself that Matt, too, had felt something changing, evolving in their own relationship. That he, too, had felt something different, something wonderful in the kiss they'd shared by the creek the night before he left. And she had almost been stupid enough to tell him so. Thank heaven she hadn't. It was obvious that Matt hadn't felt a thing.

"Let's ride," he said, grinning. "Got two or three tall tales to spin about the dark of night and the ladies of Wichita."

"Can't wait," Ammie managed weakly. "But—but I

don't want to push Tulip too hard in her condition. You go on ahead. I'll saddle Ranger and catch up."

"I'll help you."

"No. No, you go ahead." She suddenly needed some time alone.

"You sure?"

She nodded, not looking at him.

"See you in a few minutes." With that, Matt mounted Drifter and rode out.

She stared after him, unable now to take her eyes off him. An hour to the Diamond G. An hour of Matt Grayson's bawdy Wichita nights? How was she ever going to bear it?

"Oh, Matt," she murmured, "what's happening to me? To us?" But she knew. She just hadn't had the courage to acknowledge the truth until now.

Heaven save her, she was falling in love with her best friend.

Chapter 4

In love with him? Ammie rode alongside Matt, hardly daring to look at him, hardly daring to breathe. It couldn't be. They'd been friends forever. Seen each other at their best and at their worst. Shared adventure, misadventure, laughter, tears. Love him, yes. Of course. But *in* love with him? She couldn't be. Didn't want to be.

But she was.

She watched him covertly from under the brim of her Stetson. She'd known Matt Grayson since he was eight years old, yet in a curious way she was looking at him now as though she'd never seen him before in her life. She studied him, memorized him—the broad shoulders, the tanned forearms, the powerful, gloved hands that gripped the reins of the gelding, the strong angled face, a face that some might consider hard, even cold, but that had never been so to her. With her, those carved features had ever been gentled by the warmth and the humor she found so often in his blue eyes.

The same humor that was in them now as he recounted his adventures on the trail to Wichita and back. A cougar had spooked Jess Johnson's horse and nearly spooked the herd. A human polecat had tried to charge them a dollar a head to cross "his" river. Liver-curdling biscuits had been inflicted on them by their hired-on, then quickly fired, cook.

Ammie enjoyed each story immensely, especially since not one of them involved painted ladies. For that, she happily took full credit. She'd managed only a distracted

nod or two during his tales of decadent Wichita nights
and had offered none of her usual encouragement to tell
her every spicy detail. Even so, the stories had been so
risqué that Ammie began to have a peculiar hunch that
the revelries had taken place only in Matt's mind. He was
weaving these tales for her benefit, not his, apparently
because he thought she expected him to.

Ammie took odd comfort in that, pleased that he evidently had not—as her father had so crudely suggested—
sought out any Wichita cure-alls in either whiskey or
women. But that he could so easily share his trysting esca-
pades with her—real or imagined—only served as further
evidence that she was not even in the running as a potential partner for his amorous encounters. Her perception of
him might have changed, but his perception of her had
not altered one whit. She was his buddy, his pal, his com-
padre.

She was one of the boys. And it hurt.

Not that she had anyone but herself to blame. She'd
never been much for feminine fripperies and folderol. She
couldn't bat her eyelashes at a man to save her life. And in
her entire wardrobe she counted only two dresses. One
she wore to church. The other she'd bought a year ago
when the undaunted Terence Kessler had asked her to a
barn dance. She'd been so nervous, she'd spilled punch
down the front of it, leaving the dress hopelessly stained.

Terence Kessler. Ammie grimaced. If she'd had an
ounce of sense that night, she could have figured out her
feelings for Matt then. None of the stolen kisses she'd
shared with Terence behind the barn had inspired the
kind of feelings Matt's practice sessions had ignited in
her. At the time she had just thought she needed more
practice!

She blushed heatedly. Practice indeed. It hadn't been
practice she had been seeking with Matt on the creek
bank six weeks ago. It had been the fire, the magic of the

real thing. The feel of his mouth hungering for hers, the feel of his breath hot against her cheek, the feel of a man wanting a woman, his woman.

Stop it! She closed her eyes. She couldn't keep doing this, couldn't let these scandalous thoughts continue. If she did, Matt was going to read the truth in her eyes. And for reasons she couldn't yet face, it was suddenly desperately important that he not know the truth. Not yet. To divert her own thoughts, she asked, "So what did the three of you eat for six weeks, if you didn't have a cook and a chuck wagon?"

Matt snorted. "Mostly hardtack and beans. Let me tell you, I'm looking forward to tomorrow night. If there was one thing I missed, Ammie, it was your cooking. I swear, you could make a six-course feast out of an old boot."

Ammie grinned, genuinely pleased. If the old adage was true, that the way to a man's heart was through his stomach. . . . "Keep up the compliments, mister, and I might even bake you an apple pie." Apple was Matt's favorite, but Ammie only infrequently indulged him, mostly because it took her five hours to make one of the blasted things from start to finish. She preferred to have him think of them as a rare and special treat.

Matt sighed dreamily. "Make me one of your apple pies, Am, and you might not get me out of the house all weekend."

"Promise?" The word was out before she could stop it.

Mortified, she turned away from the quizzical look he shot her. Thankfully, before she could dig herself any deeper, an excited howl rose up some hundred feet to their left. They both turned in time to see Pickles streak past, tearing through foot-high clumps of buffalo grass barely a nose-length behind a terrified jackrabbit. The rabbit dodged and weaved, but Pickles matched it zig for zag.

"Five cents on the rabbit," Matt drawled.

"No bet." Ammie had witnessed this little scenario too many times before. True to form, if not to her breed, Pickles slammed to an abrupt halt just before her erstwhile meal vanished into its den. Instead of being disappointed, Pickles sat back on her haunches and looked inordinately pleased with herself.

Matt shook his head, laughing. "What do you suppose she'd do if she ever caught one?"

Ammie chuckled. "Spit it out—unless she got one that'd spent the day in a dill patch."

Another rabbit hopped into view. With a howl of canine delight Pickles was off and running again.

"Now that's the life," Matt said. "Chasing rabbits and eating."

"You'd never settle for that."

He thought about it a minute. "I suppose you're right. Maybe just eating."

She took a swipe at him. "You're terrible." She had hoped she might lead him into a conversation about his plans beyond breaking the new horses, but he was obviously in no mood to be reflective. She supposed it was just as well. Maybe she didn't want to know.

A shadow passed over them then, the sun briefly disappearing. Nervously, Ammie glanced skyward and was relieved to see that the only clouds were of the innocuous cottony-white variety.

"Any storms on your trip?" she asked.

He hesitated. "None to speak of."

Ammie gave him a wan smile. "You've never been a very good liar, Matt Grayson. At least not to me."

"I was glad you weren't there," he said, his voice serious.

Ammie had learned to tolerate rainstorms in the years since her mother's death—as long as she wasn't caught out in the open. It was as if her mind had concocted a rule to protect her. If she was inside a house or other solid structure, the storm couldn't hurt her or anyone else she cared about.

But those times that she had been caught outside, far from shelter . . .

Ammie shivered. She and her mother had been alone in a buckboard returning from a trip to town when the storm had hit. The torrential rain had turned a placid, nearly dry creek into a roiling, churning wall of death. It was Matt, as part of a search party, who had found her several hours later, half drowned, still clinging to the branches of the cottonwood tree where her mother had managed to thrust her in the instant before the raging waters swept Penny O'Rourke away.

Matt had had to climb the tree to pry Ammie's bloodied fingers loose. She remembered screaming . . . remembered . . .

Ammie clutched reflexively at the reins of the spirited bay gelding beneath her. The horse shied and almost bolted. It took her a minute to settle him down.

Matt reined Drifter close, catching hold of the bay's bridle. "I've got to learn to be a better liar."

"No, I'm fine." She took a deep breath. "The storm was rough?"

"Pretty bad. We were two days out of Wichita on the way back. Lost four horses. Just couldn't find 'em again after the rain let up." Those midnight eyes regarded her with open concern. "You sure you're okay?"

"I'm with you, aren't I? Nothing can hurt me when I'm with you."

His brows furrowed for just an instant, as though he were trying to read her thoughts, and she worried that she had let something show through in her eyes. She worked to make her expression neutral. Matt seemed to shake himself, then glanced around, as if to take note of familiar landmarks. The look on his face turned grim. "Another fifteen minutes to my father's 'welcome home' party."

"Don't borrow trouble."

"You seen him since I left?"

"No."

"Then I doubt I'm borrowing anything. Pa usually gets together with Shamus a couple times of month to jaw about things."

"Not since Clint died," she said sadly. "To tell you the truth, I was surprised when he said yes to my dinner invitation the night before you left. Your pa's pretty much slammed the door on the whole world. And my pa's been spending too much time with Mary Denby to be much help." She sighed. "Sometimes I think if Pa had just talked to Zak after Clint died—"

"It wouldn't have done any good. My father had his mind made up about what happened."

"But he wasn't even there," Ammie protested. "Oh, Matt, it must be so hard for you! It's been four months— don't you think that maybe your father could handle the truth now?"

"Four months, four years, it wouldn't matter." Matt fingered the gelding's reins. "In a lot of ways the more time that passes, the worse Pa gets. He had so many dreams for Clint. Pa literally expected him to be in the White House one day. And it was all just getting started when it ended."

Ammie winced. It had ended with a bullet in Clint's chest in an Abilene hotel room. Memories, chilling, horrifying, flashed through her mind. She, her father, Matt, and Clint had all been in Abilene to attend a cattlemen's convention. Clint was going to run for the state legislature and he was stumping for voter support among the wealthy Texas ranchers in attendance. But something had gone dreadfully wrong. Ammie had found Matt in that hotel room, cradling his dead brother in his arms. In her life Ammie had never seen such a look of undiluted anguish as she saw in Matt's eyes that night—anguish much the same as she was seeing now.

She longed to tell him to change the subject, but she didn't.

"It shouldn't have happened, Ammie. If I'd just listened harder to Clint, it never would've—" He closed his eyes. There was a melancholy edge to his voice that made Ammie's heart ache. She knew Matt had loved Clint, but Zak's overt bias for his older son had long ago stunted the relationship between the two brothers.

"You didn't know he was going to get himself into trouble that night," she said. "If you had, you would have helped him."

"He was my brother. I should've known. Somehow, I should've just known."

"It's bad enough that your father blames you. Don't you blame yourself."

He nodded, but he looked unconvinced.

This was not the frame of mind he should be in when he was about to face Zak. "Dammit, Matt," she said, feeling a little desperate. "You can't—"

He held up a hand. "I'm all right, Ammie. Honest. And I appreciate what you're trying to do. But this is my fight." He hesitated a moment, then said, "In fact, I think it might be better if I rode in alone. You go on home. Your pa wanted you back before dark anyway."

"It won't be dark for six hours!"

"Go home, Ammie. I mean it."

She sighed. "All right, Matt, if that's what you want."

"It is." He tried to smile, but he didn't quite manage it. "See you for supper tomorrow."

She watched him ride off, feeling strangely torn. She respected his right to face Zak alone, but she knew in her heart that being alone with his father was the last thing Matt needed right now. Matt had too much going on inside him, too much that was still unresolved about Clint.

What frightened her most was the thought that Zak would say something that provoked Matt into leaving Texas after all.

Ammie guided the bay toward a nearby grove of pin oaks. Her heart hammering, she dismounted and began to pace, wishing to heaven she hadn't been such a coward. Somehow she should have found the courage to tell Matt about the wondrous new feelings that were stirring to life inside her. If she had, she wouldn't have to be worrying about anything Zak said. Matt would never want to leave if he knew she had fallen in love with him.

She trembled. Would he?

She loosened Ranger's saddle and sank down in front of the closest tree. Pickles trotted over to lick her face, and she hugged the dog close. What if her love for Matt didn't make any difference to him. What if it made no difference at all? "I'll give him an hour, Pickles, maybe two," she said shakily. "Then Matt Grayson and I are going to talk."

Matt held Drifter to a walk. Now that his return home was at hand, he found himself tormented by doubts— chief among them that he'd made the wrong choice. That he shouldn't have come back at all.

True, the Diamond G was his birthright, but what good was a birthright if fighting for it meant perpetuating bad blood between himself and his father?

He reined Drifter to a halt atop the rise that led down into the sweeping, tree-studded Diamond G valley. Below him lay the sprawling corrals and outbuildings that flanked the elegant three-story house that was the crown jewel of the Diamond G. Matt felt a familiar tightening in his chest just looking at the house. The structure, primarily of Victorian influence, had been a gift from his father to his mother, built from the ground up just eight years ago.

Though most of the work had been hired out, Zak,

Matt, and Clint had constructed the mansard roof themselves. Matt shifted in the saddle now, resting his arms across his saddlehorn, a sad smile touching his lips. What a time that had been. The three of them had actually worked as a team. Once, Zak had even grabbed Matt in time to keep him from tumbling off the roof and breaking his neck. Three days later, Matt had returned the favor.

"I don't think Ma's going to appreciate any of us dyin' to put up this roof," Matt had said around a mouthful of nails.

"I guess I'm the only one who should be up here," Clint put in, his handsome face alight with a rare grin. "I'm the only Grayson who always seems to land on his feet."

"We'll just see about that!" Matt feigned a lunge at his brother, who recoiled in mock horror.

"I'm going to bounce both of you on your heads if this roof doesn't get done today." Zak growled the words, but he too was grinning. "Your mother's had to do without her piano for a week because I won't let her into the new house until the roof is done." Zak had had the piano moved from their old quarters with the promise that the roof would be finished "in a day or two." Emily Grayson had been the essence of patience when it came to just about anything but her piano.

Finally, though, the last tile was set. Zak clambered down the ladder and called for Matt and Clint to join him, then strode toward the one-story stone house that had been their home since the Graysons had first settled in Texas twenty-odd years before. The stone structure had been a necessity then—it didn't burn during Comanches attacks. But when the Indians had been forced farther and farther west by the army and by encroaching settlers, Emily Grayson had made her desire for a real house known—one like those she had seen on a trip to the East Coast before the war.

While Matt and Clint watched, Zak escorted Emily across the yard and up the steps of the new house. With an adoring smile, he scooped her into his arms and carried her across the threshold like a new bride. Laughing gaily, Emily swept into the drawing room and headed straight for her piano. She and Matt alternated playing, and the whole family sang songs long into the night. Matt couldn't remember a happier time.

Two years later his mother was dead, taken by a fever that stole her life and in a very real sense stole Zak Grayson's spirit as well.

Later, during periods that were especially bleak between himself and his father, Matt would have liked to think it was his mother's death that had been the turning point, the reason his father had become so rigid and unyielding—with him, with everyone. Except that it wasn't true. Zak had always been harder on Matt. If his mother's death had been a turning point, it was because she was no longer there to act as a buffer, a peacemaker between Matt and his father. An already-incendiary relationship had become even more volatile.

And then Clint had died. . . .

Matt shuddered. He couldn't think about that. Not now, not when he was about to face his father for the first time since their explosive parting six weeks ago. He took a deep breath. He'd put it off long enough. It was time to get it over with. Schooling his features into an impassive mask, he nudged the gelding toward the house.

Chapter 5

Matt tied off Drifter at the hitchrail in front of the house and took the six porch steps two at a time. But when he reached the double oak doors that were the entryway to the house, he hesitated, wondering whether he should knock. Then a bolt of anger rippled through him. Why the hell should he knock to gain entrance to his own home? With an oath, he slammed open the door.

He stalked inside and stopped, assaulted by sights and scents that were at once familiar and yet strangely foreign as well. This might be his home, but he hadn't lived here for years. He had moved out to the bunkhouse the night his father had sold the piano, despite an unexpected and touching plea from Clint that he stay. Only rarely since then had Matt even set foot in the main house.

His gaze flicked briefly up the stairs in front of him, half-expecting to see his father emerge from the first room on the right—Clint's room. But nothing stirred. His gaze trailed next to the drawing room on his left. It was the room that pained him most, the room in which his mother had spent so many happy hours. With the exception of the piano, everything was as it had been the night Emily Grayson died. Maroon dominated the flamboyant floral carpet, and the color was vividly repeated in the patterned wallpaper, while curtains of ivory lace gave the room an airy feel. Delicate porcelain figurines lined the mantel of the faux marble fireplace. A brocade-covered round mahogany table centered the room and was the proud showcase for numerous family photographs.

Matt's gaze lingered on the photos: a wedding daguerreotype of a starry-eyed Emily and a stiff, unsmiling
Zak; separate pictures of Matt and Clint as babes in their
mother's arms; a tintype of his mother's parents, who had
died before Matt was born; and a cracked and faded portrait of Zak's mother, also long dead. As for Zak's father,
so far as Matt knew no picture existed. Jedediah Grayson
had died when Zak was just a boy.

The last photograph on the table was a silver-gilt-
framed portrait of a seated fourteen-year-old Clint, with
Emily and Zak standing tall and proud on either side of
him. One of Zak's hands rested on Clint's shoulder. It was
a picture Clint had kept with him during his two years in
an exclusive eastern boarding school, then again later
when he'd gone off to college. Matt had had the chicken
pox the day the picture was taken. Emily had wanted to
reschedule it, but Clint was set to leave for boarding
school the following day. Zak assured Emily they would
all sit for a new photograph when Clint came home for
Christmas. But the Christmas season proved to be too
hectic that year, crammed full of social obligations. The
following summer, when Clint was again home, there was
too much ranch work to be done. Eventually, over time,
the family portrait was forgotten. No family picture was
ever taken.

Matt sighed and tugged off his gloves, stuffing them
into the waistband of his denims, then tossed his hat onto
the hall tree just inside the main entrance. He forced his
attention back to the stairway. The house was quiet—too
quiet. Where the hell was his father?

His mouth twisted ruefully. Maybe he should count his
blessings. Deciding he could use a drink, he crossed the
foyer to the library. Just as the drawing room had been his
mother's retreat, the library was his father's. Or at least it
had been until four months ago, when a lifetime of grandi-
ose dreams for Clint had turned to ashes. It was in this

room that political strategies had been mapped out, campaigns planned, and wealthy contributors targeted for special attention.

The room smelled of leather and cigar smoke, and the furnishings were as heavy and dark as those in the drawing room were light. A massive mahogany desk fronted a wall sheathed ceiling to floor with glass-paneled bookshelves. On those shelves sat scores of leather-bound books, encompassing art, science, and political opinion from every corner of the globe.

Matt ignored the books, striding over to a small rectangular table abutting the far wall, next to a fieldstone fireplace. A crystal brandy decanter filled to the brim sat atop an intricately worked sterling silver tray. Next to the brandy stood a half-full bottle of whiskey. His father detested hard spirits, permitting it in the house only because inebriated businessmen kept a much looser grip on their pursestrings than sober ones. The more generous the contribution, Zak Grayson had reasoned, the more rapidly Clint's political career could advance.

Now Matt yanked the cork from the whiskey bottle with his teeth. Neither Matt nor Clint had been permitted to imbibe in their father's presence. He and Clint had never been quite so virtuous, however, when Zak wasn't around. He poured himself a glass of the amber-colored liquid. In fact, he and his brother had both had too much to drink that last night in Abilene. Matt's knuckles whitened around the glass. Maybe if they hadn't—

He closed his eyes. How had everything gone so wrong? This was the year all of Zak's carefully laid plans were supposed to have come together, the year Clint would run for his first political office. Matt turned toward the two wing-back leather-covered chairs that faced the oak desk. He and Clint had been sitting in those chairs the night before they left for Abilene. He set the glass back down. If he listened hard enough he could almost hear his brother's voice. . . .

"What do you suppose is taking Pa so long?" Clint asked, twining his long, slender fingers together nervously as he sat in the leather chair opposite Matt.

Matt stood and paced over to the desk. "You know how he is. We're having company for dinner. He's got to make sure everything is just so. He's probably dumping some oregano into Barney's stew." He chuckled. "Anything to make it edible." Barney Hayes was the Diamond G cook and had been for nearly five years, but the man's questionable culinary skills could make cowhide seem a delectable alternative to some of Barney's mystery meals.

"I'd hardly call the O'Rourkes company," Clint groused. "Ammie might as well move in." He cast a sidelong glance at Matt. "She could have your old room, since you don't see fit to use it."

"Don't start."

"Don't start, don't start," Clint muttered, climbing to his feet. "God forbid, Saint Clint should lose his temper."

Matt winced at the pejorative he often applied to his brother when he felt especially frustrated. He didn't know Clint had ever heard him use it.

"Losing one's temper is a privilege reserved for you and Pa," Clint went on acidly. "While I can just damned well choke rather than say how I might feel about something!" He shoved his hands into the pockets of his expensively tailored gray trousers and began to pace. The back of his white silk shirt was stained with perspiration where he'd been leaning against the leather chair.

Matt studied his brother curiously. For the past three hours, he, Clint, and Zak had been in this room planning —or rather, listening to Zak plan—every moment of their next two weeks. Clint was to travel to Austin to solicit support from some political heavyweights, while Zak,

Matt, and the O'Rourkes—Matt wondered if Shamus and
Ammie actually knew what they were in for—were heading for a special cattlemen's convention in Abilene. The
convention would be attended by several rich Texas cattlemen who could prove invaluable to Clint's career.
When everyone returned from their respective journeys,
Clint's candidacy for the state house of representatives
would be announced. It was everything Clint and Zak had
been preparing for for years—except that right now Clint
wasn't behaving at all like a man about to begin his life's
dream. "What's wrong, Clint?"

"Nothing's wrong," he snapped. "Why does there have
to be anything wrong?"

"For one thing," Matt observed blandly, "I don't think
I've ever seen you sweat before—at least, not in the
house."

Clint's lips thinned. "Thank you so much for your
brotherly support. I always know I can count on you."

Temper snapped through Matt's veins, but he held it in
check as Clint continued his harangue. "I don't know why
we have to have Shamus and Ammie over tonight. With
all of us leaving so early in the morning—" His pale eyes
narrowed. "The O'Rourkes aren't spending the night, are
they?"

Matt shrugged. "I think that's the idea. They *are* going
with Pa and me to Abilene, you know."

"Don't patronize me, Matt, not now. I just—I've still
got some things to settle with Pa about the trip, about the
people I'm supposed to talk to."

"You mean the people you want to throw their hard-
earned money at you."

Clint stalked to the window. "You make it so damned
hard sometimes, you know that?"

Matt propped himself against the edge of the desk. "It's
my job. If you didn't have a devil's advocate for a brother,
how could you sharpen your debating skills?"

"Maybe I don't feel like having a debate right now. And maybe I don't feel like having an audience tonight, either."

"Ammie and Shamus are hardly an audience. Besides, a big important politician like you needs to work any assembly of potential voters, no matter how small. Who knows —if Ammie has her way about it, someday women'll get the vote, and you'll need to win her over too."

"Women are not going to get the vote," Clint snapped. "Stop being ludicrous. Women need protecting. They need—" He let out a long breath. "You're getting me off the subject."

"What is the subject?" Matt asked. "I haven't figured it out yet. I'm the stupid one, remember?"

Rage, fierce and bright, flashed in Clint's light blue eyes. "You can use that act on Pa, Matthew," he said through gritted teeth. "God knows he deserves it. But I don't. I have never in my life considered you inferior to me in any way. And I will not tolerate even an insinuation that I have."

Matt felt a hot flush of shame. "I'm sorry. I guess I'm a little edgy myself. Pa's never expected me to go along on a political junket before."

"You'll do fine."

"That's easy for you to say. You'll be in Austin wining and dining the rich and the powerful, while I'm in Abilene with Pa. If I so much as pick up the wrong fork, he'll have me arrested."

"Ammie would bail you out."

Matt grinned. "Maybe you *should* help women get the vote, Clint. She'd be a hell of an ally."

"Damned pretty one, too, if she'd ever get off a horse long enough for a man to notice."

Matt's eyebrows arched. "Ammie?"

"You don't think she's pretty?"

"Well, of course. I mean, well—I guess I don't think

about the way she looks one way or the other. She's just Ammie."

"Maybe you haven't noticed how she fills out those shirts of hers lately."

Matt shifted uncomfortably. He suddenly didn't like the direction of this conversation, though he was damned if he knew why. But he didn't have time to think about it, as Clint again began to pace, a hint of desperation creeping into his voice.

"Matt, what do you think would happen if I didn't do well in Austin? What do you think Pa would say if—if things didn't work out, if I *never* ran for political office?"

Matt straightened, pushing away from the desk. "What are you talking about? You and Pa have been laying this out for as long as I can remember. You've made dozens of trips to Austin over the past couple of years. Why should this one be any different?"

Clint didn't answer. Only then did Matt notice his brother was trembling. "What the hell's going on, Clint?"

Clint took a deep breath, his eyes wide, frightened. "Matt, I—"

A shadow appeared in the doorway. They both looked up to see Zak Grayson stride into the room. In the space of a heartbeat, Clint's whole demeanor changed. He looked calm and self-possessed. And for the first time in his life Matt saw his brother's self-possession for what it was—an act.

"Supper's almost ready," Zak said. "The O'Rourkes should be here soon."

"Barney got anything edible in that kitchen of his?" Matt asked, watching Clint with a worried frown.

"I've seen saddle leather look more appetizing," Zak admitted, "but I had him add some onions." He reached into his pocket and withdrew an envelope. "Barney finally remembered to tell me he picked up the mail this morning while he was in town." He looked at Clint. "It's from a man I have working for me in Austin."

Clint blanched visibly, and Matt was actually afraid his brother was going to faint. Zak was reviewing the letter's contents and appeared oblivious to Clint's distress.

"What's in the letter?" Matt asked.

"Trouble, I'm afraid."

"Pa," Clint blurted, "Pa, I can explain."

Zak waved his hand. "No need for explanations. It's a little inconvenient, but we can work around it."

Clint sank onto the nearest chair. "Inconvenient?"

"It seems that most of the men I wanted you to meet with in Austin will be attending the cattlemen's convention in Abilene." He read off a list of names. "They have contacts of their own to make."

For a instant Clint's relief was palpable, then Zak's next words unnerved him all over again.

"I'm afraid this leaves only one solution. I'll take over in Austin. Clint, you go with Matt and the O'Rourkes to Abilene."

"No!" Clint was on his feet.

Zak blinked, stunned. "What?"

"I—I mean, I *have* to go to Austin," he stammered. "It's all arranged."

"Nonsense. I've just unarranged it."

"Pa, please," Clint said, "you don't understand."

Zak finally seemed to notice Clint's unease. "Understand what, Clint? What is it?"

Sweat trickled down the side of Clint's face.

Tell him, Matt urged inwardly. *Whatever the hell it is, tell him!*

"I, uh"—Clint began haltingly—"I promised to take Paul Landers deer hunting on this trip to Austin."

Matt's heart sank. Landers was a bigwig with the Texas and Pacific Railroad, but he was clearly *not* the reason Clint was agitated.

"Is that all!" Zak scoffed, clapping Clint on the back. "Don't give him another thought. I'll take him out myself."

"Pa, I—"

"Wait a minute," Zak put in. "I see what this is all about."

Clint looked hopeful. "You do? Then you'll let me go to Austin."

"This is just a case of the jitters, son. Don't you worry —they'll disappear the minute you set foot in Abilene. This is the beginning, the real beginning. Everything before has been groundwork." He spread his hands wide in front of him, as though viewing an invisible canvas. "First, you'll be a state representative, then a congressman, then a senator. It's going to happen, Clint, all of it. I can feel it. I am so proud of you, son. So damned proud." He gave Clint an awkward hug. "Now, was there anything else about Austin?"

Clint shoulders sagged, and he stared at the floor. "No, Pa. Nothing."

"Excellent."

The O'Rourkes arrived then, and Zak went out to greet them. Matt held Clint back. He kept his voice low so that only Clint could hear. "What did you think was in that letter?"

Clint pulled free. "I don't know what you're talking about."

"The hell you don't!" Matt looked toward the foyer, casting a pleading look at Ammie, who quickly took the hint and distracted Zak, leading him off into another room. "Clint, if you're in some kind of trouble—"

"Don't be ridiculous."

"Tell me. We can face Pa together. Whatever it is, we can work it out."

"There's nothing to work out, Matt." And with that, Clint marched from the room to greet the O'Rourkes. He

was once again the Clint whom Matt knew too well—
hand-shaking, back-slapping, charming his way through
life as though he didn't have a care in the world. And no
amount of follow-up persuasion would get him to say otherwise, though two weeks later Matt wished to God he
had tried.

Because two weeks later Clint was dead.

Matt let out a weary sigh. That was four months ago.
"I'm sorry, Clint," he muttered aloud, still fingering the
glass of whiskey he'd set on the silver tray in his father's
library, "so damned sorry."

"Not sorry enough."

The gravel-edged voice from the archway startled Matt,
and he almost upset the glass. Slowly he straightened,
feeling his blood grow hot just looking at the gaunt, harsh-
featured man in the doorway. "Hello, Pa."

Matt had been about to toss the whiskey into the fireplace, but now, facing his father, some devil's demon
pushed him to raise the glass to his lips. With an insolent
nod he upended the glass, and the amber liquid seared
his insides all the way down to his belly.

Zak's whole body went rigid, and Matt fully expected
him to storm across the room and slap the glass from his
hand. But he didn't. He only glared at Matt, his eyes
bright with anger and something else, a bitter edge of
disappointment.

The disappointment niggled at Matt until he was forced
to turn away. Then, deliberately, he poured himself another whiskey. But he didn't drink it. He just turned the
glass in his hand and spoke in a cold, measured voice. "I
thought I'd drop by. Let you know I was back. I was sure
you'd be worried."

Zak said nothing.

"I'll be spending a lot of time over at the Shamrock
breaking those new horses."

"You've got work to do here."

"It'll get done." He set the still-full glass down and headed for the door.

"Why'd you come back?" Zak asked without expression.

"I live here. Well, at least I live in the bunkhouse. If you don't mind, I'll go to my—room. I need a bath." Zak Grayson remained in the doorway, and for an moment Matt thought disconcertingly that he was either going to have to physically move his father aside or climb out the window. Neither option held much appeal.

"There's something you have to see," Zak said.

Matt waited.

Zak reached into his inside vest pocket and extracted a folded piece of paper. "It's a telegram. It came four days ago."

"So?"

"It's about Clint."

Matt turned and walked toward the window, careful to keep his voice expressionless. "What about Clint?"

Zak crossed the room and handed the telegram to Matt. "See for yourself." There was a hint of challenge in his voice.

Matt felt a familiar heat in his face as he stared at the block letters on the paper, written in the telegrapher's hand. For long seconds he studied the message, willing the lines and curves to make sense, just this once.

But they didn't. With a savage oath he crushed the paper in his fist and shoved it back at his father, knowing the bastard had just taken his revenge on him for daring to drink in his presence. "You know I can't read it."

Smoothing out the paper, Zak read the words without inflection. " 'Will arrive River Oaks stage Friday morning. Need to speak to you of Clint Grayson's death. Have information you may find of interest.' "

Matt swallowed the savage humiliation still burning inside him. This was too important. "Is that all it says?"

Zak nodded.

"Who sent it?"

"It's not signed."

Matt began to breathe a little easier. "Where was it sent from?"

"Austin."

Matt frowned.

"That mean something to you?"

"Not especially," he lied, though his thoughts leaped at once to the night Clint had been distraught that his plans were changed. "Clint knew a lot of people in Austin."

"And there were people from Austin in Abilene when he died."

Matt shoved his hands into the rear pockets of his denims. "There's nothing anyone can tell you about that night that you don't already know."

"Maybe, maybe not. All I've really ever heard is your story."

Matt withdrew his hands from his pockets. "Meaning?"

"Meaning, I want to talk to this person who says he has information about Clint. You're to pick him up tomorrow."

"You'd trust *me* to fetch him?"

"Somehow Sheriff Haggerty found out about the telegram. He was concerned and stopped out to see me."

"Concerned?"

"Clint had wealth, status—magnets to all sorts of unscrupulous individuals. Anyway, the sheriff will see that you bring this man here."

"Just so long as you trust me," Matt sneered.

"You dare speak of trust?"

Matt stiffened, bracing himself for the verbal blow he knew was coming.

"You killed your brother, Matthew. I will never trust you again."

Not knowing why he bothered, Matt recited the accepted version of the events of that night by rote. "I was drunk. Clint had already collected several thousand dollars in campaign money. I met a man named Lance Gentry, who told me about a high-stakes poker game going on in a room at the hotel. It was a setup. Gentry tried to rob me. Clint came in. I shot Gentry. Gentry shot back. Clint got in the way. I don't know how many times I can say I'm sorry."

"Not enough," Zak snarled. "Never enough. It never would have happened if you hadn't stolen Clint's money. You killed your brother, Matt—just as sure as if you shot him yourself."

Matt ground his teeth together so hard his jaw ached, but he made no further attempt to defend himself. He couldn't, wouldn't. Not because the charge was true, but because it wasn't. The details were right enough, but Matt had made a conscious choice that night in Abilene to alter one crucial fact. It had not been Matt about to gamble away thousands of dollars in campaign money. It had been Clint.

Matt closed his eyes, reliving the horror of that night in his mind's eye. Clint had been drunk and talking crazy most of the evening. He told Matt he could double the campaign money in a single game of poker. "Pa'd be proud of me."

"He's already proud of you. Go to bed and sleep it off."

Matt had dared doze off himself, convinced he'd Clint talked out of his crazy scheme. He'd started awake minutes later to find Clint and the money gone.

Matt raced to the room where Clint had told him the game was to take place, but he was too late. A gun sounded just as Matt crashed through the door. Clint slumped to the floor in front of him, his white silk shirt a mass of crimson.

Cursing, the shooter turned his gun on Matt. In a haze of grief and fury Matt dove for Clint's derringer. Its single bullet caught Lance Gentry square in the face. Matt scarcely noticed. On his knees he scrambled toward his dying brother, lifting him gently to cradle him in his arms.

"Hang on, Clint. Hang on. I'll get you a doctor. Hang—"

"No!" Clint rasped, gripping Matt's shirtfront with surprising strength. "Have to tell . . . have to . . . can't let . . ."

"Don't talk." Matt pressed his hand against Clint's chest in a futile effort to stanch the flow of blood.

"Pa . . . have to . . . to tell . . . Matt . . . Matt don't let him . . . don't let him hate . . ." His breath caught and his eyes went wide. He was dead.

Matt held his brother tight, rocked him, soothed him, repeating his single vow over and over. "I won't tell him, Clint. I won't tell him. Ever."

Matt kept his word. Even now he kept it as he stood his ground against the condemning glare of Zak Grayson.

"I'll go to town. I'll meet the stage. I'll bring this man out to the ranch. You can interrogate him all you want. But right now I'm going to take that bath."

Without another word, he left the house. He kept his mind carefully blank as he went through the motions of rubbing down Drifter and turning him out into one of the corrals. He didn't want to think. Thinking was too painful. He crossed the yard to the one-story clapboard building that was the Diamond G bunkhouse.

He was grateful to find no one inside. This was the time of year the ranch worked with a skeleton crew. For round-ups in the spring and fall they hired on extra men. But now that it was summer, what men they had were bunked out on the range, tackling the various chores inherent in minding thousands of head of cattle spread out over thousands of acres of land.

Matt dragged a wooden tub to the center of the room, then peeled off his shirt, boots, and socks. He hefted a water bucket and headed outside. Several trips to the water pump later, he had himself a tub brimful of bath water. He found a towel and tossed it onto the nearest bunk, then grabbed a sponge and a cake of soap and plopped them into the water. Unhitching his belt and his pants, he let them slide to the floor in a heap. With a weary sigh he eased his naked, aching body into that cool, clean water.

He settled back, his knees jutting above the waterline. With slow, languid movements he caught up the sponge and began to lather his upper body. He could get used to this.

A knock sounded on the door.

Matt cursed at the disturbance, then frowned. Who the hell would knock? Any of the hands would have marched right in. So would his father, for that matter. He was too exhausted to carry the thought any further. "Come in!"

The door opened. Matt looked up, astonished to see Ammie framed in the entryway. She stepped in out of the bright sun, then stopped cold, her green eyes wide as Pickles scampered past her.

Reflexively, Matt grabbed at the towel on the bunk, sloshing water on the floor all around him as he did so. But the towel was too far away. He couldn't reach it. He shrank back into the tub. Pickles trotted over and began to lick soapy water from his knees. He shoved the dog away; she came right back. "Ammie, do you think you could get that towel for me?"

Instead of getting it, Ammie stood frozen, and her voice shook oddly when she spoke. "I, uh—I didn't mean to intrude. I was worried about—about how things would go with your father."

Was that nervousness threading Ammie's voice? It couldn't be. Hell, the two of them had gone skinny-dipping together all their lives. He should just get up and grab the towel himself.

But the towel stayed where it was, and so did he.

"Pickles," Matt said, catching the dog by the scruff of the neck and pointing toward the bed, "get the towel."

The dog drank more of his bath water.

Matt splashed water onto the dog, who only shook herself and drank more water. Matt started laughing. He hadn't wanted to be alone with his thoughts. Well, he sure as hell wasn't.

He held the sponge out toward Ammie. "Pickles is doing my legs. Maybe you could do my back?"

He frowned. She looked as if she was about to bolt out the door. Then she seemed to check herself. She strode toward him and accepted the sponge.

She started with small circles in the middle of his back, then widened the arcs until she was dipping the sponge below the water's surface. Matt leaned forward. "Mmm, keep it up, and I might think you're beginning to enjoy yourself."

The sponge plopped into the water. "I—I wouldn't want you to get spoiled. I'll, uh, wait for you outside." She all but ran from the bunkhouse.

Matt grimaced and stood up. Quickly, he toweled himself off, found some fresh clothes, and pulled them on. His shirt was still unbuttoned and he was in his stocking feet as he trailed out of the bunkhouse to find Ammie. He found her standing beside her horse, fussing with the cinch, but he could tell she was upset.

"It's okay now, Ammie," he said, coming up behind her. "I'm decent."

She wheeled, and as she did her palm brushed against his still-damp, still-exposed chest. She yanked her hand back as though she'd been burned. "Sorry," she squeaked.

"So am I."

"You are?"

"For not telling you how things went with my father."

"Oh, oh—of course." She tried to take a step back, but Ranger blocked her. "How—how was it?"

"No worse than usual."

Her eyes grew sympathetic. "I'm sorry."

"Anyway, I'm going to be heading into River Oaks."

"Now?"

He told her about the telegram.

She worried her lower lip. "Austin. Do you think it might have anything to do with why Clint was so anxious to go there?"

"I don't know."

"What if it is? How are you going to keep Zak from finding out?"

"I'll think of something."

"You don't think Clint was in trouble there for more gambling, do you?"

"If he owed a lot of money to someone, we probably would've heard before now."

"But you're afraid, aren't you?"

"All I know is that I intend to talk to whoever sent that telegram before I let him near my father."

"I'm going with you."

"The hell you are. Your father said for you to be home by nightfall. I don't need Shamus on my backside too."

"I can handle my father. I'll send word from town." She thought a minute. "I'll tell him I'm going to give Mary Denby a personal invitation to supper tomorrow night. He'll like that."

Matt looked dubious, but he didn't object. He retrieved his boots, then headed for the corral to rope a fresh horse. Ammie used the opportunity to try to recover her senses. She couldn't believe she had barged in on Matt when he was taking a bath! More than that, she couldn't believe her own reaction to it. Why had the sight of his naked chest flustered her so? She'd seen it plenty of times before.

Yes, she acknowledged, she'd *seen* it. But she'd never really *looked* at it before. Rivulets of water had trailed down the hard muscled plane, wet dark hairs had arrowed toward the waterline, and soapy lather had clung to one nipple. . . .

"Almost forgot," he said, coming up behind her.

Ammie nearly jumped out of her skin. Swallowing hard, she whirled to face him.

He was opening one of his saddlebags. "I bought you a present in Wichita."

"A present?" Her heart hammered. Matt had thought about her in Wichita and bought her a present? "What is it?"

His blue eyes alight with pleasure, he handed her a finely tooled leather belt. Ammie turned the belt over in her hand. She had to will a smile to stay on her face—it was all she could do not to burst into tears. It was the kind of present someone would buy for a man. "It's beautiful," she managed.

He grinned. "I knew you'd like it. The minute I saw it, I thought of you."

Ammie let out a shaky breath. She had some serious work to do if she was ever going to get this man to see her as a woman. "I guess we'd better head for town if we want to make it by nightfall."

Matt looked toward the house. Ammie followed his gaze and saw a figure in the window in Zak's office. "I'll wait, if you want to go in."

Matt shook his head. "I think Pa and I have said enough to each other for one day."

They mounted then and rode out, Ammie keeping Ranger several paces behind Matt's roan. She had promised herself she would talk to him and tell him how she felt, but now that she had a chance to do so the words wouldn't come. Why? She'd shared everything with Matt all her life. Why would she hesitate to share something so very important now?

The answer, she knew, was contained in the question.

She couldn't tell him precisely because it was so important. Her emotions were clouding her instincts.

Furthermore, she had no idea how he would react. He might brush it off, tell her she was being silly. Or laugh, thinking it was a joke.

Or worse. He might "understand" and be kind. He might look at her with those big blue eyes and gently explain that he could never feel the same for her.

And therein lay her biggest terror, the reason she couldn't tell him the truth. If she told him she loved him and discovered that he couldn't love her back, it would be the end of their friendship. He would feel awkward around her ever after. As much as she loved him, she couldn't risk it. She couldn't risk losing her best friend.

♧ / Chapter 6

Several times on the ride to River Oaks, Ammie considered taking Matt's advice and heading back to Shamrock: not because she feared her father's ire, but because for the first time in her life she feared sharing her deepest feelings with Matt. She tried to tell herself she was being ridiculous. That even if Matt didn't return her feelings, her love for him wouldn't do anything to alter their friendship. But still she kept silent.

She assured herself she was doing it as much for Matt's sake as her own. After all, it was obvious that his being gone for six weeks hadn't changed things at the Diamond G. Matt was still agonizing over Clint's death, and admit it or not, he was being ripped apart that his father was blaming him for it. Now, on top of that, was this cryptic telegram from Austin. Matt's greatest fear since Clint's death had been that someone else knew the truth about that night. What if the sender of that telegram were such a person?

No, there were too many uncertainties and distractions in Matt's life right now, too much pain, for her to talk to him about her feelings. She wanted the day she told him she loved him to be the happiest day of her life. For now, she would hold on to her secret. She would wait.

They rode in silence for the most part, each alone with their thoughts, and despite her worries, Ammie felt her mouth tilt upward into a tender smile. Just being with him was such sweet pleasure after six weeks of missing him. The silence gave her a chance to mull over other things, like that fledgling crusade of hers to get Matt Grayson to notice her as a woman. Heaven save her—she might even buy herself another dress!

They topped a rise and reined in. Pickles gamboled over and sat beside them, taking time out from her pursuit of a butterfly. Below them, in the wide valley of a fork in the Wichita River, lay the bustling community of River Oaks, Texas. Matt let out a low, admiring whistle. "I swear that town is growin' faster than bunch grass in a spring rain."

"I know what you mean." Ammie judged the town's borders must be pressing beyond two square miles now, and that the population was booming at well over a thousand. Pretty remarkable, considering Zak Grayson's tales of the town's less-than-auspicious beginnings. A quarter century ago, he would say, River Oaks was "nothing more than a string of tents and a lot of wishful thinking."

The first buildings, all made of wood—a general store, two saloons, and a funeral parlor—had all burned to the ground one windy night after a brawl in one of the saloons overturned a kerosene lantern. The current structures boasted a mix of stone and wood. The bank and the jail were solid brick.

To the north of town Ammie made out a clear-cut of trees. This marked the right of way that in the next year or two would become a spur line for the Atchinson, Topeka and Santa Fe Railroad. The town would really come into its own then.

"You hungry?" Matt asked.

"Starved."

"Good. Supper's on me at the hotel."

Ammie felt her pulses trip with delight. This being in love was a strange and marvelous thing. She'd shared a thousand meals with Matt, but she'd never anticipated one quite so eagerly before.

She and Matt headed down Main Street, where the

hustle and bustle of industrious townsfolk was evident in the numerous shops lining the thoroughfare—three mercantiles, a haberdashery, four cafés, the bank, a boardinghouse, a newspaper, two hotels, and five saloons, to name a few. Surrounding the business district were dozens of clapboard houses and a few more substantial homes, like the colonnaded Kessler mansion, which crowned a tree-bristled slope to the east. The Kesslers, far and away the wealthiest family in River Oaks, boasted ownership of one hotel, a livery, two saloons, and a mercantile.

Matt reined to a halt at the hitchrail in front of the four-story Kessler House. The larger of the town's two hotels, Kessler House was managed by Terence's father, Newton Kessler. Ammie knew that Terence sometimes worked evenings at the registration desk. She could only hope this was his night off. She was in no mood to fend off his advances again, which were becoming increasingly ardent. But then again, she thought suddenly, perhaps that wouldn't be entirely bad. Maybe Terence could put some ideas in Matt's head.

Besides, the hotel did serve the best food in town. The hotel itself had always impressed Ammie. The lobby was lavishly furnished in stylish French Provincial, and the walls were hung with ornately framed original paintings— one depicting swans swimming on a tranquil lake, another presenting a decidedly Parisian-looking couple enjoying a picnic lunch in a flower-dappled meadow. Ammie credited Millicent Kessler, Terence's brother's wife, with much that was tasteful and elegant about Kessler House. She had to smile, though, as she passed the arched entrance to the large dining room off the main lobby. In the painting that hung above the fireplace in the otherwise lovely room, a half-dozen gossamer-clad nymphs cavorted on a grassy knoll playing lawn tennis. The painting was a personal favorite of Newton Kessler's, and no amount of outrage on Millicent's part could get him to remove it.

"Mm-mmn," Matt said, "something sure smells good in there. But then, I'm hungry enough to eat a grizzly."

Ammie was looking past the dining room to the tall, blond, bespectacled clerk behind the registration desk. She groaned inwardly. Terence.

"Amelia!" he cried, his hand reaching automatically to adjust the string tie at his throat. "How delightful! What brings you to our fine establishment?"

"Matt and I are going to spend the night," she said without thinking.

"I beg your pardon?" Terence arched a censorious eyebrow in Matt's direction.

"Separate rooms, Terence," Matt assured him with a chuckle.

Terence still looked nonplussed—and more than a shade suspicious. But Terence was used to having his own way in life. When Amelia picked up the old-fashioned quill pen to sign the registration book, Terence leaned close, his lips brushing past her ear. "Will you be coming to town for the dance next week, Amelia?" he asked.

Ammie resisted the urge to swat at him like the pesky fly he was. He was entirely too presumptuous. Or maybe she'd just never forgiven him for that first dance, when he'd accused her of kissing like a fish. "I'm not sure yet, Terence," she hedged, casting a questioning look at Matt. "Are you coming in for the dance, Matt?"

"I doubt it. Once I start breaking those horses, I want to keep at it."

Amelia rolled her eyes. Could the man never take a hint?

"I'll look for you there, Amelia," Terence said, and then added with a sly wink, "I'll look for you behind the barn too."

Ammie flushed. She supposed she deserved that. She could only be grateful that Matt hadn't heard the lout's comment. Quickly, she excused herself and followed Matt toward the dining room.

Most of the tables were occupied. Kessler House was a popular eating spot for townspeople and visitors alike. While they were scanning the room for an empty spot, a buxom, dark-haired waitress bustled over to them.

"Why, Matt Grayson," she trilled, "where have you been keeping yourself?"

"Here and there, Theda," Matt said, grinning, not objecting in the least when the waitress looped her arm in his and escorted him into the room.

"You just come right on in, Matt. I've got the best table in the house for my favorite customer." Theda led him toward a linen-covered table that looked out onto the street, forcing Ammie to trail behind.

At the table Theda—deliberately, Ammie was certain—kept herself positioned so that Matt could not maneuver to hold Ammie's chair for her. Whether it was the result of Zak's training or Matt's own concession to her being female, Matt always held Ammie's chair for her when they dined together. Ammie had found the gesture disarmingly sweet. Now she had to watch him spread his hands in a helpless gesture and give her a sheepish smile. Ammie sat herself down.

"The special tonight is the venison stew," Theda gushed. "But I'd recommend the filet mignon for you, Matt."

"Sounds perfect," Matt said. "Make it rare."

"A rare steak for a rare man." Theda fluttered her eyelids at Matt. Ammie tried not to throw up. With a long-suffering sigh Theda turned her attention to Ammie. "Meat loaf for you, Miss O'Rourke?"

Ammie ground her teeth together. "I'll have the filet—*rare*," she emphasized, "with a side order of buttered carrots, please. And pineapple upside-down cake for dessert."

"I'm so sorry," Theda said, obviously not sorry at all, "but we're fresh out of upside-down cake."

"Fine, then I'll have a slice of blueberry pie. Oh, and bring me a dill pickle, too, if you could."

Matt grinned. "Can't forget Pickles."

"You like pickles, Matt?" Theda asked, misunderstanding. "I'll bring you a whole plateful."

Matt laughed. "You'll have yourself a friend for life."

Theda beamed. "Anything for my favorite customer."

Ammie's stomach tied itself into a very large knot as Theda just stood there, gazing at Matt. How often did Matt come in here? Ammie wondered. And why was Theda still hovering over their table?

"Something wrong, Theda?" Matt asked.

"I was just thinking," she began, looking so outrageously helpless all at once that Ammie's suspicions were immediately aroused. "Oh, no—it would be such a bother. I couldn't ask."

"Ask what?" Matt prompted.

"We-ell, later on . . . I get off work at nine, I have this big old armoire that I need to have moved." Theda had a room at the boardinghouse down the street. "And well, since you're so big and strong, Matt"—she giggled and blushed prettily—"I was just wondering if you could come by and help me move it."

"Sure. I'd be happy to."

"Oh, thank you, Matt." Her smile was all promises. "I'll be ever so grateful." At last, she headed toward the kitchen.

Ammie wondered grumpily if people could talk themselves out of being in love with someone. How could Matt be so thick-headed? "You're lucky she didn't sit in your lap."

"What are you talking about?"

Ammie batted her eyelashes. " 'A rare steak for a rare man.' 'Oh, my, you're so big and strong, Matt.' "

Matt flushed. "I feel sorry for her, that's all."

Ammie sighed. "So do I, actually." She knew Theda's history. Her husband of three years had recently run off with one of the other waitresses. Theda was probably lonely. But knowing that did little to quell the jealousy Ammie was feeling at the thought of Matt visiting the girl's room in the dark of night.

They talked for a while. Matt made suggestive comments about the painting over the fireplace, while Ammie giggled. She was pleased to see him happy, even though she knew it wasn't going to last. Later, as he was eating his steak, he leaned forward and admitted to her, "I can't get that damned telegram out of my head. If Clint was in some kind of trouble in Austin—"

"You don't want your father to find out."

"Exactly."

"How long can you protect your father from the truth, Matt?"

"It's not my father I'm protecting," he said softly. "It's my brother. I owe it to Clint not to let—"

Matt's attention was suddenly drawn toward the entryway. Ammie turned to see a stocky but hard-muscled man in his mid-fifties stride into the room. It was the town lawman, Sheriff John Haggerty.

He spotted Matt and headed toward their table. "Back from Wichita, I see."

"This morning."

"Was out to your pa's place earlier in the week. He was a little worried you might head off for parts unknown."

"Worried—or hoping?"

John's smile was sympathetic. "You two are more alike than different, you know." Then, before Matt could respond, he went on. "I hear you're meeting someone on tomorrow's stage."

"Pa told me you knew about that. How'd you find out?"

"I got my ways."

Ammie grimaced. She could guess. Finley Barnes over at the Western Union had doubtless scurried over to the sheriff with the telegram before he took it out to the Diamond G. Finley had always been the biggest tattletale in class when they'd been in school together.

"Your interest a lawman's interest?" Matt asked.

"I don't know." He paused meaningfully. "Should it be?"

Matt's jaw tightened. "You got something to say, John, say it."

"Got nothing to do with the telegram. Just wanted you to know I heard more about the man who killed Clint."

"Gentry?"

"Lance Gentry. Con man, gambler, done a couple of short terms in prison, but"—Haggerty scratched his jaw thoughtfully—"armed robbery just wasn't his style."

"It was that night," Matt said tightly.

"Maybe. I've always liked you, Matt. Even those couple of times you cooled your heels in my jail after you and the Diamond G boys hoorawed the town after a roundup. I wouldn't want you to get into any trouble you couldn't get yourself out of."

"Not plannin' on it."

John held Matt's gaze for a full minute, as though he were trying to read his mind, see inside him. Then he leaned back and said matter-of-factly, "By the way, I'm in the market for a deputy. Town council actually okayed the funds. Might be I'd consider you for the job, if you're interested."

Matt snorted. "Me? A law dog? No, thank you."

John was not offended. "Just a thought. Heard you might've been thinkin' of a . . . change of scenery."

Matt shifted uncomfortably. "Guess you heard wrong. I'm still ranchin'."

"I'd think you'd look handsome wearing a badge,

Matt," Ammie said impulsively, though her sudden, brief surge of boldness went for naught.

Matt was too busy licking his lips and looking at Theda, who had just brought him a huge slice of apple pie. The piece of blueberry that Theda set in front of Ammie was less than half the size of Matt's. But what really infuriated her was the piece of pineapple upside-down cake that she placed with grand flourish in front of the sheriff.

"Your favorite, John. I saved it just for you."

"Bless your heart, Miss Theda. You do know how to spoil a man."

Theda leaned forward, her ample bosom on ample display. "No charge, of course, for law officers."

"Maybe I *should* think about becoming a deputy," Matt said.

Ammie stood up. "I'm going for a walk." She snatched up her pickle and headed for the door.

"Wait," Matt said. "I'll go with you." He quickly counted out enough money for the meal and a generous tip for Theda, then followed Ammie out to the lobby.

"I'm glad you made an excuse to escape," he said. "I didn't feel like being a captive audience for the sheriff." With that, Ammie's hopes that he'd wanted to join her on her walk quickly sank.

To her further chagrin, Theda caught up with them before they reached the outer door. "Don't forget, Matt," she said. "My place. Nine o'clock."

"I won't forget."

Outside, Ammie breathed deeply of the clear, clean air. The sun was going down, and the temperature was dropping to more tolerable levels. She wished she could say the same for her temper.

Pickles came galumphing up and nuzzled her hand. Ammie grinned and hunkered down beside her. "Did you mooch a meal from someone in town, you big, bad dog?"

she cooed in a singsong voice. The dog barked, her tail thumping on the boardwalk.

"Well, I got you some dessert." She waved the dill under the hound's nose. Pickles wriggled and howled, then sat up and begged.

"Have you no pride, Pickles?" Matt asked.

Ammie tossed the pickle at the dog, who chomped it down in two gulps. "None," Ammie pronounced.

"God forbid there's ever a pickle blight," Matt said.

A yellow tomcat made the mistake of sauntering past. With a yelp of glee Pickles was off and running. The cat snarled and hissed, his back arching with fury. Pickles stuck her nose too close, and the cat raked at her with his claws. Pickles was again off and running—in the opposite direction.

"I'm going to pretend I never saw that dog before," Ammie said, heading down the boardwalk.

"I'm with you."

They passed a couple of matronly women who gave Ammie's tomboyish attire a summary sniff of disapproval. Normally, Ammie took no note of such nonsense, but her acute awareness of Matt made tonight different. Though vaguely irritated that she'd let the old biddies upset her, Ammie made a mental note to stop by the mercantile in the morning and look for a new dress.

Another twosome approached them, this time a man and a woman. Matt smiled and nodded at the comely Millicent Kessler and ignored the scowl that her husband, Martin, sent back to him.

"Now there goes one of the big mistakes of my life," Matt said when the couple was safely out of earshot.

"What do you mean?"

"I mean, I should've been paying more attention when that filly was still unclaimed," he said, not noticing that Ammie missed a step. "Remember that night you helped me memorize a love sonnet from Shakespeare? I recited it under Millie's bedroom window. Except that afterward it was Martin who stuck his head out at me. I thought he was gonna shoot me. He and Millie were—busy, I guess." He chuckled. "I think she liked the poem, though." Matt glanced behind him. "Yes, ma'am, that is one pretty lady."

Ammie fumed. The mercantile first thing in the morning.

They passed by the schoolhouse on their walk, and Ammie was surprised when Matt stopped there. He stood staring at the red wooden building, his expression pained and distant. Ammie knew he was remembering that last awful day.

School had been a nightmare for Matt, a nightmare of threats and humiliation. By the time he was twelve, he'd been held back time and again. His inability to read had become a personal affront—both to his teacher and, of course, to his father.

Even so, his oral lessons were consistently excellent. But that hadn't been good enough for Miss Violet Gilford. Known unaffectionately as Miss Sourball to her students behind her back, she seemed to take especial pleasure in shaming Matt.

Miss Gilford had long suspected that Matt was memorizing oral reading assignments in advance, thanks to Ammie's promptings. One day Miss Gilford gave him a book that neither he nor Ammie had ever seen before, stood him in front of the class, and told him to read it aloud.

Matt had stood there, his face burning with embarrassment as he stumbled over words that should have been easy for a first-grade pupil. Miss Gilford had encouraged the class to laugh at him. "Maybe now you'll learn not to try and fool your elders, young man," she said, then thrust a dunce cap at him and pointed toward the corner of the room.

Matt didn't move.

"The dunce cap for the dunce. Now." She picked up her hickory switch.

Ammie, tears streaming down her face, jumped up from her desk. "Leave him alone, you hateful witch!" she shouted.

Livid, Violet Gilford turned on Ammie, arcing the switch back. Instinctively, Matt dove at the woman, grabbed her arm, and wrested the switch from her grasp. In the process Violet Gilford tripped and fell heavily to the wood-plank floor.

Matt caught Ammie by the wrist, and together the two of them raced from the room.

Only her father's intervention had kept Ammie from being expelled. Still, she was suspended for a week and had to do extra chores around the school for a month. No amount of persuasion, however, could get Matt readmitted. Not that it would have mattered. He would never have come back.

At the end of that school year, though, Miss Gilford was not asked to return. Ammie was certain her father had something to do with it, but he never confirmed it.

Mary Denby had come for the next term. Her husband was an invalid, and she had to work to support them both. She proved to be a fine and devoted teacher. Ammie had liked her very much. So much so that she had even tried to talk Matt into coming back. But he wouldn't.

Mary Denby had been a widow now for two years. She lived in a two-story house next to the school and sometimes took in boarders to make ends meet. Ammie also knew she used some of her extra money to purchase school supplies for children whose parents couldn't afford them. But somehow none of that mattered now that Mary was interested in her father.

"Hello, you two," a friendly voice called.

Ammie looked up to see a plump, kind-faced woman step onto the porch of the house.

Ammie frowned. "Hello, Mrs. Denby."

Mary came down her walk to the white picket fence that surrounded her property. "Ammie, dear, how many times have I asked you to call me Mary? I'm not your teacher anymore."

"Yes, Mrs. Denby."

A shadow crossed the woman's features, a slight sadness. Ammie felt a nudge of guilt.

"Good to see you back, Matt," Mary said.

"Thank you, ma'am. I hear you'll be with us for supper tomorrow night."

"Yes, I'm so looking forward to it. Shamus and I—"

"We'd best get back to the hotel, Matt," Ammie said. "It's been a long day."

Mary's brow knit in sudden concern. "You're both staying at the hotel?"

Ammie stiffened defensively. "We—that is, Matt has to meet the stage tomorrow. And I have to pick up some things to make tomorrow night's supper an extra-special one."

Mary threaded her hands together. "You don't have to stay at the hotel, Ammie. You can stay right here with me."

Before Ammie could object, Matt put in, "Maybe that would be a good idea."

Ammie's jaw dropped. "No, it would not be a good idea. I'm staying at the hotel, and that's final." To Mary, she said stiffly, "I thank you for your offer, but I'm perfectly capable of deciding where to sleep."

"Ammie," Mary said, "I really think your father would rather—"

"It's getting late," Ammie cut in, catching Matt's arm. "We'd better be getting back. Good night—Mrs. Denby."

"I'll leave the door unlatched, just in case you change your mind."

Matt allowed Ammie to lead him off, then frowned at her. "You were pretty rude, don't you think?"

"I don't recall asking your opinion."

He gave her a sour look. "Yes, ma'am."

"Sorry. I just don't think that woman has any right to interfere in my life. And that's probably all she would do if she ever married my father."

"Your father's been alone a long time."

That was not the answer she wanted to hear from her best friend. "Mary Denby doesn't love my father!" she snapped. "She just wants his money."

Matt snorted. "I doubt even you believe that. Ammie, what's the matter with you?"

You're the matter with me! she wanted to scream at him. *For not noticing that I'm stark, raving in love with you!* "Nothing's the matter! Not a blasted thing."

"It's been a long day," he said reasonably. "Maybe you should turn in."

"What about you?"

"I promised Theda I'd come by and help her move her armoire."

That was the final straw. "Oh, by all means," Ammie shrilled, "never let dear Theda down! Run right over! Do her bidding!" With that, she whirled and ran toward the hotel, ignoring Matt's shout that she wait.

In her room Ammie sat on the bed and cried, cried because she didn't know what else to do, until finally she grew tired of feeling sorry for herself. She climbed to her feet, crossed over to the basin, poured water into a bowl, and washed her face. Then she stared at the bleary-eyed creature in the mirror.

Did love always made a person act like an idiot? she wondered. Love! "Bah!" she sniffed. She had only two questions about love: Where had it come from? And how could she get rid of it?

None of this made any sense. She'd never been a ro-

mantic sort, sitting around all day dreamy-eyed and helpless waiting for Prince Charming and his assorted minions
in shining armor to come riding by. She believed in prac-
ticality and hard work, not mystical kingdoms and hap-
pily-ever-afters.

There had been times, of course, when she'd enter-
tained vague notions of marrying, establishing a home,
having children. But in her mind it had always been reserved for some nebulous future time and place. Never
here and now. And never with Matt Grayson.

Then what was that ideal man story she'd spun for herself on the creekbank? A silly fantasy! That's what it was,
she countered testily. It hadn't meant a thing.

Matt was her friend, her ally, her confidant. They knew
everything about each other. Romance demanded mystery. Didn't it?

A light knock sounded on her door. Her heart jumped.
Had Matt decided not to go to Theda's after all?

Ammie rushed to the door and swung it open, only to
find Smoke Larson standing on her threshold. His care-
worn eyes were serious, and amazingly, he was not smok-
ing a cheroot.

"Hi, Red."

Ammie turned around and stomped back into the interior of her room. "Pa send you to spy on me?"

"No. He sent me to make sure you're all right."

Ammie refused to be repentant. "I am not a child."

"Then how come you're actin' like one?"

She stomped her foot. "I am most certainly not—" She
folded her arms across her chest. "I'll act any way I
damned well please."

"I know. That's what I've always liked best about you,
Red." He sighed. "Can I come in? Or do we have to let
the whole hotel in on this little talk?"

She pursed her lips. "Do what you want."

He came in, but he didn't shut the door. "I rode over to

the Diamond G, and Zak told me you'd headed to town with Matt."

"I was going to send word to Pa," Ammie defended. "I just hadn't gotten around to it yet. Besides, Pa knows I'm with Matt."

"What do you think your pa would have me do about this setup you've got here?"

"What setup?"

"Matt across the hall."

Ammie felt her cheeks heat. "What about it?"

"Red, honey, the only man too blind to see how you feel about that boy is Matt himself."

Ammie sank onto the bed and put her head in her hands. "Maybe I should just take out an advertisement in the *Chronicle*. How did you know I love Matt when I didn't even realize it myself until today?"

Smoke's eyes softened as his mouth relaxed into a gentle smile. "I ain't always been a worn-out ol' cowboy."

"Oh, Smoke, what am I going to do? Matt doesn't see me the way I want him to see me."

"You and Matt go back a long ways. He's like any man —he takes you for granted. Anyways, that's what my maw would always say when my paw done the same thing."

"So what'd she do about it?"

He chuckled. "She'd up and do something crazy. Get Paw to sit up and take notice, let me tell you. One time she went and applied for work as a stage driver—just jokin' of course—'cause she said the drivers was the only ones Paw seemed to hang out with and talk to, so's she thought she would just up and be one. He come around in a hurry, let me tell you."

Ammie smiled. "Thanks, Smoke. I'll think about that."

"Matt'll come around too, Red. You'll see. We menfolk can be a little slower in matters of the heart. Just give him a little time." He started toward the door, then paused and looked back. "I hope you know your pa would hang my innards on the barn door if'n he knew I was lettin' you stay here like this."

"He won't hear about it from me."

Smoke laughed. "I know that, sure enough. You never was a stupid child, Red." With that he was gone.

Ammie stood, deciding she might as well get ready for bed. Only then did she realize she had no nightclothes. She undressed anyway, deciding that buck naked felt good against the clean sheets.

She lay down and tried not to think about Matt. But she might as well have tried not to breathe. She found herself listening for his footfalls in the hall, as she watched the windup clock on her nightstand, its hand visible in the moonlight drifting through her window. Ten-thirty came, then eleven. Eleven-thirty, then twelve. Matt still did not return.

Finally, at half past midnight, she heard him. She knew it was him by his stride. Three and a half hours of moving furniture? Ammie lay there, furious and hurt, even as she knew she had no right to be either.

His footsteps stopped outside her door. He knocked. "Ammie?" he called softly. "You up?"

She scrambled to a sitting position on the bed, glancing at her clothes, which lay draped across a chair in the corner. She doubted this was what Smoke had had in mind when he talked about getting Matt to notice her. But it seemed to be the only opportunity at hand. Swallowing hard, she tugged the sheet up to cover her breasts, then called out brightly, "Come in."

Matt opened the door, his eyes apparently adjusting to dim light of the room compared with the lantern-lit hall. He took off his hat, and his hair tumbled in thick, dark waves over his ears. "I don't know what happened earlier, Am. If I said something to upset you, I'm sorry. I know I've been—"

Ammie struck a match and lit the hurricane lamp on her bedside table.

Matt's eyes widened. "I thought you said you were up."

"I'm awake."

"That's not what I meant. You're not dressed."

"So? You weren't dressed when you were taking your bath today."

"Dammit, Ammie, I don't want any old biddies in this town saying bad things about you." He backed toward the door. "I'll just talk to you in the morning."

"We've known each other since I was five years old, Matt Grayson. There's nothing either one of us has that the other one hasn't seen." She said the words even though her heart was racing madly. "Sit down. Please." Lord above, what was she doing? She'd never done anything so brazen in her life. It was as if she were trying to seduce him.

Her heart hammered. Was she?

With obvious reluctance Matt shut the door and sat down in the ladder-back chair across from the bed.

"I don't want to fight with you, Ammie. We've never had anything between us we couldn't talk about."

We do now, she thought miserably.

"It's that I was thinking about not coming back to Texas. That's why you're upset, isn't it?"

"No. I mean, yes. At least, it was. I—I don't know, Matt. It's complicated." The hand that held the sheet slipped just a little. She made no effort to catch it.

Look at me, Matt. Look at me the way you look at Theda Hopkins. The way you look at Millicent Kessler.

Matt twisted his hat brim in his hands and averted his gaze. "What do you mean by complicated?"

"Did you help Theda Hopkins move her furniture?"

His brows furrowed in confusion. "What does that have to do with—"

"Did you help Theda or didn't you?"

"We moved a few things."

Was he being deliberately vague? "Is that all you did?"

"Ammie, what's going on?"

She lowered her gaze, feeling thoroughly ashamed of herself. It was not her business what he did or didn't do with Theda Hopkins. "I'm sorry, Matt. You're right. I was upset when Pa told me you might not be coming back."

His voice was gentle. "You're the reason I did, you know."

Hope flared inside her. "I am?"

"Of course. I could hardly leave my best pal without saying good-bye."

"Oh." She prayed she hid the rush of disappointment she felt. "Then you're—you're still thinking about leaving?"

"I don't know. I'm going to help Will and Jess and Smoke break those horses, then decide."

That gave her a month, maybe six weeks.

She stretched and pretended to yawn, letting the sheet slip a little more.

Matt stood abruptly. "You're tired. I'll fetch you in the morning. We can talk over breakfast."

Ammie girded herself togalike in the sheet and climbed out of bed. She walked toward Matt, who backed up to the closed door. "Maybe we could keep talking. I'm not sleepy. Are you?"

He fumbled behind him for the doorknob, found it, and jerked it open, yawning broadly. "Dead tired, Am. Dead tired. 'Night." With that he was out the door.

Ammie pressed her head against the closed portal, letting the sheet fall from her grasp to pool on the floor at her feet. She didn't know whether to scream or cry. Her whole body tingled with imaginings of what it would be like to feel his hands on her. Had Theda Hopkins felt those hands?

Her eyes burned. How had her whole world turned

upside down in the course of only a single day? And yet, she mused, as frightening as it all was, it was exhilarating as well.

A month, maybe six weeks—not a very long time to get a man to fall in love with her. But it would be enough. It *had* to be enough.

☘ / Chapter 7

Back in his own room, Matt Grayson paced restlessly. What the hell had just happened? He'd gone to Ammie's room to apologize, deciding he'd acted like six different kinds of a bastard since he'd gotten back today. At least he figured he must have—Ammie had seemed testy enough to bite the head off a goat all evening. And suddenly the bastard he'd been all day was nothing compared to the bastard he'd just been in her room.

He stalked to the window and threw it open, staring out at the night-shrouded town. But he saw nothing—nothing save his mind's-eye image of Ammie as she had been minutes ago in that bed. Flame red hair tumbled like fire about ivory shoulders, moonlight dancing across translucent features, her breasts, lush and full, rising and falling beneath the thinnest layering of linen, her lips, pink as rose petals and, he knew from experience, just as soft.

His loins tightened *again*, and he cursed savagely.

He'd done a lot of things he wasn't too proud of in his life, but the thoughts he was having right now about Ammie might well be the worst. He pressed his head against the window, the pane cool against the heat of his skin, and he tried to slow the thunder in his heart.

His only saving grace in all this was that Ammie had no idea where his mind had been. If she had, he was certain she would have been devastated.

She was young, naive. She had no idea the effect she could have on a man.

He jammed his fingers through the tangled waves of his hair. No, that wasn't true. Not even Ammie was that naive. She'd been to a dance or two with Terence Kessler. Hell, it was Matt who had helped teach her how to kiss the scrawny little twit. Ammie knew something about a man's interest in a woman. It wasn't that she would have allowed just any man into her room just now, not after she'd gone to bed.

But she would have allowed in Matt Grayson. She would have allowed in Matt Grayson under any circumstances. Because Matt Grayson was her best friend. She trusted him completely. And he had responded like some craven son of a bitch.

Matt paced back to the nightstand and dipped his hand into the pitcher of water that the hotel had provided for his shave in the morning. He smoothed the tepid liquid over the back of his neck. Maybe he was overreacting. Maybe this wasn't what it seemed. He'd been on the trail a long time. It had been even longer still since he'd indulged his lustier appetites—since before Clint died, in fact. Surely that would account for much of what had happened in Ammie's room. Wouldn't it?

In a way, he reasoned, it had even been predictable, part of the price he paid for having been such a damned monk in Wichita. Oh, he'd gone along with Will and Jess on their forays into various saloons over the two nights they'd spent in town, but time and again he had found himself declining the favors so eagerly offered by the ladies who worked there.

Not that he could discern any noble intent on his part. If it had just been the sex, he would have indulged himself—and gladly. He could've used a respite, no matter how brief, from the pain and heartache that pervaded his life. But he'd been in no mood for the games, for hearing "I love you, cowboy" from a total stranger. Especially when he saw much of the same pain and heartache lurk-

ing in the eyes of the women, despite their bawdy laughter and lewd promises.

Matt sat on the edge of his hotel bed and tugged off his
boots. As if his abstinence in Wichita hadn't been enough
to kindle his male instincts, there had been Theda Hopkins as well. After what transpired in Theda's room tonight, it was little wonder he hadn't been thinking straight
when he stopped in to see Ammie.

He'd gone to Theda's room at the boardinghouse, as
he'd promised, to help her move her armoire. But from
the moment Theda opened the door, it was obvious she
had more on her mind than moving furniture. The buttons
down the front of her dress were undone. The creamy
flesh of her bosom quivered above the constraints of her
corset.

"Come in, Matt, come in," she said, catching his arm
and pulling him inside. "I'm afraid you've caught me just
as I was about to change into something more comfortable."

"I can come back," he offered quickly.

"Don't be silly."

She led him to a faded, threadbare love seat in front of
the unlit fireplace. "I've been on my feet all night. Won't
you join me for a drink?"

"Maybe I should just move the armoire. . . ."

She pouted. "You don't want to have a drink with me?"

He relented. "Sure. Why not?" He accepted the glass
of whiskey she poured for him, then watched her gulp
down her own. He suspected suddenly that it was not her
first of the evening.

"You all right, Theda?"

"I'm fine, Matt." She leaned close, resting one hand on
his thigh. "Thank you for asking, though."

Matt shifted, trying without success to ease his leg out
from under her hand. "Theda . . ."

"It was such a surprise to see you at the hotel." Her

hand began to stroke his thigh. "I'd heard all kinds of rumors—that you were heading to California, that you got a job with the railroad—"

Matt blinked. Had Ammie heard such ridiculous stories? That might explain—

Theda's hand roved past his crotch.

"Theda, you've had too much to drink. You don't know what you're—" His breath caught as she kneaded the bulge in his trousers.

"I know what I'm doing, Matt," she purred. "I know exactly what I'm doing."

Matt felt his loins stir, his blood heat. He set his glass down. "I can't let you—" he rasped.

"Please, Matt, I get so lonely since Sam left." She looped her arms around his neck and drew his head down. Her mouth met his. Her lips parted, her tongue teasing him, urging him to open his mouth, to welcome her erotic exploration.

Matt groaned, responded, his hands shifting to lift one of her breasts above the confinement of her stays. She arched toward him, offering the rosy peak to his mouth. Blood pounding in his head, he leaned forward.

Then with an oath he gripped her arms and set her away from him. "Theda, I'm sorry. I can't do this. I just . . . I just don't feel . . ."

"You don't have to love me, Matt," she breathed, one finger trailing enticingly around her erect nipple. "I don't expect you to love me. It's been so long since anyone— anyone even touched me." A tear slid from the corner of her eye. "I always thought—hoped you liked me, just a little."

"I do like you. That's why I'm not going to do this. You deserve better."

"Please, Matt, I want to feel a man inside me again."

Matt closed his eyes, dragging in a long breath in an effort to clear his head. "No."

Her face crumbled. She began to sob brokenly. "I'm not pretty enough, am I? Ammie has that long red hair. . . ."

Matt started. "What are you talking about? Ammie has nothing to do with this."

Theda's lower lip quivered. "I'm sorry. I thought—" She swallowed her words as more tears fell. "Hold me, Matt, please." She pressed herself against him, her arms wrapped tight around his back. "Please."

He curved his arms around her and held her close.

"Oh, Matt, you don't know how long it's been. . . ." She lifted her head, her lips brushing his cheek. "Please?"

He swallowed hard, the stiffness in his loins willing him to surrender conscience to need, but he said, "It wouldn't work, Theda. It just wouldn't work. If I honestly thought it would make either one of us feel better . . ." He cupped her cheek against his palm. "Believe me, I know what it's like to want someone to love me."

"You must think I'm horrid."

"No, I think you're lonely." He eased her away from him. "I'd better go."

She pulled the edges of her dress together. "I'm sorry, Matt."

"Forget it." He stood and started toward the door, then hesitated. He looked back at her, her face tear-streaked, pathetic. "Do you really want that armoire moved?"

She gave a watery laugh. "If you could, I'd be grateful."

Matt spent the next twenty minutes shifting the heavy mahogany bureau. He was happy for the exertion—it tempered some of the sexual tension he was still feeling. Tempered it, but didn't eliminate it. He was glad when he'd finished and kept a judicious distance between himself and Theda as he headed for the door.

She caught up with him. "Don't worry—your virtue is safe."

He gave her a wry grin. "No, it isn't. That's why I don't want you to get too close."

She giggled, then grew serious. "Thank you, Matt. For everything."

He tipped his hat. "Always glad to help a lady."

"This may not be my place to say, but—well, I just want you to know . . . I don't believe a word of those stories about you."

He snorted. "Which ones?"

She looked at the floor. "Never mind."

He chucked her under the chin. "What is it?"

She hesitated, then said, "There are some who say you —you got your brother killed."

Matt stiffened.

"I'm sorry. That was stupid. I shouldn't have—"

"It's all right," he cut in, though it wasn't. "I can't help what people say."

"I of all people should know that." She squeezed his hand. "You take care, Matt Grayson. And you tell Ammie, she's one lucky lady."

Matt had already asked one question too many tonight. He wasn't going to ask what this one meant.

Outside, he took a long, deep breath. So far, it had been one hell of a homecoming. The only good thing about the day had been seeing Ammie again, and even that had somehow gone awry. Maybe he would stop by her room at the hotel and see if she was still awake.

But first he would take a walk. He had turned down what Theda was offering, but that didn't mean he hadn't been sorely tempted. What would it have hurt, anyway? his mind taunted. Since when had he become such a saint?

The word *saint* jabbed at him, and unwillingly he thought of Clint and how often he had derided him with that very epithet. He hadn't meant to hurt Clint by using it. He sighed. Yes, he had. He had wanted to hurt Clint, because he himself was hurting. Because in Zak Grayson's eyes, everything Clint said and did was right, perfect. Clint never made a mistake. Never—

Matt stuffed his hands into his pockets, his eyes burning. God, how he missed his brother. He never would have believed it. But he missed him so much.

He supposed it was Clint's death that had made him more introspective lately, forced him to face just how finite life was. More and more, Matt found himself thinking about the direction of his own life, what he was doing with it, where it was going. There was a yearning in him that had never been there before. Or if it had been, he hadn't been aware of it. A yearning for what, he didn't yet know.

He kept walking. It was hours before he made his way back to the hotel. If he'd realized the time, he would never have stopped at Ammie's room. He would've gone straight to bed.

God, how he wished he had.

He peeled off his clothes and tossed them toward a chair in the far corner of the room. He missed. Wearing only his drawers, he stretched out atop the quilted coverlet on the bed. The night had cooled, though not much. A slight breeze wafted in from the open window and teased the perspiration that beaded on his naked chest.

His thoughts turned again to Ammie. Should he apologize to her tomorrow? And if he did, what would he say— that he was sorry she hadn't let go of the sheet?

He slammed a fist into the mattress and wondered briefly, despairingly, if Theda Hopkins would object to a return visit. He couldn't permit these kinds of thoughts to continue.

He and Ammie had so much history together. He remembered her as a little wisp of a thing the day her father had first brought her over to the Diamond G. Wisp, yes, but with the heart of a cougar.

It had been Ammie who followed him home from school just weeks after he'd met her. Ammie who'd found him crying in the hayloft, humiliated over another failing grade in reading. With her green eyes solemn she'd leaned close and peered into his own blue ones, studying them intently for a long minute. Then she'd leaned back and pronounced matter-of-factly, "Something's busted."

No judgment, no censure. From then on, she'd read to him, and her own quick study made short work of his more advanced grade level.

They'd devised a system to work around most of his written assignments. His mother had been a willing co-conspirator, though Matt had to swear never to tell his father.

"Your father wants what's best for you," Emily Grayson had said, "but he has his own ideas on how to do things, and he doesn't take to anyone else knowing a better way."

For a time Matt had even worn a splint to school, pretending his arm had been broken, so he had to do everything orally. Though his mother didn't think too highly of the scheme, she did sneak out every morning to apply the splints. Matt would then take them off every night before he got home. He and Ammie had been especially proud of that one—until that little ferret Finley Barnes had snitched on them.

Matt had to smile. He and Ammie had gotten their revenge. They'd sneaked cayenne pepper into applesauce that Finley so proudly claimed to have made especially for Miss Gilford. Finley had had to stand in the corner every day for two weeks.

Matt's smile softened. Clint had known, of course, about the ruse with the splints. It had been done a couple of years before his parents had sent him off to that fancy boarding school back east. Clint had kept Matt's secret from Zak and from Miss Gilford.

"We're brothers, Matt. We need to stick together."

"I don't need anything from you," Matt had shot back, pretending he didn't notice the hurt in Clint's pale eyes.

Matt's throat tightened. What he wouldn't give for a chance to take those words back, those and so many others! There was so much he and Clint hadn't understood about each other until it was too late.

He leaned over and picked up the crumpled telegram where it had fallen from his shirt pocket. His heart thudded as he wondered yet again who might have sent it. His worst fear—blackmail, someone who would threaten to tell his father the truth about Clint's death.

"It won't happen, Clint. My hand to God, I won't let it happen."

He closed his eyes. It was late, and he was exhausted. He would need his wits about him to face the man on the stage tomorrow. But sleep eluded him. The yearning was back. It was an ache this time, an emptiness that needed filling, if only he knew where to look. It was a long time before he drifted off into a fitful sleep.

Ammie stared at the ceiling, unable to sleep. It had been two hours since Matt left her room—ample time to reconsider her earlier behavior. She shuddered. How on earth had she dared invite him in here when she'd been stark naked in this bed? What had she been thinking? And what must he now think of her? He'd probably been appalled. If the man had been on fire, he couldn't have escaped this room any faster. At the time, she assured herself she was being subtle. In reality, she'd probably embarrassed him half to death.

She shoved to a sitting position, her cheeks heating. There was little sense dwelling on it. There was nothing she could do about it now, except pray that Smoke didn't hear of it, or—heaven save her—her father.

She glanced at the clock. Two-thirty. She was not going to get to sleep tonight without help.

Clambering out of bed, she threw on her clothes. She
didn't bother to button her shirt, but merely pulled the
sides together over her chemise. Opening her door, she
checked the hallway. Deserted. As quickly and quietly as
she could, she headed for the back stairwell. When she
had trouble sleeping at home, there was only one cure.
She hurried down the stairs, opened the rear door of
Kessler House, and whistled for that cure.

In seconds Pickles came running. Back at the ranch the
dog's warm presence at the foot of her bed often lulled
Ammie to sleep. She was hoping for a similar medicinal
benefit tonight. The dog whimpered excitedly as Ammie
ushered her into the hotel. "Shush, now," Ammie cau-
tioned, "or they'll throw us both out of here."

Pickles padded up the stairs ahead of Ammie without a
sound, though her tail waggled furiously. Ammie breathed
a sigh of relief when she reached her room undetected.
She grasped the doorknob, but before she could turn it,
Pickles skittered across the hall.

Ammie watched, horrified, as the dog began to scratch
vigorously at Matt's door. She must have caught his scent.
With a squeak of dismay Ammie lunged after her, grabbed
her by the scruff of the neck, and herded her back across
the hall.

Too late.

Matt's door opened. He stood there, barefoot, clad only
in his underwear, trying to rub the sleep from his eyes.
His dark hair tumbled boyishly about his forehead. But
there was nothing boyish about the rest of him. In the
shadowed hallway his broad chest with its fine dusting of
dark hair appeared wantonly masculine. His knee-length
drawers hugged firm, hard-muscled thighs. The draw-
string waist rode low over his hips, and the thin material
outlined a formidable bulge at the apex of his legs.

Ammie stood there, holding on to the dog, frozen,
transfixed.

Matt blinked once, twice, shook his head. "What the—? Pickles?"

The sound of his voice was more than Pickles could resist. She bolted from Ammie's grasp and bounded across the hallway, rearing up on her hind legs and planting her front paws on Matt's chest. It was something she'd done a thousand times—except that each of those previous nine hundred and ninety-nine times, Matt had been wearing a shirt.

"Yeeoww!" He cursed and stumbled back, coming fully awake, then landed in an ignominious heap on the carpeted floor of his room.

Ammie heard other guests begin to stir. Doors along the corridor opened.

Ammie didn't wait for introductions. With a flash of movement and an instinct for self-preservation she didn't know she possessed, she blew out the two nearest lamps, dove into Matt's room, and slammed the door behind her. As an afterthought, she turned the key.

The room was pitch dark. The moon must have disappeared behind a cloud bank. "Pickles!" she whispered sharply. "You are a very bad dog. Very bad!"

"Who the hell let her in the hotel?" Matt demanded. Judging from the location and the tone of his voice, he was still on the floor, still trying to ward off an ecstatic Pickles.

"I can explain, honest," Ammie said.

A fist rapped sharply on Matt's door. "Mr. Grayson!" The knob jangled. "Come out here at once!"

Ammie gasped. If they found her in here—Lord above, what if Smoke had taken a room in the hotel?

"Matt," she whispered, "what are we—"

"Hush!" He must have been thinking the same thing. Toward the door he called, "Just a minute!"

She heard him push to his feet and pad toward the nightstand. His toes slammed into one of the bed legs, and he let loose with a string of curses so blue, Ammie could've sworn the room changed color. Still mumbling under his breath, he found the table, struck a match, and lit the lantern. Then he looked down. He swore even more vividly, as he realized he wasn't dressed. In the same breath he sent Ammie a quick, hooded glance she couldn't read. He blew out the lantern.

The knocking on the door grew louder. Pickles began to howl.

"Matt, what are you—?"

"Don't say another word!" he whispered sharply. "Get under the bed."

"What?"

"You heard me. Do it."

They were both whispering, praying they couldn't be heard above the pounding and the barking.

Ammie groped her way to the bed. Briefly, she had a vision of being found by her father standing next to Matt in his underwear, or found under Matt's bed with Matt wearing his underwear. Either way, she was dead.

She crawled under the bed.

She heard the chink of coins and knew Matt was scrambling into his denims. "Please, God," she heard him mutter, "let this be a nightmare."

A pass key was being inserted into the lock, just as Matt reached the door and yanked it open. Ammie didn't dare peek out to look.

"Mr. Grayson," a highly affronted male voice intoned, "would you mind explaining yourself?"

Ammie shrank farther back under the bed. Terence.

Pickles discovered her and began to lick her face. Ammie wondered how many years her father would lock her in her room.

"Pickles," Matt called, "here, girl!"

The dog galumphed to Matt's side.

"Well?" Terence said. "I'm waiting. In fact, we're all

waiting." Ammie imagined him gesturing toward an entire hallway filled with people.

"The dog needed to go out," Matt said.

"I beg your pardon?"

"The dog needed to go out. I'm a sound sleeper. She had a hard time waking me up."

"And exactly what," Terence asked slowly, "was that filthy animal doing in my hotel in the first place? And what is it doing with you? I thought it belonged to Amelia."

Ammie could imagine all eyes turning toward the closed door of her room.

"Ammie decided to spend the night with Mary Denby," Matt said smoothly. "Mrs. Denby didn't want the dog in her house."

"So you brought it into the hotel?"

"She's afraid of the dark."

"Mrs. Denby?"

"The dog."

"Well, I want you and your animal out of this hotel at once."

"I'll leave in the morning. And so will Pickles."

Ammie could feel the tension crackling between the two men. So, too, could she almost feel Terence's eyes trying to see around Matt into the depths of this room. It was Terence who backed down.

"Be out at dawn," he huffed. "And don't even think about spending a night in this hotel again."

"Wouldn't want to," Matt drawled. "Too noisy." With that he shut the door in Terence's face.

Ammie heard the muttering of voices as the crowd dispersed, but she had little time to be relieved when two large bare feet appeared in front of her. "You can come out now."

She wasn't sure she wanted to. But she did.

As she stood up, Matt was standing there, his arms folded across his naked chest. "I'm listening."

She sat down on the bed, then remembered whose bed it was and shot to her feet. "I just wanted some company."

"What?"

"Pickles likes to sleep on my bed at home."

"Do you have any idea what could have happened, if you'd been found in my room at this hour—" He didn't finish.

"You'd be forced to marry me?" she offered hopefully.

"This is not funny!"

I wasn't joking, she longed to say, but didn't. "Well, they didn't find me, so there's no harm done."

"No harm done? You are going to get yourself out of this hotel and over to Mary Denby's and pray to God she backs up our story."

"Why?"

"Why? Ammie, these people will crucify you! You know how important a girl's reputation is."

"People know we're best friends. They wouldn't think anything of it."

"They know I'm a man and you're a woman, as you so pointedly reminded me earlier today"—he glanced at the clock—"make that yesterday." He sighed. "Ammie, the last thing I want is for you to be hurt because of me."

She stared at the floor. "You have big feet."

"We're not talking about my feet."

She was remembering how he looked in his underwear. Her gaze skated upward, colliding with the dark mat of hair across his chest. She wondered if it was as soft as it looked. Her lips parted, and her gaze tracked to his face. He was regarding her with an expression she'd never seen before—at least, not when he looked at her.

Kiss me, her mind pleaded. *Right here, right now, Matt Grayson. Kiss me!*

Matt spun abruptly and paced to the window. "I want you out of here. Now."

Had she imagined the heat in those blue eyes? Had the night shadows only been teasing her? Had she perceived desire where there had been none, only because she wished it so?

"Now, Ammie. I'm tired. I'm meeting that damned stage in six hours. I'd like to get some sleep."

"I'm sorry. I didn't mean for this to happen."

He let out a ragged breath. "I know. It's just . . ." His eyes glittered, his gaze trailing to where she had failed to button her shirt. "Get out of here, Ammie. I mean it." He crossed to the door ahead of her and peered out, making certain the hallway was empty. "Go."

She paused next to him, then on impulse reached up to touch his beard-stubbed jaw. "Matt, I—"

He jerked back as though she'd slapped him. "Dammit, get out of here!"

For the second time in less than twenty minutes, Ammie slipped down the back stairway of Kessler House. Only this time, instead of letting Pickles in, she was letting herself out. She made her way along the darkened streets, trying very hard not to cry. In that last instant before she left Matt's room, she had dared to touch him in a tender, intimate way. And he had been repelled by it.

No, she amended, maybe *repelled* was too strong a word. But he had certainly been stunned. And if she read the look in his eyes correctly, he had been not at all pleased. Maybe *disturbed* would be a better word. As though he didn't quite know how to react. He didn't want to hurt her feelings, but . . .

But he would prefer it if she didn't touch him that way again. A tear slid from the corner of her eye. How could she *not* touch him? God, all she wanted to *do* was touch him. Touch him, hold him, be with him in the most intimate way a woman can be with a man.

She had made her way to the schoolhouse, and now she leaned heavily against one shadowed outer wall. This was the first time she had fully admitted to herself wanting to make love to him, seduce him, be part of him. Her knees went rubbery, and she had to sit down. That most secret, private part of her grew warm. She closed her eyes.

Less than three hours ago, she had all but decided she had only a month to six weeks to get Matt to fall in love with her. Now she clearly saw the folly of that tactic. She couldn't make him fall in love with her, any more than anyone had made her fall in love with him. It was a subtle, gradual process that had been going on for months. She couldn't even pinpoint the moment or an event that might have triggered it. It just suddenly *was*. She loved him, period. She had to give Matt the same freedom.

She would back off, relax, as much as she was able. If she didn't, it was all too likely that her greatest fear would come true: She would destroy their friendship.

But how long could she pretend her feelings didn't exist?

"As long as it takes," she murmured aloud. "As long as it takes."

She could start practicing right now, she thought grimly as she approached Mary Denby's house. She was certainly not going to share her feelings for Matt with that woman. But how was she going to explain showing up at her house in the middle of the night?

Ammie grimaced. She would tell Mary as little as possible.

Why had Matt made up such a ridiculous story about her spending the night at Mary Denby's, anyway?

Because he hadn't wanted to risk Terence checking her room at the hotel, that was why. It might have occurred to Terence that every other guest on the third floor had been roused by the commotion with Pickles—except Ammie. Matt hadn't wanted Terence to discover her missing.

At Mary Denby's front door, Ammie hesitated. Common courtesy demanded that she knock. And yet to do so would invite endless, thoroughly embarrassing questions, questions she was too exhausted to answer right now. Cautiously, she tested the front door, grateful to find it unlocked. She eased it open and peered inside.

The house was dark and silent. Ammie let out a sigh of relief. Just inside the entryway to her left was a parlor. She crept inside and made her way to where she knew she'd find a horsehair settee. She would lie down, sleep, and give some token answers to Mary Denby's questions in the morning.

She had almost reached the settee when she sensed that she was not alone. In that same instant, directly in front of her, a match was struck. Ammie gasped, nearly screaming aloud. What she saw in the light of that tiny flame made her wish she had only an intruder to contend with. Lying on the settee, a look of supreme disappointment clouding his weathered features, was Smoke.

☘ / *Chapter 8*

Ammie weighed the possibility that Smoke would believe she was an apparition from a dream, thereby giving her the time she needed to turn and run. She could ride back to Shamrock, dive into her bed, and pretend this whole day had never happened. But her feet remained rooted to the floor as Smoke used the match he was holding to light a narrow candle atop a filigreed brass candlestick in Mary Denby's parlor.

She waited for the lecture, the explosion, the censure to come, but Smoke obliged her with none of them. He simply sat on Mary Denby's settee and regarded her with an expression that was both wounded and sad.

She should have expected as much. It was her father's way to stomp and holler. Smoke let a person stew in the imposing juices of his own conscience—a forbidding punishment indeed.

"It's not what it looks like," she blurted when he continued to say nothing.

"And what exactly does it look like, Red?" He had been sleeping in his clothes, and he tossed back the patchwork quilt that covered his lap.

"It looks like—like—" She rubbed her hand along her hip, trying desperately to think of something, anything, that sounded even remotely feasible. "It looks like I've been out for a very late walk," she stated finally.

"You always have your shirt unbuttoned on these late-night walks?" he drawled.

Ammie's gaze shot down her body, and she let out a

tiny, mortified squeak. Frantically she worked the buttons, then looked at Smoke. "It's real windy?" she offered feebly.

"Just tell me this, Red," he asked, his voice deadly serious. "Was anything done tonight that I'm going to have to beat the living tar out of Matt Grayson for?"

"Absolutely not!" she snapped, horrified. "Matt was a perfect gentleman!" Under her breath she couldn't resist adding, "To my everlasting regret."

Whatever Smoke had been about to say next was lost in the arrival of a sleep-disheveled Mary Denby, who emerged from her bedroom in the rear of the house and bustled into the parlor wearing nightcap, nightdress, and flannel wrapper. "Amelia, dear!" she cried. "Is anything wrong?"

"I apologize for disturbing you, Mrs. Denby," Ammie said, and meant it. "There was . . . a problem at the hotel."

"At this time of night?" she asked, flabbergasted.

"It was my fault."

Mary Denby and Smoke Larson exchanged looks.

"It had nothing to do with Matt," Ammie defended. "Well, not exactly anyway. It was Pickles."

Smoke rolled his eyes. "I should've known. When I seen that hound in town earlier tonight, I thought about orderin' her home, but then I thought better of it."

"What did the dog do?" Mary Denby asked.

Ammie sighed. "It's a long story, and I'm very tired."

"Of course, dear," Mary sympathized. "How thoughtless of me. Here, you come right back into my bedroom. One of my recent upstairs boarders left behind a cot that I haven't quite figured out what to do with yet. I insist you make use of it."

Ammie had no energy left to argue. Besides, to argue would only stir up more of Smoke's conscience stew. She'd had her fill for one night.

In her bedroom Mary handed Ammie a pillow. Ammie mumbled her thanks, lay down on the quilt-covered cot, and fell asleep almost at once, too tired even to dream.

She awoke to Mary's gentle shake on her shoulder. It took Ammie a minute to remember where she was. When she did, other memories came flooding back as well. She groaned and pulled the covers over her head. Could a person actually die of embarrassment?

"I've fixed us a nice breakfast," Mary said cheerfully, as though they were the dearest of friends. "You go ahead and freshen up, then come into the kitchen and eat."

Ammie remained huddled on the cot, her mind reliving in excruciating detail every mortifying minute of yesterday—from scrubbing Matt's back to clutching a sheet over her naked breasts to staring transfixed at him in his underwear. Best friend or no best friend, how was she ever going to face the man in the cold light of day again?

Then she remembered the telegram. No matter how uncomfortable she might be, she couldn't let Matt face trouble alone. Besides, there was always the chance the telegram had so preoccupied him, he hadn't even noticed how strangely she was behaving of late.

Throwing back the covers, Ammie staggered outside to the outhouse to answer a call of nature. Back inside, she washed her face and hands. She felt a little better, even though the bleary-eyed, tumble-haired creature staring back at her from the mirror above Mary Denby's washstand sparked no recognition. Perhaps she had indeed died overnight and no one had the heart to tell her.

With a resigned shrug Ammie wandered into the kitchen, where she was greeted by a veritable smorgasbord of aromas—scrambled eggs, frying bacon, warming bread, and onion laced potatoes. Ammie's mouth watered, but instead of being pleased by the feast, she was unaccountably irritated. She plunked herself down onto a cane-back chair.

"Don't you fret," Mary said as though she were reading her mind. "I could never compete with you in the kitchen, Amelia. Your father raves and raves about your cooking."

"I wasn't fretting," she said defensively, even though she was. "Where's Smoke?" she asked to distract herself. She knew she was being patently unfair to this woman, but she couldn't seem to help herself.

"He said he thought he should take a walk."

Ammie grimaced. He'd probably gone out to avoid asking her questions that he knew she wouldn't want to answer.

"You love Matt very much, don't you?"

Ammie let out a disgusted breath. She might as well hang a sign around her neck. "It doesn't much matter," she said. "He doesn't feel the same."

"Don't be too sure about that."

Ammie glanced up hopefully. "What do you mean? Did Matt say something to you?"

"Well, no. . . ."

Her shoulders slumped. "I was thinking about buying a dress today. Dumb, huh? You can't gild a dandelion."

"Oh, Amelia, never say such a thing! You're a lovely, lovely girl." Mary reached toward her as if to brush a stray wisp of hair from her face, then apparently thought better of it. She clasped her hands in her lap. "I could go shopping with you," she offered.

"No," Ammie said, then added, "no, thank you." She pushed her plate away. "I'd better go. I want to see about that dress before the stage gets in."

"I see." Ammie could tell that Mary wanted to ask more but didn't. Instead Mary said, "I was hoping that spending some time away would help Matthew, but he still seems terribly sad. It's such a shame about Clint. He would have made a fine congressman. He was such a good student."

"Clint was good at everything."

"Not everything." Mary's brown eyes clouded. "I remember he failed a history test once. He was terrified, absolutely beside himself. He begged me to let him retake the test."

Ammie made a face. "All right. He failed one test."

"It wasn't the test that mattered—it was how brutally accountable he held himself for failing. I was so concerned about him that I actually did let him take the test over."

"And he got an A."

Mary nodded, but her eyes were still pained. "He was such a driven child, but fragile. . . ."

Ammie's brows arched. She never would have described Clint as fragile. "He was five years older than I was. I guess I didn't notice much what he did in school. And then he went east to finish."

"Yes. I'm not sure that was for the best, either."

"I don't think Matt minded having Clint gone. It stopped some of the comparisons his father kept making, at least for a while."

"Parents should never compare one child with another. Matt and Clint were equally bright. It was just that Matt—" She stopped.

Ammie frowned. "You know about Matt?"

"It was in Miss Gilford's records." Her mouth tightened with contempt. "All I can say is that it's a good thing that woman was already gone before I came to town. The kinds of comments she wrote about some of those dear children. . . ." Mary took a steadying breath. "A person like that has no business being a teacher."

Ammie was beginning to remember why she used to like this woman. She stood. "I really need to get going." She started clearing the dishes.

Mary touched her arm. "Leave them. You go ahead and shop for that dress."

Ammie didn't argue. She hurried toward the door.

"See you for supper tonight," Mary called.

Outside, Ammie scowled. She'd forgotten about supper. Was that why the woman had been so nice to her? So that Ammie would return the favor tonight at Shamrock? No, that was absurd. Ammie felt a flush of shame. Mary Denby was a genuinely kind person—she always had been. Ammie knew that. It was just that lately the type of person she was didn't matter nearly as much as the fact that Shamus O'Rourke was falling in love with her.

Ammie glanced back at the house. Maybe she should apologize. Not that she was ready to give her blessing to Mary's relationship with her father, but perhaps she could be a little less overt in her disapproval. Then again, maybe she'd wait and talk to Mary tonight. She had enough to worry about this morning—not the least of which was buying a blasted dress.

Yet as she headed toward Quincy's Mercantile, she wondered why she was even bothering. If Matt didn't notice her feminine charms when she was wrapped in a sheet, what possible good would a dress do? *You've decided to be subtle, remember?* her mind chided. The dress wasn't going to be a dramatic statement. She would simply appear wearing it at some time in the near future. Her heart skipped a beat. Like tonight at supper?

She reached Quincy's, but she paused before going in, and tracked her gaze across the street to Kessler House. Everything seemed peaceful enough. After his near-sleepless night, was Matt still in bed? The thought sent a wave of heat to her face. She was suddenly glad she was shopping. She could use the distraction.

Ammie spent the next hour in Quincy's, scrutinizing every dress in the store—even, God forbid, dress patterns. But she found nothing that she could suffer to be seen in. Who designed such abominations anyway? she fumed. Sadists? If she wanted her body squashed and molded like potter's clay, she could just heave herself into a kiln.

Frustrated, she stomped from the store. There was little use denying it—the fates were conspiring against her. She had no choice but to visit the mercantile that was renowned for carrying a wider selection of merchandise.

Three doors down from Quincy's, Ammie eased open the door to Kessler's Emporium, hoping to prevent the bell above the jamb from jingling. The longer she wasn't noticed, the better. Millicent and Martin Kessler usually ran the store. Ammie was in no mood for dress-buying assistance from the beautiful Millicent.

She edged her way inside, then left the door ajar, daring a glance at the counter. A man with his back to her was busily stocking shelves. She groaned inwardly. It was worse than Millicent. It was Terence. Did the man have a twin?

He must have felt her eyes on him, because he turned around. "Amelia, what a surprise." His manner was a bit stiff and formal. His eyes were bloodshot, no doubt from having his sleep interrupted. "I'm sorry you didn't enjoy your accommodations at the hotel last night. If there was a problem, you should have come to me."

"There was no problem. Mrs. Denby invited me to stay with her, that's all." That much was the truth.

"Actually, I'm grateful to her," he said, adjusting his spectacles.

"What do you mean?"

"I'm grateful to anyone who keeps you from Matt Grayson."

"Careful, Terence."

"I'm well aware of your friendship with the man, but that doesn't mean I have to like it. Isn't a beau entitled to jealousy?"

"You're not my—" She bit off the words. She supposed she wasn't being entirely fair. She *had* accepted his invitations to more than one social. It wasn't so much that she disliked Terence than that seeing him reminded her of her less-than-commendable behavior behind the barn. Why had she ever wanted to kiss Terence Kessler?

Curiosity mostly, she admitted. And, of course, the fact that he'd wanted to kiss her had been more than a little flattering. And maybe, just maybe, some tiny unknown part of her had wanted Matt to teach her how to kiss.

"I, uh—I'd appreciate your help, Terence. I'm looking for a dress."

"For yourself?" His brows shot up in surprise.

"Yes, for myself," she returned testily. "You don't have to have a seizure."

"No, no, I'm delighted." He hurried into the back storeroom, then quickly returned carrying the most stunning dress Ammie had ever seen. She wasn't well schooled in fabrics, but she listened, astonished, as Terence enthusiastically touted the cream-colored faille with its violet satin stripes and violet crepe de Chine. "And notice the trim on the bottom, with the flounce on the bias."

Ammie didn't care about flounces or piping or gathers or pleats. She only knew that she liked the dress. She ran her rein-roughened fingers over the satiny fabric.

"Millicent had it made in Paris three years ago."

Ammie snatched her hand back. "It's used?"

"Not at all. She never wore it, in fact, and now she claims it's hopelessly out of style. To be honest, though"— he gave her a conspiratorial wink—"it seems the modiste didn't take Millicent's measurements properly, and the bodice is, shall we say, overlarge? Millicent isn't as blessed as"—his gaze flicked to her chest, and Ammie had to resist the urge to cover herself—"as some ladies are." He coughed, blushing a little, his voice timid. "I always kind of envisioned you in the dress, Amelia."

Ammie again touched the finely made garment. If even

the thought of her wearing it could get Terence all flustered, maybe it would indeed prove useful. "You've convinced me," she said. "Wrap it up."

Terence did so, happily. "Will you wear it to the dance next week?"

"Terence, I'm not even sure—"

His face fell.

"Maybe," she amended.

He brightened. "I'll count the days."

"You do that." Clutching her brown-wrapped parcel, Ammie hurried out of the store. She stood there, trying to catch her breath. Life just didn't make sense sometimes. Terence was cow-eyed over her. She was cow-eyed over Matt. And Matt . . .

She glanced up the street, an unconscious smile touching her lips. Matt was standing in front of the stage depot. Hugging her package, Ammie started toward him.

He was pacing like a caged panther and hadn't noticed her. Pickles was curled up in a ball beside a bench seat provided for outbound passengers, though there were none this morning. The stage, Ammie knew, was due any minute. As if thinking about it could make it appear, she heard the distant rumble of wheels and the pounding of hooves behind her.

Matt stopped his pacing and stared past Ammie at the approaching stage. Pickles stirred and began barking. Ammie called to the dog—the last thing anyone needed was a spooked team.

Matt's gaze flitted only briefly to Ammie, then locked on the stage again, but she had seen the uncharacteristic nervousness in that hard-angled face. He'd been more worried about that telegram than he'd let on. Ammie fought down the impulse to go to him and forced herself to stay back. Matt needed to face this man alone. The stranger might not be as forthcoming if someone else was around. Ammie distracted herself by petting Pickles.

The stage rolled to a stop. Ammie's stomach clenched, and a prickle of foreboding skittered along her spine. She had the sudden urge to set Pickles loose on the team after all, to send the stage careening out of town, and somehow prevent whoever was on it from getting off.

But she could only watch as the grizzled driver leaped from his perch and lumbered over to the coach door that faced the depot. He yanked it open, spat a wad of tobacco juice into the dust, and announced, "River Oaks. Everybody out."

Matt was already peering past the driver into the coach's interior. A look of wonder spread across his handsome features. As though in a trance, he extended his hand toward the open door. Into that big, bronzed palm was clasped a small, feminine hand encased in a black kid glove.

Ammie stopped petting Pickles. Her heart somersaulted in her chest as Matt assisted the woman attached to that hand to the boardwalk. She was without a doubt the most stunningly beautiful woman Ammie had ever seen in her life. An oval face with luminous dark eyes set off delicate porcelain-doll features. Coils of rich dark hair fell in lustrous curls about flawless ivory skin. A dress of black faille accented a tiny wisp of a waist. Her Tuscan straw bonnet was secured beneath her chin by two wide satin ribbons. It was totally ridiculous attire for a stage ride, and yet the woman seemed unaffected by the heat, with nary a hair out of place. Jealousy, more intense than any she had ever known, surged to life in Ammie, as Matt gaped at the lovely brunette with undisguised male interest.

Ammie had seen enough. She started toward the stage.

Suddenly, the yellow tomcat from the night before crossed her path. Pickles must have remembered her abused nose, not to mention her abused canine pride. The hound set up a spine-curdling howl and tore off after the astonished cat. The cat streaked down the boardwalk.

Ammie called to Pickles, but to no avail. The dog was on a mission. Pickles was hurtling toward the stage depot, the cat bare inches in front of her.

With no tree in sight up which to escape, the cat bore down on the only hiding place available: he darted beneath the brunette's voluminous skirts. Cat yowling, dog barking, woman screaming—all three participants fled in different directions.

Ammie reached the depot and rocked back onto her heels, laughing.

Matt shot her an angry glare. "It's not funny!"

Stunned, hurt, Ammie watched him rush off to rescue his damsel in distress.

The woman had stopped running and stood cowering next to the bank. Matt wrapped his arm about her shoulders, guiding her back to the depot. "I'm so sorry, miss. I don't know what got into her. She's usually much better behaved." Ammie's cheeks burned. She wasn't sure whether Matt was talking about the dog or her!

"I can't thank you enough, sir," the woman said, her voice light and lovely. Like she was. "You may have saved my life."

Saved her life! Ammie almost choked. She glared at the stagecoach, willing the person who had sent the telegram to climb out. A disreputable-looking man wearing a ragged frock coat and carrying a valise clambered down. But Matt was too enthralled by the brunette to notice.

"You're sure you're all right, miss?" he kept asking. "Maybe you'd best sit down." He gestured toward the wooden bench in front of the depot.

"I'm fine, really. It was just a bit of a shock, that's all. Thank you so much, Mister—?"

Matt touched the brim of his hat. "Grayson, miss. Matthew Grayson, at your service."

The woman paled, swayed, and looked as though she were about to faint. Matt's arms swept out to catch her. The woman leaned heavily against him. "Forgive me," she murmured. "I didn't expect . . ."

"What is it?" Matt asked, continuing to steady her.

"Your name," the lovely brunette said, taking a step back, her hand fluttering to her bosom. "You're—you're Clint Grayson's brother, aren't you?"

"Yes, ma'am, I am." A sudden disquiet crept into Matt's eyes. "You sent the telegram." It was not a question.

The woman nodded.

"You knew Clint?"

Again she nodded. Her next words nearly sent Matt to his knees. "He was my husband."

☘ / Chapter 9

Ammie stared at the brunette, stunned, disbelieving. Clint Grayson's wife? It wasn't possible. But what was even more difficult to believe was the look on Matt's face. It was not a look of incredulity, but one of curiosity, even of dawning acknowledgment.

"My name is Lynette Simmons," the woman said, gazing up at Matt with wide, sad eyes. "I didn't mean to shock you, Matthew. I . . ." She paused, apparently mindful of the small crowd that had gathered thanks to Pickles's latest escapade. "If we could go somewhere and talk privately?"

"Of course," Matt said. He glanced around, as though trying to decide where to take her.

Ammie stared at him, dumbfounded. Surely he was not giving any credence to this preposterous woman and her preposterous claim! "Matt," she blustered, "you can't take her seriously?"

"I intend to hear her out, yes."

Though she was already feeling unpleasantly conspicuous thanks to her grungy attire, Ammie marched over to face the lovely Lynette squarely. "I don't know what your scheme is *Miss* Simmons, but Clint Grayson was not married. Ever."

"You must be Amelia," Lynette said softly.

Ammie started, unconsciously reaching up to smooth her bedraggled hair. "How did you—?"

"Clint spoke of you often. Your red hair, your . . .

trousers. The fact that you never seemed to be more than two steps away from Matthew."

Ammie shifted, disconcerted, stuffing the package she carried under one arm. "Anyone could know that," she said defensively. "If you were married to Clint, why aren't you using his name?"

Those luminous brown eyes glistened, and her voice quivered ever so slightly. "That's a long story, I'm afraid." She glanced at Matt. "Forgive me, I'm very tired. If we could get out of the sun?"

"By all means." Matt shot Ammie a reproachful look. "This really isn't a conversation I want to have on a public street anyway."

Ammie flushed. She couldn't tell if Matt was being overly solicitous about Lynette, or if he was upset with her about what had gone on at the hotel last night. Ammie only knew that for the first time in her life, she felt off-balance around Matt. She was trying to conceal her own emotions and at the same time read his. But she was doing a lousy job of both.

"I know where we can talk," Matt was saying to Lynette. "Or if you'd rather lie down for a while, I could get you a room at the hotel."

"No, I'll be fine. You're very kind, Matthew, but I know you must be curious as well. Please"—she touched his arm—"I've waited a long time for this myself. I would like very much to tell you about Clint and me."

Matt slid his hand protectively over Lynette's much smaller one. "This way."

Ammie's stomach churned as she watched them head off across the street. Well, at least he was showing some sense, she thought acidly. He was taking Lynette toward the sheriff's office. Ammie followed, though she was feeling about as welcome as a priest at a brothel. She was a step behind them when they reached Haggerty's office.

Matt opened the door and gestured for Lynette to precede him. She did so. He stepped in behind her and started to close the door.

"Do you mind?" Ammie snapped, putting her hand on the door to keep it from being shut in her face.

"Sorry, Am," he said. "Didn't see you."

"Tell me about it." Feigning irritation to cover the stinging hurt she felt, she stomped inside and closed the door.

John Haggerty rose from behind his oak desk, his eyebrows arching curiously. "Something I can do for you folks?"

Matt made the necessary introductions.

"So you're the little lady who sent that telegram?" Haggerty said, his voice mild, though Ammie sensed he was as wildly curious about this woman as Matt was. And just as enamored of her looks, it would seem. The man was positively preening. Evidently hoping no one would notice, he reached into a desk drawer and grabbed a hairbrush, swiftly running it over his thinning hair. Ammie ground her teeth together so hard, her jaw hurt. Did the woman give off some kind of scent?

Lynette cast those luminous brown eyes of hers at Haggerty this time. "If I could sit down?"

The sheriff all but tripped over himself, scurrying to fetch one of the few pieces of furniture in the austere room—a straight-back chair that sat next to a small, spur-scarred table. On the table was a pitcher of water and two glasses. While the sheriff brought the chair to Lynette, Matt hustled over to pour her a glass of water.

Ammie's eyes roved to the reward dodgers posted on a bulletin board behind Haggerty's desk. She wondered what the odds were that Lynette would be on one of them. Maybe she was a lady outlaw. Ammie stepped close, scrutinizing each poster. There was always hope.

"Sorry that chair isn't more comfortable," Haggerty said.

"It's quite all right, sheriff," Lynette assured him. "I'm

fine, really." She took a sip of the water Matt handed her
and smiled gratefully, then set the glass on Haggerty's
desk.

"Now you just take your time," Matt said. "There's no
hurry. No one's going to pressure you here." He gave
Ammie a meaningful look.

Ammie stalked to the far side of the room. She shoved
the water pitcher out of the way and levered herself onto
the oak table, settling her parcel on her lap. Fine! Let him
make a jackass of himself.

Lynette opened her reticule and pulled out an embroidered silk hankie. "I hardly know where to begin."

"Take your time," the sheriff reiterated, easing himself
back into the chair behind his desk. Matt hitched one leg
onto the desk's edge. They were both now her rapt audience.

Lynette twisted the hankie in her lap. "This is so very
difficult, gentlemen. My first thought was just to come to
River Oaks quietly and announce my presence to no one.
But in all honesty, I am not a brave woman. What courage
I possessed, I received from Clint. And now without
him . . ." Her voice shook.

Ammie's eyes narrowed. She was studying Lynette's
manner as much as her words, trying to gauge whether
she was lying. To her chagrin, she detected no false notes.
Yet.

"When I finally did muster the strength to make the
journey," Lynette continued, "I decided to send the telegraph message ahead, hoping"—she paused—"hoping for
what, I'm not sure." She looked at Matt. "Perhaps hoping
for precisely what did happen. That you would be there,
Matthew."

"Why me?"

"Because Clint spoke of you so often. He loved you,
admired you very much."

Matt stood and stalked toward the far wall of the small

room. For a long minute he just stood there with his back
to everyone.

"Did I say something wrong?" Lynette asked in a worried voice.

If this was a performance, Ammie thought, Lynette's
script was working perfectly.

Matt turned, his face pained. "When did you marry
Clint, Miss Simmons?"

"We were married a year ago—secretly—in Laredo."

Matt displayed no outward reaction. "And what did you
hope to gain by coming here now?"

Her voice was quiet, but with more steel than Ammie
had yet heard in it. "Peace."

Matt came back over to the desk. "What do you mean?"

"I'm afraid that because of the circumstances of my
relationship with Clint, I was never able to properly
grieve for him. I—I thought that by coming here, I could
somehow reach some sort of acceptance about his death.
At times I still can't believe that he's gone. That he won't
be coming to see me again. I . . ." She pressed her hand
to her mouth in an effort to keep her tears at bay. "I'm
sorry."

"It's all right." Matt hunkered down by her chair and
gave her hand a reassuring squeeze. In all the years Ammie had known him, she'd never seen him act this way.
Normally it took Matt a long time to warm to new people.
Obviously, Lynette Simmons was an exception.

"It was all so dreadful," Lynette said, "as I know you're
agonizingly aware, Matthew. But think of this—I didn't
even find out Clint was dead until two weeks after it happened. I had a terrible feeling. I had received a quick
note from him, telling me that his plans to come to Austin
had been changed at the last minute. And then—then I
never heard from him again. I knew something had to be
terribly wrong."

She shuddered. "I don't often see a newspaper. I just

happened upon one in my physician's office." She straightened slightly. "I wasn't seeing him for anything serious. A little stomach disorder."

"What did the newspaper say?" Matt prompted.

"It—it told of Clint's funeral in River Oaks. It was such a terrible shock. My doctor was quite worried, and I couldn't even tell him why I was distressed."

"No one knew of your marriage to Clint?" Matt asked. "No one at all?"

Lynette shook her head. "Well," she amended, "the minister, of course." She blew her nose, somehow even managing to make that seem delicate, ladylike. "It's all so incomprehensible to me. Do you realize, I don't even know how Clint died? The article didn't say. He was so young, so alive. That was another reason I had to come. I had to know how it happened." Her brown eyes seemed filled with genuine agony as she looked at Matt. "Was he sick? Was it some kind of horrible accident? Did he—did he suffer?" She began to weep softly.

Matt looked away. "We can talk about it later," Matt said. "I think you've been through enough just making the trip to River Oaks."

"Whatever you think is best, Matthew."

Ammie didn't miss the significance of Matt's not telling Lynette about Clint's death. To repeat the accepted version of that night's events was to condemn himself as responsible in Lynette's eyes. Obviously, he wasn't prepared to do that. Not yet, anyway.

"Maybe it was meant to be," Lynette went on sadly. "My not knowing about his death right away, that is. I could never have faced attending his funeral. Never."

Ammie hopped down from the table. She'd had just about enough of this. This woman was up to something. She had to be. "How is it you couldn't face the funeral, and yet you can face coming here four months later, claiming to be his widow? How do we know you're telling the truth? How do we know you even knew Clint Grayson?"

Lynette opened her reticule and pulled out a tiny gold band. She handed it to Ammie. Ammie peered at the inscription on the inner layer of the delicate circlet: LYNETTE, ALL MY LOVE, CLINT.

"Anyone could have this made," Ammie said stubbornly, handing it back. "And since no one else seems to want to ask, I'll ask you—why was the marriage kept secret? Why didn't you and Clint announce it to the world?"

Lynette looked at her hands. "I—I'd rather not say."

"Why?"

"The reasons are very personal, private."

"That's a bit too convenient, don't you think?"

"Ammie," Matt warned, "take it easy."

"Take it easy?" Ammie cried, incredulous. "This woman appears out of nowhere and claims to have been Clint's wife—for an entire year, no less—and you say take it easy? How can you possibly believe even a word of this nonsense?"

"I didn't say I did." He gave Lynette a sympathetic look. "I'm just listening with an open mind, that's all."

"I understand, Matthew," Lynette said. "I expected you to be skeptical. Your father as well."

Matt let out a mirthless laugh. "Skeptical may be an understatement where my father is concerned, Miss Simmons. I had no idea what to expect from the person who sent that telegram. Nor did my father. But this? This, I think I can safely say, is beyond anything either of us expected. If you really did know Clint, then my next question won't surprise you. Are you even sure you want to meet my father?"

She gave him a wan smile. "Very much."

Matt had been openly admiring of Lynette's looks earlier, and now Ammie saw he openly admired that courage she claimed to lack as well. "Could you tell me where you met my brother?" he asked.

"In Austin. About eighteen months ago. I was shopping. I dropped my packages. Clint very gallantly picked them up for me."

Probably dropped them on purpose, Ammie thought sourly, then caught herself. Was she beginning to believe this woman's story too?

No. She couldn't, wouldn't. "None of this makes any sense," she said. "Clint was getting ready to run for public office. Why in the world would he take part in a secret marriage? If he loved you, why didn't he bring you here, introduce you to his father, and have a proper, public wedding?"

Lynette said nothing.

"Leave it be, Ammie," Matt said. "You can see that she doesn't want to talk about it."

"Well, she's going to have to talk about it. She can't just come waltzing in here claiming to have been Clint's wife. Don't you see what she's doing?"

"What am I doing, Miss O'Rourke?" Lynette asked. "Why would I lie about such a thing?"

"Why, Miss Simmons? Because being Clint Grayson's widow would entitle you to a share of the Diamond G, that's why. Maybe you concocted this whole scheme to make money off a dead man."

"Ammie, stop it!" Matt gritted. "If you can't keep quiet, you can leave."

Ammie stared at him, her eyes burning. How could he speak to her like that? And in front of this woman? But Ammie didn't leave. She wasn't about to leave. She stalked back to the table and stood there, shaking with hurt and outrage.

Matt didn't even notice. He was too busy apologizing to Lynette! "I'm sorry, Miss Simmons. That won't happen again."

"It's quite all right, Matthew. I'm sure she's only concerned for your best interests. And please, call me Lynette."

He smiled slightly. "I want to believe you, Miss— Lynette. I honestly do. But I'm afraid I'm going to need more tangible proof."

"Of course. You would be foolish not to." Lynette's hands trembled as she again opened her reticule. She pulled out a small stack of letters, bound up in yellow ribbon. "These are only a few of the letters Clint wrote to me over the past year and a half." She picked out the one on top and handed it to Matt. "Please, I'd like you to read it. Then you can decide whether I'm telling the truth." She blushed. "I chose this one because . . . it's not so— so intimate as the others."

Matt accepted the letter, even as he shot Ammie a silent plea. There was no way he could read the letter. She stiffened and folded her arms across her chest, her lips thinning furiously. It was patently obvious that he didn't want the beautiful Lynette Simmons to know he couldn't read. Ammie glared at him. It would serve him right if she just left him hanging.

But that she could never do. Muttering under her breath, she crossed to Matt and snatched the letter from him. "You shouldn't be the one to read it," she said, by way of covering up her apparent rudeness. "If it's from Clint, it might be too painful for you."

"You may be right," Matt said. "Thanks, Ammie."

She looked him directly in the eye. "You're welcome."

He looked away.

Ammie walked to the window to take advantage of the sunlight. "I know Clint's handwriting. He sometimes wrote to me when he was away at school. He sometimes put business between our two ranches in writing too."

Ammie unfolded the missive. She'd been hoping the script would not match. Her heart sank. It did. There wasn't a doubt in her mind that the small, precise script belonged to Clint Grayson. In fact the notion that he had handled this very letter, that he had penned these words to this woman while he was still so vitally alive, made her hand tremble for a moment. She steadied herself, then looked at Matt. "It does look like Clint's handwriting."

"Read it," he said. "Please."

Ammie read the words without expression:

> *My dearest Lynette,*
> *My mind relives again and again the glorious two days we had together on my most recent trip to Austin. And even as I relive them, I look forward to my next trip. Father has decided I should solicit votes in Fall Creek, a town about fifty miles south of River Oaks. I have enclosed currency. Please, my darling, make all haste to Fall Creek. Register under the name of Lisa Smith at the hotel. I will be in town only three days, but if you're there, my love, we can make the time last forever in our memories.*
> *With fondest wishes,*
> *Your obedient servant, Clint*

Ammie looked up. "I'm certainly glad you gave us one of the less intimate ones, Miss Simmons," she said sarcastically.

But Matt was obviously touched by the letter. "I'm glad Clint had someone to love him," he said quietly.

John Haggerty, who had been noticeably silent throughout this little encounter, cleared his throat. "The letter might prove you knew Clint Grayson, ma'am. But I'm afraid it's not proof that you married him."

Lynette handed the sheriff another folded piece of paper from the stack of letters. Haggerty studied the paper intently for a minute, then looked up at Matt.

"What is it?" Matt asked.

"A marriage certificate, all legal and proper, certifying the marriage of Lynette Anne Simmons to Clint Evan Grayson a year ago last week. According to this, the marriage took place in Laredo." The town was near the Mexican border.

"Clint felt there was less chance of his being recognized there," Lynette explained.

"Eventually, I'm going to need to know why Clint kept everything so secret," Matt said.

"I realize that," Lynette said. "And I will explain it all, I promise." She cast a slightly embarrassed look at the sheriff and Ammie. "But only to you and your father, Matthew. Please understand."

He nodded. "Now might be as good a time as any to hire a buggy to take you out to the Diamond G."

"That would be fine," she said.

Ammie could have sworn that this time there was a thread of nervousness in that lilting voice. Or was it fear? No matter how much "proof" Lynette offered of her relationship with Clint, something just didn't feel right about any of this.

But there would be time to sort the truth from the lies later. Right now, Ammie was more concerned about getting Matt away from this woman, away from her vulnerable eyes and her incredible beauty. She glanced at the clock on the sheriff's wall. "If you take her to the ranch now, Matt, you'll still have plenty of time to make it to supper at Shamrock."

Matt threaded a hand through his dark hair, sending her a regret-filled look. "I can't make supper tonight, Am. I can't just abandon Lynette to my father."

"Why not?" Ammie demanded. "If she's who she says she is, then your father will want some time to get acquainted. It's Friday. You have supper with me—us."

"Please," Lynette said, "I don't want to be the cause of any more disruption in your life, Matthew."

"It's not a disruption," Matt said. "Normally, I have supper at Shamrock every Friday. Maybe if you stay long enough, you could join us next Friday yourself. Wouldn't that be a good idea, Am?"

Ammie's head started to pound. "Terrific idea, Matt. I'm surprised I didn't think of it myself." To Lynette, she said, "But I'm certain you won't be staying that long, will you, Miss Simmons? You must have family to get back to in Austin."

"Actually, I—I have no one. I really have no plans. I thought I might prevail upon your hospitality, Matthew. At least I'd hoped—"

"You can stay as long as you like," Matt assured her, coming over to offer her his hand as she rose from the chair. "We'll retrieve your luggage from the stage stop, then hire a buggy." He glanced at Ammie. "I really am sorry about supper. But you understand?"

"Of course," she lied.

Matt gave a brief nod to Haggerty.

"I'll keep in touch," the sheriff said cryptically.

Still hovering, concerned, Matt guided Lynette from the office.

Numb and shaken, Ammie walked back to the oak table. *You can stay as long as you like.* How could he have said such a thing? How could he already believe this woman and her outrageous lies?

Ammie picked up her brown-wrapped parcel, the dress she had bought that morning to impress Matt. She stood there, envisioning herself garbed in the dress and standing next to the stunning Lynette Simmons. Gild the dandelion, indeed.

"I, uh—I'd better be heading home," she told Haggerty, hoping he didn't notice the quaver in her voice. "I've got supper to make." She all but ran out the door, leaving the brown-wrapped package behind.

Chapter 10

Matt toyed with the reins of the buggy horse, trying unsuccessfully to quell the tension threading through him. He tried to dismiss it as a natural response to his concern about how his father was going to react to Lynette Simmons. But there was more to it than that. It was a tension brought on by Lynette herself—or more precisely, his own reaction to her.

He cast a covert glance at her, seated next to him in the covered carriage he had hired. She was sitting ramrod straight, her hands clasped tightly in her lap, her dark eyes shadowed by grief, sadness. Even more than the porcelain perfection of her features, the sadness roused a fierce response in him, made him want to shield her, protect her. No matter what had brought this woman here, she had known her share of pain in her life.

"Are you sure you're comfortable?" he asked. "I can pull those side flaps down, let less sun in here."

"I'm fine," she assured him. "Having them open lets in a little breeze."

She dabbed at the beads of perspiration marking her brow, but when she brushed at her cheeks, Matt was sure it wasn't perspiration she was wiping away, but tears.

"You miss Clint very much, don't you?" he asked, already knowing the answer.

She nodded, the tears more obvious now. "I'm sorry. I thought I would be able to—to not cry so much anymore. But being with you, his brother—" She trembled. "I'm sorry."

Awkwardly, Matt wrapped his arm around her shoulder, not knowing if the comforting gesture was too intimate under the circumstances. She surprised him by leaning into him, her tears now moistening his shirt. His grip tightened.

That Clint had married this woman was something he found remarkably easy to accept. A secret marriage would explain much about his brother's behavior in the months preceding his death. Clint had made more than a dozen trips to Austin in the previous year and a half, many of them of his own volition. And then there had been the crushing disappointment Clint had displayed four months ago, when his plans to go to Austin had been abruptly and unexpectedly changed by Zak.

Matt sighed heavily. Why hadn't Clint come out with the truth then and there? If he had, he never would have gone to Abilene. He would still be alive.

Matt felt one of Lynette's small, gloved hands press against his chest as she eased back to her own side of the carriage. "Forgive me," she said. "You must think me horrible."

"No," he said gently. "I miss Clint too."

She gave him a watery smile. "He was so wonderful to me." She blew her nose. "You're so kind to take me to meet your father this way. I do hope Miss O'Rourke forgives you for missing supper."

Matt felt a stab of guilt. "She'll be fine. Don't worry." But he couldn't help worrying himself. He could tell that Ammie was upset, but it couldn't be helped. Besides, he was still feeling enormously guilty about where his mind had been when he was in her room last night, and then again later in his own room. Ammie had just been showing him a little friendly affection when she'd touched his cheek before heading for Mary Denby's—and all he'd wanted to do was pull her into his arms and kiss her. Now, if that wasn't ridiculous.

Such thoughts, he reasoned, were aberrations. He'd been tired and cranky and, if he admitted it, pretty lonely these past few weeks. Even longer. He'd been keeping to himself a lot since Clint died, trying to come to grips with what had happened in Abilene. He had shut Ammie out, unable to share the true depths of his grief even with her —or more rightly, unable to *bear* the true depths of his grief.

But he would make it up to her. He would ride over to Shamrock in the morning. It was time to start breaking those horses. Maybe if things worked out between Lynette and his father, she would like to stay on awhile. He'd meant it when he said that she was welcome to stay as long as she liked. But if Zak proved difficult, Matt would make arrangements for Lynette to stay elsewhere. Maybe even at Shamrock.

"Do you think your father will hate me, Matthew?" Lynette asked suddenly, as though she were reading his thoughts.

"Of course not," he said, because he didn't want to upset her any more than she already was. "But it might take him a while to get used to the idea that Clint had a secret wife."

"You believe me, then?" Her brown eyes were wide, hopeful.

"Yes, I do," he said simply.

She squeezed his arm. "You don't know how much it means to me to hear you say that. I was so terrified that no one—" She drew in a deep breath. "May I ask you something?"

"Of course."

"Is Clint—was Clint buried anywhere near here?"

"We have a family plot about a mile from the main house. A grove of oak trees that my mother especially loved—for family picnics and such."

"May I . . . may we stop there? I mean, before we see
your father?"

Matt smiled slightly. "Sure." They rode in silence then,
each alone with their thoughts. A half-hour later, Matt
guided the buggy into the grove of oaks and pulled up.
The temperature was twenty degrees cooler amid the tall,
stately trees. Two simple stone crosses interrupted the
lush green of the grass.

Matt helped Lynette to the ground, but he stayed behind as she made her way to the gravesites, her black
skirts sweeping along the foot-high grass. She paused between the two graves, dropping to her knees. Clint's grave
on the right was obviously the fresher of the two—the turf
was not yet fully recovered from the invasion of picks and
shovels.

Lynette slipped off one glove and ran her slender fingers along the carved outline of Clint's name in the cross.
Her shoulders heaved. She bent forward, pressing her lips
against the stone, then she leaned back and just sat there
for a long time. Matt could hear her voice, speaking softly,
but he did not step close enough to catch the words.

Several minutes later, she rose and came back to where
he stood next to the buggy horse. Her face was less an-
guished than before. "Thank you, Matthew. We can go
now."

Matt started to help her into the buggy, but she hesitated. "You wouldn't tell me at the sheriff's office, but I
need you to tell me now—how did he die, Matthew?"

Matt straightened. There was no help for it. If he didn't
tell her, his father would most certainly tell her when they
reached the ranch. Briefly, bluntly, Matt told her the
same version of that night that he'd always told his father.
Then he stood there, waiting to hear the hate he was
certain would lace her next words.

Instead her voice was hushed, gentle. "It must have
been awful for you. I'm so sorry, Matthew."

Matt experienced a flush of gratitude so acute, it left him unable to speak for a minute. To cover his feelings he helped her into the buggy, then followed. "My father hasn't been quite so forgiving, I'm afraid," he managed. "He blames me for Clint's death." He gigged the horse forward.

"Blame never gets anyone anywhere."

Lynette said the words with such vehemence that Matt looked at her quizzically.

"Oh, listen to me, I do go on sometimes. Just don't pay any attention."

"I like listening to you. You have a lovely voice."

She blushed. "You are so very like Clint in so many ways."

"I remember he told me once, 'Never argue with a pretty lady' "—his smile was self-mocking—"so I won't." They were just minutes away from the house. "How much did Clint tell you about our father?"

"I don't expect a royal welcome, if that's what you mean. Clint told me Zachary Grayson is a very determined, very opinionated man." Her smile was wan. "A little—how did he put it? Strong-minded."

Matt snorted. "Clint never was one for swearing around the ladies. I just don't want you to be upset if my father seems a bit overbearing."

"I'll be fine with you there, Matthew. And I'm sure your father can be quite charming, if he chooses. He couldn't have raised up two such fine sons without being a gentleman himself."

Matt decided to let the subject drop. He wasn't really holding out much hope for "charming," but perhaps "polite" was in the realm of possibility. They drove into the ranch yard and he reined to a stop in front of the house. He hopped to the ground, then extended his hand to Lynette. "I think I should go in first," he told her.

"There's a rocker on the porch, where you can rest in the shade." He led her to it.

"I'm fine," she said, the fear in her brown eyes giving the lie to her words. "You go ahead."

Matt hurried inside, but he stopped abruptly when he spied his father at the window of his office. "Who is she?" Zak Grayson demanded. "Where's the man who sent the telegram?"

"Miss Simmons sent the telegram."

"Who? What are you talking about? What does that woman know about Clint?"

"Quite a bit, it turns out," Matt said slowly.

"Then why the hell did you leave her on the porch! Bring her in here! I want to talk to her. Find out what she's up to."

"First I wanted to make sure you'd treat her with respect."

Zak bristled. "I've never been disrespectful to a woman in my life, you insolent whelp!" His eyes narrowed. "Why would you even think I would be? What's she said to you? What was she to Clint?"

Matt didn't take his eyes from his father's face. "She was his wife."

For a heartbeat Zak Grayson just stood there, then he swore explosively. "That's a lie! What kind of conniving little tramp—" He crossed the room, obviously intent on going out to confront Lynette.

Matt blocked his path. "I think you should hear her out."

"Hear out a tramp? A trollop who's come here to create a scandal, drag Clint's good name through the mud?"

"She's not a tramp. She's a lady. And you'll treat her like one, or I'll take her back to town now."

"You do that," Zak spat. "That'll be just fine by me."

"And what about that scandal?" Matt sneered. "If you

won't talk to her, what's to stop her from talking to the papers?"

"I thought you said she was a lady."

"She is."

"Then she'll leave quietly and go back to wherever it is she came from."

"You can't face it, can you? You can't face that Clint might have kept something this important hidden from you. And you know what? I'd bet my life you're precisely the reason he did."

"What are you talking about?"

"Why else would Clint keep quiet about such a thing? It had to be because of you. God forbid he should ever displease you."

"Why wouldn't I welcome a woman Clint loved?"

"Maybe because you didn't pick her."

"Clint was his own man."

"He was the man you made him. Scared to death to—" Matt bit off the rest, knowing he was furious enough to say something he would later regret.

A soft knock sounded on the outer door. Matt looked at his father. "Well?"

Zak straightened. "Show her in."

Matt opened the door to Lynette and led her to his father's office. "It's all right," he assured her. She was looking very pale, shaky.

"Thank you, Matthew." Her gaze trailed to Zak. "I'm so pleased to make your acquaintance at last, Mr. Grayson." She extended the back of her hand, which Zak accepted briefly, then released. "Clint told me so many wonderful things about you."

"Indeed. Well, you'll have to forgive me, Miss—Simmons, is it? Clint did not see fit to tell me wonderful things about you. In fact, he apparently didn't see fit to tell me about you at all."

"I can explain."

"I'll bet you can." He gestured toward one of the wing-back chairs. "Please," he said too politely, "sit down."

Matt didn't miss the tremor that passed through Lynette's slender body as she took a seat. "I—please, I beg your indulgence. I suddenly don't feel well."

"May I bring you some water?" Matt offered. "I think we have some tea."

"Tea would be wonderful. With a sprig of mint, if you have it. But please don't go to any trouble."

"No trouble."

Matt headed for the kitchen. He pumped water into the teakettle, then settled it on the stove. He didn't want to leave his father alone with Lynette too long. But he hoped these few minutes would somehow allow Zak to discover Lynette's sincerity for himself.

Unfortunately, that didn't happen. It was apparent when Matt returned to the study that she and Zak hadn't said two words to each other while he was gone. "I put the water on," he said. "It'll be a few minutes for the tea."

"Thank you, Matthew," Lynette said, though Matt guessed her gratitude stemmed more from his having returned to the room than to his preparing the tea.

"Never mind the tea," Zak snapped. "I want to know what your game is, missy. And I want to know now."

Lynette showed Zak the same proof she had offered in Haggerty's office.

Zak scoffed at the ring and the marriage certificate, claiming both were forgeries. But the letters stopped him. Lynette showed him several of them.

Zak's hands were trembling as he began to read the sixth one, then suddenly, with an abrupt oath, he crumpled the missive in his fist. "You hired someone to copy Clint's handwriting! That's what you did. That's why it took so long for you to come to River Oaks. It's a very elaborate scheme, little lady. But this one—he held up the crumpled letter—"this one is your downfall."

Matt frowned. He'd been certain Lynette was telling the truth. "What does it say, Pa?"

"A minor mistake," Zak gloated. "A detail that had, in fact, been reported in the newspapers, which is where this woman no doubt read about it. Except that the papers were mistaken." He smoothed out the wadded-up paper and read aloud, " 'Lynette dearest, you won't believe what I'm giving my brother, Matt, for Christmas. A colt, a black Arabian colt, boasting some of the finest bloodlines on this earth.' "

Zak looked up triumphantly. "Some reporters got wind of the gift and put it in their papers. However, it wasn't true. Clint didn't give the colt to Matt—he gave it to me."

Matt looked at Lynette, knowing his face must have betrayed the disillusionment he felt. It was true. Clint had given the colt to Zak last Christmas.

"You stopped reading too soon," Lynette said softly. "Please look at the postscript. You'll note it's dated three days later than the body of the letter."

Frowning, Zak did so, again reading the words aloud: " 'About Matt's Christmas present, my dear, I'm afraid the only ones who will ever know the colt was meant for Matt are you and Matt. My father found out about the colt and has assumed the animal is for him. He's so pleased and excited, I can hardly disappoint him. I'll try to explain it to Matt, but I have grave doubts about his taking it well. Knowing my little brother, he'll likely just call me a liar. It's too late to try for delivery of a second colt. Maybe next year. Again, my warmest thoughts for the holidays and my hope that next year we can spend them together.' "

Zak crossed over to Matt, the look in his eyes now confused, uncertain. "Is this true? About Emperor?" Emperor was the name he'd given the colt.

"Clint tried to tell me that the horse was originally supposed to be mine," Matt said, his heart twisting. "And I reacted just as he said I would—I didn't believe him."

"This still doesn't prove anything," Zak said, sinking into the chair opposite Lynette. His voice was now a little desperate. "There's still the paramount question: Why would he have kept you a secret? Why?"

"You had great political ambitions for Clint."

"Of course I did!" Zak said. "He had them for himself."

"Politicians must be above any hint of scandal."

Zak's eyes narrowed. "Are you saying you would have brought scandal down on my son, Miss Simmons?"

Her words came in slow, measured cadences: it was obviously a very difficult subject for her. "My family was originally from New Orleans. My father was . . . arrested there years ago. It seems he attempted to bribe a public official. My family had to leave New Orleans in disgrace." Shame gave heightened color to her ivory cheeks. "Clint feared that if knowledge of such a thing reached the press, his own career could be affected. Even so, he was ready to chance it. But . . ."

"But what?" Zak prompted, when she hesitated.

"I asked him not to."

"Why?"

"My father was very ill. He didn't have long to live. I wanted his last months to be . . . peaceful."

"Without the muckraking press, in other words," Matt put in.

She nodded.

"Your father is dead now?" Zak said.

"Last month. That's part of the reason it took me so long to come to you. My father paid dearly for his offense, Mr. Grayson. My family lost everything. Clint didn't want him to pay again."

Zak was silent for a long time. Then finally he said, "I would consider it a favor, Miss Simmons, if you would stay on at the Diamond G for a while. We could talk at greater length about—your relationship with my son."

There was something about his father's expression that

Matt couldn't quite read. A few lingering misgivings no doubt. Zak hadn't been entirely swayed by Lynette, but he was clearly going to give her the benefit of the doubt, at least for the moment. Matt supposed it was as much as he could hope for.

The teakettle's shrill whistle sounded, and Matt quickly excused himself and headed for the kitchen. Within minutes, he returned with the tea, but Lynette was too exhausted to drink any.

"Perhaps Matt should show you to your room," Zak said.

Lynette stood, then quickly sat back down, her hand going to her forehead.

"Are you all right?" Matt asked with a worried frown.

"Just tired."

Matt was not convinced. "How long has it been since you've eaten anything?"

She looked away, embarrassed. "I had only enough money for the ticket on the stage."

"I'll rustle her up something to eat, Matt," Zak said. "You get her upstairs so she can lie down."

When Lynette stood and again flushed a ghostly white, Matt didn't hesitate to sweep her into his arms. As her head rested in the lee of his neck, he caught the delicate scent of jasmine. He swallowed hard.

He carried her up to the first room on the right and laid her on the bed.

"This was his room, wasn't it?" she asked. It wasn't really a question.

Matt nodded.

"I loved him very much. You do believe me don't you, Matthew?"

"I believe you."

She seemed to relax a little.

"You rest. I'll bring up your things."

She caught his hand. "Thank you, Matthew. Thank you so much for all you've done."

"I haven't done anything."

She sat up, brushing his cheek with a kiss. "You've been a knight in shining armor to me."

Matt touched his cheek. "My pleasure, Lynette." He backed out of the room. "My pleasure."

Flustered, he descended the stairs, nearly colliding with his father, who was bringing up a tray of food. "Do you believe her?" Matt asked.

"I'm not sure."

"Not sure you believe her, or not sure you want to?"

Zak didn't answer, but said instead, "It's Friday. You going to Shamrock?"

"No."

Zak cleared his throat. "Then maybe you'd—you'd have supper later with Miss Simmons and me?" He coughed, adding quickly. "You don't have to."

"I'll be there."

"Oh, and there's some fence in the west forty that needs mending. Maybe you could get to it tomorrow."

"I'll be breaking horses at Shamrock, remember?"

"Right." His father's voice was testy all over again.

"I'll get to the fence," Matt said.

"I'll send one of the hands—the men who actually work this ranch." Zak continued up the stairs.

Matt cursed, tromping on down the steps and outside to tend to the buggy horse. He and his father had gotten along for their daily quota, but now the two minutes were up. He was suddenly looking forward to spending the day at Shamrock tomorrow. He would ask Lynette to join him. It would give Ammie and Lynette a chance to get acquainted. Matt smiled at the thought, certain Lynette and Ammie would become good friends.

* * *

Ammie had never prepared a more miserable supper than the one she set before her father and Mary Denby at the Shamrock's dining-room table. Somehow she had managed to burn everything: the roast, the potatoes, the carrots, the bread. She'd even burned the coffee. To make the fiasco complete, her father was furious, certain she had destroyed the meal because Mary was there.

"I expected more from you, Amelia," Shamus said, shoving away from the table. "I've been trying to ignore your disapproval of my seeing Mary. But this"—he waved a hand over the culinary disaster in front of him—"this is unforgivable."

"But Pa, I—" Tears welled in Ammie's eyes, and she bit her lip to keep them at bay.

"Shamus," Mary interjected, "the poor child is just terribly disappointed that Matt couldn't be here."

Ammie had told them about Lynette Simmons's arrival on the morning stage.

Shamus glowered. "I wish I could believe this was because of Matt."

"Then do," Mary said.

Shamus ran a hand over his balding pate. "All right." He looked at Ammie. "Not that I'm unhappy that Matt couldn't join us. I might've had words with the boy. I still ain't over his takin' you to town like that, Ammie. Stayin' overnight. It isn't fittin'. It's a good thing you stayed the night with Mary."

Ammie had already offered her grudging thanks to Mary for not mentioning to Shamus just what time Ammie had arrived at her house.

"From what you said," Shamus went on, "maybe this Lynette Simmons is the best thing that could've happened. Give Matt something to spend all that pent-up energy on. Maybe I can even quit thinking about lockin' you in your room, girl."

"Matt isn't going to spend his energy on that woman!"

Ammie shot back. "And if you locked me up, I'd climb out the window! You tell me I'm grown-up, then you treat me like an infant. I love Matt Grayson, Pa. I love him the way a woman loves a man, and I suggest you start getting used to the idea!" With that she bolted for the stairs and raced up to her room.

Flinging herself onto her bed, she sobbed into her pillow. Almost at once a knock sounded on her door. "Leave me alone, Pa!"

"It's Mary," came the gentle voice.

Ammie groaned. "Go away."

The door opened, and Ammie dragged her pillow over her head. Her voice muffled, she repeated, "Leave me alone. Please."

Ammie heard Mary pad across the room, then felt the bed give as the woman sat beside her. Ammie kept a firm grip on her pillow.

"Falling in love is a little more painful than you bargained for, isn't it, dear?"

Ammie didn't answer.

"The sheriff brought over the parcel you left behind in his office. He knew I was coming out to supper tonight. The wrapping had torn a bit, and I saw the dress."

"It turns out I don't need it," Ammie said bitterly, shoving up on one elbow, the pillow tumbling to the floor. "Matt has to spend his energy on Lynette, remember? Besides, the dress wouldn't do any good anyway—not next to Lynette Simmons."

Mary's eyes were warm, sympathetic. "You don't need to change yourself, Amelia. You're a wonderful girl just the way you are."

"I don't need your pity."

"No," Mary said slowly, "maybe you don't. You seem to have an ample supply all on your own."

Ammie closed her eyes. She wanted to tell the woman to go away. She didn't need to hear this—not because the words were harsh, but because they were true. She *was* feeling sorry for herself. "I don't know what to do. I feel like I've lost him already, and I've never even had a chance to—to let him know how I feel."

"Mercy sake," Mary clucked sadly, "the Amelia O'Rourke I had in my classroom was no quitter. You're already conceding victory to this Lynette woman, when Matt only just met her? He's known you all of his life."

"He's bored with me."

"He most certainly is not. Whenever I run into him, you're one of his favorite subjects of conversation. He always laughs and jokes and looks thoroughly cheerful when he talks about you."

"He does?"

"He does. So don't you dare give up! Look how long it's taken me to get your father to take notice."

Ammie looked at the floor. "You love my father, don't you?"

"Very much."

"I—I'm sorry I've been so awful."

"Sometimes it's hard to share someone we love."

"I want Pa to be happy."

"I know that, child." She leaned forward and gave Ammie a kiss on the forehead. "I'd best get back to him." She gave Ammie a wry grin. "I thought I'd cook him and me a couple of steaks. Would you like one?"

"I'm not hungry." She looked at her hands. "I didn't burn things on purpose."

"I know. Your father will be apologizing later, but I asked him if I could come up first."

"Thanks, Mrs.—thanks, Mary."

Tears welled in Mary Denby's eyes. "You're more than welcome, dear."

Mary went downstairs. Ammie stayed in her room.

Outside, a storm was brewing. Ammie's heart thudded painfully. Just what her miserable state of mind needed—

a storm. Within minutes the wind was whipping the curtains so hard, she was forced to close the windows.

Ammie returned to her bed and burrowed beneath the covers. Overhead, thunder cracked and she almost cried out. She hated this weakness in herself, hated her vulnerability. But she couldn't help it, couldn't stop it. Over and over, she told herself that she was safe, that the storm couldn't possibly harm her here in the house. But still she trembled.

When she could bear it no longer, she forced herself out of bed. She crept to the top of the stairs, wanting to call out to her father, to hear the reassuring sound of his voice. But something prevented her from doing so. Treading softly, she went downstairs.

She found her father and Mary huddled close together on the settee in front of the fireplace. Ammie took a step toward them, then stopped dead as realization stole over her: Her father was kissing Mary Denby!

Fresh tears stinging her eyes, Ammie tore back up the stairs and flung herself onto her bed. Lightning, fierce and bright white, painted her room in eerie shadows. Ammie waited, biting down on her lower lip so hard that it bled.

The crack of thunder that followed shook the walls, rattled the windows. Tears streamed down her face. The wind drove the branches of the oak tree beside the house to slap against the panes, scratching and clawing like some huge, menacing night beast seeking to gain entry to her room.

She remembered that horrible day when her mother died, remembered the hours of darkness she had huddled in that tree where her mother had thrust her. The wind had been howling then too, the branches buffeting her, lashing her, seeking to tear free her grip. Her mother had screamed at her to hang on, and Ammie wouldn't have let go for anyone.

Anyone but Matt. He had found her and tried to coax

her down. Failing that, he had climbed the tree and hunched behind her, cradling her against him, until finally, exhausted, she had fallen asleep in his arms. Only then had he been able to loosen her grip.

Was Lynette afraid of storms? Ammie wondered.

Hours later, she fell asleep, the sound of thunder still echoing around her, her dreams filled with images of Lynette Simmons in Matt Grayson's arms.

☘/Chapter 11

Ammie woke to the sounds of shouts and hooraws coming from outside the house. Gingerly, she opened her eyes, wincing at how tender they seemed. She frowned, wondering at the pain until she recalled she'd spent half of last night crying. Levering herself out of bed, she padded to the window, tugged it open, and looked out. She was astonished to see the sun high overhead. She rarely slept past dawn, but then, she thought ruefully, she rarely stayed awake all night, either. Patches of mud and a few isolated rain puddles were the only traces of last night's storm that remained.

More whoops and hollers filled the air. Ammie's gaze skittered to the near corral, where the controlled commotion seemed to be concentrated. Then she remembered: Matt and the boys were supposed to start breaking those Wichita horses today. She took in the scene in a heartbeat —Will, Jess, and her father were perched on the top rail of the corral; Smoke was inside the enclosure, his grip firm on the halter of a saddled and blindfolded roan; and Matt was ready to hoist himself onto the back of nine hundred pounds of equine fury.

Ammie stared, mesmerized. She'd seen Matt break scores of horses over the years, but she never tired of watching him. In fact, this morning in an odd way, it was as though she were watching him for the first time. She propped her elbows on the windowsill, fascinated by the sight of all that sinewy grace and well-honed muscle. And then she looked at the horse.

Matt mounted the roan. For an instant the animal stood stock-still, then Smoke tugged free the bandanna that covered the gelding's eyes. Like an uncapped geyser, the horse exploded, bucking, rearing, spinning, leaping. Matt matched the gelding twist for turn, one arm flung out for balance, the other gripped tight on the reins. Time and again it seemed that the power and fury of the horse would win out, that Matt's agility could not possibly outlast the gelding's brute strength and even more brutal contortions. But fifteen minutes later, it was the roan that came to a trembling halt, exhausted, frustrated, conceding victory to the human burr on its back.

Ammie grinned. Matt had won this time, but the dirt and mud on his clothes suggested that the horses had claimed victories today as well.

She hurried back to her bed and threw off her nightshirt. Today already promised to be a considerable improvement over yesterday. She had noticed one other important detail about the goings-on at the corral—Lynette Simmons was nowhere in sight. Maybe Zak had shown some sense for a change and sent the woman packing.

Dressing quickly in her ubiquitous shirt and jeans, Ammie hurried downstairs. She was surprised to encounter Mary Denby in the kitchen.

"I spent the night in the guest room," Mary explained quickly, too quickly, "because of the storm."

Ammie gave Mary an awkward pat on the arm. "I hope you slept well."

Mary smiled a shy, happy smile. "Very well, thank you."

Ammie picked up a cold biscuit and began munching it. "I'm going to be spending most of my day at the corral," she said. "Maybe get Matt to notice—"

"Ammie," Mary cut in, her soft features twisting into a worried frown, "there's something you should know."

"Not today," Ammie said, feeling almost giddy.

"There's nothing I need to know today, except that Matt's here and Lynette Simmons is not."

"She's in the drawing room."

Ammie froze. "What?"

"Matt brought her over in the buggy this morning. Miss Simmons wanted to see for herself how a ranch works." Mary grimaced slightly. "Except that she hasn't been out of the house since she got here. I'm just making her more tea. Coffee, she tells me, upsets her delicate stomach."

Ammie slapped a hand on the counter. "Is there anything about that woman that isn't delicate? I don't believe this! How could Matt do this to me?" She shot a glance toward the stairs, fidgeting with the buttons of her shirtfront. "Do you think I should go back up and change? What's she wearing? How does she look?"

"Ammie, calm down," Mary soothed. "You're going to work yourself into a state again."

Ammie let out a gloomy sigh. "Now you see what I'm up against."

"Lynette is somewhat attractive," Mary conceded.

"And the Atlantic Ocean is somewhat wet." Ammie pushed a tumbled wave of red hair out of her face. "What am I going to do?"

"Well, for one thing, you're not going to let her see how upset she's made you. For heaven's sake—the woman isn't moving in at the Diamond G, she's just there for a visit."

"I can't believe she's staying on. That must mean she's gotten Zak Grayson to believe that absurd story of hers."

"Actually," Mary acknowledged slowly, "after talking to Lynette this morning, I'm inclined to believe her myself."

Ammie shook her head. "You can't mean it."

"It seems her father was in prison for a time—a political scandal of some sort."

Ammie gasped. Lynette had refused to discuss the personal reasons for her marriage's secrecy until she'd met with Matt and Zak privately. "No wonder Clint couldn't face his father. Zak would never have approved of such a marriage. Clint's political career would have ended before it started."

"Exactly."

Ammie felt an unwelcome surge of sympathy for Lynette—and an equally unwelcome rush of admiration. It must have taken a great deal of courage to tell Zak Grayson about her father.

Mary's eyes were gentle but firm. "I think you already believed her, Amelia, even without hearing about her father. That's why she worries you so much. It's going to be a natural instinct for Matt to present himself as her guardian, her protector, especially with the guilt he feels about Clint's death."

"He does seem quite eager to assume the role," Ammie said glumly. "Maybe Lynette *was* married to Clint, but I still say there's something she's holding back, something she's not telling anyone."

Mary settled a lemon onto the counter in front of her and sliced it into wedges. "I don't know. She seems quite forthcoming to me, if a little persnickety."

"Well, I still don't think everything she says should be taken at face value," Ammie argued stubbornly. "In fact, I'd be willing to wager that at the Diamond G it hasn't been. She might have buffaloed Matt with her little-lost-lamb act, but Zak must have a suspicion or two."

"Actually," came the genteel voice from the kitchen archway, "I think Mr. Grayson does have a few reservations, but he's willing to listen."

Ammie refused to be embarrassed. "Good morning, Miss Simmons. How delightful to see you again so soon." Did the woman never have a hair out of place? And that dress! Dark blue silk, with a cinched waist and scooped neckline. She looked like she'd just stepped out of *Godey's Lady's Book*.

"Please, call me Lynette, if I may call you Amelia?"

Ammie picked up another biscuit. She could think of a
few things she'd like to call her. "When is it you're heading back to Austin, *Lynette*?"

Lynette looked away. "I haven't really decided yet."

Ammie's conscience niggled at her. Damnation! How
could this tiny woman she'd known for only a day provoke
her into abandoning the manners of a lifetime?

"The Graysons have been so very gracious," Lynette
went on, "opening up their home to me for as long as I
care to stay."

"I didn't mean to be rude," Ammie said quietly. "I'm
sorry."

"It's all right. I understand."

"You do?"

"You don't trust me. You're afraid my being here is
somehow going to hurt Matthew. And you think he's been
hurt enough."

Ammie closed her eyes, her cheeks burning. Those
concerns might have been clamoring for her attention
somewhere in the back of her mind. But if she was brutally honest, she had to admit that her primary concern
since Lynette Simmons had stepped off that stage yesterday had not been for Matt, but for herself and her relationship with Matt, and how this woman was going to
interfere with that relationship. Ammie was searching for
some kind of response to Lynette's assertions when,
thankfully, Mary came to her rescue.

"Why don't we all sit down?" she suggested, gesturing
toward the kitchen table. "I think the tea is ready."

"Thank you, Mrs. Denby. You're very kind." Lynette
pulled out a chair and sat down. "With a sprig of mint, if
it's not too much trouble."

Ammie settled into a chair opposite Lynette. She was
still reeling from the velvet-sheathed punch the woman
had just thrown at her. And she had a sudden sense that
Lynette had known exactly which punch to throw.

Mary finished preparing the tea, then joined them at the table. An awkward silence ensued. Finally, it was Mary who said, "So, Lynette, you were telling me earlier that you sing a little?"

"Yes." She took a sip of her tea. "Clint told me that Matthew plays the piano well. I thought perhaps he and I could entertain after supper next Friday night. Matthew invited me—that would be all right, wouldn't it, Amelia?"

"I can't think of anything I'd enjoy more," Ammie said, amazed that she wasn't turned into a pillar of salt or struck by lightning or something equally hideous for telling such a bald-faced lie. Her spirits sank. Surely Lynette's stay at the Diamond G wouldn't extend to a full week! "You were saying Zak had some reservations about your story?"

"It's not a story. It's the truth."

"But he didn't accept your 'proof'?"

"It's quite a shock for him. He and Clint were so close." Her teacup clattered against its saucer as she set it down. "Matthew has been my champion, though. He's made me feel so welcome. He's brought me tea, drawn a bath for me, made—"

"He what?" Ammie demanded. "He did what with a bath?"

"He carried water up to my room last night at the ranch so that I could refresh myself after my long journey." Her lips curved into a dazzling smile, but Ammie detected a hint of smugness in her brown eyes. And maybe just a little challenge. "He was most helpful."

Ammie fought down a sudden image of Lynette holding out a wet, soapy sponge, telling Matt she couldn't quite reach that one little spot on her back. . . . She shoved to her feet. "I think I've had enough tea. I'm going out to see how the men are coming with the horses."

Lynette shivered. "It all looks so dangerous. I watched one of them—Mr. Johnson, I believe his name was—get thrown off a bucking horse. I told Matthew I couldn't bear it. I had to come in the house."

"Feel free to stay in the house," Ammie gritted cheerfully. With a nod to Mary, Ammie hurried outside.

She tromped across the ranch yard, side-stepping mud puddles as she headed for the corral. She was not going to think about Lynette and her bath one second longer. Surely everything had been prim and proper. After all, Zak had been in the house.

But smugness had been in Lynette's eyes. And taunt. And challenge.

Ammie kicked at a pebble. Had Lynette affected that look deliberately, to divert her attention from Zak's suspicions about her? It had certainly gotten Ammie out of the house in a hurry. Or was she just imagining things because of her mounting jealousy over Matt?

She grimaced. Either way, she would think about it later. For now, she had reached the corral.

"Mornin', sleepyhead," Shamus said as Ammie clambered up to the top rail beside him. "The storm keep you up last night?"

"A little."

"You should have come downstairs."

Ammie almost told him she had, but she didn't want to embarrass her father. "How's it going with the horses?"

"Real good."

Matt strode toward her, his mouth curved in that lopsided grin she knew so well. "Mornin', Am." He hooked one arm over the top rail and angled a look up at her. "How's Lynette doing? Did you get a chance to talk to her?"

Ammie dug her nails into the rough-hewn rail. Two questions—both about Lynette. "I certainly did talk to her," she told him. "And what a pleasure it was."

Matt smiled, oblivious. "I knew you two would get along once you got to know each other." He ran a hand over his grime-covered face, then made a futile attempt to slap away some of the dirt and mud clinging to his sweat-drenched shirt. It was unbuttoned nearly to his breast-bone, and Ammie found herself stealing glimpses of the dark, curling hair that matted that broad chest.

"Pretty awful, huh?" he drawled.

She shook herself, dragging her eyes up to meet his. "What?"

"I said I look pretty awful."

"No, you don't. You look wond—I mean, ah, who's winning? You or the horses?"

He chuckled. "Too close to call."

She laughed.

"It's nice to hear that," he said.

"What?"

"You laughing. It's been a while." His blue eyes were serious.

Shamus coughed loudly. "Smoke's got another mount ready for you, Matt."

Matt affected a pained look, gripping his side. "I don't think I got any spots left on this body to bruise, Shamus. Seems to me, you aren't so old you can't take on one of these broomtails yourself."

"Oh, no, you don't. I landed on my head one too many times already, to hear my daughter tell it." He hopped to the ground. "Speakin' of which, I've got some paperwork to tend to. You boys keep busy now." With a chuckle he headed for the house.

Ammie was glad that her father and Matt seemed to have smoothed out some of the awkwardness that had been between them. She just prayed she wasn't the subject they'd been smoothing out.

Ammie watched as Matt swung aboard a feisty bay.

"Get him, Matt!" she yelled. "Show him who's boss!"

The horse bucked and wheeled. "Problem is—he already knows," Matt shouted.

Ammie laughed, thoroughly enjoying Matt's battle of wills with the bay. And then Lynette stepped up beside her.

The brunette stood on tiptoe and peered over the top rail. "He isn't going to hurt himself, is he?" she asked anxiously. She was clutching an unopened parasol that perfectly matched her dress.

"He knows what he's doing," Ammie said.

But the words weren't even out of her mouth before the bay fishtailed, slamming itself body-long into the sides of the corral. The whole structure shook, and Ammie had to catch herself to keep from falling in. Again the horse pounded itself into the rail. With a curse Matt leaped from its back, hit the dirt, and rolled.

The horse thundered after him. Matt dove for the lowest corral rail, snaking under it an instant ahead of the bay's crushing hooves.

For an instant he lay there. Then he slapped the ground with his fist, lurched to his feet, and cussed a blue streak.

"Oh, Matthew, are you hurt?" Lynette cried, rushing over to him.

He halted abruptly. His bronzed face flushed a deep crimson. "I didn't see you, Lynette," he all but stammered. "I never would have cussed like that with a lady present."

Ammie's lips thinned. He would cuss in front of her all day and half the night and had on many occasions! But not in front of dear Lynette. Oh, no—Lynette was a lady.

"Are you sure you're all right, Matthew?" Lynette pressed.

"I'm fine. Just damaged my pride a little, that's all."

"Maybe you've done enough of this for one day. I'd hate to think what would have happened if that horse had . . ." Tears welled in her dark eyes and her lower lip trembled.

"If it upsets you that much, I'll stop for a while. We'll watch Will and Jess take on a few."

"Thank you."

Ammie's mouth was hanging open. This could not be happening.

Lynette laid her hand on Matt's arm. "My, it is so terribly warm out here, isn't it?"

"Ammie?" Matt called. "Could you get Lynette some lemonade? I wouldn't want her to overheat. She's very—"

"Delicate?" Ammie inquired, her voice dripping with sarcasm. "A dip in the horse trough would cool her off," she muttered.

"What'd you say?" Matt called.

"I said, I'm on my way to make that lemonade."

"Great."

Mouthing obscenities, Ammie hopped to the ground and headed for the house.

"Careful, Red," Smoke said, falling into step beside her. "In some states, them thoughts you're havin' are a hangin' offense."

"Do you believe that woman?" she rasped. "She's got him wrapped around her little finger. It's disgraceful!"

"Disgraceful it ain't your finger, eh, Red?"

"This is not funny."

"It is from where I'm standin'. You really just gonna let that little lady waltz in and pick off your fella without a fight?"

"I'd fight her!" Ammie clenched her fists.

"Not that kind of fight." Smoke chuckled. "Where you been, girl? You gotta fight fire with fire."

"I can't fight that kind of fire." She stopped, looking back toward the corral. "Look at her, Smoke! Even Will and Jess are drooling. I'm surprised you aren't over there preening like a peacock yourself."

"She ain't my type. Ain't Matt's type, either, but he don't know that yet."

"What type is that?"

"All helpless and flutter-brained. She'll fool him for a while, but he'll come around."

"In forty or fifty years."

"I'm disappointed in you, Red. Didn't know you were a quitter."

Ammie straightened. For the second time in two days she had been called a quitter. She didn't like it. She didn't like it one bit. "The hell with the lemonade." She stalked back toward the corral. "I'm going to show Lynette Simmons how a woman handles herself on a Texas ranch."

She ducked into the corral and before Will or Jess even knew what was happening, she had swung onboard the bay that had just thrown Matt.

"Ammie!" Will barked.

But she was already hanging on for dear life. The horse bucked and twisted and whipped her body like a leaf in a windstorm, but she managed to hold tight for more than a minute before she shared the same ignominious fate as Matt. Only this time the horse did not charge. Ammie climbed to her feet, brushing herself off. "Got him tired out for you, Will."

"Thanks, Ammie," he drawled, "But don't ever do that again."

Grinning, Ammie glanced toward Matt, expecting him to approve of her courageous stunt. Instead, he was standing next to Lynette, trying to figure out how to open her parasol. He hadn't even been watching!

Fuming, she strode toward him.

He looked up. "Did you get that lemonade yet, Am? Lynette's awfully thirsty."

Ammie didn't trust herself to speak. What was the use? She all but ran toward the house.

In the kitchen she slammed lemons onto the counter, pumped water into a pitcher, then stood there and shook.

"What happened, Amelia?" Mary asked.

"What happened? I just about killed myself out there to get that thick-headed dolt to notice me, and all he can do is fuss over whether or not Lynette is thirsty." Tears of frustration stung her eyes, and she swiped them angrily away. "You told me to be myself—well, that's what I've been doing." Her voice broke. "But it doesn't matter. Matt doesn't want a woman like me. He wants a woman like Lynette. He wants a lady."

The tears came then, and Ammie did not resist as Mary Denby pulled her into her arms and hugged her close. "I've known Matt Grayson as long as I've known you, child," Mary said gently. "Right now, he doesn't know what he wants."

For a long minute Ammie let herself cry. It felt good somehow. Then she straightened, stepping back from Mary and drawing in a shuddery breath. "I hate him!"

Mary smiled. "Good."

Ammie frowned, puzzled.

Mary pointed toward the lemonade. "Hating him will make it easier to tell him you put salt in the lemonade instead of sugar."

Ammie dipped her finger into the pitcher and brought it to her mouth. She made a face, then brightened as a sudden, wicked thought occurred to her. "Maybe I can pretend not to have noticed and give a glass to Lynette anyway."

"With a sprig of mint?"

" 'But don't go to any trouble,' " Ammie trilled. She had to laugh. "Is this ever going to get any better?" She held up a hand. "I know, I know . . . give it time." Ammie held up a glass of the salted lemonade and looked out toward the porch. So tempting. But she didn't want to give Matt any more excuses than he already had to hover over dear, delicate Lynette.

Ammie and Mary headed outside. Ammie grimaced.

Too late. Matt was already hovering over Lynette, who was sitting in a wicker chair fanning herself.

Jaw clenched, Ammie handed Lynette a glass of water. "Sorry, fresh out of lemonade."

"If you'd like to come inside, Lynette," Mary offered, "I could brew you a little more tea."

"I'd appreciate that," Lynette said, rising. "With a sprig of mint, if you have it."

"Of course, dear." Mary sent a wink to Ammie.

Ammie grinned.

"And if you could set out some more of those little cakes you had this morning," Lynette said as she disappeared into the house with Mary. "But don't go to any trouble."

"I'm glad to see that you and Mrs. Denby have resolved your differences," Matt said to Ammie, leaning against one of the porch's support posts.

"I finally figured out I was acting like a fool. You and my father seem to be getting on better too."

"Must be a day for truces."

"A day for a lot of things." She studied him seriously. "You really believe Lynette, don't you?"

"She was Clint's wife, Ammie. I know it. I feel it."

"Then that's good enough for me," she said, and meant it.

"Thanks."

"How did your pa take it?"

"Not as bad as I thought he would. He's fighting it some, but I think he'll come around." He lifted his Stetson and threaded a hand through his sweat-drenched dark hair. "I either need to get some of this dirt off me, or go find me a hog wallow to live in. I can't take Lynette home in the buggy looking like this."

"You're leaving? It's hardly past noon."

"She's pretty tired."

"We have several beds she could lie down on."

"I think she wants to go home."

The word *home* stung. How could he already think of Lynette's home as the Diamond G? But Ammie didn't have the nerve to ask.

Matt stepped off the porch and headed toward the water pump.

Ammie followed. "What about the horses?"

"I'll be back tomorrow. I have some work to catch up on at home, you know. I've been gone awhile."

He reached the horse trough and peeled off his sweat-soaked shirt. His back was to her. Ammie recalled the feel of those corded muscles rippling beneath her fingers.

He worked the pump handle, then ducked his head under the cool stream of water that gushed out. Straightening, he tossed his head like a wet hound. Ammie felt a myriad of tiny droplets stipple across her face. "Matt?"

He turned, startled. "I didn't know you were so close." He looked sheepish. "I didn't mean to get you wet."

"It's all right. It feels good. I wouldn't mind sticking my head under there myself."

He wet his shirt down and used it as a makeshift towel to wipe off his upper chest and belly, then under his arms. "It sure is hot," he said.

"It sure is," she murmured. Without his shirt, she was acutely aware of how low-slung his denims were. She stared at the flat plane of his belly and at the dark, curling hairs that arrowed below his navel to disappear beneath the waistband of his pants.

"Got a clean shirt in my saddlebags." He headed for the buggy.

Before he could shrug into the fresh blue chambray, Ammie stepped close to pick off bits of grass that still clung to his back. His flesh was just as she had imagined it would be—hot, wet. Her hand lingered longer than it should. Her heart was pounding so loudly, she was astonished he couldn't hear it. She smoothed her hand over to where another bit of grass clung.

Matt stepped away, his laugh awkward, his eyes hooded so that she had no idea what he might be thinking. "I should get rid of these too," he said, hooking a thumb into the waistband of the denims. "But I didn't bring an extra pair of britches."

"You're about the same size as Will," Ammie offered, her tongue strangely thick, her mouth dry. "Maybe you could borrow a pair of his."

"I don't know . . ."

"You wouldn't want to get mud on Lynette now, would you?"

They headed for the bunkhouse.

Inside, Ammie grumbled to herself as Matt made her turn around while he switched into a pair of Will's denims. The thought of his leaving, and Lynette having him all to herself again tonight, prodded Ammie to be bold. She had to find out if anything more than sympathy was driving him. "How long do you plan for Lynette to stay at Diamond G?" she asked.

"I'm not sure. She doesn't have any family, and I have a feeling she doesn't have much money, either. I feel sorry for her."

"Feeling sorry for her is fine—but what are you going to do about her?"

"I'll figure something out. Clint would've wanted her taken care of."

But that doesn't mean you have to be the one to take care of her, Ammie longed to say. Instead, she asked, "Are you thinking about giving her a share of Diamond G?"

"I think that would be fair."

"Zak isn't going to like that."

He rubbed a hand across the back of his neck. "I know."

"Do you plan for her to live there or to just give her money?"

"Ammie, I don't know." His voice grew exasperated. "She's only been here a day. It's going to take time to sort things out."

"I'm sorry, I just . . . I just worry that she . . ." She hesitated.

Matt's brows knitted. "I thought you said you believed her because *I* believed her."

"I do, but . . ."

"But what?"

"If she's as desperate as you think she is . . . Think about it—we don't know a thing about her except what she's told us. Who knows what Clint even knew? They couldn't have been together that often."

"I'm so glad you trust my judgment on this," Matt bit out.

"Your judgment could be blinded by guilt."

He stiffened. "Are you talking about Clint's death?" he asked, his voice deadly quiet.

"Of course not! I'm talking about all the years you and Clint—" She paused, her eyes narrowing. "Why would you even *think* I was referring to Clint's death? How *could* you even think it?"

He looked away. "I'm sorry. I had to tell Lynette how Clint died—how everyone thinks he died, anyway. I'm a little raw on the subject, I guess."

"She didn't blame you, though, did she?"

"How did you know?"

Because whatever she's up to, she needs your help, Ammie thought, but said only, "She knew how much Clint loved you." She stepped close to him and took his big hand in her smaller one. "Take it slow, okay? I love you." She'd said the words many times over the years, but never had she meant them as she meant them now.

Something flickered in his eyes, but it was there and

gone so quickly, she had no chance to read it. He tipped her chin up. "I love you, too, Am." He scooped his hat from the bunk where he'd tossed it. "I'd better go. I'll see you tomorrow."

She didn't follow him when he left the bunkhouse. She sank onto an old wooden stool and waited. It was about ten minutes before she heard the sounds of the buggy leaving the yard. She walked to the window and looked out, staring at the retreating carriage.

Whatever she's up to . . .

Ammie shivered, despite the day's heat. Lynette Simmons, Ammie knew with a sudden, sick certainty, was going to break Matt's heart.

♧ / *Chapter 12*

Matt did not come back to Shamrock the next day—or the next. He sent word that Lynette had taken ill. Nothing serious, just a general fatigue, he assured them. But he wanted her to rest. Lynette told him she couldn't possibly rest if she was left behind to worry about his getting hurt breaking horses at Shamrock. Matt hoped everyone understood.

Ammie understood. She understood perfectly. Lynette had had one Grayson, but he was dead. She wanted another.

That cold assessment had been running through her head for days now. She couldn't seem to shake it—and there were times she fervently wished she could. The thought was repugnant, appalling. And more than a little unfair. She didn't even know Lynette Simmons. And yet as the days passed and Matt still did not return to Shamrock, Ammie couldn't help but wonder.

More than a little ashamed, she kept her thoughts to herself, even as she and Mary busied themselves in the Shamrock kitchen making ready for Friday supper. Ammie sat at the table chopping apples for the pie she knew she shouldn't bother to bake. "He isn't coming," she muttered. "I don't know why I let you talk me into this."

"He is too coming," Mary said cheerfully. "I told you, I saw Matt and Lynette in town yesterday. Lynette was posting a letter, and Matt very specifically told me to tell you that he'd be here for his Friday supper."

Ammie was not fooled. "*You* asked him to come, didn't you?"

Mary looked up from the mound of potatoes she was peeling. "I merely mentioned how much we'd *all* missed him last week."

"As if he cared."

"Amelia, please . . ."

"What will it matter, anyway? Lynette will tag along. You remember her threat"—Ammie grimaced—"I mean her promise, to sing for us."

"Lynette said she wouldn't feel up to coming and to please accept her heartfelt regrets."

"She'll come. You just wait. If Matt comes, so will Lynette."

Mary fell silent. Quickly, Ammie finished preparing the apples. She'd already rolled out the dough for the crust. When the pie was ready for the oven, she offered to help Mary with the potatoes.

"None of that," Mary said. "Your only responsibility for tonight's meal is that famous apple pie of yours." Mary reached into her apron pocket and extracted a small box tied with pink ribbon.

"What is it?" Ammie asked.

"Open it and see."

Ammie did so and gasped to find the box filled with expensive French bath salts.

"Gardenia," Mary said. "Men love gardenias."

"Mary, I can't—"

"You can, and you will. And once your bath is done, I'm going to do your hair. And then we're going to make use of that lovely dress you bought last week."

"But—"

"No arguments, young lady. A princess must prepare for her prince."

Heart racing, daring to hope, Ammie allowed Mary to pamper and fuss to her heart's content. Bathed, coiffed, and done up in a gown almost too lovely for words, Ammie felt very much like a real princess two hours later as she sat in the drawing room and waited for Matt to arrive.

And waited.

When supper was ready, she insisted that her father and Mary go ahead and eat without her. She would wait a little longer.

And still he didn't come.

"I'm so sorry, dear," Mary said, looking anxiously at Shamus.

"Maybe there was some emergency," Ammie said, though she didn't believe it. Her father and Mary meant well, but Ammie couldn't bear the sympathy she saw in their eyes every time they looked at her.

Crossing to the piano, Ammie caressed the keys. Matt's fingers could draw such magic from those keys. She had been going to ask him to play for her tonight. It had been so long since he'd done that. "I'll feed Matt's supper to Pickles, then I'm going out to the barn for a while—check on Tulip, give her some carrots."

Shamus cleared his throat. "Her foal's due soon, isn't it?" he asked, obviously groping for a subject.

"Couple weeks."

Mary twisted her hands in the apron she was wearing. "I really am so sorry, Amelia."

Ammie smiled sadly. "I know." She excused herself and went to her room. Heart heavy, she slipped out of her dress and changed into her pants and shirt. It wasn't midnight yet, but Cinderella had turned back into a pumpkin.

Out in the barn she fed Pickles the piece of apple pie she had saved especially for Matt. "I should have known better," she murmured. "Prince Charming rides a white horse. Drifter's black."

The barn door creaked, its heavy hinges protesting as the door was pushed open. Ammie looked up, expecting to see Mary or her father. Instead she saw Matt.

A rush of pure joy jolted through her. She crushed it with a vengeance. Turning her back on him, she gave Tulip another carrot. "What are you doing here?"

He stepped over to the stall and rubbed Tulip's nose when the mare shoved her head at his chest. "Pretty mad at me, huh?"

"Why should I be mad?"

"Weren't you expecting me for supper?"

Ammie pretended to consider the question. "My, my— is it Friday again already? Where does the time go? I hadn't even noticed."

He actually looked a little hurt. "I'd planned to be here, but—"

"Let me guess. Lynette wanted a cup of tea?"

He frowned. "You are mad at me."

"Lucky guess." She walked over to an old wooden apple crate, upended it, and sat down.

Matt did the same with a second crate, positioning it so that he sat facing her. "I suppose you made apple pie." His voice was cajoling. He was trying to tease her, lighten her mood. But it wasn't going to work.

"Mary made supper. Your portion was thoroughly appreciated by Pickles—about two hours ago." She crossed her arms in front of her. "You know damned well supper's long over. Why did you even come here this late, Matt?"

He tugged his hat from his head, twisting the brim in his hands. "Because whenever I've needed somebody to talk to about anything that's ever really mattered in my life, you've always been there to listen. I need to talk to you, Ammie."

"About what?" she asked, though her heart already knew.

"About Lynette."

"What about her?"

He hesitated. "She's not like any woman I've ever known. She's special. I know it sounds crazy. I've only known her a week, but—there's just something about her."

"What are you doing?" Ammie tried to laugh and failed. "Falling in love with her?"

Ammie expected, hoped, prayed that he would laugh, that he would say, "Of course not. She's a stranger. She was Clint's wife. I just feel she needs a friend right now."

Instead he looked at her, those blue eyes bright, earnest. "Maybe. Maybe I am. I don't know. I do know I like being with her. We talk about Clint. I've found out things about my brother I didn't even know." His smile was bittersweet. "Did you know that Clint liked to take off his boots and socks and walk barefoot in the grass? He used to do that when he took Lynette on picnics. Can you imagine Clint barefoot?" Matt shook his head in amazement. "She makes things easier around Pa too. He's beginning to like her. She's a real lady."

Ammie winced but managed to ask, "What do you plan to do about these feelings, Matt?" Her voice, she was certain, sounded as hollow as she felt.

"Nothing—not yet, anyway. Hell, I haven't even sorted it all out for myself. That's why I needed to talk to my best friend."

Ammie reached over and caught his hand, the contact sweet agony under the circumstances. "Matt, you've only known this woman a week. She's still grieving for Clint."

"I know."

"And so are you. And now here's someone who can share things about Clint that are very special to both of you."

"It's more than that, Ammie."

No, it isn't! she wanted to shout at him. *It can't be! I don't want it to be!* "I just don't want you to get hurt."

He gave her that lopsided grin. "I feel better than I have in a long time."

"I'm glad. If she does that for you, I'm glad." And she

was, even though her heart ached with the pain of what was ever more quickly threatening to become an inconsolable loss.

He stood. "I knew I'd feel better talking to you."

She rose to stand in front of him, and he threw his arms around her to give her an affectionate squeeze. She dared press her face against his chest an instant longer than propriety might permit. She had to swallow a sob.

"Hey, would you like to go to the dance in town tomorrow night?" he asked.

"With you?"

"With Lynette and me. I asked her, and she said yes. And I know Terence Kessler asked you. I thought you might like to ride along with Lynette and me."

"I'll, uh—I'll just ride in with Pa and Mary."

He shrugged. "All right. Then we'll see you there."

"Can't wait." How could she carry on this conversation? Couldn't he hear her heart breaking?

"You are one hell of a friend, you know that? Someday I may even get up the guts to tell you—" He broke off the thought. "Nothing. Never mind." He cupped her cheek in his rein-roughened palm, his eyes suddenly hooded, unreadable.

Ammie had no idea what he'd been about to say, but she felt a sudden, fierce rush of real hatred for Lynette.

" 'Night, Ammie."

"Good night, Matt."

She watched him ride out, wondering how on God's earth she was ever going to survive the dance tomorrow, where she would see her nightmare come to life—Lynette Simmons in Matt Grayson's arms.

Ammie sat on the settee in Mary Denby's parlor and fussed with a bit of lint that clung to her Cinderella gown. Why had she let Mary talk her into this foolishness? Unlike the real Cinderella, who'd only had to endure one night of humiliation, Ammie had now agreed to a second. Except that this night, even more than last, offered not the slightest hope of a fairy-tale ending. Tonight, Prince Charming would be at the ball with another woman.

"I don't think I feel well," Ammie said, pressing her hands to her temples.

"Nonsense, dear," Mary said. "Now, hold still." Mary stood behind the settee and added a spray of wildflowers to the coils of Ammie's fiery hair.

"I don't see why Terence has to come to the house to walk with us. I could've just met him at the dance."

"Shush, he's going to be here any minute."

"But I don't even want to go with him."

"I don't understand any of this," Shamus said, standing in the open doorway, fidgeting with the black string tie that Mary had sweet-talked him into wearing. "She's going to a dance with a man she doesn't like, so that she can spend the night watching the man she loves"—he tripped slightly over the word—"wooing another woman."

"Exactly," Mary said.

"Women!" Shamus snorted.

"I have to go to the dance, Pa," Ammie said softly. "I don't want to miss you and Mary announcing your betrothal." They had confided their secret to her on the way into town. Ammie had been genuinely thrilled for them both.

"Doesn't your daughter look beautiful, Shamus?" Mary beamed, holding out her hands as though displaying a fine piece of art.

Shamus's pale green eyes glowed with paternal pride. "That she does."

Ammie blushed.

He crossed the room to stand in front of her, his tone as serious as Ammie had ever heard it. "All I want in this world is your happiness, Ammie. That's all I've ever wanted."

"I know."

"I heard you snifflin' and cryin' with Mary in the back of the buckboard today. Now don't worry, I wasn't listenin'. I'm just glad Mary was a comfort to you." He smoothed a hand over his moustache. "What I'm tryin' to say is that it's been hard for me to see that you really are grown up now. And I was wrong to try to interfere between you and Matt. I just didn't want to see you get hurt."

"The only way Matt can hurt me is to not love me back."

"Now, now," Mary scolded gently, "that's no way for Cinderella to talk." She looked toward the door. "I think I hear Terence coming up the walk."

Ammie groaned. "Tell him I died."

"I most certainly will not. Sometimes it helps for one bee to see another bee flitting about the honey pot. Now come along."

Ammie heard music and laughter coming from Walker's Livery, and she ached to turn and run from both, but Terence Kessler held her hand in a firm grip. Together they crossed the street and covered the final two hundred feet to the huge barn. Red, white, and blue streamers fluttered from the rafters above the heads of more than a hundred ranch and town folk who were attending the monthly celebration. Several couples were already giving their enthusiastic approval to the town band's rendition of a Virginia reel.

"It's going to be a great night, isn't it, Amelia?" Terence said, grinning, a lascivious glint coming into his brown eyes. "I can't wait to show you off. You look positively glorious!"

Amelia sighed. Life would be so much simpler if she loved Terence. Instead, she wondered how long etiquette demanded that she stay before she claimed to have a splitting headache. Her gaze flitted among the numerous familiar faces in attendance, including those of her father and Mary Denby, who were proving to be one of the more energetic couples in the reel. But nowhere did she see Matt and Lynette. If she left now, perhaps she could avoid seeing them altogether. Mary and her father would understand.

Ammie pressed a hand to her temple. "Terence, I'm sorry, but I really need—"

"Do you want to dance?" he half-shouted above the din of the music. "Or do you want me to get you some punch?"

She leaned close to him, ready to repeat her request against his ear. That was when she saw them. Looking past Terence's left shoulder, she watched Matt guide Lynette into the spacious interior of the barn. Lynette, too, had to lean close to tell Matt something. His mouth broke into a wide grin, and Ammie's heart twisted.

Lynette was her usual stunning self, this time in emerald and black silk, but it was Matt's attire that arrested Ammie's attention. She'd never seen him look more resplendent. His trousers were dark, exquisitely tailored to his long, muscled legs. A white silk shirt and black leather vest set off the bronzed perfection of his features. The first two buttons of his shirt were open, revealing a tantalizing glimpse of the flat plane of his chest. Around his neck was knotted a deep blue silk bandanna.

Ammie turned, fearful he would feel her eyes on him. She still had a chance to slip away.

Terence whipped his arm possessively about her waist. "Look, it's Matt Grayson. And that must be Lynette Simmons—the woman I've been hearing my customers whisper about all week. I must have an introduction."

Her heart sinking, Ammie allowed herself to be maneuvered over to Matt and Lynette.

Ammie brightened a little to see Lynette's eyes spark

with what had to be jealousy as her gaze snagged on Amelia's dress. Her heart tripped even harder when, she could have sworn, she saw a sudden heat flare in Matt's eyes. But then he was looking at Lynette, and Ammie was no longer certain where his thoughts had been when his passion had so obviously stirred.

Matt quickly took care of Terence's introduction.

"It's such a pleasure, Miss Simmons," Terence said. "I do hope you're enjoying your stay."

"Very much." She glanced meaningfully at Matt, but Ammie had the distinct impression that that look had been for her benefit. Ammie felt her temper nudge her. Lynette wasn't even trying to be subtle anymore.

"May I have the pleasure of this dance, Miss Simmons?" Terence asked. "With your permission of course, Matt?"

"If the lady has no objections?"

Lynette nodded demurely as Terence whisked her away, though Ammie could see she was not at all happy about leaving Matt in Ammie's company. Ammie would take her tiny victories where she could get them.

"You look beautiful," Matt said, his eyes warm.

"Thank you. So do you," she blurted, then caught herself. "I mean, you look handsome."

He chuckled. "I guess we clean up pretty good. Want to dance?"

He said the words matter-of-factly as the band finished up a reel.

"I'd love to." She ignored the sudden odd alarm in his eyes as the musicians began a waltz. She went into his arms as though she belonged there, as though she would never have to leave. He slid his left hand into her right, and her heart turned over. Liquid fire skidded along her spine when he pressed his right hand against her back.

Ammie smiled, praying it was a bewitching smile, a dazzling smile. And maybe it was, because suddenly Matt was pulling her closer, her breasts a bare whisper away from the hard plane of his chest. His gaze grew dark, intense. All around them the other dancers seemed to fade, disappear.

"Ammie." He spoke her name softly, like a caress. She'd never heard him say it quite that way before.

He bent his head slightly, as though to whisper in her ear. She turned her face, and her gaze rested on the tantalizing fullness of his lips, now less than an inch from her own. She could feel her blood heat and her breathing grow shallow.

Matt was going to kiss her.

Right here in the middle of this dance floor.

And she was going to let him. An intoxicating dizziness swept over her as she raised her lips to his.

"Excuse me, Matt!" Ammie was jarred from her reverie by an annoyingly familiar voice. Then Theda Hopkins all but jammed herself between her and Matt. "I'm so sorry to intrude," she said, obviously not at all sorry.

Ammie almost cursed.

"What do you want, Theda?" Matt snapped before he drew rein on whatever emotion had been firing in those now-hooded eyes.

She handed him a letter. "This came for Miss Simmons today. The postmaster saw me on the way to the dance and asked me to give it to her, but since I don't know her" —she smiled adoringly at Matt—"I thought I'd give it to you."

"Thank you, Theda." Matt accepted the letter, though he had to tug a bit to get Theda to release it. "I'll see that Miss Simmons gets it."

"It's from Austin."

"Thank you."

"Should I wait while you give it to her?"

"I don't think that will be necessary."

Theda sighed. "I suppose your dance card's filled up, huh, Matt?"

Matt shifted, looking uncomfortable.

"I'm afraid it is, Theda," Ammie put in. "He's promised all his extra dances to me tonight."

If possible, Matt looked even more uncomfortable. Instead of feeling hurt, Ammie felt a sudden burst of hope. He had evidently been enjoying their dance more than he thought he should, considering his supposed blossoming interest in Lynette. Maybe Cinderella would get her glass slipper after all.

Theda wandered off then, looking for greener pastures. Clutching the letter, Matt headed for Lynette, who was finishing her waltz with Terence. Ammie followed.

"Many thanks, Miss Simmons," Terence said, bowing graciously.

"My pleasure, Mr. Kessler."

"Oh, please—it's Terence."

Lynette smiled.

Terence caught Ammie's hand. "There you are, my lady. Doesn't she look spectacular, Matt? I am one lucky man." Ammie winced at his effrontery when he dared kiss her on the cheek.

A muscle in Matt's jaw jumped, and Ammie couldn't help thinking of Mary's comment about bees and honey pots. "Don't forget Lynette's letter, Matt," she said, feeling almost giddy when he couldn't seem to focus on what she was saying. Maybe he really was a little jealous.

"Yes, the letter," Matt said tightly, still glowering at Terence. "This is for you, Lynette."

It might have been a trick of the light, but Ammie could have sworn Lynette paled slightly.

"If you don't mind, I'll go outside and read it."

"Of course."

Determined not to let Lynette out of her sight with that letter, Ammie told Terence she needed some air. Then she kept pace as Matt led Lynette out to an open field behind the barn, where a large campfire crackled and snapped. Several men were gathered around it, swapping tall tales and the contents of a brown jug.

"Excuse me, gentlemen."

The men scrambled in an eager wave to make way for Lynette. The lovely brunette astonished Ammie by crouching beside the fire and reading the note against the background of the flames. Why would she have to get that close? In the next instant, Ammie knew. Lynette pretended—Ammie was certain that was the right word— that the paper was snatched from her fingers by a breeze. In the blink of an eye, the greedy fire turned the missive to ashes.

"Oh, dear," Lynette said, allowing Matt to help her to her feet.

"Did you get a chance to read it all?" Matt asked, concerned.

Lynette waved her hand dismissively. "It was nothing important. Just a bit of gossip from my dear friend Pearl in Austin."

Lynette Simmons was lying—Ammie would have bet the ranch on it. And now there was no mistaking how pale she was.

"Could we stay out here a little while, Matthew?" she asked. "It's very stuffy in the barn with so many people."

Matt hesitated, then seemed to shake himself. "I'd like that."

Ammie watched them walk off together, her heart catching as Lynette slipped her hand into Matt's.

"I'm going to find out what you're all about, Lynette," Ammie muttered. "My hand to God, I will. And if you hurt Matt, you're going to curse the day you ever set foot in River Oaks."

"Who are you talking to?"

Ammie whirled. She hadn't heard Terence approach.

"Just thinking out loud," she mumbled. She walked a few yards farther on, ignoring Terence, who followed behind.

Ahead of her in the moonlight Matt and Lynette stopped. Despising herself, Ammie stepped behind a tree, watching, listening.

"What are you doing?" Terence demanded.

"Hush!" Ammie hissed. "Be still or go away."

Terence was still. Ammie listened.

"Oh, Matthew, I—I feel so guilty," Lynette was saying. "And yet . . . and yet . . ." She touched his face, and Ammie's eyes burned. "I'm so drawn to your kindness, your thoughtfulness. Forgive me. I know it's too soon after Clint, too soon for both of us."

"Too soon for what, Lynette?" he prompted softly.

"I—I think I'm falling in love with you, Matthew." She stood on tiptoe and brushed her lips against his. He did not pull away. "Maybe you love me, too, just a little?"

Ammie didn't hear his murmured response, but she didn't have to. He pulled Lynette into his arms and kissed her again. And again.

Ammie stood there, feeling for all the world as though her heart were being ripped from her chest.

"Gives a person ideas, doesn't it?" Terence whispered in her ear. Tears seared like acid down her cheeks. She didn't answer. He must have taken her lack of response as a yes. He pulled her to him, kissing her fervently on her lips, her cheeks, her neck.

Ammie felt nothing. She wondered if she would ever feel anything again.

Matt strode slowly back toward Walker's Livery and the dance, his arm resting lightly on Lynette's waist. He should have been happy, ecstatic, he thought. He'd just discovered that Lynette was as attracted to him as he was to her. Wasn't that exactly what he wanted? His head was still spinning from the heady power of her kisses.

Then what was wrong? What was missing? Why was he feeling so agitated, confused?

It had started an hour ago, when he'd danced with Ammie. Last night in the Shamrock barn, he thought he'd just about rid himself of the foolish fantasies he'd been having about her. But every time he got near her, they happened all over again.

During their waltz tonight, he'd wanted nothing more than to pull her close, kiss her. Only Theda's intrusion had prevented him from doing just that. No, he hadn't rid himself of his fantasies. All he'd done was spend a week away from her, trying to convince himself that he had!

What the hell was happening to him?

He knew—he just hadn't wanted to admit it. Hell, he still didn't want to admit it.

Amelia O'Rourke had grown up into a spectacularly beautiful woman. And he was responding to her not as her friend, but as a man. God help him, he wanted to make love to her. He wanted her the same way he wanted the other women he had bedded in his life. He wanted her hot and willing and eager.

And he despised himself for it.

Keep her safe, Matt. Shamus's words were like a curse.

Of course, Matt would keep her safe. He would never reduce Ammie to a sunset-to-dawn affair. He was losing his appetite for such meaningless encounters himself. But that didn't seem to quell his erotic dreams about Ammie. That dress she wore tonight had only exacerbated his already overactive imagination where Ammie was concerned.

Keep her safe, Matt.

Safe from himself? he thought viciously.

At least he had acknowledged his lust. Now surely it would begin to fade. He would get used to this new womanly Amelia. Just, please God, let it be soon. He was scared to death that he was going to somehow wreck their friendship, a friendship that was as precious to him as breathing.

"Matthew"—Lynette was tugging on his sleeve—"look!"

Matt followed her gaze, and his whole body went stiff with rage. Terence Kessler had Ammie locked in a smothering embrace.

With a savage oath Matt started toward them.

"Wait!" Lynette whispered. "I don't think they would appreciate an interruption."

Matt looked again, astonished that Ammie was indeed offering no protest to Terence's lusty attentions. Somehow that only made him angrier.

"Isn't young love sweet?" Lynette sighed. "Terence was telling me during our dance that he and Amelia are all but engaged."

Matt snorted contemptuously. "That's ridiculous. The only place Terence Kessler will ever be engaged to Ammie is in his mind."

"Are you sure? Look at them."

He did again, his fists clenching and unclenching at his sides. "Ammie would've told me."

"But you were gone for six weeks, weren't you?" Lynette prodded, her voice cajoling. "And you've seen her only a time or two since you got back. Maybe she hasn't figured out the right words yet."

"She would have told me," he repeated stubbornly. Hadn't he just spilled his guts to her last night about Lynette? She would have told him then. Damn—why was he getting so angry, anyway? What business was it of his? Ammie had a perfect right to fall in love with whomever she chose. And it would certainly make his life a lot less complicated if she did. "Maybe I should talk to her," he said.

"Oh, please, Matthew—promise me you won't tell her I said anything. She would be so embarrassed and hurt. Promise?"

He frowned. "Promise."

"Why does it upset you so much? You're not—not interested in her yourself, are you? I thought you were friends. That she was like your little sister."

Matt shook himself. "Yeah. Sister. Right."

Keep her safe, Matt.

Lynette ran her hand along his arm. "They do make an attractive pair, don't they?"

Matt swept Lynette into his arms and kissed her, hard, hungry, a little desperate. This was what he wanted—a woman of experience. A woman who knew what to expect from a man, and what she wanted in return. And maybe it was more than that too. Lynette needed him. She had no one. She had no one because Clint was dead.

Lynette teased his lips with her tongue. He groaned and opened his mouth, inviting her erotic exploration. His blood heated and his sex stirred, growing rigid between his legs.

Yes, this is what he wanted.

☘/Chapter 13

Ammie awoke the next morning from a fitful sleep, her nightshirt clinging to her sweat-damp body. She pushed herself to a sitting position, shoving tendrils of sweat-slickened hair from her face. She wished she could blame her clammy state on the heat and humidity of the coming day, but, in fact, the temperature had precious little to do with it.

Her cheeks burned, as memories of last night assaulted her. Surely it had all been a dream, part of the nightmares that awoke her time and again overnight. A dream that Matt had swept Lynette into a passionate embrace. A dream that he had kissed her. A dream . . .

But it wasn't a dream. It had been real. All too agonizingly real.

I think I'm falling in love with you, Matthew. Lynette's voice, soft, lilting—seductive.

A week. Matt and Lynette had only known each other a week. But then, they'd spent every day of that week together under the same roof.

And every night.

Ammie closed her mind to the images that thought conjured, but it was too late. Had Lynette whispered more love words to Matt on their long buggy ride back to the ranch? Had they pulled over and continued that kiss under a star-dappled sky? Had they made love?

Ammie shut her eyes, her head spinning. She had to stop this. Matt could not fall in love with Lynette Simmons in one week. He could be infatuated with her, bedazzled by her, even drawn to her because of her marriage to Clint. But he could not love her. Please God, he couldn't *love* her.

She trembled. A week ago, she'd been terrified Matt might leave Texas behind for good, that she'd never see him again. She had thought nothing could hurt more than that.

She had been wrong. The thought of him making love to Lynette was agony beyond bearing.

Stumbling to her feet, Ammie staggered over to the washstand, certain she was going to be sick. She bent over the basin, her stomach heaving, but she did not vomit. She might have felt better if she had.

She'd lost Matt. She'd never even had him, and she'd lost him.

Never knew you to be a quitter, Red. Smoke's words hung in the air, so clear and so real that she turned, certain he had come into her room. But she was alone.

"I'm not a quitter," she said, sounding petulant even to her own ears. She straightened, said the words again. "I am not a quitter."

Then prove it, came the challenge. *Fight for him.*

Fight how?

However it takes.

But what if it's already too late?

No, she couldn't think that way. She would send Jess Johnson over to the Diamond G and invite Matt to a picnic lunch tomorrow. She would even be magnanimous and include Lynette. She grimaced. Only because she feared Matt wouldn't come if she didn't.

She crossed to her vanity and picked up a silver-plated hairbrush, running it through the tangled waves of her hair. On second thought, she would make the ride to the Diamond G herself and invite Matt in person. The worst mistake she'd made this past week had been letting

Lynette be alone with Matt. She wouldn't make that mistake again.

Setting down her brush, she peered into the wood-framed mirror above her vanity. She winced. Was that really her? Her skin looked sallow, her eyes bloodshot. And her lips—oh, God, they were actually slightly swollen.

She pressed a hand to her forehead. Terence. He had been so eager, so mortifyingly enthusiastic. How long had she been in his arms? How long had she let him . . . ?

Don't. She stopped the self-flagellation. It was over, done. And it was certainly never going to happen again. She had one consolation, at least. No one had seen her.

Worried that her courage to face Matt and Lynette might fade, she dressed quickly. Hurrying downstairs, she grabbed an apple and munched it as she rushed out to the corral. She avoided getting close enough to anyone to actually engage in conversation. She just wanted to saddle up and go.

On her ride to the Diamond G she kept her thoughts focused on other matters, like her father's upcoming wedding to Mary Denby and what she might get them for a present. If she thought too much about what Matt and Lynette might have done last night after the dance, she wouldn't be able to look either of them in the eye when she arrived.

It was well past midmorning when Ammie cantered into the Diamond G ranch yard. She guided Ranger to the main house and dismounted. She started up the porch steps, then hesitated, her gaze angling across the yard to the bunkhouse. Matt had made his home there for years, but if he was anywhere about this morning, she knew, he would likely be in the house. Ammie's lips thinned. He would never expect Lynette to suffer the discomforts of the bunkhouse.

Ammie knocked on the front door, trying vainly to slow

the suddenly accelerated beat of her heart. What if Zak was on some errand? What if Matt and Lynette were alone together in the house? What if Matt answered the door, looking sleep-tousled and embarrassed? What if—?

The door swung inward.

It was Lynette, looking graceful and thankfully not at all disheveled. Ammie breathed a little easier. "I want to see Matt."

Lynette's eyebrows quirked upward, and Ammie knew she had sounded a bit more brusque than she'd intended. She took another steadying breath. "May I come in?" she asked, affixing what she hoped was a pleasant smile to her face.

"Of course. Forgive me." Lynette stepped aside. "But I must tell you, Matthew isn't here."

Ammie stood in the foyer. "What do you mean? Where is he?"

"A couple of the men came and fetched him and his father about an hour ago. Something about three steers stuck in a bog."

Ammie frowned. A messy, exhausting job. It could be hours before they got back.

"You're welcome to rest yourself," Lynette said. "It would seem you've had a long . . . dusty ride. I could make us some tea."

Ammie thought of declining, then remembered a remark her father had once made about warfare—something about knowing your enemy. "I'd love some. Thank you."

Lynette showed her into Emily Grayson's parlor, then excused herself. Ammie sat down on the brocade settee, feeling at home despite her trousers and boots. Emily Grayson had been a lady, all elegance and grace, but she'd also been a woman who made anyone and everyone feel comfortable in her presence. If Lynette had hoped to in-

timidate Ammie by serving their tea in this room, she had
just made her first tactical blunder.

That Lynette, too, might be sizing up the competition
unexpectedly pleased Ammie. Perhaps Ammie was making more headway with Matt than she thought.

"Do you take honey or lemon?" Lynette asked, returning several minutes later, carrying a rose-trimmed
china tea service. She settled it on the small table in front
of the settee.

"Actually, I think I'd like a sprig of mint," Ammie
drawled. "But don't go to any trouble."

"I'm so sorry, but we're fresh out of mint."

"I'm not surprised."

"I beg your pardon?"

"Nothing. Never mind. I'm fine."

Lynette sat beside her on the settee. "It's so nice to
have you over for a visit, Amelia," Lynette said, pouring
out their tea into two china cups. "We haven't really gotten to know each other."

"I was thinking the same thing," Ammie said. "That's
why I'm here. I want to invite you and Matt to a picnic
lunch tomorrow. Just the three of us. Doesn't that sound
like fun?"

"Oh, I'm so sorry," Lynette said. "I'm afraid Matthew
and I will have to decline."

Ammie ground her teeth. That Lynette could presume
to speak for Matt was annoying enough, but there was
something about the way she said the words *Matthew and
I* that made them sound like a unit, a single entity. "You
have other plans?" Ammie managed.

Lynette blushed. "He's already asked me on a picnic."

Lynette had scored on that one. Ammie knew she
hadn't been able to keep the stricken look from showing
in her eyes.

"I'd invite you along, Amelia," Lynette went on in a

low, purring voice, "but"—she blushed again—"I think Matthew had it in mind for the two of us to be alone."

Ammie slammed her teacup onto the tray so hard, the china rattled. Part of her wanted to run and hide. But another part—the part that still clung stubbornly to a rapidly fraying thread of hope—glared straight into those luminous brown eyes. "You'd better keep those claws sharp, Lynette," she said. "You're going to need 'em. I won't give him up without a fight."

"Oh, Amelia darling, did I say something to upset you? I do apologize. I had no idea your feelings for Matthew were of that nature. When he speaks of you, it's always with such . . . *brotherly* affection."

"And you'd know all about brotherly affection, wouldn't you?" Ammie snapped. "After all, you were in love with Matt's brother. Clint—remember him?"

Lynette blanched but raised her chin defiantly. "I did love Clint. Perhaps that's why I am so drawn to Matthew."

"Matt's as much like Clint as you are like me."

"Be careful, Amelia," Lynette warned, "you have no idea how very much like me you are. A person never knows what they're capable of until they get desperate enough."

Ammie's eyes narrowed, and Lynette looked away. Ammie was certain the woman had just revealed more about herself than she had intended.

"Maybe you were married to Clint," Ammie said softly. "I can almost believe that now. Almost. But somehow I can't believe for a minute that you loved him."

Lynette smoothed away an imaginary wrinkle in her dress. "I think you'd better go."

"You can bat your eyes at Matt and go all fluttery and defenseless. He's got a real soft spot for helpless creatures. But if you do anything to hurt him, you'll answer to me."

"Matt doesn't need any dusty little tomboy making threats in his behalf."

"You mistake me, Lynette. That was no threat. That was a promise."

Lynette refused to meet her eyes. "Please leave. Now."

Ammie stood. "With pleasure. Oh, and thank you so much for the tea. It was very . . . enlightening." With that Ammie stomped from the house.

All the way back to Shamrock, Ammie fumed, replaying her conversation with Lynette over and over in her head. Witty remarks, clever rejoinders, the choicest bits of sarcasm—all came leaping eagerly to mind now. Where had the words been when she was talking to Lynette?

I had no idea your feelings for Matt were of that nature.

The hell she hadn't. Lynette would've had to be blind not to see Ammie's feelings for Matt. The only person still oblivious to those feelings was Matt himself. And Ammie realized now that that was because they knew each other almost too well. They took each other for granted, saw things they expected to see, and overlooked new behaviors until they were all but bludgeoned over the head with them.

She reined over to an oak tree and dismounted, letting Ranger graze for a while. She had to decide what she was going to do about that picnic tomorrow. The thought of Matt and Lynette lying on a blanket together in some secluded meadow made Ammie's blood run hot.

At least she was reasonably certain that Matt and Lynette had not yet made love. If they had, Lynette would have been much more peremptory, dismissive toward her. As it was, Ammie may have unwittingly prodded Lynette into escalating her plans. Damn, she just wished there was some way to find out if Lynette really was hiding something.

In any event, the gauntlet had been thrown down.

There was no going back—she and Lynette were at war. Ammie shook her head. Poor Matt didn't have a clue.

And if all really was fair in love and war, what was to stop her from showing up at the Diamond G tomorrow anyway? Matt could hardly not invite her along on the picnic if she was standing right in front of him, now could he?

And maybe, just maybe, there was no picnic. Maybe Lynette had made the whole thing up.

The next day Ammie again rode into the Diamond G ranch yard, barely past the crack of dawn. She didn't want to take any chances on Matt's being gone this time.

She was surprised when Zak answered the door—although not as surprised as he was to see her. "How did you hear about it already, Amelia?"

"Hear about what?" Ammie asked. A sudden alarm streaked through her as she stepped into the foyer and saw more clearly how haggard Zak looked.

"About the accident."

"What accident?"

"Matt. He's—"

Ammie gasped. "Where is he? What happened?"

"He's upstairs, his old room. The doctor—"

Ammie took the stairs two at a time. She flung open Matt's door without knocking, a half-dozen impressions slamming into her at once. First and foremost, she saw that Matt was alive. He was sitting up in bed, propped against several pillows, his ribs heavily bandaged.

All this she took in in a heartbeat. And then she looked at Lynette. Lynette was sitting on Matt's bed, spoon-feeding him what appeared to be chicken broth.

"What happened?" Ammie managed to choke out.

Matt shifted slightly, the movement causing him to wince. "Mornin', Ammie."

"Do be careful, Matthew," Lynette chided sweetly, placing the broth on the nightstand for the time being.

"The doctor warned you not to do much moving around for at least two or three days."

"What happened?" Ammie repeated tightly, forcing her feet to move, crossing over to the bed. She could hardly bear to see Lynette sitting there, fussing and hovering.

"Pure carelessness," Matt said. "Got too close to a bogged steer just when we got him loose. Knocked me clean to Kansas, I think." There was a strange edge to his voice, and he didn't really look at her when he spoke.

"Why didn't you send someone out to Shamrock? Why didn't you let me know?"

"It just happened yesterday. Besides, it's nothing. Mostly bruises."

"If I'd been hurt, wouldn't you want to know?" she demanded, on the verge of tears.

He flushed slightly. "I'm all right, Ammie. Honest." He still didn't look at her, and Ammie had the sudden awful impression that he wished she weren't there.

"He needs his rest, Amelia," Lynette said, smoothing the bedspread that covered Matt to his waist, her hand brushing intimately past his bare forearm.

Ammie bit the inside of her lip until she tasted blood.

Matt cleared his throat. "I am pretty tired," he said.

Ammie took a step back. He wanted her to leave. He wanted her to go away. This was Lynette's doing—it had to be! "I, uh—I came to invite you to a picnic, Matt. Maybe when you feel better?"

"Lynette told me about the picnic," Matt said. "It sounds good. We could make it a foursome."

"Foursome?"

"You could invite Terence along."

Ammie's heart skipped a beat. Lynette smiled. "Why would you think I'd invite Terence?"

"I, uh, saw the two of you the other night at the dance. You seemed to be enjoying each other's company quite a bit."

Ammie wished the floor would open up and swallow her. But she refused to show her embarrassment. Not in front of Lynette. "It's like you always told me, Matt. *Practice* makes perfect."

Anger flashed in his blue eyes. Anger and something else. "I guess I didn't realize how much can happen in six weeks."

"What's that supposed to mean?"

"Nothing." He shoved a hand through his hair. "I'm sorry. I really am tired, Ammie. I need to get some sleep."

Lynette rose. "I think you should go, Amelia."

"Yeah, I'll just bet you do." Ammie had no idea what was going on, but she suddenly had the feeling she'd stepped very neatly into a velvet-lined trap. "You take care, Matt."

There was an unreadable expression in his blue eyes. "I'll do that." His hand slid over Lynette's. "I've got a great nurse."

"I'll certainly do my very best, Matthew." She leaned forward and kissed him on the cheek.

Somehow Ammie made it out of the house before she burst into tears. God, what a fool she'd been! What a complete and utter fool to think she could compete with a woman like Lynette! The war was over. She let out a bitter laugh. The war had never even begun.

She kept to herself much of the next week. Like a wounded animal, she went into ground to lick her wounds. Her father and Mary saw her pain and tried directing her attention to other things, like helping them get ready for their wedding, which was set to take place the following Saturday at Shamrock. But mostly they left her to herself, acceding to her wishes that she be allowed to be alone.

She spent most of her time at the creek, thinking and crying. Mostly crying, tormented by images of Lynette at Matt's bedside. Lynette in Matt's bed.

* * *

It was a blisteringly hot afternoon when she again headed for the creek, a week since she'd last been to Diamond G. She had no idea if Matt was even up and around yet. And beyond her savage hurt, she was beginning to get angry. How dare he shut her out like this? Whether he was falling in love with Lynette or not, how could he turn his back on their friendship? What the hell was the matter with him, anyway?

Maybe after a swim she could somehow find the courage to go over and ask him. She tied off Ranger, then headed for the creek. But she stopped abruptly when she heard splashing up ahead.

At almost the same instant she saw Drifter, tied to a shrub some fifty feet ahead of her. Her heart thudding, Ammie crept toward the bank of the creek.

She heard more sloshing sounds, the kind of noises a person makes walking into or out of the water. Ammie ducked behind a thick shrub. It was suddenly vitally important to know which direction Matt had been going. Carefully, she threaded her fingers through the branches, soundlessly easing them apart just enough to peer through. She was in time to see a flash of taut, white buttock as Matt waded in from the grassy bank, then eased himself into the deepest part of the creek.

Her throat went dry, her palms, clammy. Now what? Did she scurry back to her horse and ride off? Did she start making a lot of loud arrival noises, so that he would have an opportunity to scurry off himself? Or did she do what her desperate heart was already demanding that she do?

Ammie took a deep breath. What did she have to lose? Giving herself no more time to think, to consider, Ammie stepped out from behind the shrub and strolled, as bold as you please, to the edge of the creek.

His back was to her, and the rippling water and the soft

grasses had combined to mask the sounds of her approach.

"Nice day for a swim, isn't it?" she said, her tone a mix of anger and hurt.

Matt whipped around, his breath snagging. His sudden movement aggravated his apparently still tender, but now unbandaged ribs. "Ammie."

That was all he said. Just her name. And then he looked around, almost wildly, as though he were trying to figure out how best to escape. But he took only one step, then stopped. The water lapped at his navel. In the filtered sunlight of the trees she watched the corded muscles of his neck. He swallowed convulsively, a scarlet stain creeping into his sun-dark face. Ammie wondered if it was a sudden attack of modesty, or if he was embarrassed because he knew, he *knew,* he'd been behaving like an ass toward her lately.

She sat down on the creekbank, feeling the damp grasses soak through her trousers. She paid it no mind. She was suddenly in no hurry for her swim, no hurry at all.

"Lynette with you?" Ammie asked calmly, plucking a foot-long blade of grass from the turf and threading it through her fingers.

"Of course not," he said. "Lynette would hardly—" He stopped, his mouth set in a grim line.

"Lynette would hardly what? Go skinny-dipping? Not proper behavior for a lady, I know. Luckily, that's never stopped me." She tugged off her boots and her socks, then stood up and began to work the buttons of her shirt.

His brows knit nervously. "What are you doing?"

"It's a hot day. In fact, it's been a hot week. I've been coming here every afternoon for a swim." She tugged her shirttail from the waistband of her denims, then slid the shirt from her shoulders, praying to God that he would see her actions as unhurried, nonchalant. In reality, her heart was pounding so hard, she was surprised it hadn't broken a rib. Her nipples seemed to strain against the thin fabric of her chemise. She cleared her throat. "As I recall, that creek is big enough for both of us."

"We're not kids anymore, Ammie."

She pretended to be confused. "You mean it's not big enough?" She unbuttoned her jeans.

Matt swung around, the water swirling in his wake. "Ammie, don't."

Ammie wriggled out of her denims, and her underclothes followed. She stood there—naked, terrified, yet excited. Then she stepped into the water.

He did not turn around. "Ammie, this isn't right."

"Why?"

"There's something I need to tell you, something you don't know." He should tell her, tell her now about Lynette, but he was nearly out of his mind with what it was costing him not to turn around, not to look, see her. It had been all he could do since the night of the dance not to go to her, not to be around her. He was almost glad that damned steer had slammed into him. It gave him the excuse he needed to stay away. He was having erotic dreams on a nightly basis about a woman, a tigress, with flame red hair. The more he tried to stop the dreams, the more intense they became.

Keep her safe, Matt. He was trying. He was trying like hell. She was young and curious, just coming into her own as a woman. She was testing herself with a man she considered safe, a man who was her best friend. His mouth gave a bitter twist. Testing herself—for dear old Terence? "Ammie, this has got to stop! I don't want to hurt you."

"You've already hurt me."

He started to turn but stopped himself just in time. "What are you talking about?"

"You don't see me anymore. You don't talk to me. You're always with Lynette."

He smoothed a hand over his wet hair. "You're—jealous of Lynette?"

"You're damned right I'm jealous!"

"Ammie, my relationship with Lynette isn't going to change my friendship with you. We'll still see each other."

He was patronizing her! Ammie waded close and stopped when she was inches behind his back. She touched his shoulder. He reacted as though she'd used a branding iron on him. He whirled about, then cursed to see that the water reached just below her nipples. Droplets glistened on the coral tips, hard, erect.

"Christ! Ammie, we're not children here. This isn't a game anymore. If you're practicing for Terence—"

She gasped. "Practicing? You think I'm—?" She threaded her arms around his neck. "Tell me if you think I'm practicing." She drew his mouth to hers, her lips soft and yielding, his suddenly hard, demanding.

Ammie's heart soared. He did want her, desire her. He did see her as a woman at last. His sex was hard, rigid, straining against her abdomen.

"Oh, Matt . . . oh, Matt," she moaned. "This is what I've wanted. This. Please . . ." She would tell him. She would tell him now that she loved him. She caught his hand, brought it to her breast.

For an instant he froze, then gripped her arms and set her roughly away from him. His breathing was ragged, his voice hoarse. "I can't do this. We can't do this. Christ, what's happening?"

"Matt, it's all right." She would tell him, and he would know it really was all right. "I—"

"No!" His voice was savage. "You don't understand, Ammie. This isn't all right at all. I've asked Lynette to marry me."

☘/Chapter 14

Ammie stared at Matt. Her heart seemed suddenly to have stopped beating inside her chest. "What did you say?"

"I said I've asked Lynette to marry me."

Ammie backed up several steps in the water, her arms now wrapped instinctively about her breasts. "When . . . when did you do that?"

"This morning. We were—"

"I don't want to hear it," she rasped, fighting down a wave of hysteria. "I don't want to hear anything about it." She spun around, dropping to her knees on the muddy creek bottom.

"Ammie . . ."

"You kissed me, you kissed me like you meant it."

"I'm sorry, Ammie. I'm so damned sorry. I had no right. Forgive me." He drove a hand through his wet, tangled hair. "You're a beautiful woman, Ammie. You're all grown up. We can't play these kinds of games anymore."

She nodded, desperate to salvage some small measure of her pride. "No, no games. You're right. It shouldn't have happened. Now—now please, go away, Matt."

"I'm not going to leave you like this." He slogged up beside her, kneeling down in the water. "Ammie, please." His voice shook. "I never meant to hurt you." He curled a tendril of red hair back away from her face. "I love you, Ammie. I always will. Nothing's going to change that."

There it was, just as she had feared. Pity. Kindness.

Understanding. Even love. But not the kind of love born of passion and fire. Tears trailed down her cheeks, and she swiped them angrily away. "I'll be all right. I'll be fine. You go on back to Lynette."

"She needs me, Ammie. She really does."

Ammie winced inwardly. *And I don't? Oh, Matt, what am I going to do without you in my life?* Her heart was breaking, shattering into a million irreparable pieces. She would never be whole again. But she loved him too much to let him see that. She loved him too much to let him know he had just destroyed her.

Taking a deep, shuddering breath, she twisted around, sitting on her rump on the creek bottom. She kept her arms firmly folded in front of her chest, even though the water was nearly above her shoulders. "It's a good thing you're my best friend. I wouldn't want to make such a fool of myself in front of just anybody."

"You're not a fool," he said gently.

Don't be nice, don't be nice. She couldn't bear it. "I don't know what's the matter with me lately. I've been acting like a real goose."

He sat beside her. "I'm sorry, Ammie."

"For what?" *For not being in love with me?*

"For not seeing what you've been going through. For being so wrapped up in my own life that I didn't see how things were changing for you too." He frowned slightly. "Though maybe it would have been nice if you'd just come straight out and told me about you and Terence."

"Me and Terence? What about—?"

"I'm happy for you, Ammie. I really am."

Ammie rubbed her face with her hands. "Matt, Terence and I are not—" Oh, what did it matter? He was going to marry Lynette. "Why did you come here today? Why not one of the creeks on the Diamond G?"

"Actually, I was on my way over to Shamrock to see you. I wanted to tell you about Lynette and me." He gave

her a crooked smile. "And it was kind of like I was drawn
here. Maybe because this place is so special to me. You
and I have a lot of memories tied up in this creek. I guess
I wanted to see if it felt any different when I came here as
a man engaged to be married."

"You really love her then?" How could she talk? How
could she carry on a conversation with this man when she
was dying a piece at a time inside?

"I care about her very much," he said. "She's so alone,
Ammie. With Clint dead she has nobody. She needs
someone to take care of her."

"And you volunteered."

He smiled. "Gladly."

"When's"—she knotted her fists beneath the water's
surface—"when's the wedding?"

"If Lynette had her way, it'd be tomorrow." He looked
a little abashed. "I guess I'm pretty irresistible."

"Yeah," Ammie said softly, "I guess you are."

"Anyway, we're going to wait until after Shamus and
Mary get married. We don't want to steal their thunder.
Besides, I have to take Lynette back to Austin. She'll need
to bring the rest of her things here."

"Sounds like you've talked it all out."

"I—uh, I need to ask you a big favor, though."

"What's that?"

"Well, since Lynette and I are engaged, it wouldn't be
right if she stayed on at the Diamond G. I don't want her
to stay with strangers either. Anyway, I was wondering if
—if she could stay at Shamrock."

"Sure. Why not? And then when you come over to visit
her, I can be your chaperon."

He wasn't quite sure if he was supposed to find that
amusing or not. "Are you sure you're all right, Ammie?"

"I'm fine. You bring Lynette by this evening. We'll get
her settled in right away."

"Thanks." He started to lever himself up, but then he

must have remembered his state of undress. He sank back down. "How are we going to do this?"

"You go ahead," she said. "I won't look. I promise."

He leaned close and kissed her on the forehead. "You'll always be my best girl." With that, he rose and sloshed out of the water.

Ammie did not look up. She listened to him get dressed and felt him stand there for a few minutes as though searching for the right words, words that would make her hurt go away. But there weren't any such words. Finally, he mounted and rode out.

Only then did Ammie let the tears come.

Matt reined Drifter in at the grove of oaks that shrouded the graves of his mother and brother and dismounted. He needed to think. He needed to be alone. And yet in a curious way he didn't want to be alone.

He ground-tied the horse, letting him graze on the lush grasses, then dragged his hat from his head and walked toward the two stone crosses. The tread of his boot was muffled by the grass, and as always he was aware of the stillness of this place. The only real sound was the gentle rustling of the leaves overhead.

He reached the stone crosses and hunkered down between them. A sense of almost overwhelming loss rippled through him, and he had to fight it down. This was not why he'd come here.

He cleared his throat, twisting his hat brim in his hands. "I, uh—I came to tell you something, Clint." He smiled slightly. "But maybe you already know. It's, uh— it's about Lynette and me. I'm going to marry her. I'm going to take good care of her for you."

He took a deep breath. "It all happened kind of sudden, I know. But I think it's right. I think I'm doing what —what you'd want me to do. She's quite a lady. Even Pa thinks she's special."

He plucked at some stray twigs caught in the grasses atop the grave. "You shouldn't have worried so much about Pa's reaction to her, Clint. You shouldn't have worried."

He sat there, remembering the morning's events, not quite certain he had yet absorbed them all himself.

He'd been standing in his bedroom, still feeling odd about being back in his old room after spending so many years in the bunkhouse. He'd just finished freeing himself from the bandages encasing his ribs, when he'd caught the sounds of a rider coming in.

He crossed to the window and looked out. His brow furrowed. Haggerty. Now what would the sheriff be wanting so early in the morning? Matt grabbed his boots. He would finish dressing and find out. His father and Lynette were downstairs—one of them could answer the door.

Matt sat on his bed and leaned over to pull on his boots, aggravating his still-smarting ribs. He held his breath and got them on, then stood. All he needed was his shirt.

A knock sounded on the door to his bedroom.

"Matthew?" Lynette called. "May I come in?"

"Just a minute. I'm not quite—"

The door swung inward. Lynette swept in, looking slightly flushed but as lovely as ever. Matt smiled. "Good morning." He held his shirt in front of him, self-conscious all at once.

"The sheriff is here to see your father," Lynette said, oblivious to his discomfort. Her voice seemed just a little rushed, as though she were out of breath. Had she run up the stairs just to tell him of Haggerty's arrival?

"Saw him out the window."

Lynette paced over to him, her hands twisting together in front of her. "You're looking much better, Matthew. How are you feeling?"

"Almost good as new." Actually, he was feeling as awkward as hell, standing there shrugging into his shirt. His bed wasn't made, and somehow Lynette's being in his bedroom didn't seem right now that he was no longer a patient.

"I'd better go down and see what Haggerty wants," Matt said.

"Could I—could we talk a minute first?"

Matt frowned, only now seeing that Lynette was pensive and upset. "What is it? What's wrong?"

Tears rimmed her brown eyes. "I don't know what to do, Matthew. I'm just so confused."

"Here. Sit down." He led her to a bench seat at the foot of his bed. "Does this have something to do with Haggerty?"

Her eyes widened. "Of course not. Why would you think that?"

"No reason," he assured her. "It's just that he's here, and you're—" He hunkered down beside her. "So what is it then? Tell me."

"Oh, Matthew, I've been keeping this inside me for too long now. I'm—I'm so ashamed. Maybe I should just go back to Austin. I—"

He caught her hand. "Go back to Austin? Lynette, what's this all about?"

"I—I just keep remembering how I told you at the dance last week that I . . . thought I was falling in love with you. That was so bold of me, so terribly improper. I should never have said such a thing."

"It's all right, Lynette. You know I care about you too."

"But—but it's been a week, Matthew, and you haven't really said anything more about it. I—I just thought that maybe, maybe it would be best if I leave, since obviously your feelings aren't the same."

"No. No, I don't want you to leave."

"You don't?"

"Of course not. I have feelings for you too. I'm just

trying to sort through them all. This has been real hard for me. Somehow it's all mixed up with Clint. I don't know." He raked a hand through his hair. "I don't mean to upset you, to keep you waiting."

"But this isn't seemly," she sniffled. "I can't be here, not feeling this way. Look at me—I'm in your bedroom. And you haven't even finished dressing. Oh, what you must think of me!"

Matt quickly finished working the buttons of his shirt. "I think you're a beautiful woman."

Tears slid from her eyes. She reached toward him, cupping his face in her hands. Her skin was soft, so very soft against his beard-stubbled cheeks. He turned his face and kissed her palm. "Don't cry, Lynette. How can I make you not cry?"

She swiped at her eyes. "I—I suppose this wouldn't all seem so improper if—if we were, say, more open about our feelings. Like, if you were courting me, maybe, or something."

He smiled gently. "No, then I suppose it would be all right."

"What?" she asked, seeming confused.

"It wouldn't seem so improper if I were courting you."

Lynette's whole face lit up. With a happy cry she flung her arms around his neck. "Oh, Matthew, Matthew, you've made me so happy!"

His eyes widened. Oh, God. What was going on here? "Lynette, I—wait." He caught her arms. "I didn't mean—"

But she wasn't listening. "Oh, Matthew, I *do* love you. I'd be honored to marry you."

Marry? Matt dragged in a deep gulp of air. How had he . . . ? What had he done? He looked into Lynette's face, her eyes shining, her smile bedazzling.

"You've made me the happiest woman in the world, Matthew! You won't regret this, I promise."

He stood, his knees suddenly seeming a little wobbly. Married?

"I think Clint would have wanted it this way, don't you? And I'm certain Zachary is going to be so happy."

Matt's thoughts were jumbling together so quickly, he was having a hard time keeping them all straight. He had been trying to calm Lynette, to get her to stop crying. The subject of courting had come up, and then . . . ? Then what? How had it gotten to this?

Matt was still reeling, still in a state of shock. He could barely concentrate as Lynette went on and on about a wedding date, plans, whom to invite. But each time she paused, each time he had a chance to jump in, to try somehow to tell her that he hadn't quite meant what she thought he'd meant, he couldn't find the words. He'd never seen her look so happy. And her joy touched him, made him feel good.

What the hell? Hadn't he been thinking of settling down lately? And he did want to do right by Clint. His father was clearly enchanted by Lynette. Maybe it was a perfect solution.

Ammie.

Her name was like a splash of cold water, but he shook it off, vaguely irritated. His marrying Lynette would be better for Ammie too. It would end these fantasies he'd been having about her. Besides, Ammie would be getting settled down herself soon. All too clearly he recalled the embrace she'd shared with Terence. Ammie would never have allowed Kessler such liberties if she hadn't invited them, welcomed them. Obviously, Ammie didn't need any more practice.

"Matthew? Matthew, what is it?"

Matt shook himself and looked down into Lynette's suddenly pale features. "What?"

"You looked so—so angry. I thought maybe—maybe you weren't sure."

"No. No, I'm fine." If Ammie wanted that bland, obse-
quious little storekeeper, who was he to object? It was
certainly none of his business. He pulled Lynette against
him and kissed her thoroughly, ruthlessly.

When he released her, he was breathing hard and so
was she. Her lips were parted slightly and just a little
swollen. Her eyes were wide, glittering with a mix of
wonder and passion.

"Maybe we don't need to go down and see the sheriff
right away. Maybe"—she glanced toward the bed—
"maybe we could wait just a few minutes."

Matt's pulses thrummed harder, hotter. He wanted
nothing more than to throw Lynette onto that bed and
ease the fearsome demands of his body. But he knew he'd
be doing it for all the wrong reasons. "We'll wait," he said
hoarsely. "I wouldn't want to rush our first time together.
We'll wait."

That seemed to satisfy her. She smiled sweetly. "Then
let's go down and tell Zachary the good news."

They found Zak Grayson in the study talking to Haggerty.

"Glad you two are here," Zak said. "Come in."

"Lynette and I have some news for you, Pa," Matt said.
"The sheriff has some news for all of us."

Lynette's hold on Matt's hand tightened slightly. She
was probably a little nervous about all this. Matt's own
nerves were on edge. His whole body still felt bowstring
tight. What he needed was a quick dip in a cold stream.

"The first thing I'm going to do," Zak said, "is admit
here and now that I had some early doubts about you,
Lynette."

Matt stiffened. "I thought we'd been through all this,
Pa."

"It's all right," Lynette said softly. "I understand perfectly. A man in your father's position can't be too careful."

"I'm glad you understand, Lynette," Zak said. "I didn't like doing it, but it had to be done."

"Didn't like doing what?" Matt demanded.

"I had Sheriff Haggerty do a little checking into Lynette's past. I wanted to make sure everything was as she'd told us."

Matt looked at Haggerty. "So you're here to make your report?"

"Already have."

Lynette paled slightly. It had to be damned stressful for her to have someone poking around into her past.

"And everything Lynette said was true, wasn't it?" Matt prodded, still angry.

"As a matter of fact," Zak said, "it was. In fact, so true that it breaks my heart. It seems Lynette's father would probably never have served time if he'd had a decent lawyer. I wish to God Clint had come to me about all this."

"He was going to, Zachary. I promise you, he was. If my father hadn't been so ill—"

"I understand. It's all right. There's nothing that can be done about it now. Forgive me—I just had to know."

"Of course."

"So you're finished with your investigation?" Matt asked Haggerty.

"It would seem so," the sheriff said, although the man's tone gave Matt the vague impression that maybe he wasn't finished at all. But it was obvious his father was satisfied. And as far as Matt was concerned, that was all that mattered.

"Now, what was it you two were going to tell me?" Zak asked.

Matt looked his father in the eye. "Lynette and I are going to be married."

His father astonished him by grinning broadly, then came over to thump him on the back. "Wonderful, Matt.

Wonderful news!" He gave Lynette a paternal peck on the cheek.

"I know it's been only a short time, Zachary," Lynette said. "But—"

"Nonsense. I only knew Emily for three hours before I knew I was going to make her my bride. And somehow—somehow this is like having a little part of Clint back." Again he clapped Matt on the shoulder. "I'm real pleased for you, son. Real pleased."

Matt kept a smile on his face, but some of the joy had gone out of the moment. Couldn't his father have been pleased just for him? Did he have to bring Clint into it? Then Matt kicked himself for being selfish. Lynette had been married to Clint. It was natural for his father to make reference to it.

"I think I'm going to ride over to Shamrock," Matt said. "Tell Ammie the news."

"Maybe we should do that together, Matthew," Lynette said.

Matt hesitated for only a second. "I think it would be best if I told Ammie myself." He wasn't quite sure why that was so, but he knew he was right.

"I think you should ask Ammie if Lynette could stay at Shamrock for a while," Zak said.

"Why, Zachary," Lynette said, "whatever for?"

"Now that you're engaged my son, my dear, I don't think it would be proper for you both to be staying in the same house."

Lynette blushed. "You're right, of course. But I wouldn't want to impose on Amelia . . ."

"Ammie won't mind," Matt said. "I'm sure she'd love to have you."

"I'm sure."

"Then it's settled," Matt said. "I'll ride over there now, then come by later to get you."

He gave her a quick kiss on the cheek, but she caught

his hand, her grip surprisingly strong. "I love you, Matthew. Remember that."

He wondered at the worry lines on her brow, but dismissed them to the events of the day. He kissed her hand, then headed out the door.

From there he'd gone to the creek and had his all-too-intimate encounter with Ammie. Matt trembled slightly, plucking at more twigs on Clint's grave. The lust he felt for Ammie was becoming almost unmanageable. After he dropped Lynette off at Shamrock, he would have to make every effort to stay clear of Ammie for a while. He never should have allowed those foolish sessions of practice kissing to get started in the first place. Ammie always was a quick study at anything she tried. It was like playing with high explosives and holding a lighted match.

Well, there would be no more practicing—of that he was certain.

He tossed his collection of twigs several feet away and climbed to his feet. "I'll take good care of Lynette, Clint," he said. "I promise. I'll make her a good husband. You'll see."

Do you love her?

Matt started. Where had that question come from? Then he remembered. It had come from Ammie at the creek.

His gaze trailed to his mother's grave, and he had a sudden overwhelming sense of sadness. But it wasn't the kind of sadness that came from missing his mother. It was almost as if the sadness were coming *from* his mother.

He was being ridiculous. He had come here for a measure of peace. But he was tired, and his ribs ached. He should head home. He needed to take Lynette over to Shamrock.

Do you love her?

"Of course I love her," he snapped aloud. "And I'm going to marry her. I love Ammie, and I always—" He stopped. What the hell had he just said? He cursed. "Not Ammie, Lynette. I love *Lynette*." He'd just been thinking of Ammie, that was all. Damn.

He jammed his hat back on his head and stomped toward his horse. It was time to head home. He gathered up Drifter's reins and mounted. But even the breeze seemed to carry the question.

Do you love her?

🍀/Chapter 15

Ammie sat on a straight-back chair, staring forlornly out her bedroom window. Matt would be here soon. No, she corrected herself. Matt would be here soon with his fiancée.

"I do wish you'd come down and have a little supper," Mary said from where she stood in the doorway. "You should try to eat something."

"I'm not hungry."

Mary came over to the window. "Oh, Amelia, why on earth did you tell him it would be all right to bring her here?"

A tear slid down Ammie's cheek. The wetness surprised her. She had been certain there couldn't be a tear left in her body. She had shed them all this afternoon at the creek. "Matt asked me for a favor. I guess I've never been able to refuse him anything—not even something as painful as this. Who knows? Maybe Lynette and I will become great chums."

"I can't believe they're actually going to get married."

"Please, Mary, we went through all this when I got home."

"But it doesn't make any sense. Matt always favored the girls with a little spunk in them." Mary gave Ammie a tender smile. "The kind that wouldn't be scared silly when she found a snake in her boot."

"I guess his taste has gotten more refined."

"It isn't that."

"Well, whatever it is, it doesn't matter. They're going to be husband and wife."

"They're not married yet."

The sounds of a buggy arriving in the ranch yard below drew Ammie's attention back to the window. She peered out, but quickly looked away. Even watching Matt lift Lynette from the carriage would be painful.

"He'll expect you downstairs," Mary said.

"I know. I'm coming." She took a deep breath.

"What if you told him?" Mary asked. "What if you told Matt you loved him?"

Ammie felt her face begin to dissolve again, and she had to work hard to prevent another flood of tears. "No," she said. "Under no circumstances can Matt ever know that. Not now. He's made his choice. Don't you see, Mary, if he knew how I felt, it would make everything so awkward. Matt wouldn't want to hurt me. And yet he would start to feel uncomfortable around me, and then pretty soon he wouldn't be there at all."

"But maybe, if you told him, he—" Mary stopped, apparently thinking better of whatever she'd been about to say. She wiped at her own tears. "I guess we'd best go down, child."

Ammie paused in front of her mirror, cringing to see how red and puffy her face looked. "He's going to know I've been crying all afternoon."

Mary bustled over to Ammie's washstand and dipped the end of a towel into the water pitcher, then came over to dab gently at Ammie's face. "You look fine. We'll tell him you've been dicing onions."

Ammie managed a watery laugh.

Shamus had already shown Matt and Lynette to the drawing room by the time Mary and Ammie arrived downstairs. Ammie clasped her hands together in front of her, twining her fingers so tightly her knuckles whitened. "Hello, Matt, Lynette."

Matt was sitting at the piano toying with a few stray notes, arranging them to his liking. He glanced up at Ammie, his expression unreadable, then quickly returned his attention to the keys. Ammie knew he was remembering this afternoon.

Lynette was smiling serenely, standing behind him. Nothing in her manner suggested that her last meeting with Amelia had been anything less than congenial. "Amelia, darling, I can't tell you how grateful I am that you're allowing me to stay here with you. Now that Matt and I are going to be married"—she touched Matt's shoulder, the gesture intimate, proprietary, and for Ammie excruciatingly painful—"it certainly wouldn't be appropriate for me to stay under the same roof with him night after night, now would it?"

"It certainly wouldn't," Ammie agreed in her sweetest voice. "We wouldn't want Matt's reputation to be compromised."

Matt chuckled, taking her words as a joke. Lynette tittered politely, but Ammie didn't miss seeing the corners of her mouth tighten. Ammie gave herself a mental pat on the back.

Ammie stepped farther into the room and was surprised when a gaunt figure rose from the chair in the far corner. Zak.

"Good evening to you, Amelia," Zak said.

She nodded. "Mr. Grayson." Even after all these years, Ammie had never felt comfortable addressing him as anything else.

"I too would like to thank you and your father for opening your home to Lynette."

"It's such a pleasure," Ammie lied.

Shamus gave an exaggerated cough.

Ammie grimaced. She supposed she was being a little transparent.

To Lynette Zak said, "Remember, if you need anything

at all, just send one of the Shamrock hands over, and either Matt or I will take care of it. All right?"

"Yes, Zachary, I promise. Now please, stop fussing."

Ammie was struck speechless. This couldn't be Zak Grayson, fretting, deferring. Matt had been charmed by the lovely brunette, as Ammie knew only too well, even driven by a measure of guilt about Clint. But Zak had never seemed a man to be swayed by a pretty face, and while naturally grief-stricken about Clint, he'd never even remotely felt any guilt over his death.

Ammie watched in astonishment as Zak continued to speak to Lynette with what appeared to be genuine affection in his leather-lined face. Even the notorious father-son feud seemed remarkably absent in Lynette's presence. Lynette moved with ease between the two Grayson men, chatting, flattering, and diverting. If this was how things had been at the Diamond G for the past two weeks, then Ammie could see even more clearly how Lynette would be like a magnet to Matt, an enchantress who brought peace to his tempestuous relationship with his father.

"Well, everyone just sit and make yourselves at home," Mary said cheerily. "You, too, Amelia. I'll go into the kitchen and get us all some coffee and cake." To Lynette, she said, "Of course, I'll make tea for you, dear."

"Thank you, Mrs. Denby."

"My pleasure."

Ammie smiled grimly. She'd hidden the mint earlier that afternoon.

She was grateful to Mary for not asking for her help in the kitchen. Mary knew how much Ammie wanted to stay near Matt. After a few minutes, though, she decided she might be better off in the kitchen. That way she wouldn't have to witness Lynette's continual fawning over Matt. Anything he said, she agreed with. At one point Ammie actually heard him joke that women should never get the vote because they'd probably cast their ballots for the most handsome candidate. It was an argument that Clint had honestly believed. Ammie had nearly taken Clint's head off for it, and Matt had agreed with her. Now Lynette was giggling and telling Matt he was right! And Matt did not take the comment back.

Seething, Ammie shifted her attention to her father and Zak. If she didn't, she was going to be sick.

"Just be sure you're at the wedding Saturday," Shamus was saying as he lit up a cheroot.

"Wouldn't miss it," Zak said.

Shamus's green eyes grew serious. "It's been too long, Zak. We used to get together at least once a month."

Zak looked away. "It's been hard since Clint died, Shamus. Real hard. I had a lot of dreams for that boy."

Shamus put a hand on Zak's shoulder. "Maybe you need some new dreams, old friend."

"Maybe." Zak cast a glance at Lynette. "And maybe those dreams are starting."

Lynette looked up and smiled a smile that could light up a room. "Thank you, Zachary."

"You and Matt have made me very happy, Lynette. You've given me a new chance to see grandchildren growing up on the Diamond G."

Lynette's smile froze only a little, but enough that Ammie noticed it. And then Lynette was tittering and blushing prettily again. Ammie decided the woman had just had the good grace to be embarrassed.

Matt squeezed Lynette's hand. "Don't worry, Pa. We'll get started on that right away."

Ammie leaped to her feet. "I think I'll go see if Mary needs any help in the kitchen." She fled the room, but instead of heading for the kitchen, she bolted out the front door. She needed some air—fast. The idea of Lynette bearing Matt children brought new agony to an already gaping wound.

She stayed outside, checking on Tulip and Pickles. When she ran out of things to do, she invented new things. She knew she should go back to the house, but she couldn't face it, couldn't bear it. She stood beside the corral, listening to a hauntingly beautiful tune Matt played on the piano, then sank to the ground and cried when the music was accompanied in perfect harmony by the sweet, clear voice of Lynette Simmons.

How long was it going to hurt like this? How long would it be until seeing Matt and Lynette together would be only a minor ache instead of this crushing torture?

Ammie managed a humorless laugh. Only forever.

Muttering a curse, she swiped the tears from her eyes. She'd best start getting used to it. She couldn't sit around sobbing the rest of her life. She realized now that she'd been clinging to some last thread of hope; hope that something in Lynette's story would be amiss and her whole claim would unravel, collapse. But it was obvious now that Ammie's own desperation had made her read things into Lynette's behavior that weren't really there. Otherwise, there was no good reason for her to still feel even now that there was something, *something*, the woman was hiding.

No. It was time to face the truth. Matt was going to marry Lynette. Ammie squeezed her eyes shut to prevent more tears. Matt loved Lynette. Ammie was just going to have to learn to accept that. And precisely because she loved Matt, she vowed she was going to try hard to do just that. Taking several deep breaths, she steeled herself to go back into the house. It was time to start learning to live with the pain.

She headed across the ranch yard, then paused when the front door opened and light spilled out onto the porch. Matt and Zak were evidently preparing to leave. Ammie met up with Matt at the bottom of the porch steps.

"How's Tulip?" Matt asked. The look in his eyes suggested that what he really wanted to know was where she'd been half the night.

"Foal's due anyday now."

He turned to glance behind him, then leaned close to Ammie, his voice a whisper. "Make sure Lynette doesn't get near the barn when Tulip's in foal, all right?" he said. "It might be too . . . intense for her."

"I know," Ammie said, too miserable even to conjure any sarcasm. "She's delicate. Don't worry, Matt. I'll take good care of your intended."

"I know you will. Thanks, Am." His eyes were serious, and he seemed to want to say something else—perhaps about the creek—but just then Lynette moved out onto the porch with Shamus and Mary.

Matt took Lynette's hand. "You get all the rest you can, all right? Don't tire yourself."

"I won't, darling. You mustn't worry."

Ammie's jaw clenched. Did Matt have any idea what he was doing? At this rate, Lynette would be bed-ridden, expecting to be waited on hand and foot. The woman might be petite, but there was nothing infirm about her. Ammie couldn't believe how thoroughly Lynette had him hoodwinked. That woman was as delicate as cowhide.

Matt led Lynette several steps away from everyone else into the deep shadows beside the house so that he could wish her a lover's good night. Ammie dug her nails into her palms. She wasn't doing very well with her new vow of acceptance.

Mary and Shamus kept up a steady stream of conversation with Zak and tried hard to include Ammie. But Ammie knew they were only trying to take her mind off what was happening in the shadows.

"Oh, Matthew," Lynette cooed, walking back with him to the buggy a few minutes later, "I'm going to miss you so." She hesitated, but only briefly. "Matthew, I hate to

ask, but if you could bring by two of my parasols, I would
be ever so grateful. The peach and the lavender."

"I have to ride in to River Oaks tomorrow, but I'll have
one of the hands bring them by first thing in the morning."

Ammie's vow of acceptance crumbled just a little.

"And my bath salts. Silly me, I forgot my bath salts. The
jasmine and the hyacinth."

"He'll bring those too."

Ammie's vow crumbled a little more.

"Oh, Amelia dear," Lynette said, her arm firmly en-
twined with Matt's, "if you would be so gracious as to
draw me a bath?"

"Now? It's practically midnight."

"I can hardly sleep if I feel all dusty from the ride over
here."

"You don't look dusty to me." Although that could be
changed in a hurry, Ammie thought acidly.

"Please?" Matt put in. "I'd consider it a favor."

Ammie's vow disintegrated, vanished in a haze of fury
and disgust. She wasn't certain which of them infuriated
and disgusted her more—Lynette or Matt. Lynette—that
she could behave in a simpering, helpless manner that
was an insult to hard-working women everywhere. And
Matt—that he could be so taken in by her!

What hurt the most was that Ammie was all but certain
that Lynette didn't love Matt. Not once had Ammie ever
seen love in Lynette's brown eyes. Dependence, yes.
Even a certain measure of wistfulness. But not love.

"I'll see what I can do about the bath," Ammie muttered as Matt gave Lynette a chaste kiss on the cheek,
then climbed into the buggy with his father.

Everyone wished one another good night, and then the
Graysons headed for home. Shamus went off to his bedroom, Mary to the guest bedroom. Ammie was the lucky
one, chosen to share her bedroom with Lynette.

Upstairs under the soft glow of a hurricane lamp, Ammie pulled on her nightshirt, then arranged a pallet on the floor of her room. She would share a bedroom with Lynette, but not a bed. "Are you sure you want that bath, Lynette?" she inquired with no real interest whatsoever.

"I really would appreciate it, but"—she sighed—"if it's too much trouble . . ."

"Oh, it isn't that," Ammie assured her. "I was just thinking. By the time we heated the water and carried it up to the tub, you likely wouldn't get to sleep before three in the morning. I'm just wondering how attractive Matt would find big, puffy black circles under bloodshot brown eyes."

Fearfully Lynette touched her hand to her face as though even the mention of puffy black circles could make them pop out. "Well, maybe you're right. Matt does want me to get my rest." She turned down the fresh linen on Ammie's bed. "I do hate to put you out like this, Amelia."

"You mean you'd sleep on the floor?"

"Oh, well now, I—"

"Never mind," Ammie said. "You're the guest. You get the bed. I insist. Matt told me to take good care of you."

"He's such a darling, isn't he?"

"A real darling." A blind, totally obtuse darling, but a darling nonetheless.

Ammie lay awake long minutes later, staring at the ceiling. How would Miss Delicate react, she wondered, to a taste of what ranch life was really like? Of the kind of life Lynette would one day be expected to live if Matt ever came to his senses?

The barest hint of a smile teased the edges of Ammie's mouth as an idea came to her—a thoroughly wicked idea. *Enjoy the bed, Lynette,* it's going to be the last bit of creature comfort you'll get for quite a while. Ammie closed her eyes. She needed to sleep. She was suddenly looking forward to tomorrow.

It was the crack of dawn when Ammie stood over a peacefully sleeping Lynette with an iron skillet and a heavy wooden spoon and began to play her own version of reveille. Lynette awoke, sputtering with outrage.

"What do you think you're doing, Amelia?" the brunette demanded, peering with disbelief toward the still-gray light beyond the windows.

"I've made a decision, Lynette. You'll be proud of me." Ammie's voice was just loud enough that Lynette winced with each word. "I'm going to help you be a better wife to Matt—excuse me, *Matthew*. Now I realize you've had some trouble telling the Grayson men apart, but I can promise you it was Clint who would have wound up living in a fancy mansion in Austin, not Matt. Matt's not a city boy—he's all cowboy. If you intend to be married to Matt, you're going to need to know how to be a proper rancher's wife."

Lynette pulled her covers up to her neck. "I don't have to know any such thing! I'm sure Matthew will consider my feelings when we discuss where we'll live after we're married. He knows I'm very—"

"Don't say it," Ammie snapped. "You're about as delicate as this skillet." She smacked it again for emphasis. "You may have Matt bamboozled with that helpless act, but it isn't going to work on me. No woman could come to River Oaks by herself and present herself to a family as powerful as the Graysons without some kind of backbone holding up her *fragile* body. So get off your hind end, get on these britches"—Ammie flung a pair at her—"and get downstairs. Now."

"And if I refuse?"

"Then maybe I'll just let it slip to Matt that you despise ranches and everything on them."

"And maybe I'll tell him you're in love with him and you would do or say anything to discredit me."

Ammie was quiet for a minute. "You do that," she said at last. "You tell Matt I'm in love with him. It's the only thing I don't have the guts to tell him myself. And it's at times like this that I know I'm going to live to regret it. You don't deserve one hair on his head. In fact, you make me sick. And I don't care what Sheriff Haggerty found out in Austin, I still say something about this whole story of yours stinks. You've just spread too much jasmine over it for anyone to smell it. But so help me God, if I ever get even a hint of what it is—"

"You're crazy! You're out of your mind jealous."

"You got that right, Lynette, and you better not forget it. I told you once, if you ever hurt him, you'll answer to me. Now I'll take it a step farther—you hurt him, and I'll spend the rest of my life digging up every minute of your past until I find out what it is you're lying about. And then I'll have it printed in every newspaper in Texas."

"There's nothing to find out! You heard Zachary. He had the sheriff check. How dare you!" But there was a flicker of fear in Lynette's brown eyes.

"How dare I? I'm crazy, remember? I'm crazy in love with Matt. I'm so in love with him, that if you really are what he wants, then I won't get in your way. But you're going to have to prove you're good enough for him—not to him, but to me!" Her voice shook. "Do you know what makes him laugh, Lynette? What makes him cry? What hurts him? Do you even know what his favorite meal is?"

Lynette turned away. "No," she said softly, "but I have a lifetime to learn, don't I?"

That one hurt. That one hurt like hell. "Maybe. And maybe not. Get downstairs. We've got work to do."

From sunup to sundown Ammie worked Lynette—teaching her to feed chickens, clean chickens, groom horses, feed horses, shoe horses, muck out stalls, and har-

ness a team. If the work was even remotely backbreaking
or filthy, Ammie had Lynette doing it. And if she wasn't
satisfied with the way Lynette did the job the first time,
she had her do it again.

What astonished Ammie even more than how well
Lynette did many of the chores foisted on her, was the
fact that she did them at all. Ammie had fully expected
her to run screaming into the house before nine in the
morning, refusing to lift another finger. But though she
complained bitterly and often, Lynette continued to do
the work. Either she really was that desperate, or she had
more of a backbone than Ammie had wanted to give her
credit for.

Even so, Ammie took fiendish delight in every smudge
of dirt she saw on Lynette's perfect face, every new blister
on her lily-white fingers, every splotch of manure on her
boots. Shamus and Mary were too busy getting things
ready for the wedding to take much note of Ammie's
scheme, and Matt stayed thankfully absent.

Matt must have been Lynette's hole card. She kept
looking toward the road, expecting him to come courting
and thereby rescue her from Ammie's vile clutches. But
he did not.

Lynette was forced to endure day one of being a ranch
hand, then day two. Day three was a Friday, the day before the wedding. Shamus and Mary had gone to town to
do some shopping. The hands were out on the range.
Today would be Ammie's last chance to make Lynette see
this was not the life she wanted to live. If Matt didn't
come by for supper tonight, he would definitely be here
for the wedding tomorrow. Once Lynette complained
about Ammie's treatment of her, he would probably put
her up at a hotel in town. If Lynette was going to break, it
had to be today.

But it was already past noon, and Lynette was showing
no signs of giving in. This even though she and Ammie

were standing in two inches of matted straw and manure, after a morning of cleaning out the barn. Lynette leaned on the rake she was holding and mopped the sweat from her brow with her shirtsleeve.

"Keep going," Ammie said. "We've got another hour out here, then I want to start on the house. We're having a lot of guests in tomorrow for the wedding, and I want this place spotless."

"This isn't going to work, you know."

"What?" Ammie asked innocently.

"You're not going to beat me, Amelia. I won't quit. I won't give in. Matthew asked me to marry him, and I intend to do just that."

Ammie threw down her rake. "Just give me one answer, Lynette. Why?"

"That's my business."

"You don't even pretend to love him, do you?"

"There are different kinds of love."

"I don't believe you. I don't believe you have *any* kind of love for Matt."

"And I don't care what you believe."

Ammie sagged onto a crate. "I wish he could see you like this."

Lynette flinched, looking down at her grubby attire.

"I don't mean the pants and the boots and the sweat, but just the way you are—so cold and calculating. You turn it on and off like a switch."

"You learn to play the hand life deals you."

Ammie frowned. That was an odd phrase coming from Lady Lynette. But then Ammie supposed standing in manure could do that to a person. "Wouldn't getting a settlement for being Clint's widow be enough for you? Why do you want Matt?"

Lynette raked at the straw at her feet. "What you keep conveniently forgetting, Amelia, is that it isn't just me who wants Matt—it's Matt who wants me."

"He feels sorry for you."

Her brown eyes glittered. "That wasn't sympathy he was giving me the other night before he went home. Matthew is a very passionate man, very . . . physical."

"You do it on purpose, don't you? You enjoy hurting people. Damn you, I love him. I—" Ammie clenched her teeth together so hard, her jaw ached, but she refused to cry in front of this woman. "Was it all a lie with Clint too?"

Lynette turned away, but not before Ammie saw a brief flash of real pain in her eyes. "What I had with Clint I'll never have with another man. He was the kindest, most sensitive man I've ever known."

"Then how can you—?"

A rider galloped into the yard, interrupting. Ammie recognized him—he often rode a circuit of ranches, delivering mail. He handed a letter to Lynette. "Come for you in town, Miss Simmons."

Lynette thanked him, and the man was on his way. Lynette stared at the envelope as though it were some alien creature, poised to strike her.

"Aren't you going to open it?" Ammie prompted, recalling Lynette's equally strange reaction to the letter she'd received at the barn dance.

With trembling fingers Lynette opened the envelope and scanned the letter's contents. Her face turned such a ghastly shade of gray that Ammie actually felt a prickle of concern. "What is it?"

"Nothing."

"Don't tell me that. What is it?"

"My—my friend Pearl has taken ill."

Like hell, Ammie thought, but said, "Maybe we should go inside for a few minutes. Have some coff—tea."

Lynette offered no objections. They stopped at the water pump to clean up first, then headed for the house.

Ammie put the water on, then sat across from Lynette at the kitchen table. "So what's the matter with Pearl?"

"Who? I mean, the doctor isn't sure."

"You and Pearl are good friends?"

"Yes—I . . . she was very kind when Clint and I . . ."

"Needed to keep things hidden?"

Lynette nodded. "Clint and I would stay at this extra place Pearl had. No one bothered us there. Clint was well known in the capital, so we had to be very careful."

Lynette folded the letter and stuffed it into the pocket of her trousers. Ammie was suddenly certain she was planning to destroy it at the earliest opportunity.

Could what was in that letter be damning enough to force an end to her engagement to Matt? Ammie's heart thudded. She had to get her hands on that letter. And until she had a chance to do it, she wasn't going to let Lynette out of her sight.

"We'd best get back out to the barn," Ammie said after they'd had their tea. "Tulip was looking awfully ready this morning. I hope she hasn't decided to drop her foal while the men are away."

"Why?"

"Sometimes there can be problems."

"I'm sure you could handle them, Amelia."

The comment was matter-of-fact, but Ammie had the odd impression it was meant as a compliment. The thought made her uncomfortable. "Let's go," she said.

She had a sudden suspicion that Lynette was going to refuse, that the contents of the letter had so upset her that she was no longer willing to join their battle of wills. But she rose slowly from the table and meekly followed.

Outside, Ammie strode toward the barn. She didn't really think Tulip would foal until tomorrow or the next day, but she would use any excuse to keep an eye on Lynette.

She was stunned, then, to find Tulip lying on the floor

of her stall in the throes of obvious labor. "Oh, no." Ammie swung open the stall gate. Forcing herself to stay calm, she stepped in beside the chestnut, speaking soothingly all the while. Tulip nickered softly, a what-took-you-so-long look in her big brown eyes.

"Easy, girl, easy. That's it." Ammie never stopped talking as she smoothed her hands knowingly along the mare's middle. Tulip was definitely having contractions.

Ammie cast a glance back at Lynette, who was standing at the head of the stall. "You're going to have to help me."

"She's having her baby?"

Ammie nodded.

"Oh, dear God." Lynette murmured. "Do you know what to do?"

"Pretty much," Ammie said, trying to sound calmer than she felt. "I've seen the men handle things a few times. And I helped Pickles with a few litters of pups." Ammie was afraid that if she let Lynette see how nervous she really was, neither one of them would be any use to the mare. "We need to clean up first. Come on."

They went back to the water pump, rolled up their shirt sleeves, then used the cake of soap that was sitting there to scrub their hands and arms up past their elbows. Ammie checked her nails to make sure they were short and well trimmed. Then she took a deep breath. "Let's do it."

Lynette managed a weak nod.

Back inside the barn, Ammie tied Tulip's tail to the side of the stall to keep it out of the way, then again checked to see how close the foal was to being born. On the next contraction, Ammie saw the tip of the foal's nose and a front hoof right side up. "Thank God," she murmured. "At least it's not breech."

Ammie turned. Lynette was still standing at the stall entrance, her face as white as the blaze on Tulip's face. Ammie felt her temper nudge her. This was no time for a simpering act. She had started to say as much, when

Lynette said softly. "She isn't going to die, is she? I mean she seems to be in so much pain."

"No," Ammie said, her own voice gentle. "She isn't going to die. You and I aren't going to let her."

Lynette blinked back tears, then Ammie watched in stunned silence as Lynette walked over and knelt in front of Tulip's head. "It's all right, girl," the woman soothed. "It's going to be just fine. Amelia will take care of you." She continued to talk to the horse as though the mare were a frightened child.

Ammie again checked Tulip's progress. "Oh, no."

"What?" Lynette asked.

"I only see one hoof. It means the foal's other leg is hooked under its body inside the mare."

Tulip's breathing was growing more stressed. Ammie gestured toward Lynette. "Keep talking to her."

Ammie broke the birth sack that covered the foal's nose, gently clearing the tiny horse's airway. "It's going to be a dry birth now. We have to hurry."

Gently, gently, Ammie reached inside the laboring mare's womb, feeling along the foal's body, desperate to find its other leg. She had to get the leg turned, or Tulip and the foal could both die. "I found it. I found the leg. Easy, Tulip. Easy, girl."

"Such a good girl." Lynette cooed. "We'll get your baby, don't worry. Don't worry."

Ammie tugged on the leg, pulling, pulling.

"What's happening?" Lynette's eyes were wide, frightened, despite her continuing gentle words to the mare. "What are you doing?"

Ammie explained as best she could, then said, "You just keep talking to her. You're doing fine." Ammie worked with the leg, trying to shift it. *Hurry! Hurry!* her mind thrummed. If her arm were caught inside the mare when a contraction started, it could snap the bone like a matchstick.

There! She moved the leg, then slipped her arm free just as another contraction started. Ammie shuddered. That was too close.

Tulip was breathing harder. She was getting tired. If she stopped pushing, she could still die.

"We need to help her, Lynette," Ammie said. "Come back here with me."

Quickly Lynette did so. Ammie showed her where to grab on. "Okay, with the next contraction, we work with it and pull for all we're worth."

"We'll kill it!"

"No. No, we won't. They're sturdy little beasts, trust me. Okay now—on three. One . . . two . . . three."

They pulled as a unit, harder, harder. "Nothing's happening!" Lynette cried. "Oh, Amelia, they're both going to die!"

"No! Now, pull! Dammit, pull!"

The foal whooshed out in a rush. Lynette and Ammie both tumbled back. The foal flopped on top of them. Ammie was up first, gathering clean burlap bags to wipe down the new baby.

Lynette managed to struggle to her feet as well. Ammie looked at her. She was now truly a bloody mess—and yet somehow she still managed to look pretty. Ammie shook her head in pure amazement, then held out one of the burlap bags to Lynette. "Want to help dry off the foal?"

Lynette's eyes shone brightly as she accepted the bag. "They're both going to be all right now, aren't they?"

Ammie nodded. "You did a fine job, Lynette. A fine job. Thank you."

"Thank you, Amelia. More than you know."

They both began rubbing down the foal's dark and curly coat.

"Is it a boy or a girl?" Lynette asked.

Ammie did a little checking. "A boy," she pronounced. "A fine healthy colt."

"I think Mama wants to see her baby." Lynette pointed toward Tulip, who had raised her head and was now looking expectantly at Ammie.

"You want to do the honors?" Ammie asked Lynette.

"Could I?"

Ammie helped a little, but Lynette did most of the work maneuvering the gangly foal up to Tulip's head. The mare at once started to give her new son an avid licking.

Ammie and Lynette made quick work of the afterbirth and gathered fresh straw for the stall. Then they went out and washed up a bit. By the time they'd finished all that, the foal was beginning to fluff out like a baby duck and make its first attempt at standing up.

Ammie and Lynette stood side by side and watched the performance. First, the foal struggled to anchor its front feet solidly in front of him. When he accomplished that much, he sat there for a minute in a comical canine pose. His next attempt got him onto both his front and back feet, after which he promptly fell over onto his nose.

His third attempt, however, was a resounding success. He stood, looking quite proud of himself.

Ammie and Lynette both applauded happily.

Tulip got to her feet, looking none the worse for wear, now that the ordeal was over. The foal's tail waggled happily as Tulip urged her son's head beneath her belly. The foal found the faucet he was looking for, and both mother and son were content.

"I couldn't have done it without you, Lynette," Ammie said, and meant it.

Lynette smiled. "It was wonderful, wasn't it? He's so beautiful."

"He looks just like his daddy."

"He does?"

Ammie nodded.

Lynette went in and stroked the greedily sucking foal. "So beautiful."

Ammie watched this new Lynette almost with more wonder than she watched the foal. "Maybe you could be a rancher's wife," she said softly, and a little sadly.

Lynette's eyes were warm. "I know you love Matt, Amelia. And I'm sorry. I wish I could tell you just how sorry. But I have to . . ." She hesitated.

"Have to what?" Ammie prompted. Was Lynette actually about to tell her what she had been aching to know ever since the woman had stepped off that stage in River Oaks? The truth about what had really brought her here?

Lynette continued to stroke the foal. "I've been so frightened. I just—" Tears welled in her eyes. "Maybe if I did tell you, I don't know. Maybe it would be all right."

Ammie was afraid to breathe, certain that even the slightest distraction would rouse Lynette from the melancholy that had persuaded her to speak so freely.

"It's about Clint," Lynette began. "About Clint and me and our marriage." As she looked at Ammie, her brown eyes were so filled with pain that Ammie winced. "You see, Clint—"

The barn door creaked open.

Lynette gasped, turning almost guiltily toward it.

Ammie swore inwardly, even as she saw Matt striding into the barn. Blast! The man had one annoying sense of timing! "Hello, Matt," she grumbled, for once in her life supremely irritated to see him. "Come see Tulip's foal."

He quickened his stride. "She had it? Is she all right? I stopped at the house. Where's Lynette?"

Ammie gestured toward the stall's interior.

His eyes widened.

"Hello, Matthew," Lynette said, her hand going automatically to her hair in a hopeless attempt to straighten it. She was a grimy mess from head to toe, and her eyes still held a trace of abject sadness, which Ammie was certain Matt would misinterpret.

He did not disappoint her. He spun on Ammie. "What

is this?" he hissed. "I thought I asked you to make sure she wouldn't be subjected to—to—"

"To the birth of a new life?" Ammie inquired testily. She was determined not to let his oafish behavior affect her this time.

"Look at her!" he snapped. "Just look at her!"

"I'm all right, Matthew," Lynette said. "Honestly." She was still petting the foal. "Isn't it just the most precious thing? It's a boy, you know."

Matt opened the stall gate and stepped inside. "Come with me, Lynette. I'll help you get cleaned up."

"I don't want to go. Not yet. I want to stay with the baby awhile longer. Can't I?"

Matt frowned, obviously confused. "Of course." He looked at Ammie. "My God, she's in some kind of shock."

Ammie had to admit that Lynette did seem a bit peaked, and for once it did not seem to be just another play for Matt's sympathy.

"I think I might need a bath," Lynette said. She held her hands out, palms up.

"I'll get some water." He halted midstride, grasping her wrists. "What the hell are these?" He stared at the mass of blisters on Lynette's hands. "You don't get blisters from helping a horse foal." He glared at Ammie. "What's been going on?"

Ammie swallowed nervously. Damn.

"I asked Amelia to teach me to be a good rancher's wife," Lynette said.

Ammie's eyes widened.

"And who the hell ever said I wanted my wife to have hands like cowhide?"

Ammie winced, self-consciously stuffing her own hands into her pockets.

Matt continued to glower at her. "Can I talk to you outside?"

There was no help for it. Ammie walked with him out of the barn.

He marched a half-dozen strides, then stopped. Then very deliberately, he turned to face her. "Now, would you like to tell me what the hell you've been doing to Lynette the last three days?"

Ammie straightened her shoulders, trying not to give in to the very real guilt she was feeling. "I figured you'd want a wife who knew how to handle herself on a ranch."

"So you worked her like a field hand?" he gritted. "Ammie, a person doesn't get blisters like that from gathering eggs from a henhouse."

"She's not as fragile as you think she is."

"I don't care if she's made of cast iron. What gave you the right to do such a thing? I trusted you. I asked you as a friend if she could stay here. I thought—I thought you and Lynette would be friends. At least, I'd hoped."

"Well, you were wrong."

"Obviously. Wrong on both counts, it would seem. Wrong that you and Lynette could be friends. And wrong that I could trust you."

She flinched.

He must have noticed, because he drew visible rein on his temper. "Ammie, what's going on? This isn't like you."

She looked at the ground. *Tell him, just tell him.* But she couldn't. Why humiliate herself? He was going to marry Lynette. For Ammie to tell him she loved him would only add more strain to an increasingly unbearable situation. "I just think—I think you're going too fast with all this. You've only known her for two weeks."

He shook his head. "You know, the person I expected to have trouble with was my father. But he's thrilled about the wedding. I thought you of all people would be happy for me."

"Matt, more than anything I want you to be happy. God knows, you deserve it. But I just—I just don't think

Lynette . . . Dammit, she was Clint's wife. Since when did you and Clint have the same taste in anything?"

His jaw tightened. "That was pretty low, don't you think?"

"I'm not saying these things to hurt you. I just want you to think about what you're doing."

"I have thought about it. And a week from tomorrow Lynette's going to be my wife."

"A week? My God, it's as if you've got to hurry up and marry her before you change your mind!"

"That's enough!" He slapped his hat against his thigh, pacing back and forth in front of her like a caged panther. "That's the craziest thing you've said yet."

"Then what's the hurry?" Ammie demanded.

"We just don't want to wait, that's all."

"You don't—or she doesn't?"

"What's that supposed to mean?"

"You figure it out."

His lips thinned. "I'm not listening to any more of this. I'm going back in to Lynette."

"You do that."

"Did you even *look* at her hands?"

Ammie shoved her own hands at him. "Look at mine! So what? They're the hands of someone who works for a living."

"That's different."

"What's different?"

"Dammit, Ammie, Lynette's a lady! She's not like—" He clamped his jaw shut.

"She's not like what?" Ammie shrilled, fury and hurt snapping through her like wildfire. "She's not like me? Is that what you were going to say?"

"I didn't mean that."

"Like hell you didn't!"

"Ammie, what's the matter with you? I've never seen you act this way."

"What do you care what's the matter with me? You don't give a tinker's dam about me anymore!" The hurt, the frustration, the heartache of these past two weeks came roiling out of her all at once, and she was helpless to stop it. "You go on back to your Lady Lynette. See if I care. Have tea and cakes the rest of your stinking life! After my father's wedding tomorrow, I don't care if I never see either one of you again." She was starting to cry, and she couldn't stop that either. "I take that back. Maybe one more time. After all, my birthday's coming up. Maybe you can get me a pair of boots to go with my belt!"

She whirled and raced away, leaving Matt standing there, staring after her, stunned, speechless.

☘ /Chapter 16

Ammie spent the night in the barn with the new foal and Tulip. She much preferred their four-legged company to any two-legged creatures prowling the Shamrock grounds. Gathering up armfuls of fresh straw, she built herself a comfortable nest in the corner of the barn nearest Tulip's stall. By then it was after midnight, and she was exhausted. Even so, she awoke well before dawn.

Stretching tiredly, Ammie lay there, trying to will herself to get up. Whatever this day might hold, it couldn't be worse than yesterday. She closed her eyes: Yes, it could. Her father and Mary were getting married today. And while Ammie was genuinely thrilled for them both, the wedding meant guests. Guests meant Matt.

Ammie sighed, unwillingly recalling the aftermath of her heated exchange with him outside the barn yesterday afternoon. Matt had followed her to the house. She'd been in the kitchen, pumping water into a bucket to carry up to her bath. He had made a couple of half-hearted attempts to talk to her, but she wouldn't even turn around to look at him, let alone speak. In the end he'd stormed back outside.

She'd stood by the sink, trembling, furious—and yet feeling a sick emptiness as well. She and Matt had never had an argument they couldn't resolve. And they'd never, *ever* had one like this. This was no argument, no debate about politics or breeds of horses, or how much cayenne to put in her chili recipe. This one was personal. This one was ugly.

He'd come into the house again a few minutes later with Lynette. By then, Ammie had cloistered herself in her bedroom, disrobed, and was preparing to step into her tub. Instead, she'd stood by her door and listened as Matt took Lynette into the back bathing room—no doubt drawing water for her *lady*ship's bath.

Tears burned Ammie's eyes, and she swiped them viciously away. She hadn't blubbered as much in the last ten years as she had in these past two weeks! She was beginning to feel like a blasted water pump herself. This had to stop. Matt had made his choice, and it wasn't her. She was simply going to have to live with it.

Except that it was more than that. Not only had Matt chosen Lynette to be his wife, he seemed to be choosing her whole manner of living as well. And it hurt. It hurt like hell. Matt had never found fault with Ammie's less-than-conventional behavior until Lynette Simmons had swept into his life.

Ammie's temper stirred anew as she settled into her bath. She looked at her hands—rein-rough and not exactly dainty, but quite serviceable, thank you. She picked up her sponge and scrubbed at her skin with a barely suppressed violence. How dare he make her feel bad about herself? If the way she led her life was wasn't good enough for him, then to blazes with him! If he was so easily swayed by fluttering eyes and flattering words, then maybe *he* wasn't good enough for *her*.

Several minutes later, Ammie sloshed to her feet, climbed from the tub, and toweled herself dry, still seething. She padded to her wardrobe and cast a grim eye at the two dresses hanging there—her Sunday church dress and her new purple and gold faille. They were fine for special occasions, but her work on the ranch was better served by more sensible clothing. With a self-righteous sniff, she grabbed up a clean shirt and pair of trousers.

Maybe someday the rest of the world would catch up with her.

Wrapping a towel about her still-wet hair, Ammie marched downstairs. She wondered suddenly if Matt had had the audacity to stay in the bathing room and assist Lynette with her bath. At once her conscience jabbed her. She had just been grumbling about Matt's harsher judgments of her, and now she was doing the same thing to him.

When she reached the bottom of the stairs, she saw him pacing in front of the hearth. He acknowledged her presence with an unreadable glance, then deliberately resumed his pacing. It was apparent in every coil-tight step he took that he didn't trust himself enough to speak to her.

Ammie tugged the towel from her hair, several wet, trailing strands dampening her shirt. Without meaning to, she cleared her throat. Matt once again paused in his pacing. He drilled her an expectant look, and Ammie realized with a rush of fresh anger that he was waiting for an apology.

She thrust out her chin defiantly. He would have a long wait.

The silence between them stretched to untenable lengths. Ammie became certain that if either one of them said a word, the other would explode on the spot.

Still grimly silent, she stalked over to a chair and sat down. She wasn't going to give him the satisfaction of leaving the room. She found a dime novel her father had recently brought home. Jaw clenched, she started reading, vowing to ignore the trough Matt was wearing in the floor in front of the fireplace.

She read. He paced. Lynette bathed.

Long minutes passed.

Matt broke the stalemate first. He stomped over to the window and looked out. Evidently he needed a change of

scenery. Either that, or Ammie's studied nonchalance
with her book was driving him mad.

She surprised herself by actually becoming engrossed
in the novel. The story concerned a fiddle-footed black-
guard who abandoned the woman who adored him to become a fur trapper in the Rockies. Ammie found the de-
nouement particularly satisfying.

A bear ate him.

Another hour of excruciating silence passed before
Lynette emerged from the bathing room. Matt strode to
her side at once. Now it was his turn to drive Ammie mad
with his fussing and hovering.

"You sure you're feeling all right?" he asked. "I can get
some salve for those blisters."

"I'm fine, Matthew," she assured him. "Please don't
bother."

What stunned Ammie was that Lynette actually meant
it. She cast a covert glance at the woman. She seemed
remarkably subdued. Ammie wondered if she was thinking about their interrupted conversation earlier in the
barn, when Lynette had been about to tell her something
about Clint. Did she wish that conversation had continued, or did she wish it had never begun?

"I want to apologize again for Ammie," Matt said to
Lynette, sending a pointed look Ammie's way.

Ammie bristled. "I'll do my own apologizing, Matt
Grayson"—a satisfied look came into his eyes, until she
continued—"if and when I feel it necessary to apologize
to someone, that is."

"Dammit, Ammie—"

Lynette touched his arm. "No, Matthew, please. I don't
want to be the cause of any more trouble between you
and Amelia."

"She had no right!" he gritted.

"Perhaps she was a bit overzealous, but I'm sure she
meant well." Lynette's hooded eyes raised briefly toward

Ammie in a look that Matt didn't see. Ammie expected the coolness to be back, the calculated air of being about her business once again, but instead Lynette's eyes held a very real regret.

Ammie wondered about that, even as she felt an unwelcome wave of sympathy for the woman. Perhaps Lynette was not so much calculating in her bid for Matt's affection as she was desperate. But why? Why was it so important that she marry Matt? As Clint's widow, she had every legal right to be Clint's heir. And even if it she hadn't had the law on her side, the Graysons would have felt morally obliged to take care of her anyway. And yet as far as Ammie knew, Lynette had yet to make any demands on the Graysons—financial or otherwise.

Ammie sighed. Perhaps it was time to admit that it was her own crushing jealousy that colored her view of Lynette Simmons. Lynette wasn't necessarily harboring any deep dark secrets. She could be just what she presented herself to be—a lonely widow who very much needed a man in her life.

What broke Ammie's heart was that it had to be this particular man.

She couldn't know the pain that showed through on her face in one unguarded moment, so she was surprised to look up and see Matt standing over her, concern and confusion mingling with an odd wariness in his blue eyes. That wariness, Ammie supposed, sprang from his inability to predict whether his approach would signal the start of another round of bickering between them.

"I, uh—guess I'd best be leaving," he began a little stiffly, twisting his hat brim in his hands.

She didn't say anything. She was staring at the open collar of his shirt, unwilling now to look him in the eye. To do so, she feared, would be to tell him she loved him.

"I said some things I shouldn't have," he went on. "I

think we both did. If I hurt your feelings, Ammie, I . . . apologize."

She didn't speak. All she wanted in the world to do was to fling herself against him, force him to put his arms around her, hold her, kiss her, never let go. She pretended to cough as she tried to swallow the lump in her throat.

"I guess I'll see you tomorrow. For the wedding," he said.

If she said anything at all, she would fall apart.

He muttered a quiet oath, obviously interpreting her continued silence as anger. He turned to Lynette. "Walk me out to my horse?"

"Certainly, Matthew." Lynette followed him outside.

When the door had shut, Ammie crossed to the window. Steeling herself, she lifted the edge of a lace curtain and peeked out. Lynette and Matt were standing near Drifter, talking in quiet tones. Ammie could hear nothing of what they said, but several times Matt looked toward the house. Ammie was certain he couldn't see her, so her only conclusion was that he was talking about her. Or perhaps doing some more apologizing on her behalf. She couldn't summon the energy to care one way or the other.

Lynette stood on tiptoe and brushed Matt's lips with a kiss. Ammie expected him to respond by sweeping her into his arms. Instead he stepped back. Again he looked toward the house. Then he gave Lynette a modest peck on the cheek, mounted Drifter, and rode out.

Lynette came back inside but didn't look at Ammie as she spoke. "I think I'm going to lie down for a while." She started toward the stairs.

"Lynette, wait, please."

Lynette paused.

"I was too proud to say this in front of Matt, but I really am sorry for riding you so hard these past three days."

"I know." Lynette's eyes were overbright, as though

she were on the verge of tears. "I enjoyed the work more
than I thought I would. It helped me take my mind off
. . . other things."

"What things?"

"Clint. I know you don't believe me, but I loved him
very much."

"You were going to tell me something about him out in
the barn."

She straightened slightly. "Was I? I don't recall?"

"I can't pretend that we're friends, Lynette. I'm too
damned jealous for that. But if you're in some kind of
trouble, maybe I could help."

Lynette's smile was wan. "I told you once we were
more alike than you knew. Both a little desperate. I know
this won't be much consolation to you, Amelia, but I
promise you, I'll make Matthew a good wife." With that
she left the room.

Ammie closed her eyes. Just what she needed to hear.
*If I thought you loved him, that wouldn't hurt quite so
much.* But Lynette didn't love him—and maybe this was
just wishful thinking on her part, but Ammie wasn't altogether certain Matt loved Lynette. He had never said so
—not exactly anyway. It was a thin thread on which to
hang her hopes, but it was better than no thread at all.

Briefly, Ammie considered following Lynette to try to
pressure her into saying more, but Shamus arrived home
as she hesitated. He had taken Mary to town on this final
night before their wedding. Smoke Larson was to bring
her back in the morning. From the moment he tromped
into the house, Shamus O'Rourke gave a whole new
meaning to the term *nervous bridegroom.*

Ammie bore his grouching and stomping and nitpicking
and worrying for as long as she could. Then she fed him
his supper and fled to the barn. The end of one hellacious
day.

*   *   *

And, Ammie thought miserably as she pushed up from her bed of straw the next morning, the beginning of another.

Moving slowly, she crossed to the big door of the barn and shoved it open. Outside, the sun was painting broad strokes of crimson, purple, and gold across the eastern sky. Ammie wondered if Matt was out of bed yet, if he was watching the same thing. There had been many a trail drive when they'd rolled out of their blankets at first light just to watch the sunrise together. Ammie had thought those times special then, but now they seemed somehow even more precious as memories.

Ammie crossed to Tulip's stall to check on the mare and her foal. She took her time, in no hurry to face either her father or Lynette. She stroked Tulip's velvety nose and fed her a handful of carrots. "You deserve 'em. You worked hard to have this little guy." Then she patted the foal's neck. "We need to think of a name for you, don't we?"

The foal snuffled curiously at the last carrot Ammie was holding. "If you're anything like your mama, I'm going to need a bigger carrot patch." Ammie frowned thoughtfully, eyeing the foal's white-stocking feet and blaze face. "Carrot patch. I suppose I could call you Patches. What would you think of that?" The foal took a cautious nibble of the carrot's tip. "Patches it is." Tulip made short work of the rest of the carrot.

"I'd best get in the house. See if Pa's settled down any. If he hasn't, Mary might say 'I don't' instead of 'I do.' "

Ammie plucked at the bits of straw that clung to her hair as she strode out of the barn. She was met head-on by a black-tan-and white freight train. "Where have you been keeping yourself, Pickles?" Ammie laughed, rubbing her hands along the dog's furry sides. "Ah, wouldn't you know it." Another litter of pups would be along in about six weeks. "Lost your head to another sweet-barking mongrel, didn't you?"

Pickles whined happily, licking Ammie's face.

"You tell me that story again when you've got eight pups to feed and Romeo is off romancing some other little hound dog."

Pickles's tail thumped. Ammie shook her head.

Plastering a cheery smile on her face, Ammie continued toward the house. She found the place in a mild uproar. The wedding was set for two that afternoon, but already her father was stomping through the house, bellowing about not being able to find his tie, his razor, and his best pair of boots.

Ammie had heard him even before she'd come into the house. Whom he was bellowing at, she had no idea. As he went on bellowing, Ammie rolled her eyes and hurried back to his room. Quickly she found the items he was looking for. The next time he went charging past her, Ammie held them out to him.

"One suggestion, Pa," she said.

"What's that?" he asked, trying to put on his boots and tie at the same time.

"You might want to put your shirt on right-side out."

He groaned. "Oh, Ammie, a man just shouldn't get married at my age."

"Are you trying to tell me that you've changed your mind?" She was teasing, but he was too scattered to see it.

"No, no, I love her, Ammie. I love her." He kissed Ammie on the forehead. "I love you too. Have you seen my shaving mug? What happened to my belt?"

Ammie let him skitter off. It was five hours until the wedding—he would never last. She decided to retreat to the kitchen. It would be safer there. Besides, she should have already started on the day's food. There weren't going to be too many guests—her father and Mary had wanted to keep the event fairly small, private. But several neighbors and townspeople were coming.

Including Matt.

Thinking of Matt—when wasn't she thinking of Matt these days?—didn't do anything to brighten her mood as she walked into the kitchen. She was surprised to find Theda Hopkins bent over the sink, busily peeling potatoes.

"Hope you don't mind my starting already," Theda said. "Mrs. Denby hired me to come out and help with the food, serving it and all. She said she didn't want you slaving over the stove. She wanted you to enjoy the day."

Ammie appreciated the sentiment, but she would have preferred to bury herself in the kitchen rather than mingle with the guests. It was hard enough to see Matt these days, but it was doubly so when he was with Lynette.

"Your pa and Mrs. Denby sure look sweet together," Theda went on, obviously in a chatty mood. "They came into the hotel for dinner last night." Theda sighed dreamily. "Love sure is mysterious, isn't it?"

"That's a fact," Ammie said. "I sure can't figure it out."

"Something else I can't figure out is Matt Grayson falling for that Lynette Simmons. That was really something, wasn't it?"

Ammie dropped the spoon she was holding into a bowl of cake batter. Theda went barreling on.

"I always would of thought it was you that landed Matt."

"What makes you say that?" Ammie managed.

"Just the way he'd be when he was around you." Theda's eyes glowed with envy. "You know how men and women are, always playin' games with one another. But not you and Matt. Never seen two people so at ease with each other, so tickled just to be in each other's company."

"I think we'd best concentrate on cooking," Ammie said, desperate to change the subject.

"You know, that night he come to move my armoire— that Lynette lady wasn't even in town yet. I thought for sure Matt turned me down because of—" Theda stopped. "Never mind."

"What?"

"Nothing." She was actually blushing. She went bustling over to check on some bread dough she had set out to rise.

Ammie frowned. So Theda had indeed had more on her mind that night than shifting furniture. And yet Matt had backed away from what had surely been a most temptingly offered tryst. Why? Ammie recalled his bawdy Wichita tales, and how certain she had been he'd been making them up.

The kind of pain Matt's in, he's going to be lookin' for comfort wherever he can find it. In a bottle. Or in a bed.

But he had done neither, she was certain now. Ammie's hands trembled. The night before he'd left for Wichita, their "practice" kiss at Shamrock Creek had left them both flustered. Ammie had been awed. Matt had been taken aback.

Had he felt a rush of real desire for a girl he had for so long viewed as his kid sister? Had he been ashamed of that desire?

She remembered how he'd behaved in her hotel room when she'd been wrapped in a sheet. He'd been in a damnable rush to get away from her. Would he have done that if he felt nothing for her? And what about the dance? She had chalked up to her imagination her notion that he'd been about to kiss her before Theda intruded. But what if Theda hadn't barged in? And then there was the creek, earlier this week. Ammie didn't have a doubt in her mind that Matt had been fearfully aroused when she'd joined him in that water.

Except that by then it had been too late. By then he had asked Lynette to marry him. Why?

Because Lynette is a beautiful, desirable woman who

needs him, her mind answered grimly. And Zak had openly encouraged the match.

But could there be more to it than that? Ammie bit her lip. Could he have done it, at least partly, to avoid acting on feelings he might have considered dishonorable to their friendship?

Her heart pounded painfully, afraid even to think it. She'd been disappointed too many times these past two weeks. Yet if there was even the remotest chance that he was being wonderfully, foolishly noble . . .

Somehow, some way, she had to find out. And to do so, she would have to get him alone. There would be no practicing for this. She would have to push him to find out how true his feelings for Lynette were. If his feelings were true, he might be so disgusted with her, he would never forgive her. But it was a chance she had to take. In a week he would be lost to her forever. In a week he would be married to Lynette. Now was the time to risk everything—even if it meant losing her best friend.

Chapter 17

Ammie could scarcely concentrate. She was so nervous about what she was going to say and do when she saw Matt that she nearly laced Mary's corset to the bedpost—with Mary in it. She and Mary were standing in the guest bedroom. It was fifteen minutes until the wedding ceremony, and Ammie was supposed to be helping the bride get dressed.

"Amelia, dear, are you sure you're all right?" Mary asked, her soft brown eyes narrowing with concern.

Ammie gave herself a mental shake. "I'm fine. I guess I'm just all thumbs today."

"It's the bride who's supposed to be nervous."

Ammie finished lacing the corset. "I know. I'm sorry."

"It's all right, dear." Mary pressed a hand to her stays. "Oh, these things are such an abomination! I wonder what your father would say if I started wearing trousers and shirts instead."

Ammie had to chuckle. "I don't think you'd want to be in the room when he said it. He figures one tomboy in the family is enough."

Mary smiled warmly. "You don't know how it pleases me to hear you include me when you talk about your family."

Impulsively, Ammie gave Mary a hug. "This might sound a little odd, but . . . I think my mother would have liked you very much."

Mary's eyes glistened, then she shook herself. "Oh, my, the time! My dress, Amelia."

Quickly Ammie slipped the simply styled blue silk over
Mary's head. She'd just finished with the fastenings when
a soft knock sounded on the door. Ammie grinned. "Pa
must be getting impatient." She went to the door and
threw it open.

Her breath caught. It was Matt. Dressed in an exquisitely tailored gray jacket and trousers, silver brocade
vest, and string tie, he played riot with her already over-
loaded senses. She had to remind herself to breathe.

He nodded, a trifle stiffly, evidently surprised to find
her here. She'd come in to help Mary dress nearly an
hour ago, and he may well have just arrived.

"Good afternoon, Amelia."

Amelia? He never called her Amelia, not even when he
was angry.

"I came to offer my best wishes to the bride." Now
Matt smiled warmly as he crossed the room to hand Mary
a small, wrapped package.

"Is this what I think it is?" Mary asked.

He nodded, an oddly bashful look in his eyes.

Mary gave him a quick, affectionate hug. "Thank you."

He shook his head. "Thank *you*."

Without any further acknowledgment to Ammie, he left
the room.

"What was that all about?" Ammie asked, trying hard to
mask the hurt she felt at being so roundly ignored. He
was certainly doing a superb job of hiding all that latent
passion he had for her.

"It's a secret," Mary said, giving Ammie's hand a
squeeze. "I'd tell you if I could, but he made me promise
not to."

Ammie's spirits dipped further. He was sharing secrets
with Mary, but not with her? Oh, God—was she just de-
luding herself? Grasping at a dream? A mirage?

"He's not keeping anything from you to hurt you, Ammie. It's—it's a surprise. He'll tell you about it in his own

time. I know he will. I think he already would have if
not . . ." She hesitated.

"If not for Lynette?"

Mary gave Ammie a hug. "I hope and pray everything
turns out for you, dear."

"Thanks, Mary." Ammie called on that cheery smile
again. This was Mary's wedding day, and Ammie was not
about to spoil it. "I'd best hurry up and get dressed myself. The minister is here. Everyone's going to be ready
but me."

Ammie hurried up the stairs to her room, where she sat
on her bed and took several deep breaths. She was not
going to cry. And she wasn't going to let Matt's sour mood
intimidate her, either. If she was wrong about his attrac-
tion to him, then the worst she would be was humiliated.
At least she wouldn't have to spend the rest of her life
saying "What if?" She still wasn't sure how and when she
was going to approach him, but maybe having no specific
plan was for the best. If she tried to orchestrate things too
closely, she might only invite disaster.

She dressed as quickly as she could, pulling on her
faille dress, promising herself she would be back in her
room ten minutes after the ceremony to throw on her
jeans and shirt once again.

Starting toward the door, she halted in midstride, her
gaze snagged by a heap of soiled clothing in the corner of
her room. She grimaced. She recognized the shirt and
trousers Lynette had been wearing yesterday during the
delivery of Tulip's foal. Heaven forbid that the woman
should wash them herself. Ammie had a good mind to—

She gasped, remembering. The letter! The one that had
turned Lynette's face such a ghastly shade of gray.
Lynette had stuffed it into the pocket of those very trousers. Ammie had completely forgotten about it. Her heart
thudded. In the excitement about the foal, could Lynette
have forgotten it as well?

Ammie crossed the room and picked up the trousers, her hands shaking so badly she could scarcely hold on to them. She told herself to be calm. After all, the letter might well speak of exactly what Lynette had said it did— the illness of her friend Pearl. But Ammie knew with a sudden fierce certainty that that wasn't true, that it wasn't true at all.

She stuck her hand into the pocket. Her heart turned over in her chest. The letter was still there.

She pulled it free, staring at the Austin postmark on the envelope. Inside was a letter that held the key to whatever Lynette had been hiding ever since she'd stepped down from that River Oaks stage that day weeks ago. All Ammie had to do was read it. Read it and put an abrupt end to Lynette's engagement to Matt.

Ammie's grip on the letter tightened. She pushed back the flap and drew out the folded blue paper. Lynette would lose, be abandoned by both Graysons, sent away in disgrace.

Lynette, with her sad brown eyes and a haughty demeanor that hid a pain so raw that even through her jealousy, Ammie had seen it and sympathized with it.

With this letter Lynette might lose, but Ammie most certainly wouldn't win.

Cursing, Ammie shoved the letter back inside the envelope. She couldn't do it. In fact, she had no right to do it. She wanted to win Matt because he loved her, or she didn't want to win him at all.

Muttering another curse, Ammie jammed the letter into the night-table drawer. She had a wedding to attend.

The ceremony was blessedly short and sweet. And blessedly, too, her father didn't faint. In fact, once the "I do's" were said, he was so overcome with joy that he not only kissed Mary, he kissed Smoke, Matt, and Zak as well!

Then he grabbed Ammie in a big bear hug. "Your pa is

one happy man, Ammie girl." He planted a kiss on her cheek. "One very happy man."

"I love you, Pa," Ammie said. "And I love Mary too."

He hugged her again, then went off to reclaim his bride in a rousing Irish jig.

Ammie headed toward the kitchen to see if Theda needed any help. But first she cast a covert eye toward Lynette and Matt. They had stood together during the ceremony, but Matt seemed pensive, distracted, as he had earlier in Mary's room. His hands were stuffed into the pockets of his gray trousers. Lynette had tried to engage him in conversation, but most of his answers seemed monosyllabic.

It wasn't much, but Ammie would take her hopeful signs where she could get them. Maybe their fight yesterday had started him thinking. She continued toward the kitchen.

Into her path stepped an obviously drunk Terence Kessler. Ammie grimaced.

"You haven't been very friendly, Amelia," Terence said petulantly.

"I told you, I have a lot of work to do."

"You're the daughter of the groom. You don't have to do anything."

"Let me by."

He didn't move.

Ammie's lips thinned. She had not been at all pleased to see the man here. Her father and Mary had invited Millicent and Martin Kessler, but the invitation had not included Terence—Ammie had specifically asked that it not. Obviously, he had assumed it was a mistake and come anyway. He'd sidled up to her during the wedding ceremony and had been loath to leave her side ever since. His proprietary manner was becoming very wearing.

If she went into the kitchen, he would probably just follow her. So instead, Ammie opted for the stairs—thankfully, he didn't have the nerve to follow her to her bedroom. She stayed in her room longer than was necessary to change back into her shirt and trousers. Maybe Terence would take the hint and go home.

The skies were darkening a bit, and a storm was possible. Surely, the guests would leave early.

Ammie waited a half-hour, then came back downstairs. Terence was at her side in an instant. Ammie did her best to ignore him as she mingled with the other guests. Time and again she glanced toward Matt, who was seated at the piano providing much-appreciated entertainment. And yet Ammie had the odd feeling that his playing allowed him to ignore everything and everyone around him.

She was still hoping for an opportunity to get him alone.

But dusk came, and Matt played on. He'd said little or nothing to anyone, including Lynette, for hours.

Most of the guests were gone, as was Theda. A storm was definitely brewing, and everyone had wanted to be home before it hit.

Only the Graysons remained, Matt playing the piano, Zak dozing in the wing-back chair in front of the fireplace. The Kesslers had left about ten minutes earlier. Ammie had only too happily walked Martin, Millicent, and Terence out to their buggy.

"How about a little good-night kiss, Amelia?" Terence had asked, leaning close to her.

She had recoiled from the whiskey on his breath. "Not tonight, Terence."

His eyes had glittered angrily, but he hadn't objected when his brother got him into the carriage.

Back in the house, Shamus was yawning broadly, evidently trying to give Matt a hint. But Matt continued to play, and the piece seeming as brooding and dark as the sky. Lynette had seated herself next to him on the bench seat, but he seemed as oblivious to her as he did to everyone else. Ammie had never seen him like this, so walled in. She resisted an urge to try to draw him out. She had little doubt what the outcome would be. Tonight was not going to be the night to try to measure his feelings for her.

"I'm going to go out to check on Tulip and Patches," she said. "I'll be back in a few minutes."

Once she was in the barn, she decided she was really in no hurry to return to the house. Between fending off Terence and fretting about Matt, she hadn't had a moment's peace all afternoon. Talking to the horses soothed her, helped her relax. She'd even brought in Ranger because of the coming storm.

A sudden rustling in the straw behind her caught her attention. She spun around, and her eyes widened.

Terence.

"What are you doing here?" she demanded. "I saw you leaving."

"I convinced my brother that you'd asked me to spend the night." The look in his eyes made the hair on the back of Ammie's neck stand on end.

"That's disgusting!" she snapped. "You just borrow yourself a horse and head on home this minute!"

"I don't think so." He straightened, though not fully. His words were slightly slurred, and he was still very drunk. "I knew you'd come out to check your horses eventually."

"What do you want?" Ammie took a step toward the door, but he moved to block her path.

"I've been dreaming of that night at the dance, Amelia. I haven't been able to get it out of my head. I love you, Amelia. I want you to marry me."

"You've got a pretty revolting way of proposing."

He lunged for her, wrapping his arms around her. The kiss he planted on her mouth was sloppy, repulsive. She tried to throw him off, but he only tightened his hold.

"Stop it!" she hissed. "Let me go this instant!"

"But you wanted it the other night, Amelia. I know you did. Don't fight it, darling." He kissed her again, driving his tongue into her mouth.

Ammie gagged, then bit down hard.

He yelped, staggering back. There was a trickle of blood on his chin. His eyes went hard.

"If I gave you the wrong idea, Terence," Ammie said, trying again to take a step toward the barn door. "I'm sorry. But I was upset—shocked—about something. I didn't know what I was doing."

"The hell you didn't," he spat. "You don't tease a man like that and then expect him to just walk away. I've wanted you for a long time, Amelia. A very long time. And I'm not about to settle for a few measly kisses."

"You're drunk, and you're disgusting. This is my home. Get out."

He grabbed for her, and she leaped away, but his fingers snared her shirt. He jerked her toward him. Several of her shirt buttons gave way. Terence's eyes gleamed cruelly in the lantern light of the barn. Ammie tried to twist free, but he pawed at her chemise-covered breasts. Terrified, Ammie drove her boot into his shin.

He swore viciously, then drew back his fist.

The blow never fell. Terence's hand was suddenly trapped in the viselike grip of Matt Grayson. Matt turned Terence's arm like a corkscrew, forcing him into an agonized crouch. There was a feral light in Matt's blue eyes that Ammie had never seen before. With his other hand, Matt drove a fist into Terence's face, sending him sprawling butt-first into a fresh pile of horse manure. "You even think about coming near her again, Kessler," he snarled, "and I'll kill you."

Wide-eyed, sputtering, Terence shoved himself to his feet. But even drunk, he recognized suicide when he saw it. He staggered from the barn. A few seconds later, Ammie heard the sound of retreating hoofbeats.

Ammie drew herself up. Fighting back tears of relief, she gripped the two sides of her torn shirt. "Thank God you came, Matt."

Matt was in no mood for gratitude. "I think you'd best have a talk with your intended," he gritted. "If that's the way he's going to treat you, I may have to take his head off. What the hell were you doing out here alone with a man that drunk anyway?"

Ammie stared at him. "My intended? I don't know what you're talking about. And as for his being here, I didn't even know—" She stopped, tension and terror exploding through her in a rush. "How dare you speak to me that way! I don't need any advice from you on how to conduct myself. What kind of behavior would you expect, anyway? I'm no lady, remember?"

A muscle in his jaw jumped. "I suppose I'm going to hear about that the rest of my life."

"You don't have to hear anything. Go back to the house and leave me alone." All her plans to talk to him, to find out if he cared about her, suddenly seemed no more than a sad, pathetic joke.

"I'm not leaving until I have some answers."

"What answers?" she asked forlornly. "I don't know what you want from me, Matt."

"For one thing, are you and Terence planning to get married or not?"

She let out a humorless laugh. "If Terence Kessler were the last man on earth, I would become a nun."

Matt peeled off his Stetson and raked his fingers through his hair. "I don't get it. The way you were kissing him at the dance, I thought—"

"You saw that?" Ammie squeaked, mortified.

"I thought things must have gotten pretty serious between you two while I was in Wichita."

"Don't you think I would have told you, if they had?"

"Maybe. Maybe not. We haven't seen much of each

other lately. And when we do, we end up fighting." He
twisted the Stetson's brim in his hands. "I don't like it."

"I don't, either," she managed, her heart pounding. She
started to rework the buttons of her shirt, but her fingers
were shaking so badly, she couldn't find the blasted holes.

"Here," Matt said gruffly, "let me do that." He settled
his hat onto a hook in a support post, then caught the two
edges of her shirt, lining up buttons with buttonholes,
seemingly methodically. The two lowest buttons were still
fastened. He worked the next one up the line.

Ammie's breathing slowed. She fixed her eyes on his
face. So close. He was so very close. She could feel his
breath on her cheek. Hot, sweet. His dark hair fell in
waves almost to his shoulders. God, how she wanted to
run her fingers through it!

He worked the next button.

Ammie's lips parted. She studied the pulse thrumming
at the base of his throat. His skin was dark, stippled with
the faintest shadowing of beard.

The next button was missing.

His hands trembled slightly, and his hooded gaze
seemed to skim for just an instant past the fabric of her
shirt to the chemise-covered softness of her breasts.

He worked the next button, his hands now positioned
in such a way that if he were to shift them ever so slightly,
he could capture a breast in each palm. He was breathing
through his mouth. His fingers tensed, stilled.

Their eyes met. Ammie thrilled at the heat, at the fire
in that midnight blue gaze. She tilted her head slightly
and moistened her lips with her tongue.

His hands came up and cradled her cheeks against his
palms, and then he brought his mouth down on hers. The
pressure was gentle at first, tender. She moaned and his
tongue flicked out to touch hers. She gasped with the
shock of it, the wonder. Her lips parted more fully, and he
accepted her erotic invitation for more.

Ammie felt her blood heat, her mind whirl with the heady magic of his touch. He guided her back, eased her down into the nest of fresh hay on which she'd slept last night. She felt drugged, intoxicated, yet she hadn't had a drop of spirits all day.

They lay side by side, his fingers caressing her throat, the hollow at the base of her neck. She gasped, shifted, her body instinctively seeking his. She caught one of his hands and guided it to her shirt-covered breast, her body arching as he toyed with her stiffening nipple.

He tugged free the very buttons he had so recently fastened. His hand shoved the fabric roughly aside, then eased open the silken ribbons of her chemise. A primal sound rumbled in his throat as he captured her naked breast beneath his callused palm. She felt the need in him and reveled in it.

"Oh, Matt." She sighed, her fingers trailing along the beloved curve of his jaw. "I knew it. I knew you didn't love Lynette."

He froze. "Lynette. Oh, God—oh, my God!" His hands fell away, his eyes stricken. His breathing was harsh, ragged. "What have I done?"

"You don't love her," Ammie pressed. "You can't, if you kiss me like that."

He jammed a hand through his hair, her words a lash to the guilt that was already ripping him apart. "What the hell was this, Ammie? Some kind of trap? Another way for you to hurt Lynette?"

A strangled sound tore from her throat. "You could *think* that? You could think that of *me*?" She stared at him. How could he kiss her to madness and then accuse her of— "What's *your* excuse, Matt?" she shrilled. "Or are you just drunk too?"

He drew up sharply, as though she'd slapped him. And she wished to God she had.

He pushed to his feet. "Sometimes I don't think I even know you anymore, Ammie."

She refused to show him any hurt. She'd been hurt far too much by this man already. How dare he act the injured party? She stalked over to Ranger and vaulted onto his bare back. "Be sure to say good night to your fiancée for me."

He came after her, grabbing for the reins. "Don't. This isn't over. We need to talk."

"No, we don't ever need to talk again."

"Dammit, Ammie, it's getting dark. What happened between us doesn't matter enough for you to break your fool neck!"

"It's my neck," she rasped. "Besides, you're mistaken, Matt. What happened between us matters a hell of a lot." She pulled back on the reins, and Matt let go. "Now if you'll excuse me, I need to be alone. I guess in a lot of ways I already am." Her voice broke. "I certainly don't have a best friend anymore."

With that, she kicked Ranger in the sides and urged the gelding out into the descending darkness. She paid no heed to the storm clouds overhead.

Chapter 18

Lightning streaked across the cloud-bruised night sky, thunder rumbling in its wake. Matt stood in the entryway of the Shamrock barn and cursed. Ammie had already been gone for several minutes. He had been certain she would return before the rain started, but now the first few pelting drops had begun to fall, and she was nowhere in sight. Even if the storm stayed relatively mild, he knew she would be scared to death out there alone.

He should have stopped her, or gone after her, but he'd feared she would have only spurred Ranger harder in her zeal to get away from him.

What was this? Some kind of trap? How could he have said such a thing to her? It was almost as though he'd deliberately tried to provoke her, hurt her. Drive her away. Why?

Because it had felt so damned good to kiss her, so damned right, that was why.

He closed his eyes. He couldn't think that way. He shouldn't think that way. He was engaged to Lynette. He was going to marry Lynette.

Do you love her?

He swore savagely. Enough!

The rain was coming down harder. He would sort it all out later. Right now he had to find Ammie. He hurried toward the empty stall where he'd stowed his saddle and gear earlier that day, after turning Drifter out into one of the Shamrock corrals. Swiftly, he changed into his range clothes. He would follow her. How he was going to find her in the dark, he had no idea. But he had to try.

Shaking out his poncholike slicker, he settled it over his head, then found another one for Ammie. She'd taken nothing with her but the clothes on her back. Time and again, he glanced toward the door, hoping to see her ride in. He didn't care if she hated him—he just wanted her safe and out of the storm. But she did not come back.

Tugging his hat brim low to shield his face from the rain, he headed toward the corral. Quickly he roped and saddled Drifter, then hurried toward the house. He was not looking forward to telling Ammie's father what had happened, but there was no help for it.

Inside, he found Shamus and Mary having tea with Lynette and his father in front of the hearth. Their conversation ceased the minute he walked through the door. "We were about to send out a search party," Zak said, a curious tightness in his voice. "We thought you were going to ask Amelia to join us. That shouldn't take half an hour, should it?"

Mary was looking toward the door. "Did Ammie decide to stay with the foal?" Her hands twisted in front of her as though she already knew something was dreadfully wrong.

Matt took a deep breath. "Ammie's gone."

Shamus came around the settee, his pale eyes widening with alarm. "What do you mean, gone? Ammie would never ride into a storm."

"It's my fault," Matt said. "We had words."

Shamus's gaze hardened. "What kind of words?"

Matt flushed, looked away. "It was a stupid argument. I'd rather not go into it." He was not about to tell Shamus about the kiss he and Ammie had shared. His discretion was partly to shield Ammie. But it was selfish too. He would deserve the punch in the jaw Shamus would throw at him if he knew. But then, the blow might make him too groggy to go after her.

"Maybe she circled back," Zak said. "Went to the bunkhouse."

Matt shook his head. "She's gone."

"What did you say to her?" Zak demanded.

"That's between Ammie and me."

Zak's jaw clenched. "Maybe it is, maybe it isn't. Why in blazes were you in the barn so long with Amelia, when your *fiancée*"—he emphasized the word—"was waiting for you in the house?"

"Easy, Zak," Shamus said, obviously disliking the barely veiled insinuation in Zak's words.

Zak side-stepped just a little. "Lynette was getting worried."

Lynette had not said a word. Matt looked at her now, her dark eyes accusing, as though she knew exactly what had happened in the barn. He turned away. "I'm going after Ammie."

"In the dark?" Zak gritted. "How do you propose to track her in a rainstorm in the dark?"

"I know how she thinks." His face twisted. "At least, I used to."

"I'm going too," Shamus said. "If Ammie hasn't taken shelter somewhere she considers safe, she'll be terrified." He turned to Mary, his face grim. "This isn't what I had in mind for our wedding night. I'm sorry."

Mary squeezed his arm. "Don't give it another thought. You just find Amelia."

Shamus kissed her on the cheek. "I love you."

She smiled. "Go."

"Got an extra slicker?" Zak asked.

"In the bunkhouse," Shamus replied, sending Zak a grateful look. "I'll roust the boys, find some lanterns, get the horses saddled." Shamus hurried from the house.

Matt started after him.

"Maybe you'd best stay here," Zak said. "If Amelia wanted to be near you, she wouldn't have ridden off. Especially considering how her mama died."

Matt stiffened, partly from anger, partly from guilt. "I'm going."

The two men glared at each other, neither prepared to back down.

Lynette touched Zak's sleeve. "It's all right, Zachary," she said. "Matthew needs to go. He feels responsible."

Some of the fury went out of Zak. He gripped Lynette's hand in his. "You're more understanding of him than he deserves."

Matt winced but said nothing.

"Will you be all right here alone with Mary?" Zak continued.

"Of course." Lynette forced a brave smile. "You go ahead. Both of you."

Still glowering at Matt, Zak stomped from the house.

Matt turned to follow, but Lynette's voice stayed him. "Matthew?"

He didn't look at her.

She stepped up beside him. "You take care."

"I will. Thanks."

Her voice trembled. "Please remember, I love you."

He closed his eyes, feeling like something that deserved to live under a rock. "I'll, uh—be back as soon as I can." With that, he all but fled the house.

Outside, the ranch yard was beginning to resemble a quagmire. Shamus, Zak, and the Shamrock hands were all tromping through mud, each carrying a lantern and leading a saddled mount. Lightning zigzagged to the north. Thunder cracked, and Smoke's gelding shied. The rangy foreman managed to hold on to the reins and settle him down. Shamus handed Matt a lantern, then quickly barked out orders about who would search where.

Water cascading off the brim of his Stetson, Matt

started to mount. Shamus caught his arm. "I don't know what went on in that barn," he rasped above the noise of the storm, "but when Ammie's back home safe, I intend to find out."

Matt covered his guilt with irritation. "We're not going to find her if we stand here."

Shamus's grip tightened. "If anything happens to her—"

"Nothing's going to happen to Ammie," Matt snapped. "I won't let it."

"We goin' or not?" Smoke called from the back of his horse.

Shamus released Matt's arm, his shoulders sagging. "I'm sorry. I know you'd never mean her any harm, Matt. I'm just scared for her."

"I know," Matt said. "So am I. But she'll be all right. Ammie's tough. She can handle herself." He said the words as much for his own benefit as for Shamus's.

"Any other time I'd agree with you. But with the way she feels about you lately, she hasn't been thinkin' too straight."

Matt frowned. "What are you talking about?"

Shamus turned away. "Nothing. Let's ride."

Still frowning, Matt mounted, and the others did likewise. Each headed in separate directions. Almost at once, Matt was struck by how hopeless their task was. The lantern spread only the barest pool of light in the inky blackness, offering him virtually no guidance. He kept hold of it anyway. If he couldn't see Ammie, perhaps she could see him. Besides, looking for her was preferable by far to sitting at the ranch, waiting. He rode on instinct alone, praying Ammie had taken shelter somewhere—in a line shack or a cave—anywhere. But even that would be precious little consolation. No matter where she was, she would be terrified.

He remembered a trail drive they'd been on together a

few years back. A storm had come up, a bad one. Ammie
had been riding drag. The storm had spooked the herd,
sent it stampeding. Every man in the outfit had been con-
centrating on the cattle. It had been an hour before anyone had even noticed Ammie was missing.

Matt had gone looking at once. He rode past a huge
boulder and reined in when he heard an odd whimpering,
like some wounded creature in terrible pain. He had
found Ammie huddled on the opposite side of the rock,
soaked to the skin, trembling violently. She'd been staring
straight ahead, her eyes focused on nothing.

"Ammie?" He had hunkered down beside her, touched
her hand. She hadn't reacted at all. He said her name
again, louder.

Nothing. She'd scared him. He hadn't seen that look in
her eyes since . . . He'd swallowed hard, then settled
his body against hers, wrapped his arms around her,
crooned to her, said anything that came into his head—
just as he had that hellish day years before. Finally, after
what seemed like hours, her head had lolled back and she
had nestled into the crook of his arm. Tears streamed
down her face. "Mama saved me, Matt. She saved me.
And then the water took her. It took her."

He hugged her close. "It'll be all right, Ammie. It'll be
all right. I promise."

It was another hour before she'd regained her senses
enough to sit a horse. And then she'd been acutely embarrassed. She wouldn't even meet his eyes. He'd mounted
Drifter, then pulled her up behind him. "I can't believe I
behaved like such a weakling," she said.

"It's nothing to be ashamed of."

"It is!" she returned hotly, barely suppressing another
bout of tears.

Anytime they'd been caught out in a storm since, Ammie had made certain to stick right by his side. He hadn't
missed her white knuckles or the terror that edged her

green eyes, but she had seemed to take comfort in his presence, and he'd been glad. They had a bond, he and Ammie, an unbreachable bond that nothing could break.

Or so he had always thought.

Until today.

Matt cursed the rain, cursed the darkness, cursed himself. Ammie was out here somewhere because of him. Hurting, alone, afraid. And it was his doing, all of it. *I don't have a best friend anymore.*

What in the name of heaven had he been doing kissing her, when he was engaged to Lynette? Yet why had it felt so damned right to kiss her? If she hadn't mentioned Lynette's name, he probably would have made love to Ammie right there in the barn. And then where would they have been?

Lynette needed him, depended on him.

Do you love her?

Matt swore viciously.

Do you love her?

"No!" he shouted above the wind and the rain. "No, I don't love her. All right?" Were the gods appeased now? Were they happy? He had admitted it at last. He did not love Lynette Simmons.

But he was going to marry her anyway. He had promised Clint he would take care of her, promised Lynette as well. And he would keep that promise.

The rain was falling harder. Matt nudged Drifter into a canter. Lightning sizzled up ahead, slamming into a lone oak, starting a small fire that was quickly extinguished by the rain. Where the hell would Ammie go?

Matt's throat constricted. The creek!

Surely she wouldn't be so foolish.

But Shamrock Creek was not the creek that had killed her mother. Shamrock had been a sanctuary to them both all of their lives.

Matt spurred Drifter into the darkness.

*   *   *

Ammie huddled against the base of a massive cottonwood and stared into the dark, swirling waters of Shamrock Creek. She was breathing in short, shallow gasps,
fighting down a surge of panic.

Lightning crackled overhead, followed almost at once
by a cannonade of thunder. She was soaked to the skin,
her hair straggling wet about her face.

Home. She had to get home. She had tied off Ranger
just a few feet away. All she had to do was get to the horse
and point him toward the ranch. The gelding would do
the rest. But her muscles refused to obey her.

The rain fell harder, and the canopy of tree branches
above her provided her no protection from the wind-
whipped storm. How had she gotten here? She didn't
even remember.

She remembered being in the barn with Matt, remembered the cruel words they'd said to each other just before she'd ridden out. She hadn't been thinking clearly,
had wanted only to get away. By the time the initial rush
of pain receded, she had been miles from home. And then
it had started to rain. She remembered little else until this
moment.

She sat there, hugging her knees, rocking back and
forth, as the rain continued to beat down on her.

Get up, go home, her mind pleaded.

She did neither.

Matt. Matt would come. Matt would save her. No.
Even thinking his name was a knife thrust to her heart.
Matt wouldn't come. Not this time, not ever again. Her
worst nightmare had come true. She had dared risk everything, and she had lost. Lost even their friendship.

She had seen the look in his eyes after he'd kissed her
—stricken, appalled by the realization that he had betrayed Lynette. He had accused Ammie of trying to trap
him. Though the words had been brutal, uncalled for,

Ammie could not entirely dismiss them. It had been her plan to test his feelings. No such thought had been in her mind at that moment, but it scarcely mattered. The results were the same.

He had made his choice—and his choice was Lynette.

Lightning flashed again, and Ammie could have sworn the water in the creek seemed higher than it had moments ago. She had to get out of here. Reviling herself as a coward, somehow she managed to gain her feet. Stumbling, staggering, she made her way toward Ranger.

The horse side-stepped, whinnying shrilly. Her jerky movements were panicking the already-skittish gelding. She caught at the reins just as a ferocious clap of thunder sounded. The horse reared, and his eyes rolled back in his head. He tore the reins from her grasp. Ammie lunged for them. Too late—the gelding bolted away into the night.

Terror seized her, clawed at her like a living thing. Her only means of escape was gone. She felt as if she were suffocating. She took a step, then another, not noticing in the darkness that she was going toward the creek instead of away from it. "Mama," she whimpered. "Mama, help me."

She took another step.

Again and again Matt shouted Ammie's name, only to have it snatched away by the howling of the wind. The rain was coming down in sheets. The lantern had long since gone out, and he was riding blind. Only an occasional flash of lightning guided his path.

Another bolt flickered, bathing the sodden landscape in an eerie green light. If it hadn't, he would not have seen Ranger thunder past some hundred yards to the west. Matt's heart lurched. Though the sight of the panicked horse worried him, it gave him hope. Ammie was somewhere nearby.

He made it to the creek and dismounted, feeling his

way along a deer path on the near bank. Lightning illuminated the swift, angry current in front of him, tumbling, swirling. The thought that Ammie was even near that water sent a bolt of sheer terror ripping through him.

"Ammie!" He shouted again, his voice hoarse, raw. "Ammie, where are you?" He strained to hear something, anything out of sync with the storm. But he heard nothing. He continued to search, moving slowly, cautiously, afraid that if she was too terrified to speak, move, he would miss her in the darkness. Long minutes passed. He pressed on, his fingers cut and bloodied by numerous encounters with the thorny brush along the water's edge. He did not pause, and the rain did not let up.

More time passed, but still he found no sign of her. All he could think of was that cold, murky water. How easy it would be for her to stumble into it in the dark.

He closed his eyes. "Please, God . . ." Let her be all right. She had to be all right. He tried to imagine his life without her. He shuddered.

He would have no life without her.

He loved her. *Loved* her.

He dropped to his knees. Loved her.

Sweet God, of course. Why had he fought it so long and so hard? Why had he refused to recognize it for what it was? Not lust—love.

He remembered the kiss they had shared by this very creek the night before he'd left for Kansas. He'd felt the first stirrings of desire then but had dismissed it, telling himself it was a reaction to his grief about Clint, and to Ammie's teasing about the ladies of Wichita. But it had been neither of those things. He had been responding to Ammie herself, responding to her as a man responded to a woman.

And yet the very notion of having sexual feelings toward Ammie had scared hell out of him. He was certain she would be shocked, hurt. The more intense his feelings for her had become, the more pointed had been his resolve to stay away from her. Back at the ranch tonight, he had not wanted to be the one to fetch her to join them for tea. Only after Mary had busied everyone else with some small task of postnuptial tidying-up had Matt given in to her urging that he go out to the barn. If he hadn't known better, he would almost suspect that Mary had wanted him to be alone with Ammie.

Except that Ammie had not been alone. Matt's blood ran hot as he remembered seeing her in Terence Kessler's arms. At first glance he had believed she was encouraging the man's advances, but in a heartbeat it was obvious she was not. It occurred to Matt, even as he was punching the bastard in the face, that either truth would have brought the same response from him. There had been more at work there than the protective instincts of one friend for another. He couldn't admit it then, but he saw it now for what it was. He had been insanely jealous of Kessler.

And then he had pulled Ammie into his arms and kissed her himself, succumbing to a desire so fierce, it had frightened him. To cover those feelings he had lashed out at her, driven her away. Driven her to this.

Cursing, he pushed to his feet and again groped along the bank, his thoughts as jumbled as the waters of Shamrock Creek. "Ammie, forgive me." He tripped and fell heavily, nearly plunging headlong into the angry water. He felt beneath him, certain he had stumbled over a treefall.

His heart stopped. She was huddled on the ground, still, unmoving. She had not reacted at all to half his body landing across hers. "Ammie." She was cold, so cold. He found her chest and desperately felt for a heartbeat. But his hands were too numb. He couldn't tell. He pressed his face against hers, and his own heart started to beat again only when he felt the warmth of her breath against his cheek.

Scrambling to a sitting position, he felt along her body, trying to judge whether she'd sustained any injuries, any broken bones. He found no external wounds. He shook her, gently at first, then when she made no response, more forcefully: "Ammie!"

Nothing.

He had to get her out of there. He had to get her someplace warm and safe. Though she was soaked to the skin, he removed his slicker and settled it over her head. It would help trap her fading body heat. Gently, gently, he lifted her, cradled her against him. Her head nestled in the lee of his neck, and she moaned softly. Impulsively, he kissed the top of her head. "You're all right now, Ammie. You're safe. I promise." She began to shiver.

He started back toward where he had tied off Drifter. Time and again he was forced to pause, to wait for a flash of lightning to light the way. He was tromping through ankle-high water now, and the creek was leaving its banks.

Hurry! Hurry! his mind urged. But he dared not risk missing Drifter. The gelding was their only chance. Finally, he spied the horse.

Drifter danced sideways at his approach, his ears flattening against his head. "Easy, boy," Matt soothed. "Easy. It's just me." The gelding calmed a little, but Matt did not untie the reins until after he had gotten Ammie onto Drifter's back. The horse tried to bolt, but Matt held on, vaulting up behind Ammie. Drifter needed no urging. Matt barely touched the gelding with his spurs, and the horse lunged into a dead run.

Only after they put several hundred yards between themselves and the creek did Matt slow the horse. The gelding had always been as sure-footed as a mountain goat, but not even Drifter could spot a gopher hole in the dark. It was for that reason that Matt decided not to risk heading for the ranch. Besides, Ammie needed to get out of the rain immediately. He turned Drifter toward a nearby bluff, where there was an overhang of rock. They would wait out the storm there, wait for the first light of dawn.

The shallow cave faced in the opposite direction of the wind and was just deep enough to protect Drifter against the storm as well. Matt dismounted and eased Ammie into his arms. She made no sound. He carried her as far back into the mouth of the cave as he could, then he laid her on the stone floor. Blessedly, this far in, the floor was dry.

He hurried back to Drifter to fetch his saddlebags, then returned to Ammie's side. He struck a match. His heart turned over. She looked so pale, so lifeless.

He flipped the match into the rain, then quickly rummaged through his saddlebags and extracted a change of clothes and a blanket. Allowing himself no time to think about what he was doing, he stripped Ammie of her soaked clothing and dressed her in his dry shirt and trousers. For once, he was grateful for the darkness. He leaned forward, brushing his hand across her forehead.

She didn't move.

He kissed her cheek.

She shifted slightly and shivered again. Working rapidly, Matt gathered up bits of wood and dried grasses that had blown into the rocky fissure over the years. They wouldn't burn long, but he would use the warmth of the fire while it lasted. He peeled off his own soaked shirt, then eased Ammie into a sitting position, cradling her against him. He began to suspect that her shivering had more to do with her ordeal than with the temperature. The rain itself had been cold, but here, away from the brunt of the storm, the summer night was not altogether unpleasant.

"I'm sorry, Ammie," he murmured. "So damned sorry." He leaned his head back against the wall of stone. He needed her to wake up, needed to talk to her, tell her so many things. Like the fact that he loved her.

What would she think of his pronouncement? Would she truly be shocked? Hurt? The thought brought a sharp stab of pain with it. And then he remembered her reaction to their kiss in the barn.

I knew it. I knew you didn't love Lynette. Had those been the words of a friend who was convinced he was marrying Lynette for the wrong reasons? Or had those been the words of a woman who didn't want him marrying Lynette for *any* reason?

The way she feels about you lately, she hasn't been thinking too straight.

His heart thudded in his chest. Could it be?

That day when he'd stopped to go skinny-dipping in the creek and Ammie had unexpectedly joined him, he'd been conscious only of his own reactions to her, how fearfully aroused he'd been, how desperately he'd wanted to hide that fact from Ammie. But she'd been no playful child that day. She'd been all woman, a woman who'd pulled him into her arms and kissed him hard on the mouth. *Tell me if you think I'm practicing.*

He closed his eyes, and a strange mix of wonder and sadness welled up inside him. How could best friends be so blind to each other's feelings? He tipped her head back, studying her beloved face, even as he trailed his fingers featherlight along her cheek. "How could two smart people be so stupid?" he murmured.

Obviously she had been as reluctant as he was to acknowledge her changing feelings. "But you were about to, weren't you?" That day at the creek. And then he had told her he was going to marry Lynette.

He raked his fingers through his hair. Lynette. How in the name of heaven was he ever going to explain any of this to Lynette? She would be within her rights not to release him from their engagement. In good conscience he wasn't even sure he could ask her to release him, even though he could see now that he had been set to marry her for all the wrong reasons: To assuage his guilt over Clint. To gain his father's approval. And in a very real way, to find a haven from his growing desire for Ammie.

How Lynette would react to his confession, he couldn't predict. He would just have to wait and see. Right now, his only concern was Ammie. Outside the cave, the rain was still falling. "I love you," he murmured, stroking her hair, needing to say the words. "I love you so much."

He was certain she was still unconscious, but then he felt her tears, hot, wet against his chest. "I love you too."

His throat constricted, his eyes burning, as he hugged her tight. "How do you feel?"

She looked at him, her eyes luminous in the meager firelight. "Perfect," she whispered. "Now that I'm with you." She raised her hand and traced her fingertips along his mouth. Tears slid from the corners of her eyes. "I've wanted so long to hear you say you love me." She gave him a tremulous smile. "It was worth waiting for."

He captured her face in his hands. "You'll never have to wait again." He kissed her cheek. "I love you." He kissed her forehead. "I love you." He kissed the tip of her nose. "Ammie O'Rourke, I love you with all my heart."

He gathered her to him, and his lips found hers, her mouth even softer than he remembered. He reveled in the sweet eagerness of her response. The fire winked out, but it didn't matter. He was warmed by the heat that fired his blood. All the confusion and pain of the past few weeks fell away. Nothing mattered now but the joy of being in each other's arms. And for long minutes they settled for just that.

He longed to make love to her and knew she would have let him, but despite the aching need in his loins, in his heart he pulled away. He wasn't free to love her. Not yet. Ammie knew it as well as he did. Maybe more. Her next words confirmed it.

"What about Lynette?" she whispered.

"I'll talk to her." His heart was still racing, his blood pounding.

"She won't want to let you go."

"I'll talk to her," he said again. "She'll understand."

Ammie trembled, obviously unconvinced, and Matt felt a stirring of foreboding, a sense of loss so profound, it was like a physical pain. He had the sudden urge to grab Ammie, climb onto Drifter's back, and ride and never look back. Instead he just held her close.

"Remember the game we used to play when we were little, Matt?" she asked softly. "The one where when something bad happened to one of us, the other would wish something good. Like the time you and Drifter didn't win the race against Clint's horse. I wished you the fastest horse in the world."

He smiled against her hair. "And I remember your first batch of cookies. They were all burned. I wished you a better stove."

Her laugh was more like a sob. "Wish me something, Matt. Wish me something now."

"Anything, Ammie. I'd wish anything for you."

Her voice was so much like that little girl of years ago that it all but broke his heart. "Wish me a rainbow, Matt."

Chapter 19

Ammie awoke to silence. The rain had stopped. The cloud cover was gone. She blinked tiredly, fighting off the urge to drift back to sleep. It was still a couple of hours before dawn. Outside the cave, the tree-bristled grassland appeared more like some dark, mystical fairyland, as millions of water droplets glistened in the golden glow of a nearly full moon.

She sighed. Her muscles were cramped from being so long in the same position, but she didn't move. To do so would awaken Matt. And she didn't want to lose the cocooning warmth of his embrace, a warmth that was far more than physical. It was a warmth of the spirit as well.

He loved her.

She could still scarcely believe it.

Hardly more than five hours ago, she'd been convinced she'd lost him forever. Lost even their friendship. And now she sat wrapped in his arms, his blanket draped shawllike about them both, and reveled in the wonder of those three magical words *I love you.*

She pressed her face against his shoulder, trailing her fingers lightly across his chest. He wasn't wearing a shirt, and in the soft light of the moon she marveled at how beautiful he was, as beautiful as this night had become. She doubted she would ever fear a thunderstorm again. After all, it was the storm, however indirectly, that had led them to admit the truth at last—that they loved each other.

Her mouth curved into a tender smile at the irony of it.

To think that for weeks Matt had been as unsettled by his escalating desire for her as she had been by hers toward him! He had wanted to protect her, shield her, spare her the shock and embarrassment of what he considered almost a betrayal of trust. Even if it meant marrying Lynette Simmons.

Ammie shuddered. What a fool she had been to keep silent. It would have been better to face Matt's possible rejection than to allow his relationship with Lynette to reach the stage it had unchallenged. If she had had the courage to speak up when Matt had first returned from Wichita, none of this would have happened.

Now all three of them would pay a price for her cowardice.

Lynette would most certainly be hurt. Despite the woman's sometimes cloying pretense of helplessness, there was an air of real desperation about her that had made even Ammie feel sorry for her. The true depth of that desperation, Ammie had yet to discover. What if Lynette refused to free Matt from their engagement? Would Matt feel honor-bound to go through with it?

For all his reckless ways, Matt Grayson was a man driven first and foremost by conscience, a sense of fair play. Under the best of circumstances it would be difficult for him to back away from a commitment, no matter how ill-advised that commitment might have been. But Lynette's unhappiness, her vulnerability, and her dependence could make backing away infinitely difficult for him, if not impossible.

On top of that, Matt would have to deal with his father's reaction. From the very beginning, Zak Grayson had openly approved of Matt's relationship with Lynette. Their engagement had created the bond between father and son that Matt had been seeking all his life. How would that bond fare if and when the engagement was broken?

Ammie closed her eyes, her heart aching. *If?* Surely, there was no real chance that Matt would marry Lynette now. But then why, despite the growing discomfort in her aching limbs, did she refuse to move, refuse to wake him? Because every minute they stayed here was a minute's delay in that inevitable encounter with Lynette.

You're giving in to your fear again, Amelia, she chided herself fiercely. *You can't keep him here forever. Sooner or later, he has to talk to Lynette.*

She traced her finger along the beard-roughened line of his jaw. There was no help for it. It was time to go.

Matt stirred, his eyelids fanning slowly upward, his arms tightening about her waist. "Good morning," he mumbled drowsily.

Her heart pounded. "Good morning."

Gently, tenderly, he smoothed the tangled mass of her hair away from her face. "I could get used to this. Waking up in your arms, I mean."

"Me too." Her mouth felt suddenly dry, her breathing shallow.

Matt shook himself. "We'd better go." She would have protested, but he added, "Your pa is likely worried sick."

Ammie felt a stab of guilt. She hadn't even thought about her poor father.

Stiffly, she and Matt pushed to their feet. Matt grabbed his shirt. Ammie could tell it was still damp, but he shrugged into it anyway, his shoulders hunching reflexively at the unpleasant chill of the fabric against his bare flesh. Quickly, she broke camp while Matt saddled Drifter. When he'd finished, he turned toward her and held out his hand. She swallowed hard, then slid her fingers into his palm. She started to mount, then impulsively drew his hand to her lips and kissed the backs of his fingers.

Their eyes locked.

In that frozen instant of time Ammie saw in those open,

unguarded blue eyes all the fire, the passion, the love he
had taken such care to hide from her these past weeks.
Her knees went rubbery as her body responded to that
look just as surely as if it had been a caress.

Sagging against him, she murmured his name, all but
drowning in a whirlwind of sensation. Tilting her head
back, she opened her mouth to say something. What it
was, she later could never remember, because in the next
heartbeat his mouth crashed down on hers, and the last
shreds of rational thought fled. Hot, eager, his tongue in-
vaded her mouth, plundering its secret recesses. He
tasted her, possessed her, gloried in her, emboldening her
to respond in kind.

"I want you, Ammie," he said hoarsely, pressing her
down onto the cave floor. "God in heaven, I want you so
much."

His hands roved urgently along her body, the fierce-
ness of his need making his movements clumsy, awkward
—so much so that he apologized and forced himself to
slow down, and for that Ammie could only love him more.

He opened the buttons of her shirt, then almost rever-
ently, as if he were unveiling a most precious treasure, he
eased the material away from one breast. His eyes seared
her, her nipple hardened even before he touched her, and
then he worshiped her breast with his mouth.

Ammie cried out, arching upward, tangling her fingers
in the thick, dark waves of his hair. Her breathing grew
ragged as she held him to his erotic task. She felt that
most secret part of her grow moist, ready.

She writhed beneath him, her body tinder to his flame.
She had wanted this, dreamed of it, ached for it. And now
she would be his, fully, completely. Instinct lashed at her.
She slid one hand between their straining bodies, her fingers fumbling with the fastening of his fly. The button
yielded. Heart thundering, she slipped her hand beneath
his jeans, skating down along the hard plane of his abdo-

men and then lower. She found his heated flesh, touched him.

He gasped, stilled, the pleasure so exquisite it was almost beyond bearing.

Impatient, Ammie shoved at his confining denims, pushing them down past his hips. Her knees shifted, one of them inadvertently coming up . . .

Matt let out a startled yelp.

Ammie jerked back, heat suffusing her face. "Oh, Matt, I'm sorry! I'm so sorry."

"It's all right." He lay back, sucking in air through clenched teeth. "It's all right."

"I didn't mean—I didn't mean to . . ." She stared at him, mortified beyond words.

"It's all right," he rasped again. "I'll live. Just give me a second."

Tears slid from the corners of her eyes. "I can't believe this. I've ruined everything. Oh, Matt, are you all right?"

Gingerly, he pushed to a sitting position and adjusted his clothes. "I'm fine. I swear." He caught her hand, kissed her palm. "Oh, Ammie, please don't cry. It's not that bad. You just—caught me a little off guard." He chucked her under the chin, trying to coax a smile from her. "Besides, it's just as well."

"You're just saying that."

"No, I'm not. Ammie, I love you. But I didn't mean for us to get so carried away. When I make love to you, I don't want any shadows between us. I want . . ." He hesitated.

"You want to be free of any ties to Lynette."

He nodded.

"I understand," she said, and she did.

"Besides," he teased gently, "this stone clamshell isn't what I had in mind for the first time I make love to you. I want a bed."

Ammie managed a shy smile. "Me too."

"Come on." He helped her to her feet. "Let's get you home."

Ammie mounted Drifter, and as she waited for Matt to climb up behind her, her heart was full, her senses bursting with the wonder of knowing how much he loved her. The whole world seemed fresh and new. Her gaze shifted to the mist-shrouded meadow and beyond. She couldn't be certain, but just for an instant, she could've sworn she saw a rainbow.

They rode into the Shamrock yard just past dawn, just in time to stop her father and the others from taking up the search again. Shamus, Zak, and the Shamrock hands had returned to the house only long enough to change into dry clothes. It was obvious that none of them had gotten any sleep.

Ammie leaped from Drifter's back and rushed into her father's outstretched arms. "I thought I'd lost you," he whispered hoarsely, giving her a fierce hug. "When Mary told me Ranger came in without you . . ." He didn't finish.

Ammie blinked back tears of her own. "I'm fine, Pa. Honest." She looked over her shoulder. "Thanks to Matt."

Matt had dismounted and was standing a respectful distance away, not wanting to intrude. Though her father might have held Matt accountable for her trouble in the first place, no such accusation showed in his pale green eyes. He stepped toward Matt and stuck out his hand. "I'm grateful, Matt. Thank you."

Matt accepted the handshake. Will, Jess, and Smoke came over and gave Matt a round of heartfelt pats on the back as well.

"Good to have you home, Red," Smoke said, grinning. "I'd appreciate it, though, if the next time you scare the bezeebers out of all of us, you'd give us fair warning." He rubbed his head. "I would've drunk a lot less of that punch at the wedding yesterday."

"I promise," she managed through the lump in her throat.

Mary had come out of the house and was dabbing at her red-rimmed eyes with the hem of her apron. "Oh, Amelia . . ." Her voice faltered. Ammie flung herself into Mary's arms. They didn't say anything. They didn't have to.

Ammie felt overwhelmed, overjoyed, to be home, to be surrounded by people who loved her. And then out of the corner of her eye she saw Zak Grayson striding purposefully from the house toward Matt. Ammie stiffened, stepping away from Mary. She hurried to Matt's side.

There was no mistaking Zak's mood: it was hostile, angry. His eyes were as hard as his voice. "I want to talk to you, boy. Alone. Now."

Ammie touched Matt's hand. A mistake. Zak didn't miss the intimacy of the gesture. His gaze grew harder still.

"Now," he repeated.

"I don't think so," Matt said, his voice deceptively even. He glanced at Ammie, and she read the resolve there, the love. "First I have to talk to Lynette."

"Lynette is asleep," Zak snapped. "She was up late fretting herself sick about you. Not that you apparently give a damn, but I won't have you upsetting her."

Matt started toward the porch.

Zak snared his arm. "Just what the hell are you planning to say to her?"

"That's between Lynette and me."

They glared at each other for a long minute. Ammie was certain they were about to come to blows at last. Then Zak stunned everyone in the ranch yard by allowing Matt to step around him. In the next instant she could almost have wished for that fist fight; the words that followed Matt into the house were far more agonizing than any physical blow could ever have been.

Ammie had never heard Zak Grayson beg before. But she heard it now: "Don't end it, Matt. Please."

Matt found Lynette in the guest bedroom. The door was open, and she was sitting in the rocking chair next to the bed, the soft blue folds of her gown making her appear even more vulnerable than usual. He straightened as he entered the room. She did not look up, even when he closed the door behind him.

"Did you find Amelia?" Her voice was hushed, subdued. "Of course you have." She answered her own question. "You wouldn't have come back if you hadn't. Is she all right? She wasn't hurt, was she?"

Though he couldn't see her eyes, Matt knew Lynette had been crying. He winced. "Ammie's fine." He stepped farther into the room and cleared his throat nervously. This was going to be so damned hard. "Lynette, I—"

"You finally figured it out, didn't you?" Lynette interrupted, still speaking in that hushed, subdued tone. She was clutching at a silk kerchief in her lap.

He frowned. "Figured what out?"

"That you love her."

He blinked, startled. "How could you know what I didn't even know myself?"

She smiled wanly. "I'm a woman. Why do you think I worked so hard to keep you away from her?"

Matt didn't know what to say.

"It's all right, Matthew. I maneuvered you into your proposal. I release you from it, of course."

Matt stared at her, stunned by how easily she had acquiesced and more than a little disconcerted. There was something not quite right about this, but he was so glad to be unengaged, he wasn't about to press her on it. "You

won't want for anything, Lynette. I promise you. I'll see to
it that you're well provided for."

"Thank you, Matthew, I—"

The door burst open and Zak stormed into the room.
Gone was the man who had swallowed his pride just moments before. Now he was livid. "I asked you not to do
this, Matt! Now I'm telling you! I'm not going to let you
humiliate Lynette like this!"

"It's all right, Zachary," Lynette said. "Matthew is only
doing—"

"No!" He cut her off. "No son of mine is going to
shame me this way. Matt will marry you, if I have to hold
a gun to his head!"

Matt glared at his father, furious and strangely hurt.
Couldn't the bastard see how painful this was? Did he
have to turn it into abject torture for everyone, including
Lynette?

Lynette rose and crossed the room, placing a placating
hand on Zak's arm. "I can't make Matthew love me, Zachary." Tears slid from the corners of her eyes. "I'll go back
to Austin. I'll be fine."

"You're overwrought. You've had a long night. You don't
know what you're saying." Zak turned on Matt. "I always
knew you weren't half the man Clint was, but this— I
would thought that for the sake of your brother's memory,
you could at least summon up some sense of honor, responsibility."

Matt stiffened. "I told Lynette she wouldn't want for
anything."

"And you think that absolves you? Well, it doesn't!
You're not going to treat Clint's widow this way!" Awkwardly, Zak put his arm around Lynette's waist and
guided her back to the rocking chair. "You're coming back
to the Diamond G with me," he told her. "I won't hear of
anything else."

"I'll stay a few more days," she agreed. "But then I

really must go back to Austin. I have to start rebuilding my own life, Zachary. Alone."

Zak continued to fuss over her. "We'll talk about it later." He shot a glance at Matt. "I don't give a damn where *you* stay tonight," he snarled. "Just make sure it isn't on the Diamond G."

Matt ignored his father. "You take care, Lynette. I'll be by to see you."

She blinked back tears. "May I ask you one favor, Matthew?"

"Of course."

"When I leave for Austin, I'd like you to be the one to take me to the stage depot."

"If you insist on leaving," Zak put in, "I'll be the one to take you."

"Thank you, Zachary, but I'd like Matthew to do it."

"I'll be there," Matt said, then escaped the room. He stood outside the door, feeling shaken, exhausted. . . . *honor, responsibility.* His father's words had cut deep—partly because it was a charge he had already leveled at himself. He had never been quite sure how he'd wound up betrothed to Lynette—but he knew for certain that he hadn't done anything to disavow their engagement that morning in his bedroom. And because he hadn't, she had been crushingly hurt.

And yet which was the more honorable and responsible course? To go through with a marriage that could only leave them both miserable in the long run? Or to call it off while they both still had a chance to get on with their lives?

She might be hurting now, but he was certain she would be grateful later. She didn't love him. She barely knew him. And she was still grieving for Clint.

"It was rough, wasn't it?" Ammie asked.

Matt's head jerked up. He hadn't even realized he'd wandered out onto the porch. He looked into Ammie's

gentle, sympathetic eyes and knew that no matter what
the cost, he'd done the right thing. This was the woman
with whom he wanted to spend the rest of his life.

"I feel like such a bastard," he said.

Ammie stepped close to him, settled her hands on his
chest. "Lynette will be all right. She seems fragile, I
know. But that day she helped me with Tulip's foal, I saw
a side of her I wouldn't have guessed existed. She's a
survivor, Matt. She is."

He sighed. "I hope you're right."

"Is she leaving Shamrock?"

"Pa's taking her back to the Diamond G for a few days,
then she wants to go back to Austin." He settled his Stetson on his head. "I'd best be going myself. I don't want to
be here when my father comes out."

"Where are you going?"

"I don't know. Nowhere in particular. I just need some
time to think."

"Would you like some company?"

He gave her a crooked smile. "Yeah, I'd like that a lot."

They rode to the creek. Most of the evidence of last
night's storm was already gone. The creek, though slightly
elevated, once again rippled placidly within its banks.
"It's almost as if it was all a dream," Ammie murmured.
"Like it never happened."

Matt walked up beside her. The memory of finding her
lying so cold, so still, slammed into him like a fist. "It was
no dream. When I thought I'd lost you . . ." He drew
her to him, kissed her hard. They were both shaking when
he released her. "I love you so much," he said hoarsely.
"How could it have taken me so long to figure that out?"

"I think we were both afraid of tinkering with something very precious—our friendship."

He resisted the urge to kiss her again, fearing this time
he wouldn't be able to stop. "I want to marry you, Ammie
O'Rourke. Have children with you, grow old with you."

He tugged off his hat and threaded his fingers through his hair. "I just wish Lynette hadn't had to be hurt by all this. I don't want you to take this the wrong way, but I feel so bad about her."

"I'd be disappointed in you if you didn't. You're a very caring man, Matt Grayson."

"She's already had to suffer Clint's death."

"I think her grief for Clint is what drew her to you. She was trying to replace Clint with his brother."

"And maybe I was trying to be Clint for her. Damn, if I'd gotten to that hotel room ten seconds sooner! Ten seconds! Clint would still be alive. I'd have killed Lance Gentry before he had a chance to shoot Clint."

"Don't. The guilt isn't yours, Matt. You've got to stop carrying it. It's hard, I know, but Clint brought that night on himself."

"Maybe. But that isn't what the guilt's about, Ammie. Not his dying, not exactly—I've come to terms with that. What hurts so much is that"—his voice shook—"that I never got a chance to tell him I was sorry for being such a lousy brother and that—that I loved him."

Ammie kissed him again, wanting desperately to give him surcease from his pain. But he pulled away. "Don't."

"Why?"

"Because this isn't a time I can settle for kisses, Ammie. I want"—his eyes burned her, seared her—"I want to be inside you, lose myself in loving you. And that isn't fair."

"But I want it too."

"No." He climbed to his feet, stalked away several paces. "I have too much respect for you to take you because I'm feeling sorry myself. We'll wait."

She rose to stand beside him and took his hand in her own. "As my best friend," she teased gently, "you've had occasion to notice over the years that patience is not among my best virtues. Don't make me wait too long,

Matt. You've always been a most dedicated instructor, and I'm looking forward to being your best student."

He crushed her to him, burying his face in her hair. "We'll teach each other, Ammie. On this particular subject we'll teach each other."

The rest of the day was magic, as were the next day and the next day and the next. She and Matt were inseparable, spending every available minute together laughing, talking, planning their future. Shamus offered Matt a full partnership in Shamrock. Matt promised to think it over, though he hadn't yet given up on the Diamond G. He spent his nights at Shamrock too—in the bunkhouse. He wasn't ready to stomach another confrontation with his father. Ammie didn't know it was possible for human beings to be as happy as they were.

Friday came around, and Matt spent the morning as he had spent the past several mornings—helping the hands break the last of the Wichita horses. Just as Ammie was taking him out some lemonade, a rider came galloping into the yard. It was Joe Bradley, a wrangler who worked for the Diamond G. He rode immediately over to the corral and spoke to Matt. Joe was already riding out again by the time Ammie reached the corral. "What did he want?" she asked, though she could guess.

Matt hopped down from the corral rail. "Lynette's leaving. She wants me to take her to town to meet the afternoon stage."

"Today?" Ammie frowned. "Just like that? Why would she leave on such short notice?"

"I don't know, but I promised her last week that I'd take her." He lifted his Stetson and threaded his fingers through his sweat damp, dark hair. Ammie could tell he was uneasy about going. "You don't mind, do you?"

She twined her arms around his neck. "I mind, but I won't ask you not to go. I know it's something you need to do. But I admit I'm surprised your father didn't talk her into staying."

"He probably tried. Joe said Lynette got a letter from Austin yesterday."

Ammie suddenly remembered another of Lynette's letters. It was still upstairs in a drawer in her bedroom. She hadn't read it, but neither had she been able to bring herself to throw it away. She thought about mentioning the letter to Matt but decided against it. He would have enough on his mind facing Zak.

"Be back to kiss me good night?" she asked.

He caught her to him. "And maybe good morning. While I'm in town, I'm going to talk to the preacher, Miss O'Rourke, and see what I can do about your becoming Mrs. Grayson."

Ammie's heart did a somersault in her chest. "I've got tomorrow open."

He grinned. "Sounds good to me."

He kissed her again, then mounted and rode out. As Ammie watched him, an odd foreboding niggled in the pit of her stomach. As the day progressed, she tried to work it off by playing with Patches and Pickles, but the heavy feeling persisted. She told herself it was because she just wasn't keen on the idea of Matt seeing Lynette again. Though Ammie was certain of Matt's love, she wasn't at all certain about Lynette. After such a hard fight, the woman had given up too easily.

Again and again Ammie's thoughts returned to the letter. Maybe reading it would put her mind at ease. Maybe Lynette really did have a sick friend named Pearl.

Still warring with her conscience, Ammie went to her room. She opened the drawer in her night table and drew out the folded blue envelope. Lynette had never come looking for the letter, likely giving it up for lost.

Ammie took a deep breath. For Matt's sake, she had to know. She opened the letter and began to read.

Before she got past the first sentence her hands were trembling. Merciful God—no wonder Lynette was so desperate! And no wonder she'd been so insistent that Matt be the one to take her to the stage on this particular afternoon. Lynette hadn't thrown in her hand after all. She had one last card to play.

Ammie raced from the house to the corral. She took time only to put a bridle on Ranger, then vaulted onto the bay's back. She had to get to River Oaks in time to meet that stage. If Lynette played that final card and played it right, Ammie knew with a sudden horrible certainty that Lynette would win.

☘ / Chapter 20

Matt reined Drifter in at the hitchrail in front of the River Oaks stage depot. Beside him, his father was helping Lynette alight from the buggy in which Zak had driven her to town. Lynette's leave-taking was not going as either Matt or Lynette had planned it. Lynette had tried her best to say her good-byes to Zak back at the Diamond G, but Zak had insisted on coming along. When Lynette had requested that Matt be the one to drive the buggy, Zak had bluntly refused.

"It's a long drive to River Oaks, Lynette," Zak had said, "and I intend to use every mile to dissuade you from your foolish decision to return to Austin. Not even the generous financial settlement I've arranged for you puts my mind at ease. The thought of Clint's widow alone and unprotected in a city the size of Austin is simply intolerable." He shot Matt a look of pure venom, leaving no doubt that he placed the blame for Lynette's plight squarely at Matt's feet.

Matt had offered no defense. What would have been the point? But he'd been grateful for the sympathetic look Lynette had sent him. Perhaps by now she too had realized that she had mistaken feelings of need and grief for love. He hoped so.

And yet as Zak escorted Lynette to the wooden bench seat that abutted the depot's false front, Matt couldn't escape the niggling sense that if given the chance, Lynette would still go through with the wedding. She had neither said nor done anything, but the impression persisted nonetheless.

"We timed it just the way you wanted it, Lynette," Zak was telling her as he fussed with her parasol, popping it open to shield her from the sun. "The stage should be here any minute."

"Thank you, Zachary."

Matt frowned at how much her hand trembled when his father handed her the parasol.

"If you could get me a glass of water, please?" Lynette asked. "I'm feeling a bit overwarm."

"Of course." Zak headed toward the café down the street.

At once Lynette rose and crossed to Matt. In the harsh glare of the cloudless afternoon sky, her ivory skin seemed paler than usual to him. And then he noticed the fear in her luminous brown eyes.

"What is it?" he asked, his voice harder-edged than he meant it to be. Something in the way she looked triggered the same foreboding he had felt the other night, the night of the storm, when he had wanted to gather Ammie in his arms, mount Drifter, and ride away and never look back.

Lynette took her hand in his. Her skin felt cold, clammy. "There's something I must tell you before the stage gets in, Matthew. I should have told you before now, but I just couldn't find the words."

A familiar voice intruded. Sheriff John Haggerty called out a greeting as he ambled up the boardwalk toward them. "Thought that was you I was seein' from my office, Matt. Been a while."

"That it has," Matt agreed, trying not to show his irritation at the interruption.

"I was tied up the past couple days taking a prisoner over to the county seat, otherwise I would've come out to Diamond G. I turned up some information you and your pa might find of interest."

"What kind of information?"

"Oh, Matthew"—Lynette sighed—"I really am so very warm. I—I—" The parasol slid from her grasp to clatter onto the boardwalk, as Lynette swayed unsteadily on her feet. Swiftly, Matt swept her into his arms and carried her over to the bench seat.

"Oh, Matthew, do forgive me." She pressed her fingers to her temples.

"Don't be silly." He rubbed the backs of her hands. "Do you think you should lie down?"

"Maybe you should take her to my office," Haggerty suggested. "Get her out of the sun."

"No," Lynette said quickly. "No, please. I—I'm fine, really."

"The sheriff's right, Lynette," Matt said.

Zak rushed up and elbowed his way between Matt and Haggerty. "What is it? What's happened?" With more tenderness than Matt had ever seen from his father, Zak helped Lynette take a sip from the glass of water he had brought her. "I don't care what you say," he pronounced. "I am not letting you on that stage, young lady. You're not well."

"My, my," the sheriff said, rubbing his chin thoughtfully. "You've made quite an impression on the Graysons, now, haven't you, Miss Lynette."

Lynette made no response.

"I really think we all ought to go over to my office," Haggerty said again. "I have some things to say to all of you."

"About what?" Zak demanded.

"About Miss Lynette, I'm afraid."

Lynette's face went alabaster white.

"What's going on, Haggerty?" Zak snapped. "Can't you see you're upsetting my daughter-in-law?"

"We'd best talk in private, Zak. I—"

The sound of the stage rumbling up the street interrupted whatever the sheriff had been about to say. Lynette looked for all the world like a terrified doe caught in a hunter's cross-hairs. She gripped Matt's shirt sleeve. "I wanted to tell you—I wanted to tell you privately. I swear. Oh, Matthew, please believe me, I loved Clint with all my heart."

"Lynette, what is this? What's going on?"

The stage lumbered to a halt. The driver hopped down from his perch and jerked open the passenger door. "River Oaks," he announced.

Matt saw only one passenger inside. A plump middle-aged black woman peered out, eyeing the two-foot interval from the coach step to the ground with some trepidation. When the driver made no move to do so, Matt offered her his hand.

The woman gave him a polite, though slightly wary, smile. Then she gave him her hand, and Matt helped her to the boardwalk. "I thank you, sir. You're very kind." Her cultured voice and gracious manner suggested an education rarely afforded a black person, man or woman. Matt was impressed, and curious. He was about to ask if he could be of any assistance when his father moved aside, and the woman caught sight of Lynette.

Instantly the woman flew to Lynette's side. "Child, oh sweet child," she crooned. "What have they done to you?"

"Pearl," Lynette managed, her voice weak. "Pearl, I haven't told them. I—"

"There, there," Pearl soothed. "You hush now. Pearl is here. Pearl will take care of you."

"Did you bring—?" Lynette didn't finish.

Pearl nodded, looking toward the coach.

"Wait. Maybe I can still explain—"

"This is Pearl?" Zak asked, his brows furrowing. "From Austin? Did you know she was going to be on the stage, Lynette?"

"She knew," the sheriff put in.

Zak's lips thinned. "You're just bustin' a gut to tell us something, John. Why don't you spit it out."

Haggerty took exception to Zak's tone. The words he might have couched in an objective tone grew smug, arrogant. "You'll remember when you brought Miss Lynette in to do a little shopping a couple of days ago, Zak. Well, it seems that while you were getting that haircut and shave, Miss Lynette took the time to visit the telegraph office."

Zak looked questioningly at Lynette, but she did not meet his gaze.

"Well, sir," Haggerty went on, "it seems that the telegram that Miss Lynette sent was to her friend Pearl."

Matt wondered grimly if Finley Barnes had ever kept a telegraph message confidential in his life.

"Now, I knew Miss Lynette was leaving River Oaks today, what with the weddin' canceled and all." Haggerty was enjoying himself now. "So I thought to myself it was a mite peculiar that she was invitin' a friend to come up for a visit. And to bring a package with her to boot.

"Ol' Finley said Miss Lynette was actin' real nervous over it too. So bein' a lawman and a bit suspicious by nature, I sent off a few telegrams of my own. I guess I should have done it before, but she was such a charmin' little lady, I didn't push beyond the surface." He looked at Zak. "I'm real sorry it had to work out this way."

"What way?" Zak asked testily. "So Lynette asked a friend to come up and join her on the trip home. What's so ominous about that?"

"Not a thing. Until you put it together with a few of the answers I got to those telegrams."

Lynette blanched. "Please, Zachary. I can explain everything."

"Explain what?" Zak's voice was not harsh, but it was no longer so benevolent either.

With Pearl's help Lynette got to her feet, and together they walked to the stagecoach. Pearl reached inside and retrieved a blanket-wrapped bundle. "Slept like a little lamb, child. But he sure did miss you. Yes'm, he surely did miss his mama." She placed the bundle in Lynette's arms.

"My God," Matt whispered. A baby.

Zak could only stare in disbelief.

Tears slid from Lynette's eyes as she gazed at the sleeping infant. "Zachary, Matthew, I'd like you to meet Jeremy. Clint's son."

Matt eased Lynette into one of the chairs in Haggerty's office. She was clutching the baby and still looking deathly pale. "Would you like me to get you a doctor?" he asked.

"No, no. I'm fine."

She was far from fine—she was on the verge of collapse. He was a bit shaken himself. A baby. Clint's baby. It was wonderful. But it was also quite baffling. Why hadn't Lynette told them about the child before? A baby would have solidified her claim on Diamond G from the outset.

Matt could tell his father was torn apart. On the one hand, he was overjoyed to discover he had a grandson. And on the other, he felt hurt and betrayed that Lynette had kept the child a secret.

"Until this is sorted out," Haggerty said, "I think Miss Pearl should take the baby to the hotel."

"No," Lynette cried. "Please! I've missed him so much."

When Zak spoke, his tone gave away nothing of what he was feeling. "I think it would be for the best if the child weren't here."

But Pearl made no move to take the baby. Instead, she came over and crouched down in front of Lynette. "I thought they knew, child, or I would have stayed away."

"It's my fault," Lynette said. "I didn't know how to tell them."

"Who are you to Lynette, Pearl?" Matt asked.

"I've been with the Simmons family since New Orleans. Since before Miss Lynette was born. In fact, I helped birth her. All we've got left in the world is each other."

"By way of proper introduction," he said, "I'm Matt Grayson. I'm wondering if you knew my brother."

"Mr. Clint? Oh, yes, he was a fine man, a wonderful man. He tried to help Miss Lynette. He loved her very much."

"Enough of this!" Zak snapped. To Lynette he asked tightly, "Why didn't you tell us about Jeremy?"

"I couldn't predict what your reaction to me would be when I first came to River Oaks."

"That could explain your arriving without the child," Zak said reasonably, "but not why you continued to keep him a secret."

The baby began to fuss. Reluctantly, Lynette handed him to Pearl.

"Is there a store where I could get some milk?" Pearl asked.

"To the left and three doors down," Matt said.

"Thank you. I'll hurry." With that, Pearl took the baby and left.

Lynette began to weep softly. "Please, Zachary, I—"

The door swung open again, and Matt was surprised and pleased to see Ammie hurry in. Even in the midst of this chaos it felt good just to see her. Something in her eyes told him she wouldn't be needing an explanation of what was going on. But when she looked at Lynette, her gaze held no judgment, only sympathy.

"I'm sorry to interrupt," Ammie said. "But I had to be here."

"Then come in and be quiet," Zak said. Again he prodded Lynette. "Why was the baby a secret?"

Lynette's eyes were wide, frightened, but there was a quiet pride in them too. "I had to do what I thought best for Jeremy."

"And maybe for yourself?" Haggerty inserted.

"More from you, sheriff?" Zak gritted.

"If you'll allow me."

"Be my guest."

Haggerty walked over to his desk, opened the top middle drawer, and extracted a sheaf of papers. "Do you want to tell him, Miss Simmons, or should I?"

Lynette said nothing.

"Have it your way," Haggerty said. "I'm sorry, Zak. Truly. It seems Miss Simmons is not Clint's widow."

Zak staggered back a step.

"The marriage certificate was a fake, an excellent forgery."

"You're lying," Zak said. "Tell me he's lying, Lynette."

She remained silent.

Zak cursed and stalked over to her. "I don't understand. I trusted you, cared about you, I— damn you!" He gripped her arms, shook her violently. "I want the truth. All of it. Now!"

"Get your hands off her, Pa." Matt stood bare inches away from his father. His hands were balled into fists at his sides.

Zak let go of Lynette, but he didn't back away. He stood there, seething and, Ammie guessed, bitterly hurt. Lynette's link to Clint had gained her in mere days what Matt had fought for in vain all his life—a place in Zak Grayson's tightly locked heart. And now it was all about to turn to ashes. It was obvious that John Haggerty had learned from another source what Ammie had learned from Pearl's letter. Haggerty's next words confirmed it.

"Oh, Clint wanted Miss Lynette to be his wife right

enough," the lawman said. "But Miss Lynette couldn't
marry him. You see, she was already married to someone
else."

"That can't be true." This time it was Matt who spoke.
"It can't be."

"I'm sorry, Matthew," Lynette said quietly, "but it is."

"What a fool you must have taken me for," Zak said.
"What a complete fool. Did you make a fool of Clint too?
Or did he die before he knew of your treachery?"

"It wasn't that way at all. I loved Clint. I loved him
desperately. He knew about my marriage. We were—"

"Liar!" Zak rasped. "Clint would never commit adul-
tery! Never! If for no other reason than it would be political suicide." He paced to the far side of the room. "Oh,
it's all so clear now. As a widow, you would have a claim
on Diamond G, but as an adulteress *whore*, you would get
nothing!"

"Stop it," Matt said. "You've got no right to talk to her
that way."

"No right? This woman has piled lie upon lie upon lie.
She was not married to Clint. She was married to another
man. And this child—who's to say it's Clint's? It could be
her husband's."

"The baby *is* Clint's," Lynette said, straightening
slightly in her chair. "I hadn't been with my husband in
an—intimate way for over two years." Despite the scarlet
blush staining her cheeks, she did not look away from Zak
Grayson's furious glare.

"More lies!" he snarled.

"It's the truth!" Ammie blurted. "Lynette's husband
was a monster who used to beat her. And he was a thief.
Half of the five years they were married, he was in jail."

"I wondered what happened to that letter," Lynette
said, not unkindly.

"I only read it today, Lynette." Ammie's eyes were full
of compassion.

"Sweet Christ!" Zak snorted. "What next? Did your husband share the same cell with your father?"

"My father's story was . . . an exaggeration. It was the story Clint told me I should tell you if anything ever happened to him. He said you might overlook my father's difficulties. But you would never overlook Clint's being with a divorced woman."

"How did you really meet my brother?" Matt asked.

"It was a little over two years ago." Lynette's eyes took on a faraway look. "Clint was coming out of a saloon in Austin." She smiled, a sad little smile. "It was very late, and he was a little tipsy. He kind of stumbled into this alley. I was sitting behind some crates, sobbing. He heard me. I had run away from my husband."

She shuddered, the memories overwhelming her. "One of my eyes was swollen shut, and two of my ribs were broken. Clint took me to a doctor. A doctor who was paid to be very discreet. I was terrified that my husband would find me. But Clint went back to my place—that's when he met Pearl. Pearl took care of me and my bedridden father. My husband was gone. He would leave for weeks on end sometimes, and then just . . . show up. Anyway, Clint found a small place for Pearl and me and my father to live. He paid the proprietor to look the other way."

"Bah!" Zak said. "This is all nonsense."

"Let her talk, Pa," Matt said.

"It wasn't long before Clint and I fell in love. He found out that my husband had been arrested for cheating someone in a card game in Waco. Clint went to see him. He told him he could pull some strings and get his sentence reduced, if he would give me a divorce. My husband agreed, but he kept stalling about the divorce papers. Clint didn't dare press him on it, because—because he was always afraid that word would somehow get back to you, Zachary."

Zak ignored that. "You never did get divorced, did you?"

"Clint was desperate. I was pregnant by then, and he wanted to be married before the baby was born. Earlier this year, he sent word that he would be coming to Austin to finish up everything. He'd even arranged for my husband to be there to sign the divorce papers at last. Clint was going to pay him a lot of money. But Clint never came to Austin." She took a quivering breath. "He went to Abilene instead."

Matt's heart was thudding against his ribs. Please, God, don't let what he was thinking be true. "Simmons is your maiden name, isn't it, Lynette? Not your married name."

"That's right."

"You say Clint was going to pay your husband a great deal of money?"

"Yes. But when Clint didn't come to Austin, my husband was furious. He said the deal was off, and he left."

"Do you know where he went?"

"No. I haven't heard from him in months. I suppose he heard that Clint was killed, and figured—" She stopped.

Matt was looking at Ammie. "What was your husband's name, Lynette?" He asked the question, though he already knew the answer.

"Gentry," she said. "Lance Gentry."

"Oh, my God!" Ammie gasped.

"What is it, Matthew?" Lynette pleaded. "Tell me."

He didn't have to. She saw it in his face.

A keening sound rose in Lynette's throat, a mournful, pain-filled sound that seemed torn from the depths of her soul: "No, no, *no!*"

Tears stung Ammie's eyes, and the anguish in Lynette's sobs wrenched her heart. She crossed the room and pulled Lynette into her arms, soothing her, rocking her, as though she were a child.

Zak crossed the room, too, but not to comfort. There

was murder in his eyes. Matt stepped in front of him. "Leave her be!"

"Didn't you hear her?" he shouted. "Her husband killed Clint. Her husband murdered my son. She's not going to get away with it!"

"*She* isn't getting away with anything! She loved Clint. Or haven't you been listening?"

"He's dead because of her."

"He's dead because he tried to *help* her, tried to pay off the son of a bitch she—" He bit off the rest, but it was too late.

"What are you saying?" Zak's voice went deadly quiet. "Are you saying that it wasn't you who took the campaign money to that hotel room? That it was . . ." He shook his head. "No. No. How dare you besmirch your brother's name. He would never steal the campaign money."

Matt jammed his fingers through his hair. For a long minute he didn't speak, as he weighed the consequences of what he was going to say. But finally he decided it was what Clint would have wanted him to do. "I never wanted you to know what I thought had happened to Clint. I thought Clint had broken under the stress of running for office, and that he was going to gamble the money away. It made me crazy. I couldn't understand it. But now it turns out, it wasn't that at all. Now I know he was using the money to save Lynette's life."

"No!" Zak made a vicious chopping motion with his hand. "No more lies! I want her arrested, Haggerty! I want her behind bars now!"

"On what charge, Zak?" It was apparent that Haggerty had been moved by Lynette's story.

"She's responsible for Clint's death."

"She can't help what her husband did."

"Then fraud! She presented herself as Clint's widow! I arranged to give her money. I had it wired to an account in Austin!"

"She hasn't picked it up. I can't charge her."

"This whore killed my son! She has to pay!"

"Dammit to hell, Pa, don't you ever stop?" Matt shouted. "Lynette doesn't have to pay for killing Clint. She has to pay for making a fool of you! That's what this is all about. You believed her, cared about her, and then found out she had dared to lie to the almighty Zak Grayson."

"Shut your mouth, boy!"

"No! For five months you've hated my guts for what you decided I did to Clint. And now in the blink of an eye, you heap that same hate on the woman Clint loved. Well, it's time you put the blame where it really belongs, old man."

"How dare you?"

"Lynette lied to you for the same reason Clint lied to you: fear. Of you. If Clint hadn't been scared to death to make a mistake, scared to death to come to you with his problems, he'd still be alive. And that's God's truth. You killed Clint, Pa. *You.*"

Zak drove his fist into Matt's face. Matt staggered back, but he did not so much as raise a hand to wipe the blood from his mouth.

"You'll pay," Zak said. "You'll all pay. And you—" he pointed at Lynette. "You'll wish you were never born."

The door opened and Pearl bustled in, carrying the child. Lynette rushed to her side.

An ugly light shone in Zak Grayson's eyes. "And I know just the price. I'll hire the best lawyers in this state. I'll have your character destroyed, *Miss* Simmons. The courts will declare you unfit, then grant me custody of my grandson. And I swear to you, madam, the boy will never even know your name."

Lynette began sobbing hysterically. "Not my baby! Oh, dear God, Zachary, not my baby!"

"He won't touch your baby, Lynette," Matt said.

"You can't stop me!"

"I can and I will," Matt replied calmly. "I won't let you ruin another child's life."

Ammie gasped. The steel resolve in Matt's tone said it all. She knew exactly what he was going to do, and although she could feel her heart shattering into a million irreparable pieces, she made no attempt to stop him. She couldn't.

"If you're willing, Lynette," Matt said, "I know a way to prevent my father from having any claim on your son."

"I'll do anything, Matthew," she whimpered brokenly, "anything to keep my baby."

Matt couldn't look at Ammie. He didn't dare. He could never have gone through with this if he did. "The child will be legally mine, Lynette, if you marry me."

☘ / *Chapter 21*

The fire crackled and snapped in the Shamrock hearth. Ammie sat huddled beside Matt, staring into the flames. It was nearly midnight. They were alone in the big house. Mary and Shamus had gone to River Oaks to put Mary's old house on the selling block and to pack up the rest of her belongings. They wouldn't be back until late tomorrow.

Ammie had the feeling Mary's sudden urge to tie up loose ends in town had had more to do with the unspoken plea that must have been in Ammie's eyes when she and Matt rode in at sunset, than with any need Mary might have had to gather up old knickknacks. But whatever the reason, she was grateful. She would have this one night alone with Matt.

He had said precious little since the ugly scene with his father in Haggerty's office that afternoon. He'd left Lynette, Pearl, and the baby in a hotel in town, promising them he'd be back tomorrow. He and Lynette were to get married immediately, to forestall any plan Zachary might hatch to gain legal custody of the child.

The wedding was set for three o'clock tomorrow: fifteen hours away. In fifteen hours Lynette would do what Ammie had feared from the beginning she would do—break Matt's heart and in the bargain Ammie's as well. But not in the way Ammie had envisioned. Lynette was not a conniving vixen, plotting to snare herself a wealthy husband. She was a desperate mother, trying to give her son a name.

"It's strange," Ammie said, trailing her fingers along the back of Matt's hand, where it rested on her denim-clad knee. "But I can't even hate her. I hated her when I thought we were on level ground—when she was just a beautiful woman who wanted the same man I did. But now—now I can only feel sorry for her."

Matt didn't say anything. He only hugged her a little tighter. The fifteen hours were ticking away.

They had spent much of the time on the ride home trying to conjure some way *not* to go through with the wedding, some way to keep Jeremy with Lynette without her having to become Matt's wife. But each possibility they explored was ultimately rejected.

They couldn't run—Zak would find them, or hire someone who could. They couldn't perform a counterfeit marriage—somehow he would know. And they couldn't appeal to his mercy—he didn't have any. The only way for Jeremy to be safe was to be legally safe. Not even Zak Grayson was above the law.

And so during those last few miles of their journey back to Shamrock, Ammie had made a decision. Tomorrow Matt would be Lynette's husband. Ammie would have tonight. She would build memories with him during these few precious hours that would last them both a lifetime.

But first, she knew, she would have to overcome the man's implacable sense of morality. He would never be so unfair as to make love to her now, now that they couldn't be married. He wouldn't want to despoil her, sully her reputation for some nebulous future husband. What she wouldn't be able to get through that honorable head of his was that there would be no future husband, nebulous or otherwise.

The love she had for Matt was a once-in-a-lifetime bit of fairy dust and magic, the like of which would never come her way again. Nor would she want it to. Without Matt, she would content herself with being a rancher, maybe adopt an orphan or two. But she wouldn't marry. Ever.

Except tonight. Tonight in her heart and in her soul she would marry Matt Grayson. For this night, this one night, she would be his wife. She would slip past the barriers of what he considered his duty to her, and she would make him understand that the unfairest cut of all would be for him to deny her the full measure of his love.

Her heart pounding, Ammie stretched lissomely, easing away from him just enough to tilt her head back and kiss him fleetingly along the curve of his jaw. "I've decided," she murmured dreamily, "that I didn't just fall in love with you a few months ago. I fell in love with you the very first day Pa drove us over to meet you and your family, because you didn't laugh at a little girl in britches."

"Actually," he said huskily, "I have a confession to make. I found the daisy on your rear end rather amusing."

She giggled. "My mother always worried that people would think I was a boy."

"Mmmmm." He traced a finger down the center of her face, past the tip of her nose, then paused to memorize the sensual perfection of her lips. "No chance of that happening these days."

"There were other times when I should have known I loved you," Ammie said. "Like the first year after my mother died. You made me that panful of biscuits."

"I was pretty proud of them, as I recall."

"Until you bit into one."

"I think your pa wound up mortaring them into the fireplace, didn't he?"

"Either that, or he melted 'em down for bullets."

He laughed, and the sound warmed her heart. "Remember when we went after that beehive to try to start our own honey farm?"

"We ended up with more stings than sense." They both laughed, but then she sobered, snagging his gaze with her own. She twined her arms around his neck, praying fervently that he would not pull away. "I do love you, Matt Grayson. So much."

"Ammie, don't. Don't make it harder than it already is." He said the words, but he did not pull back.

"You rode home with me tonight, Matt. You must have known this night could happen. And I think you want it to as much as I do."

She had scored a hit with that one. He could not deny the truth of her words. It gave her hope. And then abruptly he climbed to his feet and strode over to the table near the hearth. On it he picked up a leather-bound book. Ammie recognized it as the one he had given Mary for a wedding present.

"I, uh—I've been wanting to share something with you," he said. "A secret. But then I decided to wait. I wanted it to be special when I told you." His voice cracked a little. "I wanted it to be our wedding night."

"What is it?"

He brought the book over to her and again sat down next to her. "Mary read my school records awhile back. A few months ago, she came to me and told me she had had a nephew like me. He was part of the reason she had decided to become a teacher. He couldn't read, and people called him stupid. And she knew he wasn't stupid. She taught him how to read. She asked me, would I like to try it?"

"And you told her no."

He had to smile. "Being in love with your best friend doesn't give you much room to lie. I told her no—but only the first five or six times she asked me. I didn't want to fail again."

"But then you did try."

He nodded. "Once or twice before I went to Wichita. A couple of times after I got back. Then all this week—those nights I spent in the Shamrock bunkhouse. The little lines finally started to make sense. It was like . . . like a door opened, a light shining in a dark place."

"Why didn't you tell me?"

His thumb caressed the leather cover. "Because—because I wanted to be good at it first."

Her eyes brimming with unshed tears, Ammie looked at the man she loved and whispered words she never thought she would hear herself say. "Read to me, Matt. I would love to hear you read to me."

Shyly, hesitantly, he opened the book and began to read from Byron: " 'She walks in beauty, like the night/Of cloudless climes and starry skies;/And all that's best of dark and bright/Meet in her aspect and her eyes.' "

He read on. Byron, Keats, Browning. He read the most beautiful words he could find, and he read them for her. And when he'd finished and he closed the book, Ammie found she couldn't bear the tiny distance between them for another second. She reached for him, took his hand, and brought it to her face. "You love me." She kissed his palm.

"More than my life."

"Then give me this night, Matt. Give me this one night. It's the only night we'll ever have."

His hand began to tremble. She could see the indecision in him, feel it.

"Please?"

He didn't answer, but he didn't object when she took his hand and led him up the stairs to her bedroom. There, she had him lie down on her bed. His face was haggard, drawn. She smoothed his hair back from his face and kissed him tenderly on the forehead. "Sleep, Matt. Sleep."

She drew a bath for him and brought the water up to the tub in her room. She was pleased to see that he actually had fallen asleep, some of the worry lines in his face softening.

She sat on the bed, savoring the joy of watching him sleep. This man was her best friend. He knew everything about her—she smiled—but he loved her anyway.

Gently, she shook his shoulder, rousing him. He was instantly awake. She could feel the tension in him, the despair. If it was possible, she hurt even more for him than she did for herself.

"Let me take care of you, Matt. Please, let me. Just for tonight." She began to unbutton his shirt.

He caught her hands. "Don't. Ammie, please—I can't bear it."

"Let me, Matt. Let me have this night. I want it. I want it so badly. Don't turn me away. Don't stop me. Please."

His eyes held hers for a long minute as his conscience warred with a soul-deep need. Then his hand fell away.

Ammie smiled, gently, tenderly. "I haven't had much practice at this. But you'll recall I was always a pretty good student."

He didn't trust himself enough to speak.

She finished unbuttoning his shirt, then eased the sides of the garment apart, exposing his chest to her questing fingers. "You're so beautiful, Matt. So beautiful."

His breath caught as she skated her fingers along that broad flat plane, feathering past one nipple, then the other. She leaned forward, kissed him lightly where her fingers had been. He closed his eyes.

Her hands skimmed to his belt, and she unfastened it. His breathing grew shallower, harsher. Again he caught her hand: "No." The word was a plea.

Gently, she nudged his hand away. "Let me do this for you, Matt. Let me do everything." She slid the belt free of his jeans, then worked the buttons of his fly.

He arched his head back. "Ammie, you can't. You mustn't do this."

She lay his fly open, then moved down to his feet. She tugged off first one boot, then the other. She did the same

with his socks. Then she began to knead the flesh of his
feet, working her fingers along his arches, then massaging
each of his toes. Slowly, erotically, her fingers traced delicate circles along his flesh. Where she had gotten the idea
to do such a thing, she couldn't have said. She only knew
she would have liked someone to do it to her.

Ammie eased herself back up his body and caught her
hands in the waistband of his jeans. He raised his hips
slightly, his breath catching, as she eased his pants down
his legs and off. She worked the same magic along the
hard muscles of his legs.

She did not miss the tightening bulge at the apex of his
legs, still concealed from her beneath the fabric of his
drawers. She concentrated on his legs.

She moved next to his fingers, his wrists, his arms, easing his shirt off of his shoulders completely. Over and
over she repeated her gentle command that he lie still,
that he let her take care of him.

She had him shift onto his stomach, and she began to
work the taut muscles of his back. As she slipped off his
underwear, he groaned softly.

Ammie caught his hand, convinced him to sit up and
come over to his bath. The back of the tub was high
enough to lean against. Ammie picked up a sponge and
dipped it into the warm water, then lathered it with soap.
She washed him with the same loving gentleness with
which she'd given him his massage. Then she wet his hair
and washed and rinsed it as well, working her fingers
through the long, dark length.

He stood up and allowed her to dry him off. She patted
gently, thoroughly, not missing a single square inch. Then
she led him back to the bed.

He lay there, his eyes never leaving her as she made
swift work of her own clothes, then garbed herself in her
filmiest nightgown. Her hair tumbled about her shoulders
like a cascade of fire.

Ammie settled onto the bed next to him, bestowing tiny kisses along his freshly scrubbed flesh: his arms, his neck, his chin, his forehead.

Again she got him to roll onto his stomach. She kneaded the hard flesh of his buttocks, smiling when he began to snore.

He was still asleep when she urged him onto his back. She kissed his nipples, first one, then the other. She licked, touched, sucked, sipped. His breathing grew harsher, and his head lolled from side to side.

"I don't want you to be hurt, Ammie. Please."

The vulnerability in his voice gave her pause. The last thing she wanted was for this night to be just one more thing for him to feel guilt over.

But he wouldn't. She wouldn't let him. She would love him so much, he would never regret this night.

Matt lay on her bed, his body naked, glistening from the dampness of the bath and the sultry temperature of the night. Her fingers trailed along his chest to his belly and down. It was time to introduce herself to that most formidable part of his anatomy, the part of him that made him a man. She touched him, felt the already rigid flesh grow bigger in hand.

He cried out, arched his head back, murmured her name. Tears slid from the corners of his eyes.

She took him in her mouth, her tongue swirling, exploring, delighting in the strength, the heat, the sheer maleness of him. She touched him, petted him, stroked him, caressed him, loved him, worshiped him.

For Matt, rational thought was a distant memory.

Ammie continued at her sensual task, watched his hands twist in the bedding. She brought him to the brink of madness time and again, then backed away, retreated, only to start again.

Joy, pleasure, delight, awe—she felt them all, and more. Gave each in turn to him, and more.

"Ammie. Ammie." He was past the point of nobility, past the point of asking her to stop.

He gripped her arms, dragged him on top of her, drove his mouth against hers. He groaned, cursed, kissed her ruthlessly, passionately, his body insane with its demand to take her, take her now. But even above the demands of his sex was a need to give back as much as he had been given.

His loins throbbing, he levered himself up, slipped her nightgown from her body. "Let me see, Ammie. My God, I need to see you."

His hands captured her breasts, each coral-tipped mound seemingly made for his hand. He massaged, caressed, petted, stroked. He took her breast into his mouth, darting his tongue over its tautening bud, reveling in her gasp of pleasure.

Her nipples grew hard, erect, still glistening, wet, where his mouth had loved them.

He pressed her down, then took her other breast into his hand, even as he suckled the one. She arched, moaned, writhed against him, burying her hands in his hair, holding him to his sensual task.

He grazed his hand along her slender body, past her hips to cup the velvet-soft mound, dipped his finger into the cavern of her womanhood, delighting to find it wet, welcoming.

"I want you, Matt. I want you to fill me. I want to take you inside me. Please. Please, Matt. I've wanted it for so very long now."

Her fingertips swirled around the tip of his manhood, guiding him to the entrance.

He held himself above her, staked his arms on either side of her, and eased the tip of his sex into the welcoming softness of her womanhood. She spread her legs wider, eager for the joining, then thrust her hips upward to take the full length of his shaft.

Her maidenhead gave easily, the barricade gone in but a tiny gasp. He held himself there, felt himself grow full, harder, just to feel the cocooning heat of her all around him.

Ammie twined her legs around his hips, captured him in a velvet trap from which he wanted no escape.

What had begun in tender passion finished in a thundering eruption of mutual passion and need.

"I want you, Ammie. I want you a hundred times a day for the rest of my life. I can never get enough of you. Never."

He began to move, faster, faster, their bodies fused in a rhythm older than time, yet somehow new and wondrous.

With a cry part oath, part prayer, he spilled his seed inside her, shuddering with the force of his release. And she held him there, cradling his head against her breasts, whispering that it was all she'd ever dreamed of and more.

And he wept, the tears hot and wet. Because he knew it could never be again.

The sweat cooled on their relaxing bodies, and a breeze from the open window tickled across their exposed flesh.

Her heartbeat slowed. Awareness that had included only Matt grew gradually again to encompass the sounds of the Texas night: owls, coyotes, cicadas. Pickles romping after the moon. Horses nickering. Leaves rustling. All these things that she loved—and this man she loved more.

They fell asleep in each other's arms, then awoke together in the middle of the night. Their joining was more hurried this time. Her legs fell open to welcome him, the sight lashing him to a frenzied arousal that made him take her once, twice, then again.

He lay atop her, his sex spent, but still laying claim to what was now his. Ammie. Heart, soul, body, she was his. And he was hers. All the noble, gallant motives of this afternoon fell to nothing in the shadow of the awesome power of his love for this woman. How could he ever marry Lynette?

Against his will, he thought again of Jeremy, a tiny baby being raised by a vindictive Zak Grayson. He couldn't let that happen, no matter what the cost.

"Maybe—maybe someday your father could change his mind," Ammie managed, "and you could leave Lynette."

"I could never abandon Jeremy. He would think of me by then as his father."

Ammie swallowed bitter tears. There was no hope for it. Threading her fingers through the soft waves of his hair, she gave voice to one final, desperate thought. "Lynette knows you don't love her. You can come to me, Matt, anytime you want."

"No!" The word was fierce, agonized. "I would never have you as a mistress, never allow you to throw your life away like that. You need to find someone. Find . . ." He held her close, imagining her in someone else's arms, and he thought he would go mad.

Against the pain of the coming morning, they lost themselves once more, each in the wonder of the other's love.

When Ammie awoke again, it was past dawn. Matt was gone. On her pillow he had left a note, the block letters drawn with painstaking care, the words to sear her heart.

I love you, Ammie. Matt.

Chapter 22

Ammie stood amidst the sheet-draped furniture in the parlor of Mary's old house, trying desperately not to cry. And yet crying was exactly what she wanted most to do as her gaze drifted across the narrow room to settle on the broad back of the man she loved. Matt was standing at the front window, seeming detached and resigned, though she could feel despair coming off of him in waves. His gaze was locked, Ammie was certain, on the white-steepled building up the street. In less than an hour he would be inside that building. In less than an hour he would take Lynette Simmons to be his wife.

"This is all so dreadful," Mary clucked sadly, coming over to Ammie's side and giving her a swift hug. "Are you sure there's nothing your father and I can do?"

Ammie raised her eyes to where her father stood near the front door. There was a world of pain in that pale green gaze. Her father hurt for her, hurt for Matt. "I wish to God I'd've let you go along when Matt fetched those horses in Wichita, Ammie. I wish to God—"

"Don't, Shamus," Matt put in. "You were doing what you thought best at the time. And I can't say you weren't right. I wasn't thinking too straight back then. Ammie was better off at home."

Ammie didn't argue. It wouldn't change anything. And she certainly didn't want to add to the pain her father was feeling.

"Maybe if I tried talking to Zak," Shamus offered.

"You spent half of last night talking to him," Mary said,

her mouth twisting in disgust. "You might as well talk to stone."

"You were at the Diamond G last night?" Ammie's eyebrows arched in surprise. She had ridden by the ranch on her way into town to give Zak Grayson a piece of her mind herself. But the place had been deserted.

"Zak's at the hotel," Shamus said.

Matt let out a mirthless laugh. "Probably didn't want to miss the wedding." He raked a hand through his dark hair. The gesture tore at Ammie's heart as she recalled her own fingers trailing through those silken strands last night in her bed. His gaze snagged hers, and she knew in that instant he was remembering the same thing.

His hand dropped to his side. He turned toward Shamus, dragging in a deep lungful of air. "I'd consider it a great favor, if you and Mary would leave Ammie and me alone for a few minutes. We need to say our . . . good-byes."

"Of course." Shamus took Mary's arm. To Ammie he asked, "Are you going to be at the church?"

In other words, Ammie thought bleakly, *are you going to be there to watch the man you love get married to another woman?* Ammie looked at Matt. "Do you want me there?"

The question tore his heart out, but somehow he managed to shake his head.

Ammie understood.

"We'll be back in a little while, dear," Mary said.

Ammie nodded, not looking up as they left.

"This isn't really good-bye, you know," Ammie ventured with a lightness she didn't feel. "We'll still see each other all the time. Every Friday night you and Lynette"— her voice quivered, but she plunged on, determined to be brave—"you and Lynette will be expected promptly at six for supper."

Matt's next words were a death blow to her already-shattered dreams. "I'll be taking Lynette and the baby west to California, maybe Oregon. I won't—I won't be back to Texas, Am. Not ever."

"You can't mean that!"

"It's the only way. The only way for both of us."

"You can't leave me!" She felt the resolve she'd conjured begin to teeter, collapse. She had wanted to be strong for Matt's sake. But this was too much. To never see him again? She couldn't bear it. The room tilted crazily. She felt dizzy, light-headed. She'd never fainted before in her life, she thought, as her knees buckled.

Matt's arms swept out and he gathered her to him. He carried her to the settee, unable to resist pressing his lips against the slender column of her throat. He thought he would die from the sweet agony that touching her brought him, knowing it was for the last time.

"You can't leave," she murmured. "You can't."

"I have to. Don't you see, Ammie? I could never stay here. Not now. It would be torture to see you, torture for us both. I want you to get on with your life. I want you to forget about me."

"You might as well tell me to forget to breathe."

"There's no help for it, Am. I can't let my father raise Clint's son. I can't let another child go through—" He stopped. They'd said it all before. Straightening, he said gently, "I'd better go."

"I'll hate your father until the day I die."

His back ramrod straight, Matt walked out the door. He did not look back.

Ammie struggled to her feet. She made it to the threshold, resisting the impulse to chase after him. She felt for all the world as if she were watching him walk toward his own execution and there was nothing she could do to stop it.

Nothing.

Zak's at the hotel.

Tears blinding her, Ammie hurried up the street. She stopped when she reached Drifter. Matt had tied off the gelding this morning in front of the sheriff's office—to make a last-ditch effort to find some other legal means to thwart his father. Her hands shaking, Ammie dragged Matt's rifle from the saddle boot. Her face grim, she continued toward the hotel.

Slamming open the front door, she marched through the lobby. The sight of Terence Kessler at the front desk only added fury to the emotional storm raging inside her. "I want Zak Grayson's room number. Now."

Terence stared down his nose at her. He displayed not the slightest hint of remorse for his despicable behavior in the Shamrock barn. "I don't give out that kind of information, *Miss* O'Rourke. It's hotel policy to protect the privacy of our—"

Ammie twisted her fist into Terence's shirtfront, dragging his face down to the level of her own. "Give me the number, or I'll ram my fist down your throat and tie your tonsils in a knot."

Terence told her the room number.

Ammie bolted up the stairs, still gripping Matt's rifle. She pounded on the door to Zak's room. No response. She tried the knob. It wasn't locked. She thrust it open and stepped inside.

Zak Grayson sat slumped in a chair in front of the window that faced the street. Ammie's blood ran hot. Had the bastard seen Matt heading for the church? Her hand grew clammy around the stock of Matt's rifle.

Ammie strode over to him, surprised that he reacted to her presence only then. His head turned slowly. Ammie blinked, startled. His hair was disheveled, his eyes bloodshot. In his hand he clutched a nearly empty bottle of whiskey.

Ammie had never seen Zak Grayson take a drink in her

life. But it was obvious he had done well more than that. The man was drunk.

"I want you to stop the wedding. How can you let this happen to your son?"

"He made his choice." Zak's words were slurred slightly.

"No, you made it for him. You would've taken Lynette's baby. I want you to renounce any claim to the boy."

"Matt made his choice," Zak repeated, his voice sullen.

Ammie levered a cartridge into the rifle's chamber. "You've done nothing but hurt Matt, hurt both your sons, all your stinking life. You killed Clint with your crazy standards of perfection. And now you might as well be putting a bullet in the only son you have left."

"He defied me. Matt always defied me. I couldn't let that happen."

Ammie started to raise the rifle. Zak made no move to defend himself. A sob escaped her, and she let the weapon drop back to her side. Her threats were empty. Grayson knew it. She knew it. She could never so much as point a gun at anyone, let alone shoot it.

"Please, Zak, I beg you. Don't let this happen. You're the only one who can stop it. Matt's leaving, and you'll never see him again. Never see your grandson again. Is that what you want?"

Tears tracked down that gaunt face.

"Is that what Emily would have wanted?"

"You don't understand."

The door opened. Ammie gasped in surprise to see her father. He was carrying Lynette's baby.

"We've got nothing more to say to each other, Shamus," Zak said.

"Time was, we used to talk quite a bit."

"Those times are gone."

Shamus sat down in a straight-back chair in the corner of the room, cradling the sleeping infant in his arms.

"They're so innocent, aren't they? So tiny. So needful. They are what we make of 'em, Zak. You watch out for him, love him, teach him right from wrong, and one day you've got a fine man for a son."

"Clint's dead."

"I was talking about Matt."

"You can't see it, either one of you. Matt—Matt is different. Headstrong, reckless. He needed a strong hand. He fought me at every turn. Just like . . ."

Ammie frowned. "Just like who?"

"Get out!"

Instead Shamus rose and walked across the room, still holding the baby. He hunkered down beside Zak's chair. "I remember bits of a story you told me the night we spent on the Wilderness battlefield."

"I was fevered. I didn't know what I was saying."

"You talked about your father. You told me about a mean, drunken, Bible-thumping bastard who never gave a damn for any of his children. But most especially he hated you."

"My father's dead. He's been dead since I was ten years old. He's got nothing to do with any of this."

"Doesn't he? You told me that night that you would never be that kind of father to your own sons, that you would never raise a hand to them. You would love them, teach them the evils of liquor, gambling—"

"Shut up! That bastard beat my mother every day of his drunken life." Zak pulled a picture from his shirt pocket. "I found this yesterday, going through the desk in my study."

Ammie stared at the faded daguerreotype. It was a picture of Matt at the age of maybe fourteen or fifteen. "I never saw this picture before," she said, surprised. "I thought there weren't any pictures of Matt as a boy."

"It's not Matt," Zak said. "It's my father."

Ammie's mouth fell open. Matt was the spitting image of the man in the picture, the man Zak Grayson despised.

"He drank, gambled. Never got past the second grade. Never amounted to a damned thing. I was so afraid. So afraid."

"Afraid of what? That Matt would be like your father?"

A half sob escaped his throat. "Don't you see? I couldn't stand to look at him. I couldn't stand to see that face. I saw that face in my nightmares." Zak was trembling.

"Damn you, Matt isn't anything like your father! He'd cut off his arm before he'd raise a hand to a woman."

Zak wept quietly, his voice far away now, as though he were no longer aware that anyone else was in the room. "I was only ten years old. My father was beating my mother again. Beating her with his fists, his belt, anything he could get his hands on. I begged him to stop. I begged him." Zak was sobbing. "I picked up his gun."

Ammie sagged into a chair.

"My mother made up a story, blamed it on intruders. No one questioned it. No one cared. No one gave a damn that Jedediah Grayson was dead. God forgive me—I killed my own father."

Zak shuddered. "Every time I looked at Matt, it was like a curse from the grave. When Emily was alive, she could rein in his wildness. She loved him enough for both of us. But she knew. She knew about my father, and about why I couldn't look my own son in the face without seeing myself as a murderer."

"None of this is Matt's fault," Ammie said. "All he ever wanted to do was love you."

"Don't you see?" Zak went on, as though he hadn't heard. "I wanted so much not to be like my father. I wanted so much to raise my boys right. And yet what I did was worse than anything Jedediah ever did. My father could blame it on liquor. What's my excuse? Pride, stubbornness—my own damned guilt."

"None of us can change the past," Shamus said gently. "But you can change the future. Set things right between you and Matt."

"It's too late. Too late." Zak shook his head.

"What happened with your father wasn't your fault," Shamus pressed. "But what's about to happen at that church down the street will be your fault, unless you stop it."

Zak raised his head. Ammie scarcely dared breathe.

"Help me, Shamus," Zak whispered. "For the love of God, help me."

Matt and Lynette were standing before the preacher. No more miserable-looking bride and groom could have been found anywhere. Ammie burst through the open doors and rushed to Matt's side. Behind her, Zak slowly made his way to the front of the church. He stopped several feet away from his son.

"Matt, I . . ." he began, then stopped.

"Come to gloat?" Matt gritted.

"No, I . . ." He pressed his hand to his forehead. The whiskey was making him unsteady on his feet.

Matt's eyes narrowed suspiciously. He looked at Ammie. "What's going on?"

She tried to give him a reassuring smile, but there was too much pain, too much uncertainty in Matt's blue eyes. She wished there was a way for him to know all at once everything his father had said. But this wasn't the time or the place. And anyway, it was Zak Grayson's call to make —one way or the other. Ammie could only grip Matt's hand and wait.

"There's been enough pain," Zak said, unable to look his son in the eye. "I promise you, Matt, I won't do anything to take the child from his mother."

"After everything you said yesterday in Haggerty's office?" Matt snapped. "After all your threats? Why change now, Pa, after spewing all your poison? Because if you stop the wedding now—if I'm stupid enough to believe you—what's to stop you from changing your mind? You could still steal the boy from Lynette."

"No," Zak said quickly. "I'll sign papers. I'll do whatever you want."

A bitter sound tore at Matt's throat. "You've never given a damn about what anybody else wanted—not in your whole life. You didn't care what Clint wanted, what Ma wanted. And you loved them. Me—"

Ammie could hardly bear the weight of anguish in Matt's voice.

"Hell, everyone in this room knows just what you think of me."

"I love you, boy." Never before had Ammie heard such tenderness in Zak Grayson's voice. It was a tenderness tempered with raw pain, guilt. "I wouldn't blame you if you told me to go to hell. Might be what I deserve. Things between us—they were poisoned before you were even born, by things that weren't your fault. Things stretching back to when I was a boy myself, and . . ."

He stopped, suddenly aware of the people clustered around him.

"He's telling the truth, Matt," Ammie said softly. "But there's so much more . . ." She gave his hand a squeeze. "It'll take a lifetime, a lifetime of you and your father riding together on the Diamond G. Really talking to each other. Getting to know each other, maybe for the first time."

Lynette, who hadn't said a word until now, reached over to place a tentative hand on Ammie's arm. "The wedding's off?" she asked, her voice timid, though oddly hopeful. "And I get to keep my baby?" Her legs seemed to give out and Ammie steadied her until she settled herself onto the pew in the front row. She looked wilted, and there were huge circles under her beautiful dark eyes. Ammie knew then that this lovely woman had been suffering as much as any of them at the prospect of this forced marriage.

Zak crossed to the pew and sank slowly down beside her. "I don't deserve any more respect from you than I do from my son, but—but I'd like very much for you to hear me out, Lynette. I want you and Jeremy and Pearl to live with me on the Diamond G. You don't have to decide now, and even if you choose to go back to Austin, I vow to you, you and your child will never want for anything."

"Oh, Zachary, if only I could believe that. If only . . ."

Zak reached out to take Lynette's hand. "I loved Clint. My hand to God, I did. I thought I was doing right by him. He was so bright, so damned brave. But I made him afraid to bring you home to the Diamond G. I made him afraid to bring home the woman he loved. And because of that . . . you lost your whole future. Jeremy lost his father. I can't undo the wrongs I've done. But I can take care of you, as Clint would have wanted. Matt and I—we can raise Jeremy up with the Diamond G as his legacy. Teach him what his father was like. What it means to carry the Grayson name."

Tears welled in Lynette's eyes. "But Jeremy will never have Clint's name. Can never—"

"I'll see to it. Go to the lawyers, have it worked out. Clint never slipped the ring on your finger, but you were his wife in his heart. The only place that matters."

Lynette clearly did not know what to make of this stunning turn of events. Ammie didn't blame her. It would take time to absorb it all, but Ammie was certain that the first step had been taken. That Zak Grayson was determined to set right so much that he had done wrong. She could even foresee a day when Matt would forgive his father. Maybe there would even come a day when Zak Grayson would forgive himself.

Lynette looked up at Ammie and Matt. "I don't know what to say." Tears slid down her pale cheeks. "I'm so sorry for all the hurt I've caused you both."

Ammie leaned down to give her an awkward hug. "You did what you had to do to protect your son. I doubt I would have done anything different myself."

Lynette handed Ammie the bouquet of wildflowers she gripped in her hands. "Maybe," she said shyly, "as long as we're all here, we could go ahead and have a wedding anyway." She looked from Matt to Ammie, her face breaking into a hopeful smile.

With trembling fingers Ammie accepted the bouquet from Lynette, then turned shimmering eyes to Matt.

Matt's whole face lit up. Taking her hand in his, he whispered hoarsely, "Will you have me?"

Her lips curved into a radiant smile. "Only forever."

Zak Grayson removed the gold wedding band from the little finger of his left hand and laid it in the palm of Matt's hand. "You should have a ring to give your bride, son."

His eyes overbright, Matt accepted his mother's ring, then awkwardly extended his right hand toward his father. With a glad cry Zak Grayson took his son's hand in his own, then pulled him into his arms for a stilted, but heartfelt bear-hug embrace.

There wasn't a dry eye in the church.

The wedding ceremony itself was a blur. Ammie remembered nothing except for nearly shouting, "I do!" And then the preacher told Matt, "You may kiss the bride." And he did. And then he kissed her again.

They lingered only long enough for Ammie to fling her arms around her father and Mary. Then Matt caught her hand and they all but ran from the church. In the wink of an eye he had fetched Ranger for her and Drifter for himself.

"Where are we going?" Ammie laughed.

"Where else? On our honeymoon." He grinned, but Ammie could tell that he still wasn't sure about all this. A lot of questions were dancing around in those blue eyes. And there was a tenseness in him that Ammie suspected had much to do with his eagerness to be gone. No doubt, he was afraid that any minute he would wake up and find that all this was just some crazy dream—and that he still faced marriage to Lynette and a barren life without Ammie.

They didn't stop riding until they reached Shamrock Creek. There, under the sheltering canopy of cottonwoods that had been their sanctuary all their lives, Ammie gently, patiently answered his every question, told him all of what his father had said.

When she'd finished, Matt was quiet for a long time. "So much pain," he whispered at last. "So much heartbreak." God, the agony my father must have suffered. To kill his own father, no matter how justified . . ." He shook his head, fingering the daguerreotype of his grandfather Zak had given Ammie. "No wonder there were times he couldn't seem to stand even the sight of me."

"And any time you defied him, lost your temper, took a drink—even your having trouble in school—they were all unknowing lashes to your father's guilt. It wasn't you he hated, it was himself. To make up for what he'd done, he had to be the perfect father to his own sons. And he couldn't bear it when he failed. Until today, he couldn't even admit it." She snuggled close, laying her palm against his chest, taking pleasure in the easy intimacy she shared with this most special man.

"But then the prospect of losing you forever finally tipped the balance," she went on. "He could accept your hate, but he couldn't accept never seeing you again. And

when he realized that you meant to go through with the
marriage and leave Texas, the walls he'd built around his
heart all of his life came crumbling down. And now, now I
think you and your father both have a chance to heal."

"I hope so."

"I know so."

Matt smiled at her quiet certainty, though he wasn't at
all sure he shared it.

"You remember our horrid teacher Miss Gilford?" she
asked.

"Miss Sourball? How can I forget?

"It was your father who got her fired for what she did to
you."

Matt blinked, startled. "He never said a word."

"It was his way. To tell you would have been a sign of
weakness."

"It would have been a sign he gave a damn." Matt
closed his eyes, letting out a tired sigh. "Can Pa and I
really start over, Ammie?"

"Do you want to?"

It was a question he could have answered either way
and he knew she would have understood and accepted
whichever answer he gave her. At last, he said softly, "Yes,
I want to."

She kissed him, gently, tenderly. "Then you will."

He hugged her close. "Have I mentioned lately how
much I love you, Mrs. Grayson?"

"I think I could stand to hear it again, Mr. Grayson."

He did more than tell her. He showed her. With his
body, with his heart, with his soul. He loved her with a
passion that melted her bones, left her clinging to him,
sated, gasping, spent. Yet hungry, ever hungry for more.
And when he'd finished, he loved her again.

And afterward, as Ammie smoothed her fingers along
Matt's beloved face, content beyond measure, happier
than she ever knew she could be, it was as though they'd

come through a storm together and the whole world spread before them, fresh and new. "Thank you," she murmured, bestowing a tender kiss on his cheek.

"For what?"

She smiled. "For wishing me a rainbow, Matt."

Experience the Passion and the Ecstasy

Heather Graham

☐ 20235-3 Sweet Savage Eden $4.99

☐ 11740-2 Devil's Mistress $4.99

Meagan McKinney

☐ 16412-5 No Choice But
           Surrender $4.99

☐ 20301-5 My Wicked
           Enchantress $4.99

☐ 20521-2 When Angels Fall $4.99

CHRISTINA SKYE

"A STRONG, NEW VOICE IN HISTORICAL FICTION DESTINED FOR STARDOM."
—Romantic Times

Be sure to read these novels by bestselling, award-winning author Christina Skye

20929-3 THE BLACK ROSE $4.50

20626-X DEFIANT CAPTIVE $4.50